Telepathy of Terror

Sam had not had one of these cross-over episodes in a very long time, and never one as clear as this. The longer it went on, the more vivid it became, almost as if she and the Storm Princess were truly one. They were so mentally close, so attuned . . .

"This is your sister, the one you seek to destroy," Sam told her.

"Get out of my mind, bitch!"

The thought was so sharp, so violent, and so filled with rage that for a moment Sam was taken aback, but she knew she had to press onward.

"I am not your enemy! Give me your reasoning! Show me why I should not fight you!"

The Storm Princess whirled. "Klittichorn! The bitch is *here!* In my mind! Get her out! *Get her out!"*

CHANGEWINDS III:

WAR OF THE MAELSTROM

JACK L. CHALKER

ACE BOOKS, NEW YORK

This book is an Ace
original edition, and
has never been previously
published.

WAR OF THE MAELSTROM

An Ace Book/published by arrangement with
the author

PRINTING HISTORY
Ace edition/October 1988

ISBN: 0-441-10268-9

Ace Books are published by The Berkley Publishing Group,
200 Madison Avenue, New York, New York 10016.
The name "ACE" and the "A"
logo are trademarks belonging to
Charter Communications, Inc.
PRINTED IN THE UNITED STATES OF AMERICA

10 9 8 7 6 5 4 3 2 1

For Randall Garrett,
another old friend of my youth
and a writer's writer,
gone too soon.

PREFATORY NOTE

This is the climactic book in the *Changewinds* saga, which began with *When the Changewinds Blow* (Ace, 1987) and continued with *Riders of the Winds* (Ace, 1988). Unlike a series, this is the final part of a single continuous narrative, and is intended to be read after the first two to create a single novel in three volumes.

In the second volume, concessions were made to provide a measure of recap and rationale for those who came in late; little such is provided in this volume, since it would at this point take a very long time to explain. If you have not read the prior volumes, buy this one now, so you'll have it, then check where you found it and buy the other two. A good, intelligent, businesslike bookstore or newsstand will have them; if not, order them or change bookstores. If you found this at a small newsstand or rack that simply can't have the space to put everything, buy it here and then drop by the nearest bookstore for the others, which the nice folks at Ace have tried to insure will have them.

If you must, be aware that you're going to be thrown full-blown into the long and involved climax of a major plot. You might still have a good time, but you'll never get it all reading just this one. Those of you who have been reading right along with us will pick it up rather easily—I've provided enough for you to get back in the groove, I think. You've been lulled for over two hundred thousand words into a rather small and private story of two people caught in another world at just the wrong time, but now that which has only been hinted at is to be fully seen, the questions fully answered, and now the Changewinds will truly blow. It is the time for armies and swords and sorcery, and much more, for literally anything might happen when the Changewinds blow. . . .

Jack L. Chalker

• PROLOGUE •

Seizing Destiny's Threads

She was a short young woman, in no more than her early twenties but far older in the eyes, where it revealed damage to the spirit. She was not conscious of what her eyes showed, although it drew the attention of all others, she was dressed in a full-length blue satin robe without belt to conceal the chubbiness that only she thought was important.

She stood on the balcony of the castle looking not at the vast forests and high mountains beyond, but rather at the sky, where clouds seemed to swirl and dance in unnatural combinations for her amusement, as indeed they did. They had always done her bidding, first with her mother's help, and then, after the Akhbreed bastards had slain her mother, fully in command herself of the weather and storms that most others, even powerful wizards, found impossible to control.

Her mastery over these clouds and this weather and the strangeness with which the sky moved terrified most who could see it, even those who lived in the region and were now used to her experiments, pranks, and moods, but, to her, at least, something was very wrong.

The clouds suddenly stopped their wild movements and began to sort themselves out into more normal patterns as the natural conditions were allowed to reassert their influence upon the patterns. She uttered a mild curse of frustration under her breath, turned, and stalked back inside her rooms, but she did not remain there. Instead, she went to the door, where guards with beaked faces and hands resembling birdlike travesties of her hands stood guard in crimson uniforms, pikes at the ready.

She went down the winding stairs as rapidly as her robe,

slippers, and dignity would allow and then stalked down a hallway that was the only unguarded one in the entire castle. It had no need to be; he who lived and worked on this level was one to be protected from rather than the other way around, and only she of any of them would dare even enter this one level without first asking permission.

Klittichorn, Horned Demon of the Snows, master sorcerer of the Akhbreed, was in his study working as he usually did on his magic box. No one else there understood what the box was or what it did; it was one of those great magical things that only the Akhbreed sorcerers had or understood, although it looked somewhat like a mechanical device, with a lot of little buttons all clumped together, on each of which was a different magical symbol none but the Akhbreed could decipher, but which Klittichorn used with rapidity to create his spells and do whatever else it was that sorcerers of his rank did.

The magic was in the square, barely the thickness of a hand, on which strange symbols like those on the buttons but grouped almost as if they were, well, words—occasionally with small pictures of unknowable things—would appear in bright blue against a metallic gray background.

A tiny little alarm sounded and a small red light went on just above the buttons, and Klittichorn cursed and sighed, and for perhaps the millionth time since he himself had arrived unexpectedly on this strange world of Akahlar, he wished at least he'd had an extra battery charger. It had taken him a good two years after setting up here just to rig a way to adapt the localized and unstable current used in the Akhbreed castles for basic electricity so that it would recharge the damned thing.

The woman burst into the room at just that moment—always the worst moment, he grumbled to himself, when he was in the foulest mood. She alone could get away with it and know he would check his considerable wrath, although he had fried people with a glance or turned them into stone for less effrontery than this. It wasn't out of any love or respect for the woman, or any relationship, either. She wasn't all that bright, really, which was to his advantage, but he needed her as he needed his magic box and all his other tools of power, and she knew it.

"You might try knocking," he said acidly.

"This is serious," responded the Storm Princess sourly, in a surprisingly deep, almost mannish voice. "It has happened again. First the dizziness, then the sudden weakening of power and control. It was intermittent, but stronger than any of the last times. I have not felt such a lack of control since control passed to me upon the murder of my mother. Something is very, very wrong, wizard. Dangerously wrong at this stage."

He tried not to betray the fact that he was as concerned about this as she was by maintaining a calm and clinical tone. "Yes, I have been increasingly concerned about these lapses of yours and I have been trying to analyze what is causing them."

"It's that girl! The one you have failed after all this time to locate, let alone kill. She invades my sleep and creeps in corners of my mind."

"Your twin, in fact," he responded, nodding. "I agree that she is at the root of this, but not in the way you think. She has the same power as you, but it is untrained, armed only by emotion, and would be no match for you. No, it's something else. A new factor has been added to the equation, and, yes, you are right, our inability to nail her hide to the wall is the root of our problem. Somehow she, or fate, or, more likely Boolean, has come up with something we failed to anticipate, some new equation that is challenging the neat and ordered set we were dealing with. Do not be too hard on me, my dear. I have killed you in a hundred worlds a hundred times; it was inevitable that I'd miss at least one of you. The problem was that there were too many of you in various worlds of the outplane; our very attempt at insurance drew attention to what we were doing and allowed Boolean to finally figure it out. Forget recriminations. We must now deal with what conditions we have."

"And just what *are* those conditions?" she demanded to know. "Am I losing my powers or what? And, if so, what comes of all our planning, all our schemes, all the blood and hopes of our vast but fragmented army and the oppressed people all this would liberate?"

He sighed. "You aren't losing your powers, but they are being diluted, almost as if yet another version of you was—"

He snapped his fingers. "No! Blast me for a fool! It's so obvious that it never once occurred to me! In spite of my precautions the worst happened anyway! *Blast!*"

He was clearly angry as hell with himself, and even she grew a bit nervous when he was this way. He didn't like to show that he still had a human side left to anyone. Under normal circumstances she might have left him for a while to cool down, but this was a unique circumstance. It was her powers that were in question here, and her powers were all she had.

She would never have believed that she had a near total immunity from his true rages; at least, she would never have believed why she did. He needed her very much, simply because he needed someone he could talk to, rant and rave to, just *interact* with, who wasn't so terrified of him that they were clearly play-acting. The fact that she was neither smart enough nor sophisticated enough to understand much of what he discussed was actually a plus. Ignorance was often the safest confidant.

"You know what is causing this?" she prompted him, trying to divert him from his anger.

"Yes, yes! It's obvious now! And Boolean probably had nothing at all to do with it. I have kept you too sheltered, my dear. Had I considered this threat I could have dealt with it, but no more. That girl out there—Boolean's Storm Bitch—she's gone and gotten herself pregnant!"

The Storm Princess looked surprised. "That is all it takes to cause *this?* that she be *pregnant?* Why did I not hear of this before? Out there, on her own, it was almost inevitable sooner or later."

He sighed. "I—I thought not. When I sucked them down to Akahlar I had them in the Maelstrom you created for me. I was about to shove them into the storm when Boolean appeared. He took me completely by surprise—I had no idea until that moment that even he suspected what was going on, nor certainly that he would have the skill, let alone the guts, to tempt the Changewind. I had to draw my attention away from the girls in order to block him. He actually *challenged* me in there, knowing that if either of us so much as touched the walls of the Maelstrom we would be consumed by the Changewind. It took more skill and concentration to just remain there than even I thought possible. I refused, but realized that so long as he was there and the danger so real I had no chance to make a stab at the girls, who were being drawn down and past me. I could have removed them, but to take my concentration off Boolean would have given him the opening to destroy me. Still, with Boolean in the act, I knew that there was at least a slim chance that our quarry might elude us in Akahlar, where they could not be so easily located. The flow of air from the storm is always an upward spiral, as you know. I risked a small spell, down, below all of us, figuring that Boolean would not notice such a minor thing directed elsewhere than at him or the girls—and he did not. The spell caught in the spiral and came up, lost in the overwhelming blast of power coming from the storm's walls.''

''Just—what did you do?'' she asked him, not quite following all this.

''They looked so similar I couldn't tell which girl was which,'' he replied. ''Two terrified teenage girls pouring out every emotion possible—it was confusing. As the resemblance struck me, though, I knew it would also strike Boolean. I know how he thinks—now. I knew what he would do, and I knew that one had to be in so many ways your duplicate. He would inevitably make one look just like the other to carry on the confusion, but it would be merely physical. I knew that at their age and stage they would not be certain of their own minds and feelings, and so I made them choose and harden the extremes which conflicted within their natures. A yin and a yang, as it were, so that they could be differentiated. Our target would become a lover of women and gain no pleasures from a man; the other, the false one, would tilt to the other extreme. A simple system, and, yet, one Boolean could do nothing about without negating the duplication as well, and one that would make our quarry stand out in our society and, not incidentally, would prevent the natural experimentation that might have resulted in a pregnancy.''

''With all that I have undergone I am yet a virgin, although I do not know why I was not violated in those early days. I have *chosen* celibacy, which she certainly has not.''

''You weren't violated because it was your power that interested everyone, and there was a great deal of fear that virginity was a part of it. Needless, as it turns out. You are celibate by choice because your nature makes you incapable of desiring a man and you hide, as she did, from your attraction to other women by denial. Yet your mother was like that, and hers before her. It is a part of it.''

"How could my mother have been thus?" she demanded angrily. "She had *me* and her mother had *her*, and we were not products of virgin births!"

"They carefully picked the fathers in elaborate rites, and then stood for it in order to bear their heirs," he responded. "The gift, or curse, of the Storm Princess included this always, because one of such powers must be apart from society, both above and different from its rules and conventions, so as to never compromise that position of power. In the absence of a Storm Prince, who does not exist, it was the way to distance the paranormal from the normal, and as a part of the gift itself it is an essential part of a Storm Princess's makeup. But she had not yet fully realized or accepted her different nature and was still experimental. I thought by freezing it I would preclude a child."

She frowned. "Well, consider it now, because it is done. Boolean must be laughing at you now. You can not deceive the master deceiver."

"Boolean!" he spat. "He has a damnably charmed destiny! Head to head Boolean is easy to deceive. His brilliance may be equal to mine, but he lacks both talent and imagination. He is the brilliant thief, the master trickster, bright enough to comprehend what the greatest minds come up with, and steal it and make it his own, but incapable of coming up with it himself. Why, right now I have him convinced that four Akhbreed sorcerers await his exit from Masalur; four who together could crush him or keep him for me to finish. That is what imprisons him there—that belief. It was easy enough to fake convincingly. We sorcerers have certain procedures for checking for dangers. It was enough to show him that danger clearly lurked in sufficient force by all the signs. Would that I truly *had* four such allies!

"Still," he added, "it is a trick more in his style than my own, which is mostly why it worked. He has preyed upon me for a decade because of my naiveté in such things, but I am capable of learning a lesson well."

"And yet she is pregnant anyway, and possibly by Boolean's own machinations."

"Nonsense!" He spat. "The failure was mine, so easy to see in retrospect. I, who have sent thousands to Hell, somehow never considered rape. And by our own agents, too! Those bestial idiots with Asterial's band were dumb enough to probably gang rape the lot of them. Blast! And probably the only time she was or ever will be penetrated by a man happens to be the time she is most fertile! Destiny fights my attempts at meddling with it!"

She shook her head in puzzlement. "Still, how can this matter? It only incapacitates her and makes her more vulnerable. Another one who can control the storms I can understand, but a *baby?* An unborn one at that!"

He sighed and looked at her as if she were a small and not overly bright child. "You are the only daughter of an only daughter who herself was an only daughter, and so on, as far back as your line goes. That is the only way to pass along the powers of the Storm Princesses, and that is why it is such an exclusive club. The power connects the child to the mother. That power is not within you; it is, rather, drawn to you. You are a magnet, a lightning rod, for it. The power is finite, and connects you to her and her to you as well in a nebulous way. That is why you dream sometimes of her and she must of you. But now there is a child and it grows within her and is *physically* connected to her. You are magnets, all three, but together those two are a larger magnet and therefore a stronger one. Whenever she draws power in, the power draws also to the unborn child. You get less. The older the child grows, the more power she will draw as well as the mother, and you will be the loser. Do you understand?"

The Storm Princess felt like she wanted to sit down and fast. "You—you mean that the mother and child together will draw so much power to them that eventually I will get none?"

"Well, not none—you will always attract that part that is closer to you and far from them since you will be a stronger *relative* magnet—but it is true that you are being slightly weakened now, on an intermittent basis, and it will get worse. It is also true that the two of them together, even one as a babe in arms guided by her mother, would be able to totally drain you if you were within the same sector. This is very dangerous, and may just be what Boolean is counting on. Time, which has always been on our side up to now, has become our enemy and Boolean's friend. We can wait no longer.'' He strode over to a massive and mystical red tapestry-covered wall and pulled a bell rope.

''Then the solution is obvious,'' she said, steeling herself. ''No matter what, I, too, must arrange to conceive a child.''

He sighed. ''My dear, there can be only one heir to the powers in all Akahlar. If we fail to eliminate her before the child is born, there will be no other. The moment she conceived, your own capacity for conception ceased. No, we must act pragmatically now with what is possible.''

The Executive General of the Armies entered in response to the bell pull, his toadlike face and bulging eyes seeming strangely incongruous atop the resplendent blue, gold-braided uniform and shiny boots. He stood there and bowed slightly to both of them.

''General, we have two problems and we must now advance our timetable to meet them,'' Klittichorn told him. ''We must have the duplicate. It's the fat one we want, and there is no reward too high to pay for her—dead. I no longer need to see her. The one who kills her need only bring me evidence of the deed and he can name his own price.''

A snakelike tongue ran around the upper lip of the toad-faced general. ''Very well. Do you still want the decoy? I ask although it appears they both lead extraordinarily charmed lives.''

''No, don't capture the pretty whore, but put people on her and keep them with her. She and that crazy artist both. They are the magnets that may draw our quarry out from wherever she is. Just do not allow them to get all the way to Masalur hub and Boolean. Take them alive if possible at that point but not before, and hold them for me. Something in the back of my mind keeps telling me that they are the key to locating the duplicate but I can't put my finger on just how yet, so keep them ready. I want to know where they are and be able to put my hands on them if it comes to me.''

The general bowed. ''Very well.''

''That's not all,'' the sorcerer added. ''We have a growing danger to all our plans the longer we wait. The duplicate might still continue to elude us, since we haven't been able to find her in almost two years and we now have far less time and Boolean might be well served to just hide her. How long would it take to get the word to all the armies in the field to assemble?''

"All of them? For the full assault? Months. There are many hundreds of worlds that would have to be notified, given orders, and there's assembly time, and, of course, it must be done without alerting the Akhbreed," the officer replied.

Klittichorn did a little figuring in his head. "Let's see. . . . Assuming it was those apes with Asterial, it would be—hmm— six months, give or take." He thought a moment. "You have eight weeks, General. Exactly fifty-six days and not one more. No excuses. Those who are not ready at that time we will do without. We will attack in full force starting at precisely twelve noon, our time here, progressively around all of Akahlar. You must not give me any excuses or objections, General. I tell you that if we do not attack then we may *never* be able to attack. There is a new and potentially fatal element in our game and only this timing will block it.''

The general clearly didn't like it, but he made no objections to the basics. "Still, though, I am uneasy and so will our allies be at the lack of a truly valid test. It is one thing to create dust-devil changewinds in the deserts and high country here and there, but an Akhbreed Loci is a totally different matter. They will not rally, sir, in sufficient force to do the job, unless it can be proven that a hub, an Akhbreed hub, guarded by a great Akhbreed sorcerer and supported by thousands of lesser ones, can be as easily taken out. I mean no disrespect to you, Ma'am, or to you, sir, nor do I reflect my own confidence in saying that. It is a practical matter.''

"The masses are sheep, General! You do not need any mystic powers to hear them *baaing,* nor to know that there are precious few wolves. We are all either predators or prey, General. You have only to pull the right levers to get the sheep marching to the slaughterhouse, one by one. If you can not do that, then you are a sorry wolf indeed and perhaps not the man to lead this great crusade.''

The General was not intimidated. "Then give me that lever. Give me something so startling that there can be no resistance. I can move them, but distance and the need for secrecy ties my hands. Give me something that will not betray us but which will none the less be so loud I will not have to raise my voice to reach the farthest colony of Akahlar.''

The sorcerer nodded. ''Very well. I have been itching to do this ever since we managed to contain Boolean inside Masalur. I was going to do it anyway, but you and others pressed me not to out of fear it might tip our hand. I think we can do it so that it will not. I think we *must* do it, both for the reasons you name and to eliminate the only effective threat we have. Without Boolean, the threat is lessened greatly. Without the girl, it is effectively eliminated.''

''Then you intend to move against Masalur as a demonstration,'' the general said more than asked.

''I do. It will be an excellent test no matter what, and we might just eliminate Boolean in the process, although I fear he leads a life as charmed as that girl we have been chasing.'' He paused a moment, then said in disgust, ''*Augh!* He has bested me for so long he has gotten me trained to his mind-set. Damn him!''

He got control of himself, then added, calmly, ''We already have forces in the region. They can seal it off, block immediate word of the tragedy, and control that word when the navigators dare approach.''

The general nodded. ''And when do you plan this demonstration to occur?''

''It must be early enough to serve as such, *and* build confidence. I assume that you will be assembling the General Staff for the final preparations. That will take a few weeks. All right. Four weeks. Four weeks from today, at precisely two in the morning Masalur time. That will mean most of them will be asleep and there will be little time to flee or act on a major alarm. That date and time and the object are classified from this point. General Staff only, not even aides. We need enough people to know that we are the ones who did it and to be able to get that word back. Not enough to leak to Boolean or be intercepted by spies. You understand?''

''Perfectly, sir. The timing will also be right in that it will spur our forces onward to assemble on the ready and will also be rather short even if the Akhbreed suspect. We will know if they do by whether or not an assault is made upon us here.''

Klittichorn chuckled. "Yes, and even if they do they will find us gone, and there will be too little time to take proper countermeasures. Very well, General, it is decided. In twenty-eight days Masalur will cease to exist. And perhaps Boolean and his fat bitch as well."

The Storm Princess stared at the sorcerer. "Then I should get in some last-minute practice with you, I should think. I am relieved that the waiting is over and that we will finally act. The General can take care of the military matters here. You and I, Lord Klittichorn, should leave for the Command Center as quickly as possible."

The horned one nodded. "I agree. It is all or nothing. The die is here irrevocably cast. Now we will seize the threads of Destiny and play them to their ends, and, no matter what comes of this, or what decision is ultimately reached, all the worlds of Akahlar and perhaps all the worlds of Probability will be transformed forever."

· 1 ·

The Mirrors of Truth

IT HAD NOT been a good trip, and it hadn't gotten any better. Now, at least, they were with a qualified Navigator's train heading in the right direction, although that didn't give Sam a lot of comfort. The last time she'd been in such a train, it hadn't helped at all. In fact, she was one of the few survivors.

Maybe the only one by this point. She had thought long and hard about that and all it did was make her own personal depression worse. The kids at least had some kind of peace back at Pasedo's with their minds mercifully cleansed of the ugly memories of rape and murder. Charley and Boday—who knew if they still lived, or where, or under what conditions? Even Boolean might not know, or might not care to know. She was the only one that was ever really important to him.

She only thought she used to have nightmares; now she awoke, sometimes with a scream, drenched with sweat and shaking like a leaf. Her attempt to overcome the demonic fat she carried was out the window as well; she no longer had much energy, and she often felt a bit sick or strange, and she really no longer felt like doing much of anything other than eating and sleeping.

The worst part was that she was having trouble remembering things clearly. She knew she had come from another world and had spent most of her life in that other place before being drawn here as a pawn in these sorcerers' games, but she couldn't really remember it, sort it out, or make sense of it. She had no clear vision of her old, pre-Akahlar self, nor any real memories of her family, although she must have had one.

Rather, it seemed, somehow, that she'd always been this way, had sprung as she was, as if one of Boday's fantastic creations, cast out into an angry world she didn't understand as the plaything for others, the quarry in some fantastic supernatural chase. And now she moved towards Boolean, whether she wanted to or not, in a seemingly endless journey divided between those who wanted to kill her and those who didn't care about her, both companion and prisoner to the strangest split personality she could imagine.

By day, her companion was Crim; a big, brawny, powerful man wise in the ways of Akahlar, a mercenary who, at least, was on her side. By night the big man vanished, replaced with the beautiful but no less tough Kira, a mysterious woman also from another world and place but now very much at home here. Once they had been two, but now, cursed, they shared an existence, the man by day, the woman by night, each otherwise a passive observer in the other's mind, an unimaginable marriage. It was hard enough to get to know or understand another person; Crim and Kira remained ciphers, friends or not.

"We're going to have to cut out of the train," Crim commented to her as he sat on the wagon seat staring into nothingness. "We're coming in to Covanti hub, and the heat will really be on there. I'll want to scout it out before we risk passage through the city-state."

She nodded absently, not really caring any more.

"Perhaps," Crim mused, "we can make use of the lay-over. Kira's quite concerned about your mental state and moodiness, and I think she's right. If you don't care if you make it or not, then you won't make it. Monanuck, the Pilot for this leg, tells me of a reliable physician in Brudok, a town near the border. I think we'll stop in there."

Physicians here were different than what the word conjured up in her mind from some past, little-remembered life. They were sorcerers, usually Third Rank, but with particular skills in the healing spells and generally teamed with a top alchemist for those ills and injuries requiring potions.

"I want no more drugs," she told him flatly. "They have been the cause of much of my misery, I think. Drugs and potions that bend and erase the mind and play nasty tricks on it."

"Not that kind of physician," he responded. "But I think

you ought to try her. There's little to lose, and you might find out what's wrong.''

Actually, Crim knew most of what was wrong with her even though she did not, but he had no quick fix for the problem nor any confidence she could deal with much of it if she heard it from him.

"Why not?" she sighed.

It was Kira, however, who took her to the physician's office in the small but prosperous-looking colonial border town. There was no telling who might be about looking for her in this sort of place, and night was far safer, even for two women on their own, than day.

The physician was a woman in her mid-thirties, with a bit of prematurely graying hair she hadn't bothered to color out but had cut very short. She wore a satiny yellow robe, no makeup, and her only jewelry was some fancy, overlarge rings and some sort of charm necklace with various tiny things attached to them. That wasn't unusual for a sorceress—those were various magical things or symbols used for invoking powers, Sam knew.

It was immediately clear why Crim and Kira were keen on this particular one; she asked no probing questions about why they were there or where they were going or anything like that. In fact, she asked very few questions at all except for her age and the usual vital statistics. Then she probed, by laying on of hands, various parts of Sam's body, particularly her fat stomach, and then placed both hands on Sam's head, one on each side, shut her eyes and seemed to go into a light trance. Sam found she didn't really mind the exam; the sorceress was kind of attractive and the feelies evoked pleasant memories.

Finally the physician broke her trance and sat down in a chair opposite Sam. She seemed to be thinking for a minute or two, then she said, "Well, you are not suffering from any physical diseases other than a minor and easily treatable infection that could lead to boils—and you may have a cold coming on. However, there are some severe complications here that will take more than I can give, I'm afraid. You have a number of complicated spells acting on you, some of which are acting against others and causing some of your problems, and a couple of minor ones old enough that they are integrated into your very being. That was what took so long to detect. You further have some serious neurological problems stemming from an ingestion within the past year of a powerful potion that is unfamiliar to me. I could treat any one of them, but the combination is far too complex.''

Sam sighed. "Tell me something I don't know. So there's really nothing you can do.''

''Not me,'' the physician agreed, ''but I think there is someone who can. In Covanti hub itself, however, is, I believe, someone who can help you a great deal.''

Kira cleared her throat. "Uh, it is not easy for her to go through the hub, and it must be done quickly and without delay. I had hoped to have her stay over here for a day while I went over and checked things out, but for her to go into the hub to actually see a specialist is, uh, *indelicate*. I am afraid I can not explain further, except to say that there are people there who would do her harm.''

The sorceress sighed. "I see. Well, there is no way around it. If you do not get this straightened out, I'm very much afraid that it will consume and destroy you. It has already gone on far too long. The one I would send you to does not live in the city proper but in the hills along the eastern border. If you must pass through anyway, it seems far more dangerous to me, as a physician, not to make the stop than to make it.''

Kira nodded. "I see. Well, give me the details and I will see what can be done. Sam, go get dressed and I will be out in a minute.''

Sam was under no illusions that she wasn't being shoved into the next room so the two could talk, and she very much wanted to hear the conversation, but short of making a scene there wasn't any way they were going to say what they wanted to say with her there. She sighed, got down from the table, and went off to dress, figuring she could worm it out of Kira somehow later.

As soon as Sam was out of the room, the physician whispered to Kira, "She doesn't know she is pregnant? Even though she is clearly more than six months along?''

''She doesn't,'' Kira responded. "There has been no good way to tell her without depressing her even further. You see, the odds are quite good that it was the result of a rape. As for her ignorance, she is so used to thinking of herself as fat and ungainly that the additional burden, while it saps her strength, isn't the sort she would notice, as opposed to either of us.''

"Well, she's going to find out in another eight to ten weeks," the physician noted. "I think this specialist will be the right way to solve that and many of her other problems. I have known great successes from Etanalon, although there is danger. In such a mixture of spells and experience, she alone can be the ultimate physician to herself. Even Etanalon can only give her the means to cure herself as much as she might be cured. She should not have gone this long without a Second Rank specialist treating her. Her depression, her nightmares, her moodiness, her lack of control, which is only exacerbated by the pregnancy, saps her soul. Without the will to cure herself, she will go mad with the treatment or die without it.''

Kira considered that. "She is stronger than she thinks she is. Deep down, she has shown great courage and resourcefulness when she had to. I think it's still there. Tell me where this Etanalon is, and I will do what I can.''

It was a quick and relatively easy passage into Covanti hub, much to Kira's relief. There were only two sleepy soldiers on guard, no particular hangers-on except a couple of dogs sound asleep on the border station porch, and the document checks were perfunctory at best. It was, in fact, so easy that Kira began to worry that some kind of a trap lay ahead. Either that, or they had successfully shaken their pursuers at this point and they were now regrouping beyond this point, where they knew that Sam would have to pass. She didn't like the idea of having such a solid and waiting line ahead, but at the moment she preferred it to complications here.

Even so, they took no chances, travelling the outer loop road around to the east. It was well after midnight when they reached the small village nestled in a valley surrounded by low, rolling hills, and if anyone was about at that hour they certainly kept to themselves.

Covanti was wine country, both the hub and some of its colonies. The vast bulk of Covanti wine came from colonial vineyards, but the really good stuff, the select stuff, came from small privately held vineyards within the hub itself. The sense of it being a peaceful and highly civilized region continued along the roads, which were generally well lit with oil lamps on high poles. The village had electricity, a rarity outside of the big cities, and looked less like a remote town on a mystical world than some tiny and quiet European village, right down to the red slate roofs and white stucco buildings.

Etanalon lived above the village, in a small house overlooking the town and the valley. The road up was steep and not as well lit, and it took them almost an hour to get up there. Still, Kira didn't want to wait for daylight. She preferred to be up there before anyone saw them, and to remain up there until darkness again could shield a proper exit. Covanti had been easy to get into, but it might be hell to get out of.

Sam had been all right up to this point, but, now, looking at the ghostly small house with only the hint of a glow inside, she began to grow nervous. Nothing really good had ever come of her experiences with sorcerers. She didn't trust the ones she knew, let alone ones like this about which she knew nothing.

What was a Second Rank sorcerer doing living in a gingerbread-style house up here, anyway? They were all crazy as loons from their power and experiments—particularly the ones that went wrong—and all they seemed to ever be interested in was increasing their own power and knowledge no matter who else got hurt.

Looking at the house in the dim light and thinking that way, a thought came unbidden into her mind from that part that was mostly cut off. Hansel and Gretel. This didn't look like the kind of place where you'd want to help the old witch light her oven, that was for sure.

Even Kira seemed a bit nervous. "It certainly doesn't look like a sorcerer's den," she noted, then sighed. "Well, here goes."

She raised her hand to knock on the gnarled wooden door, but before she could do so it opened with a strong creaking sound and a dark figure stood just inside.

"You are Etanalon?" Kira asked, wondering somehow if this wasn't a sophisticated trap, with them now irrevocably committed. A Second Rank sorceress out of the political way would be just the kind to be a friend to Klittichorn.

"Oh, do come in, both of you," responded a pleasant, high, elderly woman's voice. "I have some tea on the stove."

They entered, primarily because there was no graceful way to back out, and found themselves in a cozy living room, with overstuffed chairs and a couch with flowery upholstery, a big, loud grandfather's clock that ticked away, and rugs of exotic and colorful designs on the walls in the Covanti fashion.

Etanalon reentered from the rear of the house bearing a tray with a teapot and three teacups. She looked a lot like everybody's grandmother should look—seventies, perhaps, but in fine health, with thick gray hair and a cherubic face, round spectacles perched on her nose. She was wearing a long, baggy, print dress and looked nothing at all like any Second Rank anything. About the only odd thing about her was the glasses, which were consistent in fashion but looked to Sam as if they were entirely black and opaque.

She put the tea down on an antique coffee table, poured, then got herself a cup and settled back in a padded rocking chair.

There was a sense of unreality, sitting there in dim light in this Victorian setting with an old granny, sipping tea at two in the morning.

"We are . . ." Kira began, but Etanalon stopped her.

"I know who you are. I have been expecting you. When Amala contacted me and described you, I knew just who you must be."

She saw Kira start at this, and raised a hand. "Oh, rest easy," the sorceress said reassuringly. 'If I were going to betray you there would be nothing *you* could do to stop me."

"Then—you are on our side?" Kira asked her.

"I take no sides, dear, in such mundane conflicts. I withdrew from that a couple of centuries ago. Such mundane political maneuvering and bully boy contests are so *boring* after awhile, and they never settle anything except which new bully is going to be king of the hill. Since then I've been engaged in pure research, to expand knowledge, and I help out people now and again without regard to who or what they are if they come my way."

Even Sam was shaken a bit from her lethargy by the attitude. "They say that if this one goes bad it will destroy all life everywhere. That doesn't bother you?"

"Oh, pish and tosh! It is far more difficult to destroy all life than these petty materialistic bully boys think it is. Even if it did, the Seat of Probability would eventually reform it anyway. And if it doesn't, then it changes little in the basics, does it? A study of what really is gives one *perspective* after a while."

She finished her tea, then sat back and looked at Sam through those dark glasses. "Ah, well, I see the problem, or, rather, problems," she commented. "It brings up an interesting question, though. Do you want to live, child? If you don't then there's nothing more I can do."

Sam thought about that. "Yes—and no," she responded carefully. "I want to live, yes, but not like now. Not alone and wandering around with everybody after me and no end to it. There has to be an end to it."

"There is an end to everything," Etanalon told her. "Some of it is Destiny, predetermined by Probability, but some of it is our own choices, right and wrong. Your problem seems to be that you don't really know what end you desire. You think you were happiest when you had no choices at all and let destiny sweep you along, but that's not happiness. Mental oblivion isn't happiness. Drifting isn't happiness. It is turning oneself into a vegetable. Most vegetables are ignorant and happy as long as it rains enough and gives sunshine enough for them. But the end of a vegetable is stew, and even then it doesn't really care. So far you have been content to be a vegetable and let all the choices be in other's hands, lamenting those choices you were uncomfortable with and either blaming or accepting fate. And see where it has brought you—to this state. Most people are like that, which is why they end up carrots or stew themselves. Excitement, energy, comes only to those with the courage to kick destiny in the rear end, take its thread, and shake it. They might end badly, or well, but at least they will have *lived*."

"What kind of choices could *I* have made?" Sam asked her.

Etanalon stood up. "What's done is done. What matters is where you go from here. If you really want to live, to grow, to make a mark, then you must undergo a trial that will not only give you those choices but compel them. It requires no strength of body but it does demand character and the courage to face a single enemy on the level of your soul, that enemy being yourself. You will either emerge strong and alive, or you will fall into the pit of your vegetative half and will consume yourself. This is your first choice. Take the treatment, as it were, or walk away, out of here, as you are. That pit will consume you if you do, but more slowly, and you will be absolved of any responsibility because you will be incapable of action.''

Sam grew uneasy. "What kind of trial?"

Etanalon shrugged. "I can not say because it is never the same for any two people. There may be other methods, but this is mine. Even I have no idea what you will face since all that you will face is inside you right now. What do you say? Take a chance—or walk away?"

"You want me to decide on this *now?*"

The old sorceress smiled. "Why not now? You can debate it endlessly and never resolve it. You have been moving more by night than by day of late, as I can see, so you should not be any worse off now than later. Call this your first test. Your first real decision as a newly independent person. Choose!"

"I—I—" Sam was caught completely off guard by that. Choose some kind of unknown sorcery *now,* without even thinking it through? This wasn't fair! This wasn't the kind of choice she craved!

"In life," said Etanalon, "you don't get to pick what choices are there, only from those that present themselves or ones you make yourself. You very rarely have time to think about the ones that count until after you have made them."

Suddenly Sam realized why the sorceress was putting on the pressure. This was just what she'd been talking about. The choice at least was clear—a risky cure or walk out the door. Yeah—walk out the door to what? More of the same? Hell, they were probably gonna blow her head off before this was through anyway.

"All right—I'll take your test," she told the sorceress.

"Ah, good! Then something still burns inside you after all. Come and follow me. No, Kira, you remain here. Have some more tea. You can not be a part of this one."

Sam expected them to go down into some great magician's den, with bubbling pots and eyes of newts and all that stuff, but instead Etanalon led her into a small but cozy bedroom that matched the living room in decor. About the only unusual thing in it was a large, thin object against a wall covered by a black drape.

"Remove your clothing, any jewelry, anything else you might have on," the sorceress instructed. "Just lay it here on the bed. This little journey must be taken with nothing but yourself."

Sam did so, then stood there, wondering. Etanalon went over to the thing masked in black cloth and carefully removed the cloth, revealing an antique full-length floor to ceiling mirror. It was quite beautiful, and for a moment Sam couldn't see why it was covered. Then she looked again. The reflection was—odd. Brighter than it should be, but, more, it reflected back only herself and Etanalon, not anything else in the room, against a shiny mirror finish.

"Step up to it and look at yourself in the mirror," Etanalon told her, while getting out of the reflection and back into the doorway. Everything will be more or less automatic from that point. Go on—there is nothing there that can hurt you externally. The only wounds that you can suffer will be self-inficted, and that's always up to you, isn't it? Go on—look in. That's it. Just look into your own eyes."

"The last time I did something like this I had a demon possess me," Sam commented dryly, but she did as instructed.

There was a moment of contact—eye contact with her own reflection, and a sudden but very brief sense of disorientation, and suddenly she was no longer standing in the bedroom of the sorceress but instead within the mirror itself. She looked back but could see nothing but another mirrored wall. She turned again and looked ahead at her best reflection, such as it was.

Now what? she wondered. *Do I just stand here staring at myself or what?*

"What do you want to see?" her reflection asked her in that deep, gravelly voice she'd been saddled with since childhood, a voice that had grown only deeper with age.

She jumped, startled, and the reflection didn't.

"Who are you?" she asked it.

"You," the reflection replied. "I dwell here but I have no existence, no reality, until someone is reflected within me. Then I become the mirror image—left-handed to your right, and so on. But only the image is reflected, inside and out, not the baggage you bring with you. Not the spells or potions or any external things. Still, I am you. I have your mind, your memories, all of it, for as long as you are reflected in me. I am a separate entity, but I can exist, can live, only as another.''

"Well, you didn't get much of a bargain this time," Sam responded.

"Oh, I don't know. When you have no body, no memories of your own, it is good to be alive. I would be quite happy to step out, to live your life, if I could. What do you see in your reflection that is so wrong?"

Sam chuckled dryly. "Well, for one thing, I'm *fat*."

"Yes. So? Why is being fat so terrible and thin so good?"

"Well, people look at you different, treat you different, when you're fat. They make fun of you. Kind'a like you're cripple or something, only it's your fault."

The mirror considered that. "Then why are you fat?"

"You know, if you got all of me in you. It's a curse."

"Did the demon make you fat?"

Sam thought about that. She'd blamed that demon since the start, but it really *wasn't*. "No, I did it to me. Kind'a fast, too. Boday encouraged it. She drank that love potion so I'm always attractive to her, but she didn't want nobody else to feel that way, I guess."

"Oh, so now Boday did it. *Which* of you drank that love potion?"

"*She* did, of course!"

"Uh-huh. So, after that, she was no longer a free agent in these matters, but you were. You ate out of boredom, perhaps, or perhaps it was just because you felt secure and didn't have to put on for other people. You have a family tendency towards overweight on both sides. Your father was heavy, and your mother was once very heavy, wasn't she?"

Memories, forgotten until now, reaching around the blocking points in her mind, flooded into her. Her father—big, strong, built like a wrestler. Her mother—heavy, not obese but definitely well rounded during her early memories. Herself, at nine or ten, chubby, being teased by the other girls, coming home crying, hating herself. In her teens struggling to take off the weight, fighting to keep it off . . . She thought she was still fat then, but how she'd love to be that weight now.

Back in Boston, that girl—Angela what's her name. Pigging out and nearly skeleton thin. One time walking into the lavatory after lunch and seeing Angie deliberately forcing herself to puke up the lunch she'd eaten so it wouldn't go down and make her fat. . . .

And then, after the breakup, how hard it had been to keep from eating and how her mother struggled with near starvation and every fad diet in creation to get down, so she would be "presentable" to get hired. Mom always on that, "You're too fat" kick and "Thick thighs" comments. Mom went nuts keeping it off, but not Sam. Sam got to a certain point and could, it seems, go no further.

"Then why did you stay fat?" the reflection asked her.

"*That* was the demon. It cursed me not to lose weight until I got to Boolean."

"That curse ended when the demon was removed from Akahlar," the mirror told her. "And yet that spell remains. It remains because you didn't really want it vanquished. Tell the truth, now. You can not lie to me, because I am you, so tell yourself the truth. Don't you really like not worrying about it?"

The truth, huh? Well, the truth was that the reflection was right. She *was* generally eating right, without denying herself some pleasures. She was no glutton, no compulsive over-eater, not in the past few months, anyway. Oh, she might like to be a little lighter than this, but she was sick of trying to be thin for other people or watching some girl eat two ice cream bars and stay thin as a rail while she gained walking past a bakery and smelling. Even thin, she never was gonna be no glamour queen. And, well, yeah, on her own, she liked big tits, she didn't feel all that awkward, and she thought she was kind'a cute.

"Yeah. I'd like to take off some pounds, but it ain't worth that kind of fight," she admitted, knowing that billions of women would groan and gnash their teeth at that comment.

"So being fat is no big deal to you," the mirror concluded. "That means, then, that you're only unhappy with it because of the way other people treat you. Perhaps that would be true back home or under other circumstances, but what about here and now? You envied Charley her slimness because she didn't have to work at it. But, here and now, knowing how people never seem to look inside a person or past their skin, have you noticed that people here treat you as an adult, a social equal, where Charley is always assumed to be an airhead and a bimbo? And that is so transitory. We grow older. What demand is there for a fifty-year-old courtesan? Was she not always the smart one, always getting the best grades? Give her that curvaceous body and sweet face and look what she not only becomes but *enjoys being*. She would be more formidable in your body than in hers.''

Again, she had to admit that the reflection spoke the truth. She had envied Charley's looks because it was an idealization of her own self, but that's what it was—an idealization. Without magic and alchemy it could never have been truly attained. And it had both limited and imprisoned her friend.

Hell, Charley's body really was designed for only one thing: attracting men. And that it did really well. As for herself, well, that wasn't what she wanted at all, although that, too, bothered her.

''Accepting bein' fat is one thing,'' she told the reflection, ''but I'm a fat dyke. Always an outsider in any society. It's against God and nature and it bothers me, but it's there.''

''Indeed? If there is a God or gods, perhaps it or they have lapses. There are far worse afflictions to bear. Birth defects, retardation, cerebral palsy, whatever. And if it is mental, it is certainly preferable to becoming a catatonic or a homicidal maniac, a beaten wife or a child abuser. It harms no one, forces no one else into it, and allows the person to become a productive member of society at peace with themself. Your tendency was reinforced by Klittichorn while still on your way here, as a way of insuring that if you survived him you would remain childless and thus give the elementals who empower the Storm Princess and her double an additional one with whom to divide their powers and thus weaken his own.''

She was startled at that news. ''You mean—it wasn't just me?''

''No. There is a point early in childhood where the unisexual bonds are strongest, when girls prefer playing only with girls and boys only with boys. Even in the teens these boy and girl groupings exist, with your closest friends and emotional bonds being with the same sex while your sexual urges draw you to the opposite one. There is a point where the barrier is crossed, where it is possible to be as close to a member of the opposite sex as to your own and where physical gratification between the opposites is strong as well. That insures children and a next generation. For some—not a lot but a very large number in real terms—that barrier is never crossed. For some it is physical—a minor birth defect, one might say, with the chemicals of the mind not dropping wholly into the right places. For others it is mental. For many it is only a combination of the two. You always thought you should like boys, and wished you did, and you even resigned yourself to marrying one day, but it wasn't what you felt, it was what society and family and other people expected of you. It was worse than being fat in a society that prized thinness; it was something society considered so repulsive they campaigned against it.''

More memories of the past. Of Daddy, idealized, heroic, wise, tough, strong, yet loving her always and spending all that time with her. It was Mom—cold, always clear that she was an intrusion; an unplanned, long-term inconvenience, slapping her around for the tiniest fault, taking all her frustrations out on her kid. Yelling, screaming, fighting all the time with Daddy, too. She remembered the pain, the hurt in Daddy's face after one of those bouts. And yet, when Mom finally got her degree and decided to split, she'd fought like hell for custody, and when they'd awarded joint custody Mom took that job twenty-five-hundred miles from Boston just to spite him. And joined that Bible-thumping evangelical, Hell and Damnation church to boot. Trying to fix her up with all those dumb guys in suits who were weenies when compared to Daddy or even to normal humanity. Not that the guys at school were much better. All that pawing and strutting and shit they did that was so, well, juvenile. The only thing in their minds was to stick that thing of theirs up every girl's dress. She needed love, not—that. . . .

"You can't really fight it any more, you know," the reflection commented. "You could have, once, even up to the point where Boday took that potion. You might still have lost the fight, but you might not have. It is hard to say. But the tendency was there, and the spell forced a choice, and considering your background and how you felt, there really was no option. It was there inside you, but you chose to fight it. Klittichorn ended the battle; his spell compelled that you win the fight or stop it. You could never totally win, and conditions were always against any other way, anyway. Deep down, you have been so satisfied with that choice that the spell is hardly detectable; you have made it a part of yourself. The only thing you have never done, never faced, is acceptance of it. That is what tears at your mind. Not that you are this way and will be so, but that you still feel unnatural, an outcast, somehow wrong or deformed. You keep treating it like some kind of disease that will pass or waiting for a cure to be discovered. It hampers your actions, limits your freedom. It is killing you.''

"What the hell can I do? It don't seem *right*, somehow, that's all.''

"Forget that. What's right is what's right for *you*, not everybody else. It's not what could be, it's what *is*. You didn't pick it, and it's not your fault, and you can't change it now. You really don't want to at this point. It's not a crime, it's part of what you are. Who really cares? Society? Yeah, they'd rather see you miserable or trapped forever in a loveless, sexless marriage and getting so miserable you finally become a drunk or an addict or kill yourself. That would make them happy. If it wasn't your choice to be this way, then you're as natural as they are. You just scare 'em 'cause some of them are afraid maybe it's in them, too. That same society that doesn't blink an eye when young girls are sellin' themselves on street corners, or thinks it's too bad but not scary that other girls are rotting their minds with drugs and booze, or who can accept the idea of teenage girls havin' babies and rotting on welfare—yeah, they're the ones who say you're a greater evil than the others. They can forgive the others, right? But not you. You're not hurting nobody, not even yourself. Makes you think, don't it?''

"So what's your grand solution?'' Sam asked the mirror.

"I can only work with what's in you that's reflected in me. I'm the other side of what you are, remember. I say you got a right to be as unconventional and abnormal according to their lights and set your own standards rather than live with somebody else's. I can tell that's what you really want, too. I say don't pretend for nobody, and if they don't like it, to hell with them. You got Boday. She's still alive and out there someplace and your destiny is to see her again. The spell of union still exists and I can see it. So what's your problem?''

Sam sighed. ''Boday,'' she replied. ''The attraction on her part is chemical, not real. What if it wears off? What if a spell frees her, or something else, and she suddenly finds me repulsive? *Then* what do I do?''

''It probably won't happen, but what if it did? You know you aren't the only one like yourself. If you're comfortable with yourself and out in the open and honest to everybody else, you'll make out. Go out there with a feeling that you're gonna *live* your life with the cards destiny deals you, not curl up and die in a self-pitying cloud that you and things aren't what you want them to be. Consider that society's happiness does real harm to you, but your own happiness really doesn't hurt them at all. It's an easy choice. Be strong, be decisive, live on challenges, don't run from them or worry about what might be.''

It was good advice, advice that was, she realized, really what, deep down, she had wanted to say to herself but never could. ''It'd be easier if I had Charley's brains, though,'' she commented. ''God knows she ain't usin' 'em.''

''So who said you were dumb? Some junior high guidance counselor waving his I.Q. tests around in so stupid a manner? Coming straight out and saying you were dumb, so you believed it, just like you swallowed the rest, and you stopped trying. Your grades were fairly good until that time when he told you you were below average. And who was he to tell you that? You picked up the tools and skills of carpentry just watching your Dad. You know, in every case where you haven't just given up and surrendered, you've out-thought and out-maneuvered just about everybody. You escaped from Klittichorn back on your own world. You escaped from traitors on this one, and you have survived quite well here. It is only when you quit, when you listen to *them* rather than just go out and do what you want that you fail. Forget about *them*. A lot of great minds flunked out of school but not out of life. Ever wonder what that guidance counselor's I.Q. was? Or how much of it he used? Who cares whether you're smarter than some and dumber than others? That's another thing that is. What do those numbers mean? There are always people smarter than somebody else, and lots dumber, too. You're probably a lot smarter than some smart people in some areas as it is. So, forget it. If you can't learn something you figure out a different way to do it and you go on. How many brains could have survived what you've already survived? You got big problems to solve ahead. Get rid of the old ones. You can't afford 'em.''

She stared at the reflection, as if sensing for the first time that this was a true dialogue and that this creature that looked like her was anything but.

"Just who and what *are* you?" she asked the reflection suspiciously.

"You might say a spirit. A kind of life that exists outside the kind you know or understand. All things which are not energy are created by energy. That trapped energy breeds us; the matter contains us, or natural laws shape us in energy itself. My kind is called by many names by many people of many cultures. Some call us elementals, some ghosts or spirits, *manitou* and *turgerbeist*. I was born within the casting and polishing of the mirror, and am sustained by its perfection. Because I reflect you, I become you, for a time, as I said.''

"But you aren't reflecting my thoughts, not even deep down! I never thought this heavy or thought any of this through.''

"Because you reason, so can I. I know all that you know, and all that you are, but it is secondhand. I did not live it or experience it. I can, therefore, be objective about it. First we deal with what is and is unlikely to be changed, for good or ill, right or wrong. You are a Storm Princess, a magnet for the elementals born of storms and a mistress of them. Those are powerful ones who have no feeling for matter; they are bursts of pure emotion who must live their lives in the briefness of the storm rather than within the lifetime of a tree or a rock—or a mirror. They obey neither sorcerer nor demon, although they might cooperate if they feel like it—or turn on them and devour them. Those of magic fear them, as do even the other elementals. But, long ago, there was a compact of some kind. Some great one performed a service which even they can not now know or understand, but a debt, an obligation, was created. Girl children of that one line, descended from that first who created the debt, they will obey and never betray. They are the Storm Princesses.''

"But I'm not born of that line."

"Perhaps not, although who's to say? They recognize you as a legitimate heir to that debt and that is all that matters. They can not tell you and the one born in Akahlar apart. As you already know, they will come if they are summoned, and they will obey you, at least as you are in Akahlar or connected to it in some way, by interacting with those forces that flow from it."

Sam sighed. "So how the hell do you get to tell me the way I should act and think?"

"As I say, first we take what is. You are a Storm Princess and you can't change that. You are fat, and unless you intend to be constantly at war with your body for the rest of your life you are going to stay fat. And, you find men sexually unattractive and not even all that interesting on the whole. You have been fighting that up to now and you can fight that for the rest of your life and pretend it is not so and be unhappy because of it *or* you can just accept it as something no different than a tendency to be overweight or being short the rest of your life and get on with living. Your problem is that you have not thought it through. You think of these things as wrong rather than as simply different. Do you remember your life as Misa on the farms of Duke Pasedo?"

She nodded. "Yes. That, too. In many ways it was a happy time."

"Yet almost all of the peasants and workers there were different. Victims of the Changewinds, or of other spells and curses that made them abnormal, unnatural. The Duke's own son has hollow bones and wings instead of arms and flies as a bird might fly. Did you find all those who were there who were not totally 'human' to be repulsive? To be unfit company? To be denied your friendship and help? Should they be treated as animals, as less than humans?"

"Of course not!" she retorted immediately. "They were some of the nicest people I found here. A lot more human where it counted than most of the Akhbreed."

"But many were ugly, deformed. Surely they bore the mark of sin and the wrath of God and were punished by God, condemned to look like that and live like that."

"No, no! They were all victims. Just victims of circumstances beyond their control!"

"Do you believe, then, that the Akhbreed are the inheritors, the truly superior race who has a right to forever rule hundreds upon hundreds of other races on other worlds who do not match their own physical standards or accept their culture?"

"Of course not! The system here is obscene. Kind'a like the worst parts of all the racism and sexism and shit back home."

"And do you remember your vision of the Changewind?" the elemental pressed, reading her memories. "Of a young boy caught out in the great storm and changed by it into an inhuman, demonic creature?"

She *did* remember. "Yes! And when the soldiers found him afterwards he pleaded with them that he was the same boy on the inside still, but they murdered him! It was—awful!"

"Then we should accept them as they are? Treat them according to how they act and contribute, whether they are good or evil people, without regard to their looks or what they eat or what language they speak or what culture they follow? Or should we consider the different our inferiors and treat them as such, and perhaps kill all the maimed and deformed and the crippled among even the Akhbreed who do not attain the Akhbreed standard of physical perfection and behave exactly as all Akhbreed are expected to behave?"

"That's stupid! Where are you goin' with all this?"

The reflection looked her straight in the eye. "How major are your problems compared to theirs? How can you condemn them while eating your heart out that you yourself don't quite meet their standards? You are no different than those people at Pasedo's, than the colonial races, than the cursed and deformed and handicapped, except that your differences are so minor you can even exist in Akhbreed society. How can you at one and the same time condemn the Akhbreed for their ways and yet be upset because you can not fully meet the Akhbreed standards yourself? You would not be upset if you were caught in the Winds, if you suddenly had a tail or grew wings. Or even if you caught a terrible infection and lost your hearing or an arm or a leg. You admired those people for overcoming their differences, which were in most cases very severe."

For the first time, really, she *did* see the mirror's point, and see, too, how very silly her own feelings must look to such a one.

The reflection, however, wasn't true. "Now think of yourself in their position. They could be horrified at what they had become and give up, become vegetables, die by inches in a morass of pity. They might have been so forlorn that they committed suicide. Many do. Those who you saw were the survivors. The ones who decided to accept what was and *live*. That self-loathing, that lack of ego and self-worth that consumed many of the ones who did not survive, is what also is consuming you. And for what? That, through no fault of your own, you aren't what other people think of as normal, attractive, perfect."

Damn it, the thing was a hundred percent right. She knew it now, understood it, and also understood what kind of a hypocrite she had been. She would have saved that boy. She would liberate the colonies. She wouldn't care a bit if she shared more meals and living quarters with the folks at Pasedo's.

And yet, without that potion, she might well have shrank from some of them, or been worried or revolted by them, and that knowledge made her feel ashamed. The potion had done more than wipe away memory; it had wiped away hangups as well. Because she did not remember then, those people were the only ones she knew.

They were normal.

They were a far better lot of human beings than almost any of the so-called "normal" humans she'd run into. Those bastards back at the cliff—they were "normal" humans. Zamofir was "normal." Probably even Klittichorn was "normal."

"Just understanding and realizing that makes you wiser than almost all of the Akhbreed of Akahlar," said the elemental. "And most of those of your home world, too. One who matches all of society's rules and perhaps is even a genius can still be insane or even evil. But the only true measure of superiority is one's wisdom."

Sam sighed. "What do I have to do?"

The reflection smiled. "Look inside yourself and then look at your reflection and decide that it will do just fine. Be ashamed of nothing not of your own doing, and cast off all the worries over things that have no meaning and no relevance and which can not be changed.''

"I—I want to very much, but I'm unsure that I can! I grew up set in one way, and even though I hated it, it was still a part of me. That's what I've been trying to get rid of by my memory lapses. I understand that now. But I'm back. I'm Samantha Buell again. It's not that easy to do it all at once, like this, now, and know that it'll stay.''

"If that freedom is what you truly want," said the reflection, "then I can give it to you. I can not force it. I can not do it for you. But if you truly wish it, if you let me in, if you do not fight or fear or doubt, then, now, at this point, at perhaps *only* this point, I can heal you.''

Choices. . . .Crossroads. . . .This way or that. This is what Etanalon meant. This is the moment of decision. Not to be transformed into some artificial beauty as Charley was, nor to become anything other than what I am. Rather, to accept what I am and go on from there. To be content to be just me. . . .

It wasn't an easy choice for all that, for it meant surrendering forever the fantasy of changing, of giving up even the desire for the magic wand that would make her perfect. Instead a Sam with no illusions, and content with that. One who would never please the public, but might well please herself. It was a tough thing to choose. Nobody outside of fairy tales ever really lived happily ever after, but it was damned tough to give up the dream of it.

The reflection seemed to shimmer, and parts of it began to fade, and Sam was suddenly afraid that she had made a choice by not making it.

"Wait!" she called. "I—I'm ready.''

The reflection solidified once more, this time becoming very much her reflection, her perfect mirror image. She stared into her big brown eyes and the image seemed to come closer, floating to her rather than walking, until they were nose to nose.

Then the image and her own body merged, and inside the mind, throughout her whole body, there was almost an explosion, a tingling, an excitement. Barriers within her mind fell like dominoes, one after the other, until she remembered her whole past, her whole self, right up to this point, but with a kind of clinical clarity she had never known before.

Yeah, she'd been dumb, all right. Dumb all the way through. All the time it was *them* she listened to; all the time it was herself she'd been fighting. The barriers continued to fall. *What a mess I made for myself—back home and here,* she thought sourly. *Well, I'm not going to give a shit about them and their standards and their rules and demands anymore. It's time to stop being afraid of living. Okay, I'm not like them. I'm different, in a lot of ways, and they aren't really so bad at all.*

It was as if she was suddenly reborn, grown-up and wise. She liked herself now, and she found her old self pretty damned pitiful and repulsive. She liked the image of herself as a survivor, as somebody with power who might be able to do important things. No more dishonesty, not with herself, not with other people. Anybody who didn't take her as she was, wasn't worth knowing anyway. Let other people be embarrassed for her differences. She wasn't gonna be, not ever again. Who the hell wanted to be "normal" anyway? That was just another word for "dull."

So now what? She was sick and tired of being led around by the nose, of running and hiding and being scared of shadows and the future. She had power here—great power. Maybe it was time she used it. Maybe it was time to test it out and see if the journey was really worth the trip.

She turned, and suddenly realized that she was no longer within the mirror but back in Etanalon's bedroom, just standing there. She turned back and looked into the mirror once again—and there was no reflection there at all.

Etanalon came back into the room and covered the mirror once more. Sam went to the bed and got dressed once more, then sighed, turned, and looked at the sorceress. "I think I can handle it now," she said simply.

"Indeed?" Etanalon replied, sounding a bit skeptical. "Then you believe that there is nothing that can crush you, nothing that can stop you, even unto death. You're now ready for any new challenge. Is that it?"

"I think so. I'm gonna try and avoid that death part as long as I can, though. I ain't sayin' I'm not gonna fall flat on my face, but at least it'll be my decision, up front. I'm through running. From myself, from others. I didn't pick gettin' dropped here or what I have to do, but it's right that I do it. That I face her down and screw her ass into a thunderstorm. Not 'cause Boolean wants it, but because it's the right thing to do.''

The sorceress nodded. ''That's nice, dear. Come back in and I'll hand you your first crisis of your reborn self.''

Sam was suddenly wary. ''Something happen while I was—in there?''

''Oh, no. Nothing's changed. In fact, the entire process took only a few minutes, no matter how long it seemed to you. It's something that already was, but which has been kept from you. Both a severe complication to your plans and, well, a potential advantage as well. But you should be sitting down for it.''

Kira was curled up on the couch but looked up and then sat up. ''That was fast.''

''I'm a lot better, Kira. Inside, anyway. I still feel like I'm carrying a ton.'' Sam settled down in one of the padded chairs.

''Not a ton, dear,'' Etanalon said softly, ''just a baby.''

Sam stiffened in shock. *''What!''*

''You're pregnant,'' Kira responded, affirming the news. ''Six months along.''

''Holy shit! You *knew* about this? And you didn't tell me?''

Kira shrugged. ''In your mental state it was tough to know whether or not the news wouldn't push you off the edge. But, as the physician said last night, you weren't too far from finding out with a vengeance.''

Sam sank back down. ''Jeez! Pregnant! I come out of there ready to march into battle against the forces of evil and now maybe I can waddle a little. I know I ain't had a period since lord knows when, but I figured it was the potions or the shock or the weight or something. Jeez! One of them bastards back with the Blue Fairy in Kudaan, probably.'' She paused a moment, thinking, all the memories now clear in her mind. ''Or maybe not. God, I hope not!''

''The rape was the only sexual experience with a man?'' Etanalon asked.

She thought a moment. ''No, it wasn't. A day or two earlier, really. I realized I had this—power—with that demon amulet, and there was Charley screwin' half the train, and I just *had* to know. I just picked a strong, nice guy and kind'a bewitched him into seducing me. It was no kick at all. I didn't even get off.'' She thought a moment. "But he did. Jeez, I *hope* it's his! He was a pretty nice guy for all that and I think he was killed in the attack. Huh! I guess we'll never really know, unless he or she grows up to be an ax murderer or something.''

"She,'' Etanalon told her. "Storm Princesses have only girls, and generally only one child. She, too, will be a Storm Princess, at least as long as she remains on Akahlar. More importantly, it will preclude the native Princess from a child, since such things are determined by the elementals. More and more they will take you for her, dividing their support less and less between you.''

Sam was still pretty shaken by the news, but she was thinking clearly now. "Wait a minute. Are you telling me that because *I'm* havin' the kid she can't? And that once the kid is born she'll lose her powers?''

"That is the way we believe it works, yes,'' the sorceress replied.

Kira, too, was fascinated by this. "Then we might already have won. The only way they can retain their power and keep to their plan is if they kill her and her unborn child. There are a number of very pleasant, tranquil places deep in the colonies where someone could hide for a year or more. We need only take Misa there and wait until the child is born. Then the Storm Princess's power dies and with it Klittichorn's dream of controlling the Changewinds.''

"Sam,'' she responded. "Misa was just another place to hide. Susama in Akhbreed, Sam for short in any tongue. I like the picture you're painting, but it's all wrong.''

"Huh? What do you mean? Etanalon just said—''

"—What Klittichorn already knows,'' Sam finished.

"We don't know for certain that he knows,'' Kira retorted. "We don't even know that he's not chasing Charley all over the map.''

"Maybe he is, but I doubt it. For one thing, I tune in every once in a while to the Storm Princess. I got to figure she somehow tunes in on me. And I don't sell old Horny short.

They got a pretty good idea of me by now, I think. We had to fight off the hired guns back off Quodac, remember, and I think maybe that slimy bastard Zamofir has got to know more than he's putting out. He saw me on the train, maybe even arranged the attack because I was there. He was there at the rock camp, too—the only survivor from their side. Figure he saw it all, heard everything. Then, later, he shows up at Pasedo's and narrowly misses me.''

Kira sighed. ''Yes, and Pasedo's people knew you were pregnant at that point. Crim should have drowned that little creep. All right—so Klittichorn knows. What good does that do him if he can't find you?''

Sam sighed. ''Well, suppose I was him. Six months. . . . So I got three months to go, give or take, right? He'll figure from the rape Zenchur would have reported to him, which is good enough. Now, he's spent *years* building his armies and making his plans. Years finding and shaping and building up this Storm Princess until she'll do exactly what he wants her to. He's got Boolean bottled up, everything shaping up nice whether I'm around or not, and then he finds out he made one tiny mistake. He kept her a virgin instead of getting her knocked up when he had the chance.''

''It would have been difficult unless the soldiers who took her from her homeland had ravished her, and no doubt they had strict orders on that,'' Etanalon noted. ''This is a lengthy plan of Klittichorn's, carried out with much patience. He arranged everything so that she would be his willing accomplice, from the massacre of her people and mother onwards. Do not doubt it. He manipulated the threads of her destiny to create what he had. A child would have interfered with that.''

''Yeah, and I guess he kept her on a tight enough leash so she couldn't fool around on her own,'' Sam noted.

''Most certainly. She would have been most public, you see, and always guarded. But remember, too, that she is in all senses except her background *you*—another version of you. On that level, she might have been no more likely to 'fool around,' as you put it, than you would—at least not with men. Of course, she would not admit it, even to herself, and she would expect an arranged marriage at some point, but she would run from such feelings in horror, as you tried to do. It was a factor that Klittichorn overlooked. Or, perhaps, one he simply took for granted and reinforced in you. It simply never occurred to him that there were other ways than romance to cause pregnancy. In his own way, he's rather conservative and old-fashioned in his outlook. It never seems to have occurred to him that, in spite of all, Storm Princesses are still born. At any rate, it is done.''

"Yes," Kira put in, "but now what can *we* do? All it's done is to start the clock ticking on the end of the world.''

"I don't see how, even with all his tricks, he can get her to go along with him on this," Sam commented. "I mean, no matter what, I don't think I could trust that horny bastard.''

"Hatred and revenge fuel her," Etanalon told them. "She is convinced that only as the liberator of the colonial races and the destroyer of Akhbreed power and rule can she both avenge and give meaning to the deaths of her mother and her people, as well as give meaning to her own life.''

Sam nodded. "Frankly, I wouldn't mind being the liberator myself, but not at the cost of having old Horny around to pick up the pieces. The system here is bad, but I can imagine worse.'' She turned to Kira. "Don't you see? If I was old Horny, faced with all this work and all this power goin' down the tubes, I'd move it up. I'd go with what I had and take a chance, ready or not. He's gonna do it, Kira. He's gonna do it before my baby's born. I don't want my baby growin' up in *his* world, or even in the wreckage a defeat would leave behind. We don't have much time, Kira. You got to contact Boolean. You got to tell him that the whole deal's off. Tell him either we hit them now, or it's going down and soon. We need to get together whatever forces we can and move on them before they move on us. No more bullshit. No more sneaking around. We hit them first, quick and dirty, or it's all over.''

· 2 ·

Political Pictures

SUCH WAS THE luxurious and glamorous reputation of the Imperial High Court of Covanti that Covantians had a saying that it was better to be the one who emptied the King's toilets than to be a merchant prince. And, after a few days there, even Charley and Boday had some reason to believe it.

Halagar, the old friend and one-time schoolmate of Dorion who was now an Imperial Courier for the Court, had brought them straight in to the palace without incident, and in record time. It was far easier when one was travelling with clear Imperial protection; there might have been all sorts of thugs, thieves, and murderers waiting to claim Klittichorn's reward for them, but none of them dared act against people under the protection of one from the Court. Rewards were only of value if one lived to spend them, and Halagar's large, jewel-encrusted ring gave him some kind of psychic contact with the Akhbreed sorcerers who maintained and guarded this land.

Of course, that protection extended only to the land and colonies of Covanti; once outside of that domain, they were also beyond the reach of any sort of Covantian imperial protection, supernatural or otherwise. And there was still five worlds, four of which were under other kingdoms, before they reached Masalur and Boolean.

As far as Charley was concerned, she didn't care if she *ever* reached Boolean now. She had been giving a lot of thought to that, although, to be sure, the decisions about her future were not hers to make.

She had come to Akahlar not by anyone's grand design but simply because she had been with Sam when the two great wizards had come for their Storm Princess clone; one to kill,

38

the other to save. Like the innocent passenger in a car crash, she'd had nothing at all to do with the accident but she nonetheless suffered all the consequences.

Then Boolean had taken advantage of her presence and her superficial resemblance to Sam to make of her a decoy; to make her appear as Sam would have if everything had gone exactly right, if the idealized potential in Sam's genes had been a hundred percent realized. She was beautiful, sexy, perfectly proportioned, and, after falling into Boday's alchemical hands, virtually engineered to be a courtesan, a high-class whore, whose sole function was to give pleasure to men and to find high pleasure in that as well.

And although she had had "I'm gonna conquer the world" Superwoman ambitions in her old life, and now sometimes felt guilty remembering them, the fact was, she liked the job and the situation. The only problem she really had with it, and it was a big one, was that she was designed to stand out in any crowd, the better to attract the attention of those forces seeking Sam who would see the resemblance and take her for her friend. She was the decoy, dependent on her own wits and the powers and authority of others to save herself without benefit of Sam's powers or anything else. That was why she was here, on the road, in the middle of a strange world, on her way to Boolean. Until she, or Sam, reached that safety neither could hope for any long-term peace.

Or so she'd thought. Now, in the Imperial Court, she was beginning to wonder. For the first time since she'd worked the high-class geisha route back in Mashtopol, she felt safe and comfortable.

More, the odds of her really getting any further were slimmer even than the odds she would have gotten this far. Set upon by the gang in the Kudaan Wastes, she'd managed to escape and to rescue Sam and Boday and the others, but at the cost of her eyesight. Witnessing the supernatural battle between Asterial, Blue Witch of the Kudaan Wastes and Klittichorn ally, and the demon from Sam's amulet had caused some kind of radiation effect. All sorcerers who dealt in or with such powers had suffered the same fate and had alternate ways of seeing, but they knew magic or had powers she did not. Even Dorion didn't see with his eyes, although nobody could really tell that just from meeting him.

Not that she was totally blind. Rather, her eyes could see things of magic; the supernatural had its own colors and auras that were revealed to her when she was in proximity to them, but there was a lot less magic in the world than even most of the inhabitants thought. She had been able to see the terrible Stormrider in the Quodac void, a sight she might have chosen to avoid, but most of the time the world was a dull and meaningless gray null. It was an irony, really; most people in Akahlar, from the lowest to the highest, feared magic and the supernatural because they were things they could neither see nor understand. Magic, however, could not sneak up on her, but she was totally defenseless and at the mercy of the normal world.

More, having fallen into captivity in the Kudaan and sold into slavery, the small gold ring in her nose bound her with strong magic as a slave who could not escape her master and who was compelled to obey that master. Right now that role was delegated to Dorion, a rather sweet and shy sorcerer's apprentice who couldn't make himself take advantage of the situation, but, thanks to Yobi, the powerful witch and his own mentor, Charley really "belonged" to Boolean.

Her only convenience was Shadowcat, a medium-sized tomcat somehow bound to her as she was to Boolean. Through a tiny sharing of blood, she and the cat were somehow linked, and if she willed it and concentrated, she could see, in the strange fish-eyed and monochromatic way a cat saw, and from that small and low vantage point, just what the animal could see. This was handy only to a degree. Shadowcat might have been something supernatural, but deep down he was a cat, and cats didn't go where you wanted them to, nor necessarily look at what you wanted to see.

The other advantage Shadowcat gave her was a two-edged sword. She had been unable to master the complex polytonal language of the Akhbreed; it was doubtful that anyone not born to it or who had not absorbed it in some magical way as Sam had done, could ever master it. After all this time she understood it well enough to get by, although following a fast-talking multiparty conversation was sometimes impossible, but that was about the limit. She could understand Boday, for example, but not speak to her, except in the servile Short Speech of the courtesan whose few hundred words were designed strictly for the job of woman of pleasure. Many magicians, including Dorion, could handle English, having learned it by spell, since for some reason English, or a form of it, was a major language of the high Akhbreed sorcerers, but without Dorion or Boolean around she was cut off there, too. On her own she was effectively both blind and voiceless.

The Shadowcat binding spell also gave her a way out of that; when she held the cat others in her immediate vicinity could read her thoughts. The problem was, everybody could read *all* her thoughts, so she didn't use that much unless it was an emergency.

Still, for the only thing she could really do, and the thing she like doing the most, she didn't need to see or speak. She had concentrated not on dwelling on her problems but on coping with her situation, and, with a lot of patience and thought she was as self-sufficient as she needed to be or could be. She could memorize the basics of almost any room of normal size in a half hour; she could find the bathroom or chamber pot or whatever was available for the need and tend to herself. She could dress herself as much as one of her class and station dressed, fix her jewelry and her hair, apply perfume and even some limited cosmetics. There were tricks you just worked out for doing that. Even pouring a drink—the finger unobtrusively just below the rim of cup or glass telling her when it was full. That sort of thing. She'd arranged what little supplies she'd picked up so that she could find them and use them in the same ways every time.

In the Covanti court, they had placed her with the royal concubines, in a sort of loose harem that was pretty good and had a lot. There were real hot showers, and slaves to do your hair and nails and the like, a pick of perfumes, cosmetics, and assistance for her in putting them on, along with good-tasting things to eat and fine wines of the region and coffees and teas served regularly. Each concubine slept on satin sheets and pillows atop feather beds and had little to do until summoned but play around with the luxury. There wasn't much of a level of conversation that she felt left out of; while the Short Speech was reserved for when they were outside, just about all the women had been born and raised to this position and purpose. They were all illiterate, and appallingly ignorant of the world or much of anything outside the immediate Covanti royal grounds. They mostly did superficial comparisons of the men of the Court, and how they were in bed, and did and redid their own and each other's hair, makeup, and the like, did exercises and tried out dances. They were all pros, just like she was, only they had a kind of status and a gilded cage and they knew of nor wanted much else. This was the highest level to which they could aspire.

Charley found herself quickly slipping into their vacuous lifestyle without any problems. If they had no depth, they were at least all friendly and sympathetic, their competition between themselves limited mostly to boasting about their own sexual prowess or trying to top one another in style. It was more like a girls' luxurious summer camp back when she was, say, thirteen or fourteen. That lonely, friendless feeling she'd had since losing track of Sam in the gorge back in the Kudaan Wastes was filled, to a degree.

Too, she had not realized just how much pressure she had been living under until it was removed. Here, with the Royal Courtesans, protected, cared for, she felt reasonably safe, and slept long and well without nightmares. Particularly considering her handicaps of language and sight, this was also the highest level to which *she* could reasonably aspire. Even in twenty years or more, when beauty was fading and demand for older women was lessened, the royal honor was kept, and all needs would be attended to for life. No worries, no insecurities, no real responsibilities—it was a seductive thing, empty as it might be, particularly when you considered how she was, what she'd already been through, and what was waiting out there should she leave.

And if it got too boring, there were the wines of Covanti and an endless supply of mild drugs that would take you for as long as you wanted into a state where everything was pleasant and wonderful and the silliest little things were endlessly amusing.

She indulged herself in all the pleasures because she knew it *would* end, probably sooner than later. She was property, and not of Covanti's royal family as the others were, and she was being taken to her master.

And then there was Halagar. She had seen him only through Shadowcat, but she had known him far more intimately than that. He was a big, strong, muscular man with an equally strong and handsome face, with a bodybuilder's frame and muscle control, and so worldly wise and experienced that he had taught *her* some new things in the bedroom. He was rough, yet tender, too, somehow, and he seemed to be as smitten with her as she was with him. On his part it was a strictly physical attraction, but that was the only kind she really knew and it fired up her ego and self-image to think that out of all the choices available to him he had chosen her.

It *had* to be physical; somehow, for some reason, every time she was alone with him Sharlene Sharkin just ceased to exist, leaving only Shari, her perfect courtesan alter ego, who had no memories beyond being a courtesan, thought only in the Short Speech, and existed only to serve and please. There was a spell that would do that, of course; Sam had created it so she could have some fun back on that wagon train without betraying anything by accident. But that spell's words were English and known only to Sam and herself. Even on her own and without the spell, she could slip into Shari as easily as slipping into a dress, but she had always been there, as a sort of rider, able to regain control if needed. It was her "professional" persona. But this was different.

She wondered, sometimes, if perhaps that spell were breaking down. That maybe it was her subconscious doing it; that, deep down, she really just wanted to be Shari and to hell with anything else. In Akahlar, Shari was all that she needed, required, or could actually be. The rest, Charley, was excess baggage. She knew, at least, that if she ever did wind up permanently in a harem like this, she would quickly become all Shari and remain that way. And, truth to tell, she wondered if that wouldn't be all for the best for her own sake. She would always prefer to be in total control of her own life, but, if that could not be, and if there was no hope of ever returning home and she had to live her life here, as she was, wasn't it better to forget what wasn't relevant and just enjoy, like the girls here?

Sure, she was the brave, blind courtesan who'd outwitted and caused the destruction of a feared demon Stormrider by merely remembering a bit of high school physics, but there were only so many times you could get away with that, and she knew how lucky she'd been. One of these times, she'd lose. If not the next time, then the next, or the next. And, although one of her fantasies from the old days back home had been as the fierce and feared Amazonian warrior, it was different when you really faced those kind of things. On the whole, in real life, she knew that if she had to choose between being a warrior or a lover, she'd much rather be a lover.

Boday remained as personal slave to Dorion, although the plump, sandy-haired apprentice sorcerer would much rather have had Charley around. At least Boday was also subject to his commands, although, truth to tell, Dorion just wasn't all that comfortable in the role of master. And Boday was just a bit too weird a personality even for him.

Boday, tall and thin, now had a dark, chocolate brown complexion just like Charley, and for the same reason. Boday's body, tattooed from neck to feet, made her instantly recognizable anywhere and hardly somebody you could sneak through civilized areas. The sorceress Yobi had, therefore, dyed them both with an incredibly natural-looking skin dye to cover the designs. In Boday's case, it hadn't helped much. Neither did the fact that she assumed the name of Koba (and Charley was Yssa) so their names would not only not be obvious flags but also would match their new apparent nationalities. Neither dye nor a mere alias could hide Boday herself.

"Your humble slave is desolate!" she wailed to him in private. "When will we leave this velvet prison and resume our journey?"

Dorion knew well why Boday wanted to go. Early on, she'd accidentally swallowed a powerful love potion of her own design and the first person she'd seen after waking up had been Sam. It was incredibly strong—it had to be, since Boday often made references to one or another of her seven previous husbands—and its composition was known only to Boday, so only she could mix an antidote for it. And, naturally, under the potion, the last thing she wanted was an antidote or anyone else to slip it to her. She had even registered Sam and herself as a "married" couple in the Kingdom of Tubikosa, where it was allowed with disdain for the convenience of the authorities as a strictly legalistic means of straightening out inheritances, powers of attorney, and other such complexities that would otherwise tie the State up in knots. She certainly considered herself totally and monogamously married to Sam; how Sam felt about it Dorion didn't know, never having met that member of the trio, although Charley had indicated that Sam was the sort who liked it just fine.

Dorion, as a magician, could understand Boday, but ones like Sam made him well, *uncomfortable,* somehow. Boday was not a woman attracted to women, even now; she was just compelled by potion to be madly in love with one of them. But somebody who, without benefit of spell or potion, was still attracted only to members of the same sex was, well, creepy to him. He had known only a few in his short life, mostly men, and didn't know whether he was more disturbed that they were that way or that the ways to change that were available by spell and potion were rarely ever used.

"We're waiting for a report on what's ahead," Dorion told Boday for the umptyumpth time. "From here on in there's no choice of routes, and things are going to get tight and more dangerous than before, and before was dangerous enough for me."

"Koba knows you just like sitting here eating and drinking fine food and wines and ogling all the half-naked slave girls, some of whom might believe your tales of mighty sorcery and battles, but you are on a mission, commanded by our true master to bring us to him. How long do you believe that he will like us being kept here?"

Dorion sighed. She was dead right, of course, but the encounter with the Stormrider had unnerved him. Truth to tell, although his brown robe marked him as Third Rank, he really wasn't much of a wizard. His spells rarely turned out right or did what they were supposed to do, and he did as little as possible in that area. He also wasn't in the best physical shape and most weapons scared him; he would hardly have been his own choice for doing this job, and suspected that he'd been given it because, if he died in the attempt, it would be no great loss.

About the only reason he really was thinking of pressing on wasn't any fear of Boolean or Yobi, but mostly Charley. Halagar had been more an acquaintance than friend in their youth. In point of fact, time had dimmed the old feelings he'd had for the man, but now they were brought back full.

Halagar, in fact, was the kind of guy that boys like Dorion had hated. Handsome, sexy, debonair, the best athlete, the master of all he attempted, the dream of every local girl. Hell, even though he'd tested near the bottom of the "magically talented" group, he'd gone off to his apprenticeship mostly to get away from Halagar.

Halagar, on the other hand, had joined the army, risen rapidly in rank, gained position, then quit and become a mercenary and gotten pretty rich at doing that. Now, here he was, Imperial Courier to the King, and, worst of all, Charley had clearly fallen for him like a ton of bricks just like all the other girls always did. Hell, every time she was around Halagar she just seemed to melt away, leaving only a servile, mooning airhead. He liked Charley for her looks, sure, and he was as guilty as any man of looking at the pretty ones first, but it wasn't just the looks or even the moves, no matter how alluring they were. But he also was enormously attracted to the Charley who, blind and helpless, when faced with the monstrous, demonic Stormrider, had calmly figured out its weakness and directed its destruction. It was the strength and brains and nerve beneath the beauty that was, in fact, the most important to him.

Sure, she was a slave and compelled to obey him. He could have forbade her making out with Halagar and in fact commanded her to make love to him, but he didn't want it that way. He was a sorcerer, at least of sorts. He knew how easy it was for spells and potions to substitute for what was real. To compel it was no different to him than going down to the low-life district and buying it. His mind and heart just had no craving for or even use for gratification like that. Magicians above all others prized most that which was genuine and real.

It was the thing that puzzled him most about women, particularly strong and decisive women. They all said that they hated and detested men who treated them like sex objects rather than people and judged women by looks alone, Charley included—and said so often. Then they'd make real good friends with the kind of man who saw them the way they said they wanted to be seen and treated them accordingly—but they'd then walk off to bed with the guy who was best-looking and treated all women like sex objects and leave the guy who treated them first and foremost as people, the way they said they wanted all men to treat them, and who didn't look like a god but just ordinary. And then when you asked them why they were saying one thing to a guy and then teaching him the other, they turned and snapped and said, "You treat sex like it was a reward or something." Well, it sure wasn't punishment and it was sure a pleasure, and a guy who didn't get much sex himself sure couldn't figure why a woman would want to go to bed with a guy who acted all "wrong" and leave a guy alone and without sex who was their kind of guy.

In the absence of love, sex was either a commodity or a reward, at least to any guy he'd known. If there was any other thing that it was, it was unfathomable to the male mind.

Women and men sure didn't think alike, that was for sure. To him, Charley was basically sending the message that he was a sucker for not treating her as his sex slave and to hell with all that respect crap.

The trouble was, while he got the message, he just couldn't bring himself to be that way. Halagar, too, had gotten the message long ago, and he sure was never shown any reason to change his views, either.

Still, Halagar had been vital; Dorion had to admit that, even to himself. Were it not for the courier, his contacts, his quick sword arm and sure shot, and his rank in Covanti, they might not have made it this far. And now he was using the same power to get the information they needed to complete the journey that, like it or not, they had to complete.

He sighed and got up from the comfortable divan on which he'd been sitting. "All right—I'll see just what's up. I know how anxious you are to go on, but the gods know we needed this rest."

So far he'd been pressing Halagar for news; now he sought out others, the bureaucrats of the Court through which all such information had to flow, to see if maybe he was being played for a sucker in other ways. It took a little sweet-talking and a bit of bravado and bluster, but he finally wormed out the situation.

First was the interesting news that the dogs had been called off of Charley. That alone was amazing, wonderful news to him. Apparently it had happened many days earlier, and was now common knowledge among the underworld of Covanti, who had shifted their search to "a fat and probably very pregnant girl" exclusively. This took enormous pressure off; surely Halagar had known of this as soon as the word had been put out. Why hadn't he told them?

Of course, the answer was obvious. Now that there was no longer any manhunt, or, rather, womanhunt, for Charley, there seemed no particular reason for them to hurry on to Boolean. They had become, very suddenly, no longer really relevant to events. That meant that Halagar could enjoy all of Charley's favors until he tired of them without actually affecting the course of history or even events, and without getting a big-shot sorcerer mad at him.

Of course, Dorion's reaction at the news was just the opposite. His charge was to get the women to Boolean; now this seemed less an impossible task than a relatively straightforward affair. Not even Boday was at serious risk; it was she had the love potion, not Sam. It wasn't all that certain that holding Boday hostage would cause Sam to do anything dangerous or foolish—if, indeed, she even heard of it. Indeed, now that Klittichorn knew that Charley wasn't the one, the smart thing to do would be to facilitate their journey and do so in a manner that they would feel no reason to continue to be secretive themselves. That Sam was still trying to reach Boolean was a foregone conclusion; Charley and Boday, then, became valuable travelling the same road as bait.

To have revealed this to Dorion, or even Boday, would have meant their immediate departure.

Not that things were risk free. Covanti had mobilized some of its reserve forces and moved most of the regular troops from the colonies back towards the null zones. Rebellious forces composed, incredibly, of mostly colonial races had begun actual attacks on Akhbreed outposts and had also begun to marshall forces near the inner borders with the hub. The level of coordination was amazing; hundreds of colonial worlds, separated irrevocably by their lack of hub access to get communications or coordination between their various worlds *still* were moving as if under a unified command. Such actions were not merely dangerous, they were unprecedented.

They were also inexplicable. No matter how many forces they marshalled at the null's edge, the armies of the Akhbreed

could always defend the nulls with superior weaponry and
in-place defenses, and even if the colonials gained a bit and
managed to cross worlds—what then? They'd be cut off from
their own supply and support, unable to blend into the new
world, and would only present an easier target for Akhbreed
forces to mop up. Without control of the hub, what they were
doing defied all sense. And they could never control the hub
so long as the Akhbreed sorcerers guarded it so well and so
effectively. It was the hub, its circular shape so perfect for
military defense and supported by the vast powers of the great
sorcerers, the heart of the Akhbreed kingdoms and of the
race's control of all the worlds of Akahlar. Without the hub,
they could be deadly, costly, even inconvenient, but they
couldn't really win anything except their own death and the
harshest repression for their worlds and peoples afterwards.
They knew this. Why other than mass insanity would they
now organize and march?

Dorion frowned. "Then is it safe, or even possible, to get
through the colonies at all?"

The bureaucrat nodded. "Oh, certainly. Their worlds need
the trade from the other worlds just as much as always. It is
their interdependence that gives us power over all of them.
They might stop or overhaul a train, but except for Mandan
cloaks and blankets and weapons, they take nothing and let
the trains continue. Most, travelling with sorcerers and under
strong military guard, get through not touched at all. I wouldn't
want to go through that kind of colonial territory on my own,
but in some of the bigger trains it's still as safe as always."

Dorion thought it over. "Yeah, until the troops and sorcerers leave at the border and we cross from Covanti territory
into Tishbaal."

"Oh, this is happening all over, not just in Covanti," the
clerk assured him, sounding rather blasé about the situation.
"In fact, it's worse in Tishbaal and they're thick as flies in
colonial Masalur. But they seem impossibly well disciplined,
and, while cocky and confident, they still seem to be letting
most everybody and everything through. The High Sorcerers
of all the kingdoms are in almost daily conferences over what
it all means, as are the general staffs of the armies, but, so
far, there's been no consensus. Your friend Halagar has been
arguing with the King, advocating that we go almost to a

seize mode and close the borders and shut down the trade.
Right now, though, the economists agree that such an action
would harm us far more than the colonials. I would be
careful, though, my friend, if I were you. You are associated
with Boolean and many of the monarchs and sorcerers believe
that he might somehow be behind this.''

"That's insane!" Dorion retorted. "He's been trying to
stop this! He saw it coming years ago and has been trying to
warn and unify everybody, and nobody would listen to him!"

The clerk sighed. "Yes, well, that's the problem, or so the
rumors I hear go. He's had a hateful rivalry with Klittichorn
of Marépek for decades, and he's been trying to gain allies to
defrock or destroy—or whatever it is you wizards do to one
another—his rival ever since. Klittichorn has always treated
Boolean with contempt but has never tried to get sorcerous
and political action against him. Also, Boolean has been
outspoken for years in his contempt for the Akhbreed way
and consistently a defender of colonials, as if they were
capable of governing themselves. Comparing the two's actions and words over the years, there are a lot of people who
don't like Boolean very much and who think he might be mad
enough or frustrated enough to have somehow orchestrated
this just to force them to act against Klittichorn."

"But it's the other way around!"

The clerk shrugged. "Perhaps. Consider, though—the cham-
pion of colonial rights is saying that he is defending the
system he abhors, while a defender of Akhbreed rule stands
accused of being a mastermind that the colonials will die for.
Which would you believe? Remember, too, that you are a
sorcerer yourself and you work for Boolean. If you were a
neutral party with only a stand-off knowledge of the pair, you
might feel differently. Klittichorn's domain is cold, poor, and
remote, and he has done many favors for his brethren in the
other kingdoms and never asked much in return. Boolean is in
the middle of the richest and most powerful kingdoms on
Akahlar and he's not been known for doing favors for anyone
nor being particularly nice or even civil. You see where this
leads?"

"Yes," Dorion muttered angrily. "To Klittichorn's victory
and the destruction of Akahlar."

Still, it presented him with several immediate problems and

many decisions to make. Until now, he's never really understood how Klittichorn could be so brazenly successful and Boolean so ignored. Now it was at least clearer—the Horned One had laid his groundwork well, being the wonderful fellow, the man with great power and knowledge who would always help, always share, and demand nothing but cordiality in return. Boolean, he knew, had a less than wonderful and outgoing personality and tended to lecture those who, whether they were or not, considered themselves his equals, and he had little or no patience with stupidity, nor had he ever been quiet about his contempt for the system. Now Klittichorn's glad-handing was paying off. He was moving his forces openly, making low-level attacks and high-level threats against the kingdoms in the most brazen manner, and because they liked Klittichorn and considered him a good-fellow-well-met who said all the right things, and they had a personality problem with Boolean, who always spoke his mind, it was the latter who was getting the blame and taking the heat!

If this was really becoming official policy in Covanti, then if they stayed, they'd *stay*. Grotag, the chief sorcerer of Covanti, was known as a pretty genial fellow, but strong. Dorion knew he'd not be a match for the power in one of Grotag's hairs. He'd take no chances; he'd turn Dorion and maybe Boday into a pair of pet monkeys and give a re-enslaved and newly bewitched Charley to Halagar as his pet.

Damn it, it was time to use what powers and abilities he had and get the hell out of here!

He was heading back to tell Boday to make arrangements for their immediate departure when he ran into Halagar.

"Hold, old friend! Where are you going in such a hurry and with such a wretched expression?" the courier asked.

"We've been here long enough," Dorion answered carefully, "and if we're here much longer I'm afraid we'll be interned until the duration."

Halagar shrugged but did not deny the possibility. Instead, he argued, "Would that be so bad? This is not exactly the worst place in Akahlar nor a bad place for withstanding a siege, either."

"That is true," the magician admitted, "but I'm afraid that such safety would be very short-lived. I have been talking with various officials here and they have told me the, uh, political situation, as it were. They are fools to be taken in by a popularity act; the objective situation is upside down from their view. They are too safe, too fat, too confident that the way things are are the way things will always be and that no one can change that.''

To Dorion's amazement, Halagar didn't seem offended by the remark nor defensive about it as well. Instead he replied, ''Yes, I agree. The massive coordinated movement of raw colonial troops who have theoretically never been schooled in the military arts shows much cunning and long work. One would have to be incredibly clever to have organized that sort of thing, and someone clever enough to do that and brazen enough to do that is not stupid enough to make the old mistakes. You only come out in the open to this degree if you've found a massive chink in the enemy armor. Still, what is the percentage in moving? What can any of us do about it?''

That was a stumper. ''Not much, perhaps,'' the magician admitted, ''but if a great war is upon us and if the power of the Akhbreed is so threatened that even the hubs are not safe, I think at least I would rather be with one of power who will fight to the last. Perhaps there is nothing we can do. Perhaps there is nothing Boolean can do. But, so long as there is a chance of anything I prefer action to complacency. I know Boolean, although he and I are not exactly on close terms right now. It is true he would not lift a finger to defend the system unless it was threatened with replacement by a system far worse—or even direr consequences. Imagine a wizard who could control the Changewinds, Halagar.''

The big man *had* considered it. ''I am most troubled by that, and it is clearly the object,'' he admitted. ''However, it might not be as clear-cut as you think. Do you really believe that Grotag and the King and all the high advisors are that dense? Or that the other kingdoms and Akhbreed sorcerers can't figure out the plot? They are scared—make no mistake about it. They are still unconvinced that it could occur on a global scale, though. Many see it as a basically localized fight between old rivals. Klittichorn with *his* Storm Princess versus Boolean with his, if he can ever find her or she him. One on one. The greatest colonial rebel massing is against Masalur and the approaches to it; that is clear. Klittichorn's ambassadors have been going around assuring everyone that it's a local fight, and that he is considering a preemptive attack with all his powers on Boolean before Boolean can attack the rest of them. The sorcerers and kings are mostly willing to sit it out, perhaps rooting a bit for Klittichorn, seeing who wins. Then if the winner moves against any of the others the rest will take him on. Because of his views, they consider a Boolean victory more of a threat to them than a Klittichorn one.''

"I don't know how the horned one is going to do it, but I am convinced that this will be no localized quarrel. If Klittichorn can sit off safely with his Storm Princess in his remote northern citadel and still somehow draw and guide the Changewind through Masalur, then he already has the means to hit anyone, anywhere, that he wishes. Boolean may wish he could do that, but if he could, he would.''

"There is currently a wait-and-see attitude among the sorcerers," Halagar told him, "but once they see how things are developing they will most certainly mass on the victor to force him to share his new powers or be taken on.''

Dorion considered that. "But if they take him on, they will have to mass together to fight him. What a tempting target for a Changewind to blow through!''

"Huh! I hadn't thought of that! I'm a fighting man, not a sorcerer. I take your word for it, though. You have convinced me, Dorion, although we would never convince the others. They are, as you say, too sure of themselves. As for me, I would rather die fighting than sitting here with the winds blowing.'' He thought for a moment. "The odds of getting a train towards Masalur are slim right now. Few are willing to risk ambush by the colonials, particularly with Mandan cloaks in such short supply and the colonials practically holding some roads hostage. Armed escorts would only be good to the Tishbaal Null. We could make better time going overland ourselves, avoiding the main roads and routes.''

Dorion's head looked up at the courier in surprise, " 'We?' ''

"Why not? With my gun and sword arm and your sorcery we ought to be able to stand up to any minor colonial backwater irregulars we might be unlucky enough to come across. And I can have the maps and learn the roads and routes straight to Masalur, particularly if you can navigate at the nulls. With any luck at all we might reach your Boolean in, oh, three weeks."

"The King is not going to like your change of loyalties," Dorion noted, not at all enthused by the prospect of having Halagar along, nor all that happy that he might well be called upon to show how hollow his own boasts to the big man were about just what magical powers he might have. He wondered, too, if Halagar was *that* infatuated with Charley or if he was instead leading them into some sort of double-cross. "Nor am I that comfortable with someone who would shift loyalties so casually," he added bluntly.

Halagar shrugged. "I am a mercenary, an employee. I have been such almost all of my life. I give my utmost loyalty while I am in anyone's employ, but this will not be the first time I've quit a job. I am sick of arguing myself hoarse for a solid and unified defense of the hub with fat generals who have never fired upon anyone who could fire back. When I must commit to dull and stupid minds, then it is time I sought a different employ."

"Boolean or Masalur would certainly welcome your services, but I have nothing with which to buy your loyalty and arms."

Halagar looked at the magician, a strange, crooked smile on his face. "You have command of Yssa," he noted. "Delegate that command to me."

Dorion was shocked but not really surprised. "How can I do that? She and the other belong not to me but to Boolean personally. And she has an overriding compulsion to seek Boolean with or without me. I can not give what is not mine."

"That is understood. The commission is to get the three of you to the sorcerer Boolean, and that I will do and in the most direct manner. My fee is that she will be mine absolutely during that period only. Once there I must negotiate a new commission with Boolean. Once there, she is of no more value either as decoy or lure. I have sufficient money spread around and reserves hidden for when I truly need them. I have no wish for political power; I have seen what it does to men like me. I am certain that your Boolean will find my fee quite reasonable and affordable, and I will give my all for it."

Dorion was amazed. "She attracts you that much? You who have all the women swooning over your every move? Are you certain that you are not under an enchantment?"

"Sometimes I think so," Halagar replied. "And it is true that I can lie with most any woman I choose, although a few have eluded me. I have lost count of the number of women, free and slave, noble and common, that I have lain with, but she is, somehow, different. I have never married, not out of lack of suitable candidates, but rather because my life and chosen occupation would make it unfair to any woman and subject her to either far too much danger and strange places or force me to give up the life I love and settle down. Any such woman would also be a sword my enemies could use at my throat if all else failed. Courtesans of her caliber were always the best, but they always belonged to someone else and were heaven for merely a night, and not a one can hold a candle to her. She is blind, yes, but it hardly slows her, and she can see magic, which I cannot, and that gives me an advantage I did not have before."

"How did you know that?"

Halagar shrugged. "She remarked on the color of some charms I have carried for some protection that first night back in Quodac. I knew then that she could see the magic, although she did not understand what it was."

"Oh," Dorion responded, interested that Halagar had still never seen or experienced, nor even suspected, the real Charley.

"She would be always loyal, totally obedient, would be uncomplaining no matter what the conditions or situation, yet she would serve me in all ways and ease my loneliness. She is the best of her class that I have ever seen and the first within reach. She is a pretty jewel who can neither be purchased with money nor taken by force, and, with her, I need not compromise my lifestyle nor situation."

Dorion nodded. "I see. And this period would be a sort of—trial run, as it were." He only wished Charley could have heard the way Halagar was describing her. He envisioned a time when a lustful Halagar would bring another woman to his tent and order Charley to serve them both. Still, the deal wouldn't be made unless Boolean okayed it, and Boolean knew just who and what she really was. In the meantime, perhaps three weeks or so as Halagar's "property'' might reveal his true nature to her. Either way, this seemed the only reasonable chance of reaching Boolean under current conditions. He just hoped he wouldn't go mad watching the two and listening to them from the next bed.

"What occurs once we reach Boolean is your affair," he told Halagar. "I will accept your bargain as much as I can in the meantime, though, provided we leave as quickly as possible."

"It is late now, and there are preparations to make," Halagar noted. "Still, if you all can be ready, we could leave just beyond first light tomorrow. I will have everything ready by then, and will have cleared things here as delicately as possible. Is that soon enough?"

"I would as soon leave tonight," the magician told him, "but it will have to do."

Boday was no longer the first destination. He turned and decided that he'd better inform Charley.

She emerged from the harem, where men were not permitted, into the anteroom where he waited for her, looking puzzled but expectant. She no longer looked merely gorgeous; after some time and a make-over by the Imperial courtesans, she looked spectacular. Dressed in the light, gauze-like finery of the harem, with long, painted nails perfectly manicured and toenails to match, her hair streaked with blond, her lashes long and luxurious, she was the epitome of male fantasy. By the gods! How he wanted her, and how he hated himself for this!

"We leave tomorrow, just past dawn," he told her in English. "Be prepared."

"I am prepared," she replied. "I don't exactly have much to pack. They don't have riding outfits for people like me, but I'm sure I can find something that'll do."

"Halagar is coming with us."

That news excited her. "Really? I hoped against hope he would!"

"He is leaving the service of Covanti and coming over to us. His fee for taking us all to Boolean is you."

"Huh? How can that be?"

"He wants me to delegate my authority over you to him for the journey, which will still take several weeks. Once there, he expects Boolean to give you to him permanently in exchange for his service in the defense of Masalur.''

She was intrigued by that, but not as delighted as he'd expected her to be. ''I know this ring in my nose is kind of a turn-on, but I'd kind'a hoped that once we got to the old boy he'd at least neutralize it or something.''

''You object to this arrangement?''

She thought it over. ''No, not for a few weeks, I guess. But, you know, something funny happens to me every time he's around. I go bye-bye and Shari takes over. I love Shari when I can turn her on and off, but bein' her all the time isn't my idea of a future. I don't like the idea of being out there in the middle of nowhere without my brain in my head, either.''

''Well, I don't like what happens, either, and I can't explain it, but I don't see we have any choice.'' Quickly, he filled her in on the whole situation.

''I get the picture,'' she told him. ''I also get a real feeling that you don't like this arrangement much.''

''I don't,'' he admitted, ''but he's just the sort of person we need to have a chance of making it.''

''Well,'' she sighed, ''it's got to be. I don't have much choice these days anyway. At least it's kind'a flattering for me to find a guy with that much experience wanting me so much.''

''Uh—Charley, he doesn't want to *marry* you, he wants to *own* you. Or, rather, he wants to own Shari. I, uh, well, he doesn't think you're the perfect woman; he thinks you're the perfect slave.''

''Yeah, I figured it was something like that. And, as Shari, I *am*. I guess I should feel lucky. Very few people are ever perfect as anything. Still, it's not exactly been a burning ambition of mine to even discover that I'm the perfect slave. It's sort of like dreaming you're gonna be a great genius or something and discovering that you are really the world's greatest toilet cleaner. Still, it's in other people's hands now, really. If Boolean goes along with me, then I'll sure give Halagar his chance and see if he wants me anyway, but if Mister Green decides I'm no longer of any use then I guess I'll spend eternity washing his socks and loving it.''

''You've gotten so cynical and too fatalistic,'' he responded, a bit angry at her. "That's not like you. You're sounding more like the local women here."

"Yeah, well, show me where I've had a crack at anything else. Seriously, though—you worked with Boolean. How do you think he'll take me?"

"It is hard to say," Dorion replied honestly. "Under normal conditions you would be free, liberated as much as he could, and treated extremely well, but these are not normal conditions. What's right and wrong under normal circumstances seems out the door now. Too much is at stake for ones like him to think much about an individual's rights."

She nodded. "Yeah, sort'a like Bogart in *Casablanca.* That's what I figured."

"All we can do is get there and see. Now, listen to me and obey my commands. Until I say otherwise—and, I emphasize, until *I* say otherwise—you will regard Halagar as your lord and address him as Master or however he commands. You will obey his every command as you would mine, as if your commands were from me or from Boolean—with a few exceptions. You will not obey any command that would betray us or our mission but will instead immediately report it to me. You will obey no command that would harm yourself or Boday or me, or cause us to come to harm, and you will report as soon as possible to me if any such command is given you by Halagar. Further, if anything happens to me, or we are separated, then you will be a free agent commanded still to reach Boolean as quickly as possible thereafter by any means you can find. And you will neither reveal nor repeat these conditions and exceptions to Halagar and you will deny to him that any such exceptions exist. Those are my commands. Obey them exactly."

She heard herself responding, "I hear and obey, Master."

At that moment, she felt a sudden, strange disorientation. Dorion, somehow, seemed to be less overpowering to her, more like Boday or anybody else she knew. He seemed, maybe for the first time, just kind of, well, *ordinary.* Her Master, whose voice must be obeyed, was elsewhere, and as of yet she had no commands from him. It was a weird sensation.

"I have to go," he told her. "Boday still has to be told and we have to get packed and ready. That's if Covanti lets us leave. If not, all bets are off.''

She could hear the regret in his voice, and thought of saying or doing something, but she wasn't sure what to say or do. While she was still a bit confused, he left her standing there, alone, in the harem anteroom.

Neither Dorion nor Boday got much sleep that night, not only from the nervousness at going on, but also because of Dorion's fear that Halagar was either pulling a fast one or that the powers that be in the Court would stop them as soon as Halagar made ready to leave with them. Boday, who had no real liking for Halagar at all, saying she'd seen a thousand like him in her time, slept uneasily within reach of a whip and a short sword, ready for any sort of late-night intrusion. However, when light began to creep into the windows, and they began to hear the first stirrings of life in the castle area, nothing had happened.

Boday had agreed with Dorion that Halagar, if he were being straight with them, was an asset they couldn't afford to turn down, but she swore to Dorion that before she would let Charley be permanently given to the mercenary, she would kill either Halagar or Charley.

It was difficult to tell if Halagar had gotten much sleep, either, but he seemed to be true to his word. Two household grooms came for Dorion and Boday and their things, most of which were replacements picked up in Covanti, and took them down to the courtyard, where Halagar was waiting. He was dressed now in a plain black riding outfit with leather jacket and broad-brimmed black hat (none of which were adorned with any symbol or insignia), matching boots, and a thick, black sword and pistol belt.

Charley was with him, dressed in calf-length high-heeled black leather boots from which thin black leather straps came, interlaced up the leg and thigh and forming a cross-hatch pattern that led to a pair of black satin leather panties. Above the waist she wore an overlapping gold-braided neckpiece, matching gold bracelets and earrings, and a light, satiny black cape tied at the neck, but not much else.

Boday leaned over and whispered in Dorion's ear, "You see? Boday said she knew his type."

Dorion shrugged. It seemed an odd comment for Boday, who was rather fond of revealing leather outfits herself and, indeed, had one only slightly more modest on herself. "Seems like kind of an exposed riding outfit for so long a journey, but we're still in the warm latitudes. Still, it's in character with him and not as bad, I guess, as what she was forced to wear before." He frowned. "I see three horses, but one's a pack horse. Where's he expect *her* to ride?"

The answer was the kind of leather saddle placed on Halagar's big, black stallion. It had smaller, independent, leather stirrups attached forward, and the saddle was a bit longer than the norm. A saddle built for two. Either Covanti had two riders common enough so that such saddles were made routinely or Halagar had had this fantasy of his for a long time.

Charley was clearly in her Shari mode as well, servile and submissive and empty-headed. She always was around Halagar, something Boday and Dorion had both noticed and which had confused and disturbed Charley for a while as well. None knew the cause but while Dorion didn't like not having Charley's quick mind and courage on hand, he certainly didn't want Halagar to see that part of her, either, nor anyone else. Shadowcat in her lap broadcast her thoughts; as Shari, those thoughts betrayed nothing.

Still, Halagar's dominance and use of Charley disturbed the magician on a less practical and more emotional level. The idea of seeing her moon over Halagar and kiss him and maybe even make out with him on the trail raised emotional wounds in Dorion that he hadn't even suspected were there.

Still, he consoled himself as best he could and hoped he could stand it, knowing that just as Charley was now a tool of Halagar's, so Halagar would be a tool of Dorion so long as it served his purpose to get them to Boolean. Once inside Boolean's circle of power, Halagar was going to find his dreams a bit harder to hold on to.

It wasn't that Halagar was an evil man, it was just that he'd been, by benefit of being handsome and strong and the best at everything physical all his life, a spoiled and pampered center of attraction. Egotistical, self-centered, Halagar just wasn't the type to ever consider others as anything but tools or employers. Even now, he didn't really understand why he was lonely, or why he was so fixated on Charley even at this level—and he probably never would.

"We want a minimum of sixty leegs a day," Halagar told them, "and more if we can get it. The packhorse is strong and will keep up the pace. With so much of the colonial country infested by rebels, I intend to keep off the main roads if possible and travel mostly by day. Dorion, if you can manage solid Navigation, I intend to pick worlds where there is little report of rebel massings and plentiful water and reasonable terrain. There are a few in each track we must follow. Still, we can't count on anything, and there have been reports of minor Changewinds in the least active colonial worlds. I've got Mandan cloaks for us on the packhorse, so don't let us lose him, but that could also make us a target. They've been gathering Mandan in great quantity on their raids and I can guess why. If you could do the impossible and actually predict a Changewind and have troops ready at its periphery, you'd want to carpet your people in Mandan gold."

And that, of course, was the crux of the whole battle to come. Klittichorn and the Storm Princess together could somehow summon a Changewind to any spot they chose; the Princess could then do what even the greatest and most powerful sorcerer, demon, or magical creature could not—she could direct even that great storm, at least to a degree. Not what it could do, of course—that was beyond anyone to predict or determine—but it didn't really matter to Klittichorn what it did. It changed, it transformed, it replaced for all time (or until the next Changewind) what it touched, and if you could send such a storm roaring into the hubs of the Akhbreed, even their greatest sorcerers and spells could not stop it or even slow it down. And if you had a rebel army, well armed, well trained, and united in its hatred of the Akhbreed, following that storm quickly in, before even those who could get shelter had come back up, you would have an enemy army in your midst that perhaps even sorcery could do nothing against.

Halagar checked out everything, then put Charley up on the saddle and climbed on behind her. At the last moment a small, fast shape darted out from the shadows and leaped on to the big saddle where Charley and Halagar sat. Halagar was startled, and reached around her to pick up the creature and throw it off.

"No!" Dorion shouted. "They need each other. Remember that! The cat is a familiar and essential to her well-being."

The mercenary hesitated, then sighed. "All right," he growled, "but I'll not have a cat in my way here."

"Cats will do what they want to do—particularly this cat," the magician told him. "He will stay out of your way generally, and he will hold on as he must. But they go together, the girl and the cat. It is both or neither."

Shadowcat spent some time figuring out a comfortable place, irritated that his carrier sling was not fixed, but finally found a position that would do right against Charley and settled in, oblivious to argument.

"All right," Halagar growled at last. "But he better stay out of my way and hang on or he will be cat meat no matter what you say."

Dorion and Boday mounted their own steeds, and Dorion looked around at the luxury and comfort they were leaving and gave one last sigh, and then they were off, heading back into dangers worse than any yet faced. The only solace, and it was cold comfort to him, was that within a few more short weeks they would either be with Boolean—or in Hell.

· 3 ·

Practice Session

ETANALON WAS STARTLED to find Crim relaxing on her living room couch when she awoke, even though her magical sense told her that this was no enemy. No one, and nothing, could pass her threshold without being invited, and she'd never seen this fellow before. Most disturbing was that she got the same feeling from the stranger as from the pretty woman who was there the night before.

"Don't be alarmed," he said reassuringly. "I am Crim, Kira's—other half, you might say."

Etanalon frowned. "A curse? A very strong one, by the looks of it."

Crim nodded. "Kira resides within me as a passive passenger by day, and I inside her by night. It was a bargain to save her life, and, while inconvenient at times, it has not been a terrible thing. I believe, knowing what we do now, that we would still have made the choice."

Etanalon looked thoughtful. "Fascinating. A strong, handsome man of the world and a beautiful young slip of a thing. . . . Yet, listening to you and feeling your energies, I can see how intertwined the patterns are. I can also understand why Boolean chose you for this task. You have grown much alike, one to the other."

Crim's eyebrows rose. "Really? Nobody ever said *that* before."

"Not in the mere physical or sexual sense, but where it counts. In your manner of speech, choice of words, radiation of strength. I see not two auras there but more a greater whole. You have her memories, her innermost thoughts, and she yours?"

He nodded. "Yes. That was the hardest part at first. There was almost a descent into madness until such things could be sorted out and dealt with."

"Many would not have had the strength to do so. Almost all who know you both believe you to be separate people, I suspect. Perhaps you still think that way yourself—but you are not. In spite of what you say, the auras tell me that she does not ride with you now, nor you with her last night. I would have known. There were two of you once, quite different, but you escaped madness not by acceptance but by becoming as one. When you are a man, big and strong in the daylight and with the body's natural masculinity, you interact with the world as totally male; when you are a beautiful woman by night, you interact with the world as totally female, but you carry the same mind, aura, and inner strength in both incarnations. You have made a fascinating, almost unique, adjustment. Every male has some feminine aspect to one degree or another or they would be mere brutes, and every female has some male aspect to one degree or another or they would lack the hardness to survive on their own. Only in you, it is equal and without a dominant side."

Crim thought about that. "Maybe. I hadn't really thought about it that way. I certainly never felt attracted to other men, nor Kira to other women, though."

"Each aspect dominates with the body you wear," the sorceress noted. "That is how you avoid madness and enjoy what you have no control over becoming, but each of you draws what is needed from the other aspect. Strange, is it not, that you, who are truly two opposites in one, have no sense of confusion, while the girl, who is herself a single individual, does. Indeed, many would feel threatened or uncomfortable by you if they knew, yet I get the impression you actually enjoy the duality and would feel its loss greatly. Yet even you are uneasy with the nature of our outplaner Storm Princess."

He nodded. "It *does* make me uncomfortable, but I can't really explain why."

"Her situation is not as uncommon as we tend to think it is. It is only that it is out in the open with her that is uncommon. Sex is such a complex thing, such a part of us, both physical and mental, and yet, next to eating and sleeping, it is the most overpowering thing about us. The wonder is not that it goes awry now and then, but that it does not in so many more of us. Still, the combination, physical and mental, biology and environment, is complex and filled with countless variables. Hence, we get the pedophile and the nymphomaniac, the sexual murderer or sadomasochist and we get the impotent and frigid. The variations are endless. One wonders what the so-called 'normal' folk who would condemn her do in their own beds, or in the brothels and entertainment districts. Take any crowd of men and women and you will have a vast horde of sexually abnormal folk there, far more than her relatively minor situation. No one really cares, so long as it is swept under the covers and out of sight, any more than anyone really cares about your own true nature unless it is brought forcefully to their attention. Would a man attracted to Kira lie comfortably with her if he knew that in the morning she would be a tall, strapping, muscular and masculine Navigator? Would the women who swoon over you react the same if they knew that at sunset you would become more beautiful and feminine than they? I think not.''

He shrugged. ''It is true that I feel more comfortable the few who know my situation, and we have encountered far stranger aberrations in bed than we would have dreamed of otherwise. But we are a special case. Barring the unlikely meeting and compatibility of our opposite number, who might be female by day and male by night and both parts attracted to the other, we are best living somewhat separated lives. *She*, though, is not cursed.''

''Of course she is! Not by magic spell, perhaps, but by being different in a way that society strongly disapproves. Still, so long as she hid it, from society, even from herself, she could function—except that she was neither happy nor comfortable hiding. Like Kira inside Crim or Crim inside Kira, it was creating great stress and unhappiness and had the potential to drive her mad—a potential almost realized in her initial situation with this potion-created mate of hers, and after, where she has always taken the easy way out to flee her own inner demons. She has been victimized repeatedly here by an inner drive to forget who and what she was, to cease her own growth as a person. Many people can afford that luxury, although it is difficult to see how it is a positive thing.

She can not. She has a destiny from which she can not run, and if she tries then it will destroy her.''

Crim nodded. ''So you decided that she had to like what she was and feel confident and comfortable with it, no matter what the social cost.''

''In the end, it was she that did it. I simple removed the fear inside her, the social inhibitions that stood in the way of her accomplishing what she must. She now is happy with herself and absolutely uncaring about what others think about it. With that comfort comes confidence. Her ego, which the inhibitions kept fragmented and weak, strengthens constantly now. She will probably grow less pleasant and a lot harder to take, I fear, but this is the sort of person needed to stand up to the challenges ahead.''

It was late afternoon when Sam finally woke, after the best sleep she could remember having in a very long time. Her old memories, her complete self, was back, but she didn't think about that past too much because it wasn't all that pleasant. In fact, it was almost an alien past, really; she could hardly believe how fucked up in the head she'd been all her life.

A fragment of a Golden Oldie song from that past rumbled through her mind, though, and she found herself humming it.

You can't please everyone, so you gotta please yourself.

Not, however, that she was particularly thrilled with the situation as it now stood. Now that she finally felt comfortably at peace with herself, she wanted to go out and pick up her life and *do* things and *see* things and enjoy that life, but her changed attitude towards herself hadn't changed the situation at all.

She was still a fugitive, still lined up for a battle she didn't really know much about or what was expected of her or how to fight it, and she was still pregnant to boot and none of that had changed.

Oddly, it was the pregnancy that dominated her thoughts. She preferred to think that she got knocked up that first time, when it was her own will and choice, and that this was no rapist's child, but it didn't really matter. The kid was still a kid no matter what the father had been.

The crazy thing was, in spite of it all, she *liked* the idea that she was going to have a baby. She wanted that child more than she had ever wanted anything in her whole life, but it stuck her between a rock and a hard place. If she didn't go into this fully, if she didn't face down this Storm Princess and beat her at her own game, then the child had very little future and she even less of one. She wasn't scared for herself, but what if it came down to victory or the child? That slimy, horned bastard always knew the weak points in anybody's armor, and it was a real concern.

But everybody had weak points. Even this guy Klittichorn must have them, or he wouldn't have had to take so long and be so sneaky to get to this point. Maybe the trick wasn't to dwell on the weak points but just try and cover them as much as you could and instead concentrate on your strengths. Or maybe use the weakness—the child inside gave her incentive to win, a motivation to dominate those forces that threatened her. Frankly, she wanted to take on her opposite number right now, one on one, and get it over with, but that wasn't the way things worked.

Damn it, I need a gynecologist, not a green-robed sorcerer, she though sourly. Etanalon was different—she was kind of a shrink, and she certainly was at least as effective as any of the shrinks back home. She just didn't make any bones about working voodoo and doing it with mirrors, that was all. This was different.

She sighed, pulled on the old dress, and wandered into the main house. Baths were few and far between here, but at least breakfast was still breakfast.

"I wish you would join with us," she heard Crim saying, presumably to Etanalon. She walked into the living room and saw the two of them sitting there, talking.

"At the moment—no," the sorceress responded. "I have retired from all that. Someone else must save the world once in a while. I'm tired and pretty well disgusted with the affairs of kings and back-room magicians. Grotag had a meeting just the other day to press for a united front against Boolean, who he is convinced is the really dangerous one. Many of the others who are still sane enough to care agree with him." She broke off the line of conversation and turned to Sam. "Well, hello! How are you feeling?"

"All right, I guess," Sam replied. "Not as ready to take on the world as yesterday, and maybe a little over-tired, I dunno. At least now I know that the reason I been feelin' so weak and washed out lately is the kid. Any chance of getting something to eat? I'll fix it if you tell me where all the stuff is."

Etanalon chuckled. "No need. Sit there in the chair and just think of what you're most in the mood to eat."

Sam sat, and it wasn't hard to come up with a vision of breakfast, even if it was late in the afternoon. Lots of hot cakes, melted butter, real sausages, maybe with some fruit and powdered sugar, with a pitcher of orange juice, fresh squeezed. It had been a long, long time since she'd had a real breakfast like that.

Suddenly, in front of her, was a stand-alone tray with dishes containing just exactly what she'd dreamed of. It was a startling appearance, and she jumped, almost spoiling it by knocking it over. "Hey!" she shouted in surprise.

"Relax," Etanalon told her. "There are several advantages to being a sorceress. No shopping, cooking, cleaning, dusting—unless you want to. Go ahead—it's real. *You* bite *it*, it doesn't bite you."

Sam stared at it for a moment, though. In all the time she'd been in Akahlar, she'd seen demonic spells and mystic potions and strange and magical creatures, but she had never until this moment truly seen flat-out magic. The smell of the food and her hunger drove out any further hesitation, though, and she tore into it. Still, as real as it seemed and as good as it was, it just seemed, well, impossible. You didn't get something for nothing, *that* she'd learned.

Etanalon seemed to read her thoughts. "Sorry—I forgot. You haven't had much experience face to face with Second Rank personnel, have you? If you want the complete technique and its complexities I can give it to you, although it will do you no good. Only those with the power can do it, and only those with a great amount of power and control can do it that effortlessly. No, it is not materialized out of nowhere—I simply took the image from your mind, extrapolated the ingredients, and then did a simple matter-energy-matter transformation on it. So long as we have molecules of anything, even air, to work with it's not that hard."

"You sure don't have to worry where your next meal is

coming from," Sam agreed between bites. "Uh—you get hold of Boolean?"

Crim nodded. "I made the call early this morning using the witchstone. He agrees with you that it is far too dangerous for you to attempt the last leg to him at this point. The lands between here and there are filled with colonial rebels, and they have figured out that Charley isn't you, which is good for her but means you're the sole object of everybody's attention now."

"Yeah—thanks a lot," she responded glumly. "Uh—does that mean they got Charley? I mean, we've heard so little. . . ."

"No, right now they're safe, and even in Covanti," Crim told her. "But they have already crossed the null and are heading towards Tishbaal. A pity—had we known we might have linked up again to form a company of sorts."

She sighed. "Yeah, I could really have used them now, just for shoulders to cry on. All right, so what's his idea for us?"

"We know that Klittichorn is planning something, but we aren't sure what," Crim said. "Spies in the lower ranks of Marépek, which is Klittichorn's domain in the frozen north, report that he and the Storm Princess left there a day ago. No one is quite certain where to, although there are rumors of some sort of fortress or redoubt Klittichorn has used in the past when he wants absolute secrecy."

"You're tellin' me that we don't know where they are?"

He nodded. "That's about the size of it. We don't even know if they're heading for this fortress, even if we knew where it was. They could be headed here, or anywhere."

"Yeah, but how far could they have gotten in just a day?"

"A lot farther than you seem to think," Etanalon put in. "Do not forget that he is a master sorcerer. Within certain complicated limits we can move very far very fast if we have to."

"Oh, yeah? Then how come I been goin' through Hell to get even this close to Boolean? And why hasn't Boolean just used this power to get to me?"

"Klittichorn has convinced many of the sorcerers of the Second Rank that Boolean is the threat," The sorceress reminded her. "Boolean can't move without some of his colleagues knowing where and when. If he were to leave now it would simply cement in the minds of many Akhbreed sorcerers that he is deserting his position and is indeed behind what is happening. He can take Klittichorn, or so he believes, but not several sorcerers of that rank working in concert against him. I believe he is fairly itching to break free, and has been for some time, but he dares not until forced to do so, and that means waiting for Klittichorn to either make a move or make a mistake.''

Sam discovered that this was indeed a magical breakfast. So long as she was still hungry, the moment she cleaned the plate it was renewed. She enjoyed it without guilt, knowing this might be the last decent meal for a while. ''So—we're back to square one, like all the shit we were put through never happened. I can't get to him and he can't get to me and we don't know where the enemy is. So where does that leave me?''

''Not here,'' Crim responded. ''That's a small town down their and the odds are pretty good that within a short period of time our entry into Covanti hub and village curiosity are going to come together and reach the ears of folks we don't want to know about us. Right now we're going to pick a comfortable colony east of here which doesn't border on Tishbaal and lie low. When Klittichorn tries something it will take energy—lots of energy. Boolean is monitoring all over and he hopes to be able to trace it when it comes. *Then* we can move on them.''

''Uh-huh. Hurry up and wait as usual. Seems to me, though, that we got in here real easy. If this local sorcerer is against us and if they now know Charley's not me, it might be a lot harder gettin' out.''

''Searching everyone who comes into and out of a hub is difficult,'' Etanalon noted. ''Concentrating just on those leaving is far easier and more efficient. From this point the hubs are in hands friendly to your enemies and the colonies are heavily infiltrated. I agree, though, that caution outweighs everything else and that you must leave and quickly. I can not really use much sorcery on you since that would disturb the aura of the Storm Princess that is the key to all this. There are a lot of people who fit your general description, so perhaps subtlety, doing just a few minor things, might be far more effective than an elaborate disguise.''

*   *   *

The racial restrictions of the hub system and the nature of Covanti's economy made for some unusual and exceptional sights for an Akhbreed hub region. Periodically, when the grapes in the small private vineyards were ready for harvesting, a fair number of agricultural workers were needed. In the colonies, where most of Covanti's wine and all its export was grown, this was no problem, but only those of an Akhbreed race could enter the hub. Grape harvesting was not unskilled labor—especially when specialty grapes and the royal vineyards were involved. And few of the Akhbreed race had ever bothered to learn anything so menial as grape picking!

Out of this need had grown the tradition of the clan call, in which leaders of family clans would call upon the women members of that clan to come aid the harvest in the name of clan unity. Such a gathering of the females of the Abrasis clan was even now in its final stages at one of the clan estates near the border, and it was there that Etanalon sent them, after suitable preparation. The harvest and subsequent stompings and the like involved hundreds of women, many from different colonial worlds who knew each other not at all, although all were at least very distant cousins.

Small spells that did not involve any sort of molecular transformation would not have any real effect on Sam, and they were rather simple for one such as Etanalon. It was a rural tradition in Covanti that a woman's hair might be trimmed but not cut. Hence, a small spell that caused her hair to grow right down to her ass overnight was in order. Sam had always preferred very short hair because it was almost effortless to care for, but she accepted this both out of need and because she knew it could always be cut later. The hair was also darkened to inky black, but with some white steaks that were a particular characteristic of the Abrasis clan. Not everybody had them, of course, but it was more common than not. More irritating to her, at least at the start, were the very long teardrop-shaped silver earrings that were fixed permanently to her earlobes. The only time she'd ever really worn earrings was after Charley had convinced her to get her ears pierced at the mall, but they had been little fake gold and pearl things and she'd eventually taken them off. These things weighed a ton and weren't removable.

But it was another Covantian custom, and she accepted the discomfort as part of the disguise. She *did* have to admit to herself that the very long hair and the long earrings did in fact suit her fat face and form pretty well.

Finally, some very bewitched eyeglasses that really changed her general appearance more than she expected them to. When she wore them, they were clear transparent glass, of no real effect except as a nuisance. But, if they were removed and someone else looked into them, they would present a convincingly distorted and blurry picture as if she had serious eye problems. It was one of those neat little touches a major sorceress could give you.

Covanti hub was both peaceful and pretty, but it was carefully guarded. A check of the border showed regular patrols by civil guardsmen and a fairly thorough scrutiny by militia at the border posts of anyone leaving. Clearly somebody had put two and two together and concluded that perhaps she was indeed within the hub.

Sam had spent most of the civilized part of her life since being dragged to Akahlar in Tubikosa, a rather strict and somewhat fundamentalist place with covered women and lots of hang-ups, and even though she'd lived all her time there in the inevitable capital city entertainment district, she had a strong idea of just what the typical Akhbreed were like and she'd been none too thrilled by them. They had their lapses, usually for their own convenience, but they were basically straight, uptight, and kind of like those pictures you saw of the most backward parts of the Middle East back home. Since then she'd come more or less through the back door from place to place, mostly hiding out, or sneaking through.

Covanti, however, was a much looser place. It was almost too bad that it was ruled by such dumb guys at the top, since otherwise it was almost the opposite of what she thought of as proper Akhbreed society. It was more class-bound, sure, but she had never identified with anybody other than the lower classes here anyway and so that didn't really bother her. The big city folk dressed more comfortably and with a lot more variety than the suits and baggy dresses of Tubikosa, and, while nominally all Akhbreed followed the same general religion, there was nary a veil in sight and a lot of skin. Upper-class women were still somewhat cloistered and withdrawn, but middle-class women were at ease in colorful saris and light sleeveless tops and short skirts, and even the men wore loose-fitting colorful shirts and slacks most places.

The peasants were even looser, more so than even some of the colonials she'd seen. The climate was warm and wet, at least in the hub, except in the few high mountains areas to the north and west, and it was kind of startling to see peasant women, often with huge jars or boxes on their heads, walking topless down the road wearing only a colorful, light-colored sarong or short skirt, apparently all of cotton. The peasant males weren't above being bare-chested, either, although their normal dress was a kind of white or tan baggy shirt and matching pants, usually with sandals, and wide-brimmed white or tan leather hats.

"In many places it's hard to tell the classes apart," Crim commented, noting her surprise. "In the subtropical and tropical regions things are clearer. Somebody with royal blood wouldn't be caught dead even in this heat and humidity without being fully and formally overdressed to the point of heat stroke, which is why you never see them much in the day. The middle classes show off their relative wealth—or hide their lack of it—with fashion. The peasants—well, you see how they dress. It's not only tradition, it's the law, really. The gradations of class are actually a lot more complicated than that, but you can actually get thrown in jail for dressing inappropriately to your class."

"I'll stick with the peasants," she told him. "No complications or hang-ups and they just let it all hang out and to hell with it."

He nodded. "Now, the vineyards of the Abrasis clan are loose, and the women brought in from the colonies to handle it are all officially peasants here no matter what position they might occupy back home. It's not quite as loose as it looks, either. There's an effective if unobtrusive security guard for them and the women don't go anyplace alone, only in small or large groups. The women don't have much more in the way of political or civil rights here than anywhere else in Akhbreed society, either, outside the family. The only real exceptions are those with magical powers and those with political connections, who have a kind of *de facto* position and respect. Needless to say, the plantation owners and colonial managers don't send their own wives and sisters and daughters to these obligatory things—they send the peasant-class women in, usually the daughters and such of the field supervisors, overseers, and the like. Lots of peasants hire on cheap to the colonial corporations because, while they're the lowest here in the hub, and the lowest Akhbreed in the colony, they always have a whole native race to feel and be superior to out there. It's an ego thing. You'll find most of these women ignorant, totally unschooled, lacking much imagination, and about the most bigoted group you ever met. Take it easy in there. The object is to blend in, not draw attention.''

She nodded. "I'll try. How long do I have to stick it out in there, anyway? I know as much about wine—other than it comes from grapes and if you drink enough you can get tipsy—as I know about, well . . .*babies.*''

Crim grinned. "You won't have to know much. You're starting to show and that means they'll make you a cook or something like that. Women are coming and going all the time there during this period so it's unlikely anybody will think your showing up is anything unusual. For most of them it's an excuse to get out and away and many of them spend more time in the villages, maybe buying stuff or just seeing the sights, than actually working. You just walk in, keep your story and your accent straight, and do a little acting so you won't pick fights and draw attention to yourself. I'm going check the lay of the land and security on the eastern borders. I'll stick myself in as a Navigator going into the colonies as a dead head interested in escorting any who want to go home and thereby picking up some spare change. I've got about fourteen different Guild cards, so don't panic if I come in with a different name and a slightly different look.''

"I still ain't too sure about this," she said worriedly. "We're gonna hav'ta pick up a small bunch of girls to make it a group, and unless we ditch 'em fast Kira's gonna be kind'a obvious, but if we do they'll be after our heads.''

"Don't worry about Kira," he soothed her. "For one thing, these are colonials, not hidebound hub-huggers. I've had a little experience here. Just make friends, not waves—understand?''

She nodded. "I'll do what I can.''

Infiltrating the harvest gathering proved to be very little of a problem. Sam looked right, talked more or less right, and the security men weren't about to even ask whether or not every woman in the group she joined had been there from the start. The idea of a woman actually sneaking into one of these peasant camps just would never enter their head.

Sam had always thought of wine as something that came from more or less cold regions, and, back home, she would at least have not found lush wine grapes in a tropical setting. This was not home, though; this was Akahlar, and the rules were quite different here, as were the animals and vegetation, even if much of it looked the same.

The festival looked less like hard work and more like the Campfire girls, although the Campfires never dressed like this. The ancestral castle was off on its own grounds so far away from them it was simply a distant and tree-shrouded speck; the women were put up in open-sided buildings with thatched roofs, about twenty women to a unit, or block, sleeping on straw mats. There were communal cooking areas between each unit; generally fire pits and crude stone ovens that looked like giant backyard barbecue pits. The makings came out in wagons daily from the estates, were prepared, then distributed on a regular basis to the women unit by unit. To eat, you lined up, grabbed a hubcap-sized wooden plate, got what you wanted, then went over on the grass and had a picnic. The food was of surprisingly good quality—these *were* of the clan, after all, peasant branch or not—and drink was, naturally, local wine.

It seemed to Sam almost like an all-girl's picnic and camp-out. Nobody seemed to be working very hard, most seemed to be enjoying it, and almost all of them were young, the majority in their mid or upper teens and the oldest perhaps in their mid to upper twenties. They came from every kind of colonial world Covanti controlled—Sam counted maybe sixty variations of telltale earrings before she stopped counting.

And, although married women were rarely sent to these things and she met none in her first day there or after, there were a fair number of pregnant girls around, many looking no more than fourteen or fifteen. Kids having kids. Peasants couldn't afford the magic charms and alchemical potions that were the only forms of birth control in Akahlar, and abortion was quite literally a mortal sin to the religion—you did it and got caught, you died by public dismemberment. That was what drove many young colonial peasant girls to run away to the hub cities, where, of course, they wound up feeding the appetites of the patrons of the entertainment districts.

Of course, it depended on the locals and the clan, and the local priests as well, how such a bald indiscretion was taken. The pregnant girls here were sent here mostly to get them out of sight for a while, or until the family back home could figure out what to do next. Legally, none were allowed to have their kids in the hub, though; that would make them hub citizens, not colonials, and the government would then have some responsibility for their support and upbringing. Some would think just that way, sneak off to the city, have the kid and have it taken away and given to the church, then delivered to the pimps and lords of the entertainment district if they refused to be neutered and made wards of the church—usually janitors, housemaids, and the like, de-sexed and then cloistered for life—although few if any of the colonial girls who ran off to the city either knew or believed this. The rest would go home, but Sam wasn't sure what kind of reception they'd get at that point. She decided she'd try to find out, although she was pretty sure it wouldn't be a great life or a happy one.

This system not only oppressed and controlled the nonhuman and not-quite-human colonial populations, it was also quite effective in making even a large number of its own miserable for life.

Few of the pregnant girls with whom Sam was naturally quartered and placed seemed to think about that, though, or the alternatives awaiting them. Some of it was just the usual teenage "It'll work out" or "It won't happen to me," and some was just trying not to think about the future so long as they could be here.

She picked up her assigned goods, which weren't much—a couple of light brown panties, her personal cup and plate, and her small toiletries kit of comb, brush, and the like that she'd brought with her—and found her assigned sleeping space. Not much, but at least there was a bit of breeze and not many bugs out here.

"Hi! Welcome to the Disease Pits," she heard a pleasant teenage female voice say in a very provincial but understandable accent. Sam turned and saw a pretty young girl of perhaps sixteen or seventeen, maybe five-five or six, her waist-length hair held in a great ponytail and slung over her left shoulder so it hung down the front. She was very well along in her pregnancy, her natural thinness just making her distended belly all the more prominent, and she was wearing just a yellow panty almost like a bikini bottom. The brief dress was practical; there was no way she was going to get a sarong around her that would stay on. The fact that almost all the women around were wearing the sarongs but Sam had been issued panties indicated that dressing by class was taken here even to the lowest common denominator. "My name's Quisu," she added.

Sam kind of stared at her distended belly for a moment. It was the first time she'd ever seen a girl this far along—not in a maternity dress—this close up, and the sight was unnerving. Unlike Sam, who was fat anyway, this girl really looked like a normal teenager who somehow had swallowed an entire undigested watermelon. Quisu held herself oddly, didn't look either well balanced or comfortable, and waddled when she walked.

Is that the way I'm gonna get in another month or two? Sam couldn't help thinking. Aloud she said, "I'm Sahma, of Mahtri. Uh—how far along are you?"

"A few days over eight months. Less than a month to go." She sighed. "They're gonna throw me out'ta here this week, looks like."

"Oh yeah? Then what?"

Quisu shrugged. "I ain't decided yet. Guess I got to real soon now, though. I been thinkin' of sneakin' out in the city but I don't know nobody or nothin'. I ain't never been in no city before. Hell, this is the biggest group of Akhbreed I ever been around at one time. I don't even know how far it is or how to get there. You *believe* that?"

Sam nodded. "You're better off not knowin'. You get out on the road here, some guy'll come up and promise you all sorts of stuff and take you there. I saw some of the vultures and I know the type. I been in cities. Girl like you, they'd let you have the kid then slip you some stuff so you wouldn't remember nothin' 'bout yourself, your past, even what you looked like, and you'd be just nice and cooperative. You'd just be another street whore on some guy's string.''

"Aw, we all heard all that shit. Maybe it's true for some, maybe not, but it beats goin' home for a lot of girls.''

They walked out to the grass and sat, Sam curious and wanting to make a few friends right off the bat. "Is it that bad?'' she asked Quisu. "Goin' back, I mean?''

"*Uh!* I hate this part of it. You can't even get comfortable sittin' or standin' and you got to pee every ten minutes. Uh—I dunno what it's like in—where'd you say you was from?''

"Mahtri.''

"Yeah, Mahtri. But you take like Dolimaku, where I come from. The natives look like big lizards, even hiss when they talk. Ain't that many Akhbreed there, and the ones what are, are real strict. If I go back, they let me have the kid, then I get strung up, get enough lashes on my back to make permanent scars, then they carve my face up so's I won't never tempt no more boys. Like the boys ain't never at fault! Shit, I bet Coban maybe got a lickin' and grounded for a couple weeks or somethin', if that. His dad's the chief overseer. Kind'a big shot. Big deal! But that Coban's so damn cute, with the tightest little ass and the deepest big brown eyes you ever seen, and he was so smooth, I—I guess I fell for him like everybody did, only I was dumb enough to think he was gonna marry me.''

Sam was appalled at the first part. "You mean they'd actually carve your face up?'' No *wonder* the girls lit out for the cities, dangers and dismal futures and all.

Quisu nodded. "Yeah. Only thing is, though, the kid would be accepted like a regular member of the family. Have a chance, a future, you know what I mean? And I could see it, hold it, even care for it, watch it grow up, you know? Even if I couldn't never tell it I was its Momma. Things any different where you come from?''

Sam felt a little sick, but didn't want to press on for now with the subject.

"Well, I ain't gonna be exactly welcomed with open arms,'' she responded, being careful, "but I'm in a little different way than you. Train I was travellin' with, comin' back from visitin' relatives in the city, got hit by bandits. I got raped.''

"Wow! And I thought *I* was through somethin'! Now

Putie—you'll meet her, she's a nice kid—she got raped, too, but it was by the Company Supervisor's brother. He claimed she seduced him and was only claimin' rape 'cause she got knocked up and, well, you know which one they believed. She's from Gashom. She says they shave your head there, then rub some gunk on it so it never grows out, stick a brand on your forehead, and then you become the property of the Company, which in this case includes the guy who raped her. Ain't much, but the guy gets the kid, and in her case that means the kid's raised with the upper class, so it's something. Her friend Meda's also from Gashom, but she's from a town and got knocked up same as me. She'll get the same shave and brand, but her kid'll go to some orphanage someplace and she'll wind up property of the town—kind'a like what they say you get in the city, only without the forgettin' juice.''

"I guess you're all sort'a thinkin' 'bout goin' back or not,'' Sam responded, "and maybe comparin' notes.''

"You try not to think about it,'' Quisu said softly, then patted her bulge. "But sometimes you just can't get away from it. Meantime, we're kind'a the bad examples here. Not that you're treated bad. There's some that're holier than the gods or real smug and superior, but most of 'em'll talk to you, sometimes ask you what it's like, that kind of thing, even be real sympathetic or extra kind. We don't do no work here 'less we want to, and those of us this far along don't want to much. It's kind'a borin', but it's the way things are. Sometimes you get to hatin' the kid, sometimes you get to hatin' yourself, sometimes you just lie there and cry a lot, but mostly you just relax and try not to think much. There's always some girls assigned to watch us, like them over there tryin' to pretend they ain't, just to make sure we don't try'n kill ourselves or somethin', but nobody stops you if you just slip away and off the grounds.''

"Are there many girls who try and kill themselves?'' Sam asked, wishing she could do something, anything, for these girls.

"Sometimes. One tried it while I was here. Real sloppy job, though. Many got a lot worse to go back to than me or the others I told about. I mean, what's a little balding or scarring compared to havin' your tongue cut out, your eyes put out, and your eardrums shattered, like they do in Fowkwin?''

There wasn't much to say in answer to that. And this festival would be winding down in a few weeks; they'd all be forced to choose at that point.

Damn it! Boday used to take kids like these and make them into mindless sex bombs, while others on the street sold the less desirable ones into slavery or worse. The lucky ones would wind up permanent, free, peasant labor at a Pasedo-type place. And she'd sat there and accepted it!

The fact was, she'd just ignored all the bad parts and hadn't looked very hard or thought about it at all. It didn't make her feel very good right now.

If she had her way, and the power, she'd create some land somewhere on one of these colonial worlds as a refuge where all these kind of girls could go and have their kids and have a kind of life without being slaves or property or worse! A Pasedo kind of place without a Duke or hierarchy at all. But she didn't have that power, and so long as the Akhbreed maintained their rigid cultural attitudes and tight colonial grip there never would be such a place, not really. And she was supposed to save these damned Akhbreed from such destruction! Hell, this was just one small part of one branch of one clan! How many girls like this *were* there? Maybe, just maybe, she was coming around to the real Storm Princess's point of view. She'd been around Klittichorn a long time— she *couldn't* be *that* dumb.

Could it be that the Storm Princess knew just what she was doing, but could not imagine even dominance by a godlike Klittichorn any worse than what was now here?

Her old problem was coming back now, in spades. The problem that had overshadowed all her other problems, all her personal problems, and the one no magic mirrors could resolve for her. It was the one she'd been running from, consciously or not, since it had been first put to her, and she was no happier with it now than before. Sure, Klittichorn was a damned murderer and something of a power-mad maniac, but what in hell was Boolean? Etanalon had said that Boolean disliked the Akhbreed way and was outspoken in that dislike, and that was, more than anything else, why nobody else liked him or would help him or even believe him. But he'd done nothing to change the system and was still working against the odds to preserve it. Nor was Etanalon a really good source on this—she, with her power, could never comprehend the horrible choices these girls faced, and the most she might do with the system was fine-tune it, remove some of its more gross features, but leaving everything else in tact. Etanalon, at heart, was a believer. Why else was she still on the fence?

Damn it, she didn't have enough information! Never had. She needed to meet Boolean, talk to him, take his measure, not as some distant and mysterious ghostlike figure but man to woman. How the hell could she muster the confidence and will to beat back the Storm Princess unless she was sure she was doing the right thing?

She felt a sudden, sharp, uncomfortable twinge in her belly, and must have registered surprise or discomfort on her face.

Quisu chuckled. "I think you just got kicked."

But the kick had made Sam abruptly aware that the hot sun was no longer beating down and she looked up and saw swiftly moving clouds gathering, and she forced herself to relax. *That* was the way to draw a lot of attention fast, and that was in nobody's interest right now.

"Wanna meet some of the others?" Quisu asked her.

"Yeah, sure. Why not?" Sam responded, needing to move or do *something* right now.

"That line of trees over there is the river," the girl told her, pointing. "That's the bath tub around here. It's shady and a little cooler there, so it's kind of a hangout for those of us with nothin' much else to do. I used to be there a lot this time of day, but you get to feelin' so awkward and dumb-looking and so damned tired quick."

Sam got up slowly, then helped Quisu to her feet. It wasn't all that far, but it really was hard on Quisu, and Sam let her take it slow and easy and knew that, fat or not, this was her in not too much longer a time. If, of course, she lived that long.

There were a dozen or so visibly pregnant girls there under the trees, and it was a sort of instant comraderie that made things a lot easier for Sam. Quisu's friend Putie was something of a shock; she was so tiny she looked maybe twelve or thirteen, no more than four-foot-ten and if she weighed eighty pounds, even with her extra baggage, she'd be at fighting weight. Putie was, in fact, simply very small and slight, but she was among the older girls in the Disease Pit at seventeen. Quisu was sixteen, and Putie's fellow Gashomian Meda, a chubby girl with very large tits, was fifteen. All were well along, although in Putie's case it was hard to tell since she was so very tiny and the child was certainly at least normal size and the distention was gross. Sam couldn't help but wonder if Putie was too small and weak to survive the birth.

Sam let them do most of the talking, if only to avoid having to come up with details of a world she'd never actually been to, or making references to people and places she shouldn't know about. They talked freely, and, as Crim had warned, it was kind of tough not to object to some of it, as when Meda referred to the native population of Gashom as Slimeys, but Sam restrained herself, realizing that, no matter how wrong it was, these girls right now desperately needed somebody, some category, lower than they were, and they took the first and only cultural target of opportunity available. Okay, terrible things portended for them; they were headed for the very bottom of the Akhbreed ladder—but they would still be higher than the natives. It wasn't much, but if it's all you got, you go for it.

Sam had always kind of wondered how, back home, in Civil War times, all those thousands of church-going southern people, most of whom had never and would never own plantations or any slaves, would be willing to march out and fight and die for slavery. Maybe this was the answer. If you were some dirt-poor Appalachia farmer plowing rocks and in hock up to your ears and had kids you couldn't feed and very little else except what you might get sharecropping for the rich, you were pretty damned low. But so long as there were slaves, there was somebody lower. Like these girls, lowest of the low, who would still be so appalled at a colonial native uprising that they'd fight and die rather than let the natives take over.

Well, she was learning a lot about people and about herself, Sam thought. The trouble was, the lessons didn't seem to lead to any clear conclusion.

The ignorance of the girls was appalling, too. As much as

they were being screwed by the system, they still believed in it and could conceive of no other. They thought the sun moved around the Earth and that the stars were holes through which a little of the Kingdom of the Gods shone through. They had seen so little electrical that they considered it in the same realm as magic, and the concept of flush toilets or cities larger than small towns was just not in them. None could conceive of snow or really being cold.

None of them had ever seen any real magic, yet they believed that the spirits were everywhere—in the trees and wind and water and even the rocks—and they prayed to them or asked them for favors.

Most amazing was their total acceptance of their class. They could no more conceive of being anything but peasant class or lower, than they could conceive of suddenly turning into a dog or a lion. The very idea of *aspiring* to move up in class or position or that it was possible or done in other places was so totally alien to them that there was no use in trying to explain it. This was why even the stories of what happened to girls like them in the towns and cities held little terror, but it was also why only a small percentage of these young unwed mothers really did run away. They had a near total fatalistic outlook that sustained them and kept them from madness, but which would lead most of them to mutilation and dishonor back home simply because that was the way things were.

That was frustrating. They couldn't help their ignorance, but the idea of accepting even this was really too much for Sam, yet she didn't try and argue them into any kind of alternative action.

The fact was, they *had* no alternatives she could recommend. Oh, they had choices, all right—mutilation and permanent dishonor back home, becoming a whore or a slave or a eunuch in the city, or maybe death. And no matter what they were feeling inside, they accepted that. The completeness of Akhbreed political, religious, and cultural control was amazing and something she had never really fully faced before. And by so tightly controlling themselves they were able to control so many other worlds and people and cultures.

And the future was always on their minds.

"Men," Meda said in the same tone you'd use for vermin. "They always got to be the bosses, push everybody around.

We bear 'em and raise 'em and they grow up to be strutting assholes just tryin' to overpower and outdo each other, and the ones that can't come back and beat up on the women. It ain't fair. There oughta be someplace where the women are the bosses. Yeah, I know, it's sacrilege, but who says it is? Priests, right? Men. I ain't felt too religious lately.''

"Well, I dunno," Quisu responded. "I still like men. I guess I'll always like 'em no matter what. There's lots of good ones—my dad, for one, and my brothers ain't all that bad, 'though I'd never say that to their faces. It'd be nice if we had some equal say in things—I mean, they trust us enough to eat our cookin' but not to do business or sit in on councils. There's good and bad men just like there's good and bad women. It don't make no difference. We just run into the wrong sort once too often, that's all. I ain't even really blamin' the boy that knocked me up. I mean, I was crazy for him and I wouldn't listen to nobody. I never even thought about *this*." She patted her belly. "Never entered my head, and probably not his, neither. I ain't sure if I could do it over I could stop myself from havin' him inside me again.''

"Yeah, but most girls got crushes on somebody, only they don't go all the way," Putie noted. "Most stick it out 'til they get married. *I* stuck it out, but it didn't do me no good. He was a damned spoiled brat who never thought 'bout nothin' 'cept what he felt like and he was half again as tall as I was and three times my weight, and his girlfriend just broke up with him and got engaged to somebody else. He couldn't take it out on her so he took it out on the first girl he saw, the bastard. And when I went and told about it they all acted like it was my fault or somethin', like I came on to him. That's the way *he* told it and they all just believed it even though they knew what a louse he was. Uh—I just about made up my mind I ain't goin' back, you know.''

The others turned and said, "Huh?" almost in unison.

"I don't care 'bout me," Putie told them, "but he ain't gonna have this baby. No way. I don't care what happens to me or where the baby winds up, but he ain't gettin' it. Shit—what if it's a girl? Imagine *him* with a girl kid! Uh-uh.''

Sam could sympathize. "Where will you go?" she asked the tiny woman. "Into the city?"

"Uh-uh. I ain't never been in no city but what I hear 'bout

it I don't like. I'll cross the null and take the first colony that comes up that I can sneak into.''

"Putie," Quisu said softly, "if you have that kid without a midwife and maybe a healer around, you'll probably die.''

Putie shrugged. "Maybe that's for the best. But it'll drive 'em all nuts in any case 'cause they'll never *know*. None of 'em'll ever be sure. Maybe I'll luck out and get some colonials that'll help me.''

"Yeah, that'll be the day," Meda responded in disgust. "They'll probably eat your baby and then chain you as a pet. 'Com'on! Everybody rape the Akhbreed girl!' Uh-uh. Not for me."

It went on and on like this until Sam could take it no longer. Finally she and the others wandered back to the camp, where hordes of young women were now gathering for the meal or helping prepare and dish it out. Sam ate well, but didn't rejoin in the constant conversation testing out all the alternatives these girls were playing with. She was so damned depressed she wanted to have a good cry, but there wasn't even a good place to do that.

Lying there later on her mat, she tried to sleep, tried to put all thoughts out of her mind, to at least not face the darkness that the thatched roof covered long enough for sleep. Blank your mind, relax. . . .

She was wearing a full-length fine satin dress with gold belt and jewelry, and she was walking down a set of stone stairs to a great chamber. It was a very strange place, sort of like a great hollow dome, only it had concentric stone steps going down in row after row to a round and flat stage at the bottom, kind of like some great ancient theater.

On the floor of the chamber were several designs painted on the floor. The designs were all identical—perfect pentagrams—but were arranged in a kind of mathematical symmetry and each was a different color, the pentagonal centers all pointing inward. And, at the center of the chamber's floor, there stood a strange, violet-colored, pulsating, round globe, transparent enough so that you could see the other side through its outer skin, and the globe was moving, slowly but surely, west to east. On it were evenly spaced dots of bright orange light.

There were others in the chamber as well. She glanced

over and saw Klittichorn, in full crimson robes and horns, sitting on one of the stone rows and working with some kind of strange object.

Suddenly Sam recognized that object with a shock. A computer! The son of a bitch had a portable computer! How the hell did he get it or know how to use it?

The others were also in robes, although of dull greens and browns and blues. There were both men and women there, and while none looked like very strange creatures, all seemed to have something odd or amiss about them, something not quite right. One had tremendously pointed ears and a giant cyclopslike eye that seemed segmented into at least three parts; another appeared to have a broad tail sticking out from under her robe, and the last one she could see might well have had batlike wings. Yet all were dressed as sorcerers, and all seemed busily checking out something or another in various parts of the chamber.

Three of these oddities, plus Klittichorn and her. Five. Five pentagrams on the floor, each color coded to the robes of the others, except for the golden one that was obviously hers.

The Storm Princess turned and approached Klittichorn. "Well, wizard, has your demon box given you what you sought?"

The sorcerer didn't answer right away, but finished up on the keyboard, then watched as the small screen filled with incomprehensible numbers. He nodded to himself, smiled slightly, and looked up at her. "Indeed yes, my Princess. It would be nice to test it out, though, before going straight against Boolean. We know it works, but accuracy and control are crucial."

The Storm Princess nodded. "Very well. Whenever you're ready. This place is unpleasant, almost haunted. I would soon do what it was built to do and do so quickly."

"Patience, patience," Klittichorn responded. "You won't believe what went into its construction, let alone its powering. What brings you here now?"

"I had another brief weakening. I felt it, this afternoon, even though I was doing nothing. It disturbs me."

"Yes. If we only knew where she was. . . . A good test, I

*would think. Go, rest, practice your control. We will need it
soon enough.''*

*The Storm Princess turned and walked back up the cham-
ber, lifting her dress slightly so as to keep from tripping and
falling back into that pit.*

Sam had not had one of these cross-over episodes in a very
long time, and never one as clear as this. The longer it went
on, the more vivid it became, almost as if she and the Storm
Princess were truly one, and it was Sam and not her duplicate
who was now walking in that chamber. They were so mentally close, so attuned, Sam couldn't help wondering. . . .

"Wait!" Sam called out to the Storm Princess.

The Princess stopped suddenly, then turned and looked
around, but saw no one. Clearly, though, she had heard!

The old Sam wouldn't have dared this, and maybe the new
one would have been more cautious, but the day spent with
the poor girls had disturbed her deeply, causing her to dare
the risk.

"This is your sister, whom you seek to destroy," Sam told
her.

"Get out of my mind, bitch!"

The thought was so sharp, so violent, and so filled with
rage that for a moment Sam was taken aback, but she knew she
had to press onward. She had to know.

*"I am not your enemy! Not necessarily, anyway! This
system sickens me! I don't want to defend it! But all you and
Horny there have done is tried to kill me, and I know that you
know he's a slimeball! Give me your reasoning! Tell me your
plans! Show me why I should not fight you!"*

The Storm Princess whirled. "Klittichorn! The bitch is
here! In my mind! Get her out! *Get her out!*" The unnaturally
low voice she shared with Sam echoed across the chamber and
everybody else froze.

Klittichorn looked up at her, then stood up and stared
straight at the Storm Princess. The distance was fairly great,
yet it seemed as if he were looking not only at the woman but
through her. A tiny, thin beam of white light seemed to shoot
from him to the Storm Princess, ricochet off the woman, and
land somewhere on the pulsing violet globe.

One of the yellow lights on the globe changed to white.

"She—she's in Covanti!" one of the others shouted. "In the damned *hub!* Low hills . . . near the border. . . ."

"Got her!" Klittichorn shouted. "Princess, get back down here at once! Places, everybody! Full power up! We got her!"

Suddenly contact was broken—completely, absolutely, leaving Sam there wide awake in the darkness. It was still—Jesus! So fucking still you could cut it with a knife!

What have I done? she wondered to herself.

She got up, and managed to carefully step over and around sleeping girls and get to the edge of the enclosure. There was a fire still burning in the fire pit, although it was slowly dying, and she went over to it and tried to think. Five places, five pentagrams—but only one Storm Princess. That spinning violent globe—Akahlar? The shining yellow lights—hubs? *Think! Think!* How much time? Had to be. Had to be hubs. The white one had been near the middle, where the hot places were, and this was sure one of them. Covanti, then.

Five places but only one Storm Princess. That was important, somehow. What the hell did the globe do? The five of them stand there, they concentrate on someplace, the pentagrams point, and where they all come together is the target. That had to be it. Made no sense but what did around here? Four of them . . . sorcerers. Akhbreed sorcerers, probably, the others like Yobi, misshapen, changed, by their own misfired powers, but powers they still had.

What would they send? Some great demon stormriders, perhaps, or great magic spells, or what? No time to run, no place to run to. Ten minutes alone in the dark on that road, right around here, and she'd be in the hands of slavers and it would be bye-bye Sammie anyway.

Wait a minute. . . . Wait a minute. . . . Stormriders, big spells—they wouldn't need *her* for that. The Storm Princess could do only one thing, and it was the one thing none of them could do. Could that gizmo maybe *broadcast* that power? Send it here like it was some kind of radio or something? But what good would it do to send even a hurricane here? Her powers were at least the equal of the Storm Princess's, and she now knew how to draw the power from the storms, shape them, direct them, and she'd be closer to the storm than the Princess, closer to the elementals, whatever they were, who guided and fueled it and obeyed the Storm Princess. They would know that.

Changewind!

The term itself explained everything and yet was the greatest terror she knew. That big gadget—some way to focus magic power. Could those four sorcerers do what no sorcerer dared to do and actually cause or call or create the conditions for a Changewind? Poke a hole someplace?

Call it, yeah, but they were powerless to control it or do anything with it. The Akhbreed sorcerers feared Changewinds as much as anybody, since they were just as much helpless victims of the storm as the average person. But they were far away, inside that domed chamber, far from the Changewind they would call, safe from its effects.

Could the Storm Princess even command a Changewind?

The temperature seemed to be dropping, the very air thinning. Deep within the darkness there were terrible rumblings that caused the ground to vibrate. Sam stood up, turned, and looked around into the darkness. The conditions and the vibrations were already waking up most of the women, but they were sleepy and confused.

Let's see. . . . You could save yourself from a Changewind by covering yourself completely with Mandan gold, the only stuff that could shield you. But there was no Mandan here—not in hubs. They carried it on the trails and in the colonies and in Crim's wagon, but not here, in a place like this. It would take a lot, anyway.

She had never faced a Changewind in person, although she'd seen one in a vision, through other eyes. These fancy places were supposed to have crypts, big underground chambers lined with Mandan, for everybody to run into! That's how it had been. But even if the manor house had one, it wouldn't be big enough for everybody here, and the house was like three-quarters of a mile away. Forget it. They'd panic here and most wouldn't make it anyway.

Think. . . . Think. . . . Damn it, something in what you just thought. Think, Sam!

If they sent a storm she was of equal power at least to the Storm Princess, and closer.

Was the Changewind, for all its fearsome results, actually

just another big storm? It *had* to be! Otherwise none of Klittichorn's shit would work!

There! Tremendous sound and lightning just off to the east, between here and the border. Tremendous explosions, and women screaming all around her.

Far off, the sound of a siren kind of like a volunteer fire department came to her ears, and to the others, and immediately the large number of women began screaming in panic, "Changewind! Changewind! Make for the house!"

Sam moved away from the panicking mob, away from the enclosures, towards the storm. Was she enough? Was she up to this yet? Was she forgetting something, maybe?

She realized, suddenly, that she'd picked up a long stick from the cooking area without even thinking about it. She made to throw it away as the sounds of panic receded behind her, then stopped as she was about to throw. A pointer. Something to focus on, like *they* had.

She pressed the stick in the dirt and with all her might began to trace a circle, unsure in the darkness whether or not it was even taking real shape in the ground. Then a line here, then there, then again, and again, and again. If there *was* a pentagon in the middle of the star, she was within it, and it was pointed towards the terrible lightning and thunder and explosive sounds that now seemed so close.

She heard some people behind her and turned. "Who's there?" she called. Even now, the wind was starting to pick up, to blow things about, but that was not the Changewind, only the effects from its leading edge. It was coming, but it was not here yet.

"It's Quisu and Putie!" she heard Quisu's voice call. "Come! Get under some shelter! It *might* help! There's no way we gonna make it up there in time!"

"Stay back!" Sam shouted to them. "Don't go into the shelter! Get everybody still there out in the open but behind me! You understand? Out in the open and *behind me!* Sit on the ground! This wind's gonna be real fierce real fast!"

"You crazy!" Putie shouted. "Nobody faces down a Changewind!"

"Maybe I am," Sam called back. "We'll know in about two minutes! Now—do what I say!"

Tremendous gusts now hit her, and the leading edge of rain

that would become quickly intense. She heard somebody yell as they were knocked down, and she heard the sounds of things blowing this way and that, things that were normally too heavy to blow anywhere. Within another minute she could hear the sound of thatched roofs coming apart, and the cracking sounds of some of the enclosures starting to give way. There were screams as well, but she couldn't pay attention to anything now except that coming storm, invisible in the darkness.

Strangely, she felt remarkably calm, as if something inside her was relieved that a climax had actually come, that action was required without nagging questions of right and wrong.

She reached out into that thundering that seemed marching straight for her, not denying it, not hiding from it, almost welcoming it. She felt the strength, the energy, flow into her and she suddenly stiffened, a look of pure amazement on her face in the lightning's glow, as her whole body felt not the sudden, pounding rain and wind but rather the most intense, sustained orgasmic feeling she had ever known. The power flowing to her was enormous, beyond belief, but all she could think was, *Come on, you stupid bitch of a princess! Let's see how you take on this fat, pregnant, peasant dyke who hates your god-damned guts!*

· 4 ·

The Victorious Trap

THE STORM WAS small by weather standards, but what it could do was something no ordinary storm, regardless of size or power, could do, and that was why it was so feared.

And yet, as she concentrated on it, as she felt its power and grabbed for it, she understood that, for all its strange nature, it was still a storm. She reached out in ways she could not explain to anyone and saw it as an entity, raw yet conforming to the rules of storms so long as it was within Akahlar's domain. It had some dominion over matter and energy, of what it touched and what it might do, yet upper steering currents still held it in some tight fashion; landforms, even those it could transform, none the less bounced and jostled it, turned it, and reshaped it even as it reshaped them.

All storms had a distinctive shape and obeyed their own internal rules of consistency, and lost their power once those internal rules were altered. With an ordinary storm that was not impossible to do, but with this one the internal rules were hard to find in all the confusing masses of hissing, snapping energy. Fed as it was by a tiny particle of the monoblock whose instability had created all that was, it was the most alive and active thing in all nature, spitting off particles of matter and energy, mating with what it found and changing it in ways that seemed at first totally random but which she came to realize were in some way mathematical. The random bursts of particles and waves from its tiny but super-powered center were only half the equation; the process was only completed when they interacted with what was already there, binding the random fury to their laws and creating a fearful symmetry in what was created.

There was no way to grab that center and guide or direct it; it was unfathomable, a brilliant, sputtering, incomprehensible mass. The trick was to control the storm by its edges, to shape it, pick up the myriad whiplike appendages of energy that flew from it, and hold them in the mind like reins on a herd of wild horses.

And something, *someone* else, was busily locating and getting hold of those whiplike energy reins. Sam could sense the other, feel it, watch just what was being done. She didn't understand it; she didn't *have* to understand it; the practical demonstration was enough.

The other's power stemmed from intense but measured hatred; Sam used rage, which was rawer and less controlled but in its own way just as strong. She began to reach out to the energy reins that the other had so considerately already grabbed and stabilized and began a mental tug of war for their control.

For a while, it seemed an even match, the storm oscillating first this way and then that, but having something of its own way as the struggle for its steering energies was in dispute, but there was a grave difference between Sam and the Storm Princess, one that had nothing to do with children in wombs or experience or even proximity.

If Sam did not stop the storm, it would quickly swallow her and all the others helpless in the open behind her; the Storm Princess was safe far to the north in her dome, under no threat no matter which way the storm or struggle went. In the test of wills, experience versus self-preservation, self-preservation had the emotional intensity to give Sam a slight edge..

One by one, she pried the tendrils of the Changewind from the grip of the Storm Princess and gathered them to herself. The first few did not come easy, and there was much back-and-forth tugging and twisting. The Storm Princess tried strategy, letting her enemy have several very suddenly while making a grab for others to hold tightly, but it was a tactic that worked only once. Slowly but inexorably, with a building sense of power and satisfaction, Sam gained complete control. Klittichorn had miscalculated; even with all his studies and planning, he had too much fear and respect for the Changewind, too much faith in its ability to dominate. Now he would know.

You do not send a storm to do in a Storm Princess.

Sam felt the other's control weaken and then fade away, and she quickly gathered up the balance of the whiplike energy leads and gained complete control of the Changewind. She had it, absolutely, and she was exultant. *She'd done it!* She'd beaten the Storm Princess and Klittichorn and now was mistress of the one thing in Akahlar everybody feared!

The godlike feelings were punctured by sudden confusion. Okay, she had it—now what the hell did she *do* with it?

Clearly so long as it remained relatively in place it was drawing strength—intensifying if anything—and that was the last thing she wanted. She had to get rid of it, send it on a course that might cause terrible effects but which would dissipate it as well, send it, weakened, up into the outplane. To kill a storm you spent its fury.

It was close enough to the null that she tried to send it there, but while it shifted a few miles it could go no further. Powerful energies and upper air currents forced it back upon itself, refusing to let the storm approach the null. The conditions the null exerted against storms from the worlds was what kept Akahlar functioning; there was no way out there.

The hub, then. It had to be the hub. There were mountains someplace, mountains that could dissipate a storm, but she didn't know where they were or how to find them. All her concentration had to be on holding that storm; there wasn't much of a chance to check a road map even is she had one.

The circle around the star. Hubs weren't perfect circles but they were close; she was on the eastern border, so west, or north and west, were her only alternatives. She searched for upper air currents high above the storm, found them, and began to tie the upper tendrils of the storm's steering energies to them. She began to tie them—one, five, ten—and still the storm remained, so she frantically began to tie all that she had in messy clusters, until she reached the critical number where she felt a sudden wrenching, felt the storm begin to move, lumbering, but away. She realized that now was the riskiest part, for the only way to send it was to let it go, and she didn't understand enough of the complexities of storm movement and the influence of other things on it to be certain it would not double back on her. Still, there was no other way.

She released the reins and suddenly felt as if a great weight had been lifted from her and was speeding now away.

She was suddenly standing ankle-deep in mud with wind and torrential rain cascading over her body, the darkness so absolute she could see nothing at all. She felt a sudden rush of self-satisfaction, and in the midst of the more ordinary storm still raging around her, she laughed and raised her arms to the heavens.

Oddly, she felt neither tired nor drained; in fact, she felt really alive, energized, as if somehow the energy she had absorbed from the storm's periphery had somehow supercharged her. Not only did she feel so incredibly alive, but her mind seemed to be working with the crystal clarity only absolute self-confidence brought. She knew she could not celebrate for long; they had failed to kill her with all their power and gadgetry and magic, but they knew just where she was now. The Changewind would wreak havoc in the local area and that and the aftermath of the more conventional storms that spun off the great wind would make it as difficult for her pursuers as for her, but it wouldn't take long for them to compensate for that. Not even the mighty Changewind could touch her; she knew that, now. But a bullet, or a sword, would have little trouble making that fact irrelevant.

She also remembered what the Akhbreed did after a Changewind, how they mercilessly came down with their armies and massacred the changed victims. She could do nothing to stop that, not now, but it would mean the Covanti army would be moving this way as soon as it was clear and there was light. The fact that she had saved the Abrasis estate meant little except that this region would be an ideal staging ground for the soldiers going into the Changewind-ravaged areas. And with them would come men contacted by Klittichorn, charged to find her at any cost.

The wind, the rain, were dying down rapidly now, as the great storm sped swiftly away on its new track. Sam was able to hear herself once more, and immediately turned into the darkness. "Anybody!" she shouted. "Shout out! Is everybody okay?"

There were a number of cries in response, some quite close to her, and soon there were a few dozen voices yelling back.

"All right! Listen to my voice and come to me!" Sam shouted. "Everybody who can hear me shut up and come to me!" She kept repeating that over and over, and, slowly, they came. With the skies still totally overcast, the fires and torches all drenched into uselessness, and all lighting, even in the distance towards the manor, out, they were still effectively blind but Sam's solution began to gather them.

"Sahma! Is that you?" she heard Putie's voice call out.

"Yeah! Over here! Everybody over here so we can find ourselves and figure out what to do next."

Others were now shouting off in the distance, but they didn't seem close enough to hail. One by one, though, the drenched and mud-caked survivors made it to Sam.

The Disease Pit, as the enclosure for the pregnant girls was nicknamed, was the last in a line and a bit off to itself, and it was no surprise that almost everyone who came to her was from there. The ones left were the ones like Putie and Quisu who *couldn't* run in panic and knew they'd never make the manor house and so had simply remained to meet their fates.

The rain had become nothing more than a fine mist in the air now, and the wind was down to a gentle breeze. Sam took time to grab her Covantian super-long hair and try and squeeze out what felt like a ton of water. It was like putting a wet mop in a wringer. Maybe very long hair really did make her look better, but she wondered if appearances were worth the price.

Nine of the fifteen girls sleeping in the Disease Pit, including Sam, were there. A few from the other enclosures also showed up, but Sam told them to go see if they could find others and gather them to themselves. The ones who weren't pregnant had a lot better mobility and were in general in a lot better shape.

Not that anybody who'd undergone the storm's approach was in *that* good a shape. All were soaked, mud-covered, and scared. Sam noted that the pregnant contingent seemed, oddly, to be holding up better than some of the others, judging from the yells and screams and hysterics coming to them in the dark. She wondered just how many of them, if only for a fleeting instant, had hoped that the fearsome storm *would* come their way, overwhelm them, and end their problems.

"Ain't nobody gonna ride down here and get us together?" Meda asked nobody in particular. "They just can't let us rot here in the mud in the dark."

"They can and they will," Sam assured her. "I've seen this kind of thing before, only in daylight. They'll wait in their shelters until they are dead certain the storm's gone, then slowly come out. First thing then they'll ring this place with what security they can until the army gets here, and then they'll wait for dawn. They're scared, too. They know a lot of us got caught out here but they don't know how close the storm got or what it might have done or not done. They won't take any chances until they can see properly. Anybody checked the shelters?''

"I was near one when it collapsed," somebody said. "Made an awful racket and just missed me. With that wind I bet there's not a one standing, or, if there is, not a one anybody but a fool would get under."

Sam nodded to herself. "That's what I figured. Can't see a thing in this pitch dark, and I ain't so sure I even know which direction's what, so there's no use in moving right now. Best thing we can do is kind'a huddle down here and wait for light. It's gonna be a pretty miserable night, but until we know what's what, there's nothin' we can do."

That fact made Sam even less happy than the others. She wondered if Kira had been out there, maybe camped on the way here from whatever she was checking out. What if Crim was now cut off? If the storm cut the roads between here and the capital they'd be blocking them off and nobody would be allowed through for days. More than enough time for Klittichorn's henchmen to come here and ferret her out. Worse, it was equally possible that Kira had been caught dead center in the storm. If that was the case, nobody would be coming for her.

"I wonder what they gonna do with us?" Putie wondered aloud. "If everything's wrecked and all, there ain't no way we can just go back to normal here no matter what.'' She sighed. "I gettin' tempted to just start walkin' towards the null at first light."

Sam chuckled dryly. "Yeah? And just how far do you think you can walk, Putie? Or most of you? Even if you got some food and water, it's maybe ten leegs to the border and another thirty or forty leegs across." That was, at best, something like twenty-five miles, a fair day on a slow horse. "Besides, they'll be heavily patrolling all the way. There was lots of folks living in the path of that Changewind and they ain't dead, but they ain't folks no more, neither. We got to play it by hunch, that's all.''

"Who you all kiddin'?" Meda said derisively. "We ain't got no say in it at all. We gonna sit here 'cause there ain't noplace else to go, and then when day comes we gonna do just what they tell us t'do, like good Akhbreed girls. It just the way things *are*, that all. Only time I disobeyed and did somethin' on my own, 'gainst the rules, I got myself knocked up. The gods made the rules and every time we go 'gainst 'em we get screwed.''

That started up something of a debate that, while on a basic level, was actually over the proper role of women in this society and also the class system. Sam listened to them, slightly bemused by it. Not that any of them sounded like revolutionaries; every one of them would have been over-joyed to just go home and pick up where they left off, get married if anybody would have them, and keep house and have lots more babies. But that wasn't a choice they had, and so there was a natural human tendency to try and cheat fate. Finally Sam decided to take charge.

"Hold it! Hold it! Look, I don't know how long it is 'til dawn and I don't know what the hell will happen then, but it's startin' to get a little bit better here and there's a fair amount of grass. Each of you take a hand of the one closest to you, and let's get over where it's more comfortable and try and settle down. We're not doin' ourselves or our babies no good by sitting up all night in rotten muck.''

They did get together, and she led them to an area she could feel was fairly thick grass. It wasn't dry, but it wasn't muddy, either, nor did it have a lot of debris, and in the swiftly rebuilding heat and near-suffocating humidity, it was an island in the midst of chaos.

"Everybody just sit or lie down and try and get a little sleep,'' she told them. "I know that probably isn't possible but give it a try. It's been a hell of a night.''

A single firm voice and a little confidence was really what they needed, and she was a bit surprised although pleased at how her authority, even though a newcomer and stranger to them, was accepted. For a while there was quiet, and then somebody whispered to somebody and finally there was some-thing of a set of whispered conversations. Sam didn't try to hear them nor care what they were saying; she moved a bit away, staked out a plush plot of grass, and sat, staring out at the darkness.

Contrary to all that Meda said, there was at least one woman in the group who wasn't about to wait around for the men to decide anything. The darkness was frustrating; there was a little light now as the clouds broke and some stars shone through, but there wasn't any sort of moon around Akahlar, at least not the sort that would illuminate the landscape well enough to see.

At least now she knew she could do it—turn and twist the Changewind. The most feared thing in this whole crazy world was the one thing that did not threaten her at all. She already knew that she could summon more common storms and use their power as a weapon; she had killed with that power. There might be more things one could do than that, but she hadn't been able to test it all. It didn't matter. What she did know was enough. No matter what happened from this point on, she would no longer be defenseless, nor hesitate to use that power when necessary.

The reaction of the Storm Princess infuriated her still. She couldn't comprehend it, not really. If this Princess was her twin, then she at least had the same amount of brains. She had to know it was Klittichorn who killed her mother and that he was using her. Maybe she was bewitched, under some kind of spell—but it didn't seem like it when she was inside the Princess's skull.

Revenge, they'd said. She was fueled entirely by a fanatical desire to revenge herself and her people against the Akhbreed kings and their sorcerers. Did she, could she, hate so much that she didn't even *care* that she was being used? That the only thing that mattered to her was the destruction of the Akhbreed empire? My god! Did she see her relationship with Klittichorn as a sort of deal with the devil? Had she willingly sold her soul to evil so long as it carried out her hateful wishes?

No matter what, Sam knew, from now on the Storm Princess had to be treated as an insane enemy. There could be no more attempts at reaching a compromise or understanding with her. Perhaps that was why Boolean stood so firmly against them in spite of his own alleged lack of enthusiasm for the system.

Or was Boolean just a sort of reverse Storm Princess, hating Klittichorn so much that he'd preserve the power and the system and oppress billions forever—pay any price just to get his own revenge?

Shit—she wished she knew the answer to that one.

If she knew what direction was what, if she had any real landmarks, she would have set out that night to get some distance between her and her inevitable pursuers. It certainly wouldn't do to just start walking and perhaps walk right into Covanti, or worse, into whatever the Changewind had wrought. They wouldn't have as easy a time cleaning up *this* mess as they had the previous one she'd seen in her vision. The area was much wider, the warning had been too short, and the region too densely populated. Well, whatever they were now, they also had the night to prepare, to evacuate, or to make ready to defend themselves. It might take an Akhbreed sorcerer as well as an army to control that region, and that was one type of person she didn't want to meet here right now.

She was also more physically limited than before, when she'd built up all those muscles and done all that running and lifting. She would walk if she had to, but if there was a way to ride somehow she preferred it. As for Crim—well, she'd make it possible to follow if she could, but no matter what, Crim was gonna have to find her.

Someone approached her in the dark, and she turned and strained to see who it was. Putie, from the smallness of the figure.

"I thought I told you to try and get some sleep," Sam admonished her.

"Couldn't. Ain't had much sleep nohow, so out here and on grass it ain't possible. That's true for most of us. We sorta been—well, talkin'."

"I noticed."

" 'Bout you."

Sam frowned. "What's this all about? You speakin' for the group?"

"Sorta. See, most of us, we was right behind you, no more than two hands back." A hand was roughly six feet. "In the storm, I mean. Everybody else was runnin' 'round in panic and scared shitless, but you was real calm, you told us to sit down, then you walked to the storm. We could see you clear—first in the lightnin', then even more when you started glowin'.''

Sam was startled. ''I *glowed?*''

''Uh-huh. Swamp fire we call it back home. Green light that just come from the sky and set you glowin'. Real spooky. But there you was, just standin' there, facin' the storm, and gruntin' and groanin' and sometimes wavin' your hands in the air and the like, like you was pushin' that Changewind away from us.''

That was uncomfortable. ''Putie, you know nobody, not even the greatest sorcerers and high priests, can do anything with a Changewind.''

''Yeah, maybe. That's what we all was told. But, back home, the Slimeys, they got this crazy goddess they call the Queen of Thunder. They make these crazy carvin's of her and they worship her. They say she's an Akhbreed goddess who can control the Changewinds and got sent someplace 'cause the others were jealous of her. That she's plotted revenge for thousands of years and will one day come back and strike down the sorcerers and their gods with the Changewind, and that all the lesser races who come to her side and fight for her will be raised up over the Akhbreed. They spend a lot of time findin' shrines to her and destroyin' them. But Quisu says that the lizards in Dolimaku have almost the same thing, only it ain't just Akhbreed but the rule of men she's gonna get rid of. That she rules a goddess court of women only and she bears a daughter as a virgin. Another girl said she's in her world, too, only a peasant goddess, who brings the rain to breathe life into the soil.''

''Well, that's not exactly true,'' Sam responded, trying to limit her reply and having an uneasy feeling where this was going. ''There is somebody who has power over storms, and she did come from peasant stock, but she has only that one power. Otherwise she's as human as anybody else—and forget that goddess and virgin crap. There's a bad sorcerer who's got her and he's using her and these cults to build an army so he can knock off the Akhbreed sorcerers and take over.''

''Yeah, well, I thought you'd say somethin' like that. But you ain't really one of us. Like you was talkin' just now—

low but some big words, too, like you was tryin' to hide
yourself. We noticed. And the way you take charge—give
orders. More like a guy would, or somebody from high up,
anyways. You wasn't scared of that Changewind. Ain't nobody not scared of the Changewind, but you wasn't. And
now you tell me all this 'bout this storm goddess and this evil
sorcerer. Ain't none of us ever heard anything like that. Who
are you, Sahma? And what?''

Sam sighed. ''It's kind'a hard to explain to you who I am,
but I'm human, you got to believe that. No goddess, no
princess, no Akhbreed sorcerer or magician. My name is
Susama Boday, and I come from Tubikosa.'' No use in trying
to explain the concept of outplanes and worlds beyond Akahlar
to Putie; she barely understood the other worlds adjoining her
own.

''You're *married*, then?'' It was the almost universal
Akhbreed custom that you had but one name and that you
took your mate's surname when you married.

''Sort of. Yes. I know about the evil parts of the cities,
Putie, because that's where I came from and lived. Boday is an
artist and alchemist who took pretty young refugee girls on
the run like you and makes them into beautiful, living works
of art—so they can work for a master and he can sell their
bodies to the higher classes. Not just women but men and
even kids are turned into playthings for those with strange
appetites who can afford them. Those who can not be made
attractive for that flesh trade are turned to slaves to do all the
dirty work and cleanup. That's where the ones from the
colonies wind up when they run to the cities.''

''But you weren't no slave.''

''No,'' Sam admitted. ''It's made me feel guilty for a
while now, that I didn't feel guilty then. Oh, I *might* have
wound up a slave, but in a complicated set of things Boday
swallowed a strong love potion and I was there and so the
potion fixed on me. That is why I say I am sort of married. It
gave me someone to protect me and my friend who became a
high-class whore, so I went along. I—well, I found out things
about myself, that I had some strange needs, too, and it kind
of worked. What I didn't know was this storm and evil
sorcerer business. Another sorcerer who wants to stop the bad
one found that I was another, maybe the only other, who was

born with that power. Even I didn't know it at the time. He forced me to try and come to him, since the evil one has him kind'a pinned down. That's how me, Boday, and my friend Shari got on a Navigator's train, and the enemy hit it, killed most, captured me, and that's when I was raped. Not once. Over and over, by lots of filthy creatures who called themselves men, while I was tied to a rock.''

She was suddenly aware that she had more of an audience than just Putie, and sighed again. What the hell? They'd seen her in action. If she couldn't win them over they could buy favor, maybe even out of their misery, by turning her in the next day.

"So did they kill your husband and friend? And how'd you wind up *here*, of all places?"

"No, my mate and my friend are still alive, or at least were the last time I got word. It was my friend and a badly wounded man from the train, the father of two captive girls, who rescued us. But more bad guys chased us, we got separated, and that was the last I saw of them. I worked on a plantation for a while as a picker and they gave me a potion to forget all, but the sorcerer who needs me didn't forget and sent a mercenary to get me out and get me to sorcerers who restored my memory. The rest up to here is a long story, but we got to here and found that Covanti decided to throw in with the bad sorcerer 'cause they're scared of him, and they figure if they can turn me over they'll buy out of whatever he's plannin'. I got in okay but gettin' out is the trick, so we came up with this idea when we heard of the gathering here. Tomorrow or the next day my mercenary, who's a Navigator, would show up and volunteer to take some girls home who might be on his route. I'd go along, and just be one of the girls. No papers, no mess. That's how it was *supposed* to work. Now, if he wasn't devoured in the Changewind, he'll be cut off for days, maybe weeks, and I can't wait around for him. They know I'm here. Not just in Covanti, *here*. They'll be comin' for me. They tried with the storm but we were even there. Now they'll come with men and guns.''

The audience was spellbound, not so much by her real predicament as by the romance of it all.

Quisu's voice came from the darkness. "You mean you

made it this far, against all those forces? And you're gonna try and keep ahead of them, even now?''

"Sure. I'm not defenseless, no matter how I look, and I've got a lot of experience now. I'm not gonna get taken in or screwed again."

"But—one woman, pregnant, alone, *out there*. . . ."

"You had your brains washed with your faces! Meda was right in one sense—the system's set up by men for men. But that's the system, not any edict from the gods! Maybe we're not as tall or as strong as the men, but people didn't get to living in houses and growing food and having all the things they have and do 'cause they were bigger or stronger. The *narga* is both bigger and stronger than any man, but who works for who? Do horses ride *us*? So long as we're just as smart as men—and we are—we can do what they do. If I was a man I'd still be in the same fix as I am now and chased by the same folks."

That silenced them for a moment, and then Putie said softly, "Take us with you when you go. If brains are all that matters, the more brains the better."

"I wish I could. Lord! Do I wish I could! But you're all further along than me, and my fat hides some of mine. I mean, they might not notice one woman, but a cartload of pregnant women are gonna be kind'a hard to miss. And what happens when you're due? And I ain't even headin' for the sorcerer any more. They'll be lookin' for me that way most of all. I'd love to take you all, but I don't even know where I'm goin' myself, or if I'll get there. You see how it is. Now, go on back and get some rest. And, remember, my life depends on you not giving me away tomorrow. These vultures are going to attack much of Akahlar soon, I know it. Perhaps I can do nothing, but so long as I live I might be able to fight them. No one else could."

They didn't respond, but slowly drifted away, back to their grassy plots, visions of romance and adventure still in their heads.

Putie, however, did not go back, but waited for the rest to get out of earshot, then lowered her voice.

"This Boday's not your husband, right?" she said more then asked. "It's a girl, isn't it?"

Sam was startled again. "What makes you think that?"

"The way you talked. I ain't had no learnin' but I ain't dumb. Boday is female case, and the only time you didn't say the name you used a word ain't nobody uses for their husband. That, the bit 'bout the love potion, and how you found out you was kind'a strange, too, all fit with the goddess stories. And there you was married, but the kid's a rape child. It all fits."

"You *are* pretty smart," Sam responded. "But I told you to forget the goddess bit. It's more like a curse on the family line than any kind of big magic. Does it bother you that I'm married to a woman?"

"It might bother some, but not me. I uh, well, that is . . . I love you, Sahma."

Sam wasn't shocked, merely exasperated. "Putie, you've only known me for most of a day! And I bet you had crushes on lots of boys."

"A couple, when I was a kid," she admitted, "but not like this. When we met by the river, I couldn't keep my eyes off you, and when you helped me up you was so *strong* and I felt my whole body shiver. When the Changewinds come I came to be with you, and then you saved us all and stopped the Changewind and you wasn't scared or nothin'. I ain't never felt such love, Sahma, but I didn't know what to do 'bout it. Then when it was clear 'bout Boday and all, I couldn't keep quiet no more."

"Putie, you're still just a kid and this is just a crush like the others, maybe made worse by the scare we all got tonight and the fact that sometimes this bein' pregnant plays hell with your emotions."

Putie took Sam's hand and put it on her swollen belly. "Nobody with a tummy like this is still a kid," she responded. "And we all got them rushes when all you do is bawl for no reason, or all of a sudden want to do everything at once or stuff. Sometimes I just feel so small and helpless and lost and I need somebody bad. You can't tell me you don't feel that way sometimes, too, and you're gonna feel it a lot worse, and when you don't want it the further along you get. You need somebody along who knows what you're feelin' and can help. And who's gonna deliver *your* kid?

You? I helped bring a baby brother and sister into the world. It ain't that hard, but it ain't somethin' to do alone.''

Sam had the uneasy feeling that some wisdom was coming out of this desperation crush, and she didn't like the message.

"All right," Sam replied. "Depending on what the morning brings and what we find, and depending on the opportunities, I'll try and take you and others who might want to take the chance with me, at least until we can find some better places for you. It still might not be possible, but, if it is, I will. That's the best I can do."

"Maybe *we'll* figure it out," Putie responded, sounding very happy. "Outsmartin' men one way or the other has been women's way since the beginnin'."

Finally, with Putie beside her, she managed to doze, but it was a light and troubled sleep filled with terrible images from her past. Stretched out on that rock, with the eerie glow of the fires against the cliffs, as those filthy men came at her again and again. . . . It was a recurring nightmare that she had never been able to banish. But, this time, there was an overlapping, distant image, of a place of near darkness with just a small light within, casting a demonic, horned shadow on the walls.

"There is no way to get from the city over to the district; they've got everything sealed off," a man's ghostly and distant voice was saying, *like out of a bad transistor radio. "The army will cross in there. Why not get them to do it?"*

"No!" replied the horned one sharply. *"That would involve the law and procedures and we can not chance that Grotag might do a full examination of her and determine the truth of the situation. He is a fool but a cautious one."*

"Well, we have a few men on the eastern border and they're going to move towards the Abrasis lands at first light, but they'll have to sneak in. The incoming border is sealed. I have at least two dozen good men over in Dhoman, but it will take them at least a day to get to the border and cross the null."

"No. Even if let in, their options will be limited, for by that time the army will have a division in there. Have them camp in the null and ride picket along the vulnerable crossings of the border. There is no civil authority or army in the null. No

witnesses. We know that she is with child and probably disguised as an Abrasis."

"Yeah, but that's a pretty vague description. Are you telling me to simply murder any pregnant women who try and cross the null?"

"I leave the details to you," responded Klittichorn. "We will never have this specific an opportunity again, though. If she slips through, you and your men will wish you had been more imaginative and more ruthless."

Sam sat up suddenly, sweating.

First light showed a disaster of a magnitude even Sam had not imagined. There wasn't a single structure standing anywhere in the encampment area, and many of the shelters were unrecognizable as anything other than kindling wood.

There were bodies, too. Not many, but some who apparently were crushed in the shelters or struck by flying debris and a few who might have been trampled in the mad, panicky stampede. There was also a wide variety of injured, some with pretty bad-looking wounds or breaks.

Most startling was the view to the north of the encampment site. Where the day before had been rolling hills and countless vineyards, now stood a vast and eerie plain of purple grasses and bright orange mud, and here and there steam seemed to rush from the ground and spout plumes of water high in the air from time to time.

And scattered around, thicker the further in you looked, were groves of tall trees much like great pines, but with huge red and yellow ball-like fruit or flowers clinging to them.

Of people there was no sign, but they would have lived beyond the vineyards, beyond the road that now was cut and gone, and out of immediate sight. Sam was grateful for that; she had no desire to see what they might have become, what new race might have been formed here. If they still had their wits about them, though, they'd be off for the null *en masse* about now, before the army got here in strength. The law called for the systematic murder of every Akhbreed transformed in a Changewind, and it was ruthlessly applied.

Estate and clan personnel, with the healthy girls organized into details, managed to get their own area straightened up, the wounded onto wagons for the trip up to the manor house where healers were even now converging, and to collect and remove the dead for return and burial. The rest of the girls combed the rubble for personal effects.

Sam hadn't lost much, although she did locate the twisted and smashed pair of enchanted glasses. They hadn't even survived long enough to be used as a disguise.

They bathed in the river in groups. The river had also been changed, going underground now at the new area, but it flowed north, so the water coming past the estate was from unchanged sources and thus was judged safe. They also got fed, cold and not elaborate but it was the best they could do, and got a fresh set of clothes—which in the case of the pregnant girls wasn't much—although they were very short of combs and brushes, each of which seemed to go through countless hands.

By mid-day contingents of troops, mostly from the colonies, were coming in to cordon off this side of the "infected" region and work out plans for going in and "disinfecting" it as soon as sufficient forces arrived. At least they paid little attention to the estate and the encampment, except, of course, to ogle the girls as all soldiers did.

Also by mid-day, civil authority had moved in and attempted to impose some order on things. Rumors swept the gathering that they would all now be sent home as quickly as possible and that plans were being made to do just that. Sam hoped to get a ride to Mahtri, since that was certainly where Crim would look first, but she wasn't particular. If the first batch was for someplace far away that she'd never heard of in her life, she fully intended to go there. They set up tables on the grass with clerks behind them to take names and destinations.

Sam grew nervous when they ordered all the unwed pregnant women to one side; the vividness of the dream she had had was still very strong and the sense of ruthless menace stayed with her. She wondered if she could somehow sneak off in this mass, maybe steal a horse. She wondered, too, if some of the other girls, Putie in particular, would let her do it. *Damn!* It was always the worst case!

Still, Sam wondered just how many would actually come along when the adventure—and risks—were so immediate. Putie, certainly—the small girl hadn't left her side and kept trying to show real affection. That was tough because Sam really had the need for some of what Putie offered right now but couldn't bring herself to encourage the kid.

But before she could do much of anything, one of the clerks emerged from the crowded area of tables and records and came over to them.

"Is this everyone?" he asked them, sounding official. He was carrying a clipboard and pen but not the sheaves of documents that the clerks at the tables had.

"All right, listen up, and shut up," he said brusquely. "You've been real lucky up to now. First the Changewind abruptly changes course at the last moment and moves away from you. Now I got some more luck for at least some of you. We're trying to move everybody out as quickly as possible and send them home, but we haven't got Navigators or Pilots on the other end set up for everybody yet, and it's gonna be unpleasant here for a while, but you know what's waiting for you when you go home. You're all whores who have dishonored your families and the Abrasis clan. Don't give me any lip! You know what you are. Now, a clansman arrived here yesterday, mostly in the hopes of working out something about a few of you. We were going to take more time and interview you, but under the current emergency he can't stay and doesn't want to."

They listened silently, some seething at his terms for them, but they said nothing, not knowing just where this was leading.

"I won't mince words. Now, there's a colony called Nayub. Probably you never heard of it. It's not the world's most wonderful place, but it has among other things an Abrasis-run company that was started up a couple of years ago as an experiment with a small group of convict laborers. It's now starting to pay, and the laborers are being offered full commutation if they settle there and keep working at it. And, yes, none have seen a woman in at least two years. There's little of any civilization near their camp and it's off the beaten track. We'd like to get a true colony going and make the place permanent. We're offering to send you there instead of home. Any questions?"

"Uh, sir—you mean send us to these *criminals?*" one girl asked, a bit taken aback. "Guys who haven't seen a woman in *years?*"

"They are no longer criminals. They have been paroled under condition of exile. As for the other—well, I'd think that girls like you would have a ball as the only women for twenty love-starved men. Eventually it'll be a full-fledged colonial outpost, with lots of regular people, but that's going to be a slow build, and they'll be professionals with their own families, so it won't be rugged forever."

"You mean he wants twenty of us to go with him out there?" another asked.

"He does, but due to the emergency he's limited to his own wagon and existing supplies. Everything else was commandeered. We had planned on doing this methodically, over time, but the Emergency authorities have ordered all non-residents out as quickly as possible. That means no round trips, and by the time he might get through to hire other wagons, you will all be gone home. At the moment we can take only five. We'll take the names and homes of the rest who might want to go, but there are no promises."

No one said a thing, but they all could do at least that much arithmetic. *Each of us with four husbands* . . . . It wasn't the turn-on it seemed. Even if all four turned out to be decent sorts, which wasn't all that likely, you'd have to be wife to all four. Not just conjugally, but cooking, cleaning, keeping house, and all the other drudgery multiplied by four. The clerk knew they understood that, but, like the clan lord and the man with the wagon, was counting on it still being a more attractive alternative than going home.

"Uh—what kind of crimes did they do?" someone asked.

"What's the difference? You go home, you become a slave. You go this way, you gain some legitimacy. But, remember, they all volunteered for this colony and permanent exile afterwards rather than take their sentences, so they probably were hanging crimes. It's up to you, though. We legally can't order any of you to do this, but you have to decide and now. He's being forced to leave today, and we have your routing papers to send you home over there if you don't want to go. Lord Abrasis has cleared and approved this, and will clear all legal hurdles."

The vision still clear in her head, Sam tried to weigh the alternatives while wishing desperately that she had more time. The trouble was, this colony was most certainly not anywhere near the intersection point between the colonies and the hub. As Crim had reminded her, those weren't little slivers of land, those were whole *worlds* of which only a narrow strip a few degrees wide overlapped. How would Crim ever find her, or she escape, from such a wilderness?

She thought furiously. Maybe, though, there was another line to take here. This guy taking them in would expect no trouble from five pregnant girls who volunteered. The guy would have the same low opinion of them that the clerk did, and would consider them helpless nobodies. If they couldn't overpower him and take the wagon over once inside this Nayub, she could fry him with lightning. It seemed an ideal solution. A wagon, nargas, supplies, and probably only one road to retrace. And it would get her out of here *today*.

"I'll go," she said loudly.

The clerk nodded. "Step over here. Who else?"

"Me, too!" Putie yelled. The clerk almost hesitated when he saw her tiny size; she noticed it immediately and added, "I'm a lay midwife as well."

The clerk's hesitation disappeared and he sighed. "All right, over with the fat one. Three more."

"I shall go," announced a rather sexy-looking young woman of perhaps sixteen or seventeen, pretty and nicely built, she managed to look ready for a man and a bed even at maybe six months or more pregnant. "I have known men with three wives. Far more interesting to have four husbands."

"You'll be very popular, I'm sure," the clerk noted, not being sarcastic, and gestured.

"All right, I will, too," said Quisu, stepping out and over with the rest.

"One more," the clerk announced, looking at the group. Sam, Quisu, and Putie all stared at Meda, who seemed trying to avoid their gaze. Sam couldn't help wondering if she was either all talk and no guts or if she just hadn't caught on to the plan.

"I will," a short, stocky, buck-toothed girl of fifteen or sixteen said in a soft, shy voice, and stepped over with them.

"All right, that's it, then, for now," the clerk announced. "Everyone else get in the proper lines for your homelands and register to be taken out. When you get to the front, if you're interested, give the clerk your name, village, and family and, if things work out, we might notify you. You five, follow me.''

Sam dropped back a bit and whispered, ''Just go along with everything until we're completely out of here.'' The others nodded sagely.

They were put on a wagon and taken up to the great manor house itself, then off and down a small set of outdoor marble steps to a basement area. The other girls were almost awed by the size and splendor of the place, which was more than they had ever seen. Then they were taken into what looked to be a kind of waiting room with some comfortable chairs and told to sit. ''We want you to be off within the hour,'' the clerk told them, ''so we'll get through the formalities one at a time as quickly as possible.''

Sam felt suddenly uneasy about this, almost expecting to see some of Klittichorn's men come out and grab her as she sat more or less trapped. Why this delay if they were in a hurry? They had no particular belongings or wardrobe or the like; just load up and go.

The clerk emerged, pointed to Putie, and said, ''You. Come with me.'' The small girl looked nervous but went inside and the door was shut. The five minute wait or so seemed interminable, and when the door opened again it wasn't Putie but the clerk, who pointed to the sexy girl. Another five minutes, and Sam began chewing her nails. What was going on here, anyway?

Again the door opened and the clerk pointed to her. ''Now you,'' he said, and she got up and went inside.

There were no gunmen or uniformed officers there, but the place was the sort that filled her with instant apprehension. Suddenly she wondered if history hadn't repeated and, in spite of her confidence and cautions, she hadn't walked into another trap like she had at Pasedo's. The place was clearly a magician's office, probably the chief clan sorcerer, and he was there, a rather young fellow with a goatee wearing a loose light blue robe.

Shit! It is *another Pasedo deal!* she thought, panicking, her eyes darting around to look for the exits. The sorcerer saw her reaction and simply waved his hand at her and suddenly she felt all her fears and anxieties drain away and a sense of peace and well-being came over her.

"Don't be nervous, child, this will only take a moment," the sorcerer said in the kind of voice your family doctor used just before he gave you a shot. "Just sit in the chair here a moment and give me your hand. Yes, that's nice. Left hand, please."

There were burners going and the smell of something unpleasant cooking. He reached around, picked up a small object, tossed it a few times in his hand and then blew on it. She saw it was a thin gold band, like a wedding band, only it had four tiny different colored gems set in it. He took the ring and slipped it snugly on to her ring finger.

Instantly she felt strange, different. She had all her memories, she knew who and what she was and where she was, but something inside her head had changed. She realized that the ring contained a spell or a combination of spells that acted on the wearer, and that if she removed the ring the spells would not longer be active.

The trouble was, she had no desire to remove the ring, not ever. She felt good, happy, even content, and excited as well about the future. She remembered everything about the Changewind and the Storm Princess and Klittichorn and the rest, but somehow they were no longer important to her, no longer even relevant. She knew it was the spell doing that, but it didn't make any difference. For the first time she realized what Boday must have felt like when she'd taken that strong love potion. The fact that she knew better, knew that there were other important priorities, knew that she was the victim of a spell, didn't matter in the least. Even that was irrelevant.

Her whole view of herself and society had been turned upside down in an instant as well, and it, too, didn't bother her. She was a helpless, pregnant girl, out on her own, and she couldn't make it on her own. She wanted her baby and a home and solidity. She wanted somebody to take care of her and support her and she wanted to take her place in that household and have lots of babies and be an uncomplaining wife and mother. She was excited by the prospect, anxious to begin. Her world was instantly redefined as her husbands and children and home to be; all else was irrelevant.

Even sexually, the world was turned upside down for her, although right side up from most points of view. A few moments before she would have thought the idea of a husband, a man, silly, and as for the idea of desiring and needing a man—ridiculous. Now, strangely, the idea of having not one but many husbands excited her all the more, even turned her on a little.

The sorcerer helped her out of the chair. "Now go join the others out the back door there and wait in the wagon."

She got up and went out the door as directed and found a tall, burly, bearded man there next to a covered wagon. He helped her up the back steps, and she appreciated it, and found Putie and the other one already sitting there. Putie looked up at her and smiled. "It's all changed, hasn't it?" she asked in a voice that seemed softer, dreamier, and gentler than before.

"Yes," Sam replied, her own low voice sounding softer and sexier in her ears. "Isn't it *wonderful?*"

Boolean, Lord High Sorcerer of Masalur, was royally pissed. "What do you mean, you *lost* her?"

Crim's voice came distantly out of the glowing green crystal. "I lost her, that's all. All hell broke loose in Covanti all of a sudden. As near as I can figure out, somehow, Klittichorn found out where she was. Not generally—*exactly* where she was. I don't know how or why, but that's the word I'm getting. That Changewind that roared through was their attempt to nail her."

"It didn't. I had definite energy readings afterwards showing she was still very much alive and still whole. Then, very abruptly, the readings stopped. Cold. Like she no longer existed. It wasn't the Changewind, so what the hell happened?"

"I couldn't guess," Crim responded. "It wasn't Klittichorn's men. They're all over here now moving heaven and earth to block her exit and nail her. If somebody'd gotten her, the news would spread around here like wildfire."

Boolean thought for a moment. "I'm still getting some readings indicating that the fetus is whole, a new proto-Storm Princess. But they're weak and vague and don't allow me any sort of location except that she's still somewhere in the hundreds and hundreds of possible worlds of Covanti. That means she's been neither killed nor transformed, which is something, but something upset her matrix, her mathematical perfection that made her a Storm Princess. She's not now. I can only guess she's under some sort of spell that's changed something about her that the matrix deems essential. Timing is everything now, Crim. You should not have left her.''

"What could I do? They got drawings of a fattened-up Storm Princess at all the exit stations now, and the border's pretty well monitored here. It seemed the easiest way to slip her past, and it was—until that damned Changewind. Now we got a state of emergency here, martial law in the immediate Abrasis area, and a hundred of Klittichorn's guns on both sides of the border, not to mention colonial forces out looking for her. The only good thing about this is that they can't find her, either.''

"Well, the radiations from the fetus are enough to convince me that it's no big deal of a spell, nothing that I can't reverse in an instant,'' Boolean told the Navigator, "but first we have to find her. Are you in a position to move?''

"Depends,'' Crim replied. "I can get around the Changewind mess okay, but they're using the Abrasis estates as the eastern staging ground for their operations into the new region. I'm going to try and get in there from the south if I can and see if I can get any information at all about her, but it's such a mess that they may not let me.''

Boolean sighed. "Well, do what you can. If you can get in and find out where they sent her and what's happened to her, well and good, but don't waste time if you can't.''

"Well, I can't exactly scour the colonies for her when I don't have the slightest idea which one. We don't have years, you know, and lots of the Covanti colonies have their main settlements, even Akhbreed settlements, far from the intersection points.''

"If you can't get anything definite and fast, then don't try,'' the sorcerer told him. "There is another way. The other group, the one with Charley and Boday, is still headed here. They have suddenly become very important again.''

"But that other girl is no longer a decoy; they're wise to her. And she certainly has no powers.''

"I wasn't thinking about Charley. That crazy artist with the love potion had a legal registry of marriage performed between her and Sam back in Tubikosa. I noticed that they used a connectivity spell for the seal when we treated Sam after pulling her out of Pasedo's. A typical bureaucratic simplicity, but short of death or a Changewind, it'll stick, so there's a tenuous thread of magic energy linking the two. I believe that if I had Boday, I could use that thread to find Sam. That group left Covanti starting for here only yesterday, so if you can't find anything on Sam, or get into the Abrasis estates, then don't bother. I have no way of tracking them now, but I know they went via Ledom, so you ought to be able to pick up their trail from that point. As soon as you reach them, notify me, and I will get them into here.''

"Don't they have a magician with them? Why can't you reach them through him?''

Boolean gave a dry chuckle. "Dorion? He means well, but he's a total incompetent and a klutz to boot. That's why we sent him with them. He was more than expendable. In any case, they were the decoys. No particular need to have contact with them. Frankly, I didn't think they'd get this far, let alone still be loose or even alive. That's irony for you. Now they're the only hope we have of finding Sam. The clock is running, son. Sam's disappearance and the sudden full restoration of the Storm Princess's powers will not escape Klittichorn, but he'll also get the vibrations off the child. He'll figure it the same way. He'll send Hell itself after Boday if he has to, and the worst part of it is, that they've been told the heat's off and they're no longer being chased.''

He snapped his fingers. "Wait a minute! There *might* be a way to warn them after all, although I'm not sure what good it'll do. I'll give it a try, anyway. In the meantime, you make sure you reach Boday before they get her.''

Crim sighed. "Damn it, they're riding right into the thickest concentration of rebel forces in all Akahlar, and they got one hell of a lead.''

"You don't try, you *do* it," Boolean responded. "Otherwise Hell itself will be preferable to what will happen next.''

· 5 ·

The Darkling Plan

THE FIRST TWO weeks out on the trail had been surprisingly easy, or so they all felt.

The colonial world that Halagar had picked for their exit from Covanti had proven comfortable, if a bit rugged. The intersection point, which wasn't something anyone could change, was a region of high, rocky desert, strange and eerie landforms, and little to support a population. The road, of course, was well maintained with a complex series of junctions that apparently took you to anyplace worth being in that world, but Halagar wanted to stay away from the main roads and they certainly had no need of junctions.

The country seemed even more desolate than the Kudaan Wastes had felt, although that might be hindsight now that they knew some of the Kudaan's secrets and secret places. Still, this was a world that seemed to have no secret places, or towns, or thieves' hideouts, or even anything flying about far above. Even the silence was deafening.

They had crossed at an unmarked border point, well up and out of sight of the official road and known only to officials of Covanti. None of them were really certain why such an alternate way in was there, except that it might provide a less public entry or exit without going through prying eyes or fooling with officious bureaucrats. And there were more than their share at the ''official'' crossing; the main road was a rather stiff toll road, to cover the cost of water and grain waysides at the various junctions.

Halagar kept them well away from that road, on rocky ground without so much as a trail, navigating, it seemed, from old experience. Each night, after they would make a cold camp, he would go off with the horses, leaving the rest of them there, alone, and very nervous. He took the animals to the road under cover of darkness and found the waysides where travelers were not camped, and there was able to feed and water them.

When he first did that, Dorion in particular was nervous, although Halagar did not take Charley, and it provided a chance to have something of a normal conversation.

"Well, Charley, what do you think so far?" Dorion asked, hoping she was already a bit sick of being treated like one of Halagar's possessions. His hopes were quickly dashed.

"It's not bad," she responded cheerfully. "I wish I could see, but from your comments I gather I'm almost better off keeping this place in my imagination. I kind'a hoped, though, that he'd take me with him tonight. It must be a lonely and dull job out there in the dark with just horses."

Dorion translated, rather glumly, for Boday.

"Boday just hopes he comes back at all," the artist grumbled. "There is something about that man that gives her unease. She has seen his type too many times in the back rooms and dark alleys of Tubikosa's entertainment district. No man, or woman for that matter, remains so handsome and so competent after all that experience without it costing something in the soul."

"Well, he didn't sell it, anyway," Dorion commented. "That's something I could pick up, and even Charley might be able to see. He has a few magic charms and amulets for various minor protections, but nothing else. They aren't much, but he chose them well. No, he's always been like that. A charmed life, everything going his way. That's why I accepted his offer to take us the rest of the way."

"Bah! Sooner or later all that unnatural luck will be used up, and he will be collecting the unpaid balance of disasters," Boday responded.

Dorion chuckled. "If there was justice in the world none of us would be here now—or need to be," he pointed out dolefully.

"I think he's just *wonderful*," Charley said, sighing. "If I could only see, I'd go with him on my own in a minute. I might anyway."

"As his personal slave?" Dorion was shocked.

She shrugged. "What the hell is better for somebody like me? This world always seems to be trying to eat anybody with ambitions alive. Let's say we get to Boolean, he restores my sight and takes away the slave ring, then he and Sam go off and beat the bad guys and have a real happy ending to all this business. Then what? I can barely speak the language, I can't read or write it, and probably never will. I have no magical powers or knowledge or abilities, and only one sure way of making money. The only independent women seem to be ones with magic powers or who are educated in something that's useful here. I'm stuck back in the Middle Ages, and that means you find a strong and powerful guy to hitch on to."

When Boday got the gist of it—Dorion had some problems with the term "Middle Ages" since it meant nothing to him—she spat and responded, "You have more potential than you realize! That breast halter you created back in Tubikosa should tell you that! Such ideas mean money, and a woman with money in Akahlar is in many ways as powerful as a man with money. Men may have the power, but most men are for sale if you just find the right price."

Charley chuckled. "The bra, you mean. I didn't exactly invent that, but, yeah, you're right. I probably could come up with a lot of good ideas for the women of Akahlar, since nobody else seems to be bothering, but it would mean going back, building a stake, settling down, and, somehow, that's not what I find appealing. It's pretty much what I set out to do a million years ago back home, I guess, but it hasn't got the same appeal here. No movies, no TV, no pink Mercedes and Dior gowns and all the ways you show off your wealth or really enjoy it, and I couldn't even really run the thing. I'd need somebody just to write a letter or make a sale or sign a contract or just write the instructions for whatever I came up with. And for what? So I could live in a place that got the cool breeze and maybe had inside plumbing and a couple of erratic electric lamps and where—no matter how much money I had or how many princes I could buy—I'd still be looked on as a low-class common whore. Uh-uh. If I'm gonna be in a place like this, it may as well be with a classy Conan out seein' and conquering the world."

Dorion tried to translate, but when he got to "movies" and

"TV" he became exasperated. "You must stop using those alien terms," he told her. "Where is Shadowcat? At least with Shadowcat you can project your thoughts and save me this mental torture!"

Charley frowned. Where *was* Shadowcat? She relaxed and sent her mind out to find him, expecting to tune into some night tableau she'd rather not see with the big tomcat stalking or devouring some cute little desert creature, but she was receiving nothing. Where *was* he? Why couldn't she summon him or see with his eyes?

She'd taken him for granted up to now, hadn't really thought much about him, but this was worrisome. "I can't seem to make contact with him," she told Dorion.

"Huh? That means he's out of range. I hope he has enough sense not to get lost in this territory. He's a familiar—he can't survive indefinitely without you."

That worried her. "I never knew there was a range, or that he could survive without me at all."

"Oh, the contact spell of that sort is basically line of sight. He could still find you, though—the two of you are psychically linked—if he could catch up with you before his psychic energy was depleted. If he could find someone of the same blood type who was willing, he could probably survive for a week on his own, maybe longer, but it wouldn't be the same as if it were you, and he'd draw less and less each time until he couldn't get enough to keep going. I'm afraid I don't remember much about that course beyond that, but I do know he'd have trouble finding anybody with any blood type in this forsaken place. Don't worry—he'll be back at the last minute tomorrow morning as usual."

"Yeah, maybe," she responded, still worried.

He decided to redirect the conversation back to its roots to take her mind off the cat. "I'm still amazed that you'd consider going with him, even if I admitted your points. I don't know if you noticed it, but he has a rather odd effect on you. You stop being yourself and just become that vacant-eyed, empty-headed courtesan."

"Yeah, I know. I can remember all that when I'm me, but I can't remember me when I'm her, if that makes any sense. It's actually easier that way. It bothered me at first, but now I find it, well, sort'a convenient. There's not much conversation in this kind of riding, even if I could get into it, and I'm not equipped for sightseeing, so I'd just be sitting there getting bounced around and brooding and feelin' sorry for myself and maybe going nuts. Maybe that's what triggers Shari around him; I dunno. But Shari, now, she isn't a real person, sort of, at all. She's got no ego of any kind; she exists only in reaction to somebody else. Except in the courtesan role, where she's still on a kind of automatic: she doesn't brood, she doesn't wonder, she doesn't really think at all—she just exists. She doesn't even have any sense of time or place. I tell you I'm scared to death—I been scared to death most of the time since I got here. Not thinking for all the boring times just makes things more peaceful, that's all.''

"But if you were with him all the time you'd be like *that* all the time," he pointed out. "To me, you might as well be dead."

She shrugged. "Maybe. He's not the type to be around all the time, though. Maybe you're right, though. I'm just not the type to kill myself—the old way I was raised still has hold of me, I guess. Maybe just becoming Shari is a way out that gets around that. There's a way that only Sam and me know that forces me to become Shari and just Shari. There's been lots of times when I was tempted to use it, to solve all my problems, and nobody could ever know how to get me back."

He was shocked. "Don't do that! In the name of all the gods, don't even *think* of doing that! I don't think I ever saw anyone so smart and capable as you, who had such a low opinion of themself. Besides, what about your friend Sam? What about all this impending conflict we're trying to avoid?"

"I no longer care about Storm Princesses and Changewinds and the like. It's not my fight, Dorion. It's *never* been my fight. For a while I was a decoy, and all that did was almost get me carried away by a monster and scared to show my face in public. Now, well, I heard it being talked about back in Covanti hub. They know I'm not Sam, so that's it. My one remaining bit of usefulness to your cause and boss is over already. I can't lift a sword, I can't see to shoot anybody, and it would take a second and a half for a wizard to turn me into a toad or something. It's like atomic bombs back home. I was against them, and scared that one of two old guys could destroy the world in a flash, but there wasn't anything I could *do* about it. And I don't think protests and petitions would do as much here as they did back there, which was nothing.''

"And Sam?"

She sighed. "Don't translate this for Boday—since I don't need shit fits right now by anybody, least of all her—but if I hadn't been around Boday all the time I wouldn't think of Sam at all any more, and I don't think of her much anyway. We were teenagers together, yeah, a million years ago, but my life got shorted out because I went beyond the call of duty to help her and got sucked here with her, and since that time we've gone such different ways that I don't think we have anything except the old times in common any more. It's like somebody in the neighborhood when you were growing up— they're not a part of your life any more. She got me into this, and since that time I been ying-yanged around and here I am and I'm stuck. Stuck in this world, stuck in this class, stuck blind and mostly dumb to most everybody. Yeah, I hope she gives some meaning to all this by getting to Boolean, becoming the Storm Princess, being a combination of Mommie and Joan of Arc, becoming rich and famous and powerful and a legend in her own time, but it's nothing to me. To me, she's as remote as Boolean and less interesting, who's done nothing but mess up my life, and I have to take the cards I was dealt and live my own life. I just don't give a damn about Sam.''

Dorion *didn't* translate, but he opened his mouth to reply and then closed it again. There wasn't really anything to say. In her own way, she was absolutely right—this was no longer her fight and there seemed nothing at all she could do from this point, and she had little cause to love Sam or bother with all these matters of high importance. Struck by her beauty, personality, and intelligence, he'd put her on a kind of pedestal, never really considering just how much a helpless victim she was in all this, how totally out of control of her life she had been since being caught in the maelstrom with Sam. It was a shock to realize that she was not here out of choice, nor because she was any more part of it, nor did she really even have a stake in meeting Boolean, in having curses lifted or anything else. She was here only because that slave ring ordered her to be; she had no choice. She'd had no real choices since coming here, and not much chance of future freedom, either. In Akahlar, her intelligence wasn't a blessing but a curse, since she understood her situation full well and had no real hope or stake in much of anything. No wonder she envied being Shari! She couldn't even marry and have children—Boday's long-ago alchemy had seen to that.

"This is Akahlar," he reminded her, trying to sound like he believed what he was going to say. "*Anything's* possible here, you know. You're not like the peasants or low-class riffraff of the entertainment districts and courts. You have powerful friends, with real power. There is a way out for you. There is always a way out. Not everybody has the connections or the patience or the will to find it, but it's always there. Don't give up until the last possibility is explored. Never give up."

"Yeah, a way out. Find one of those Changewinds and walk into it. Come out some kind of monster or hybrid or something. I don't know those powerful friends you're talking about. Boolean's no friend. He's cowered for years from his enemies and subjected us to this, and he's so busy with his plots he doesn't give a damn about the discards. If I could be released from this compulsion to go to him, and not have to, that's all I would want as a gift. I'd like my sight back, yes, but neither you nor he nor any other magician has normal sight yourselves, so I figure if you can't heal yourselves you're not likely to be able to do it for anybody else, either. Oh, I know, your magic lets you see not only normally but all over, but I don't have that magic and you can't give it to me. With that in mind, the *last* thing I want is to see Boolean."

"But he'd lift all the spells, all the compulsions!"

She chuckled. "Dorion, I didn't look like this when I grew up or when I got here. I was frumpy, buck-toothed, and I was in the process of growing thunder thighs. Boolean made me look like this, and I believe you that he's a man of his word, so he'll remove the spell when I get to him and I'll go back the way I looked before. Dorion—this *body's* all I got in Akahlar. The only payoff this trip'll have for me is to take away the last and only thing that I want or can use. I won't even be desirable. I'll be a nothing. And that's even worse than what I am now."

They were asleep when Halagar returned and bedded down himself, but in the morning Shadowcat was there, with no real indication as to where he'd gone, nor could Charley get much indication. She fell asleep as Charley but awoke as Shari and stayed that way through the day and, it turned out, the night to come and several after, since after the first night Halagar did indeed take her with him when he went off to feed and water the animals, confident now that they weren't being trapped or trailed.

Indeed, to the null that separated the entire kingdom of Covanti from the hub and satellite worlds of Tishbaal, they were inseparable, and, at least for now, Dorion felt a little better about it.

Even so, he spent most of this time trying to figure out a way through her arguments and her brooding pessimism. As long as she had it, she'd have this modified death wish, which would become a self-fulfilling threat if it went on.

Damn it, *He* would take Charley in a moment, even if she changed outwardly into a rather ordinary-looking young woman. That wasn't what had attracted him so much to her; he'd seen enough Sharis—made gorgeous by sorcery or alchemy and reduced then to mere sex objects. In fact, he almost preferred her to be less attractive. That didn't mean less sexy, but it sure meant a little more security.

Halagar sure wouldn't be interested in her any more, not then. But, damn it, he was no classical male god himself. He had a sort of cherubic look but was by no means handsome, and carried a bit of fat himself. Women had never exactly fallen groveling at his feet and never would. Oh, he could buy a potion or cast one of the standard spells, but what the hell did that mean? Lust fulfilled. But if he didn't love her for her body, then her body without her will wasn't at all attractive.

Guys who looked less than great, or were anything but Mister Masculine, and didn't have the benefit of family-arranged marriages, still did attract women, of course, but by other routes. By being rich, or powerful, or famous, or supertalented, or superheroic. He had no money, and Boday had pointed out that Charley had the ability to make it if she wanted to—and Charley had shot that down.

He was a magician, yes, but one who hoped that nobody found out how lousy a magician he really was. Oh, he could use The Sight and all the other basic tricks, but you were either born with that or you weren't and he was. But he wasn't just Third Rank, he was third rate, and he knew he'd never get much beyond that. Give him a book of formulae and spells and good instructions and he could work all the classical things, do amazing stuff—amazing, that is, to somebody who neither had the power nor knew what it really was capable of. A competent Third Rank magician could create spells in his head, invent some new ones, maybe, and certainly do all the classical stuff without needing reference books and instructions for all but the most incredibly complex work. Without his books, like now, his magic was pretty damned poor and erratic, and usually unpredictably awful.

He'd been little more than a janitor for Boolean, but just a little experimentation, a little fooling around, and he'd caused a lot of disaster and wound up getting kicked out on his face. He remembered Boolean's rage, his yelling about some sorcerer's apprentice, and someone or something called a Mickey Mouse. You didn't need the references to understand the meaning. Exiled to the Kudaan, "where nobody will notice your disasters and mistakes," building fires for Yobi's cauldron, and straightening up the laboratory, because at least he knew the contents and uses of the various jars.

No, he'd never be powerful, not in that sense.

Famous? He hardly had a hope of becoming infamous, let alone famous. And as for talent—well, maybe he had one, but he hadn't found it yet. And while he wasn't a coward, or he'd never have gotten this far on this journey, he wasn't much of a fighter and he'd rather hide than battle if it could be arranged, and nobody gave medals for skulking.

Although he had more freedom of action, in his own way he was just as much a loser at life as Charley, he thought. Worse, really, since her fall had come from attempting to do good above and beyond the call of friendship, and hadn't really been her fault, while he'd had all the opportunities and blown every single one.

He had tried to promise her that there was a way out, that there was always a way out, but she hadn't believed him, and why should she, coming as it did from somebody who hadn't found a way out himself.

There was little evidence of rebels anywhere in this desolate place, or anyone else, for that matter, but that changed when they reached the null that formed the border between Covanti and its colonial worlds and the outer colonial worlds of Tishbaal. There would be no hiding from Covantian forces here; at least two divisions of its army were deployed in specially prepared defensive lines just inside the null; the men, horses, and equipment, their tents with small pennants flying, sticking eerily out of the fog-enshrouded region.

It certainly made sense to defend the kingdom from its side of the null; an attempt to guard the borders of hundreds of Covanti colonial worlds that might come up and interact with the null at any moment would have required a population many times that of the entire number of Akhbreed in all Akahlar. The question was, would they let travelers through at all, and, if so, did they have some orders about them in particular that would make this a short journey.

Halagar surveyed the scene grimly, then lifted Charley down, and turned to the others. "I'm going to go down there and see what's what," he told them. "The odds are that I know some or most of the officers setting up here, and I might get both a pass and some information on why the army would be establishing such a frontier at this point. I hate to betray our otherwise successful exit—it makes all the discomfort of the route meaningless, damn it!—but unless they have warrants for us, I'm sure I can talk our way through to Tishbaal. I'm more concerned with what I'm talking us into, considering this size of fortification."

He rode off, down into the null, while they got down and tried to make themselves as comfortable as possible. At least Charley was returned in mind for the first time in a week.

"Looks like a war," she commented.

Dorion was surprised. "You can see it?"

"I can see the null, and I can see where there isn't any null, kind of like a shadow play against the brilliance. It's all in silhouette, but it's not hard to see what's out there."

"Halagar is more concerned with what is beyond, and Boday agrees," the artist commented worriedly. "Tubikosa has a small army that is mainly used to guard the crown jewels, the palace, march through the streets on parade days, and handle emergencies, but this is more uniforms than Boday has ever seen before in one spot. If they are also covering the other borders, then they must have half the men of Covanti under arms.''

''I doubt if they have anything like this at the other borders,'' Dorion replied. ''Maybe they should, though, if there's a threat this big. If I was a rebel with some way to get colonial fighters from one place to another, I'd do a big show of force in one area and then attack from the rear while the whole army's over here.''

''Good point,'' Charley agreed. ''As Boday said, most of the armies of these kingdoms are toy soldiers—big on uniforms and brass but most of 'em never really had to fight anything big. They're used to marching into some colony and putting down some strike or local uprising by some poor natives without the weapons or organization to do much against them. They're not used to thinking in terms of armies against armies, both sides with weapons and generals and all the rest, and trained to fight, and they're sure not used to defending hubs. They depend on their sorcerers to keep the non-Akhbreeds out.'' She chuckled. ''You know, while this all makes sense on paper, I guess, I kind'a wonder what the hell all those guys could do if Klittichorn just sent a bunch of the Stormriders in here. They wouldn't even kill many of these guys. Just a bunch of 'em making passes and zapping a few tents and horses and big-mouthed sergeants, and the rest would run like hell for back here, leaving their equipment behind 'em.''

Dorion sighed. ''This is ridiculous! We, a two-bit magician, an alchemical artist, and a courtesan who came from another world, are all able to sit here and figure out all the intricacies of what these professional military men are doing wrong and how to whip them easily. If the likes of *us* can see it, why can't *they?*''

''Cockiness,'' Charley sighed. ''That and arrogance. They been the bosses so long, taught from their mother's breast that they're the superior race, the lords of creation, that they just can't get it into their heads that maybe the only thing they're really superior at, is a few good sorcerers and the keys to the gun locker. How many colonial worlds intersect this null? Hundreds? Thousands? I dunno. But if ten thousand of those not-quite-right humans from those colonies showed up here, each with a gun, they'd grind these guys to pulp. These guys, though, just can't imagine such a thing happening.''

"And why should they?" Dorion asked her. "Even if the colonials somehow got together in the nulls and even if they hit and destroy this army out there, they still can't enter the hub. Grotag and his unknown number of acolytes and assistants have the spells sealing off entry to the hub from all non-Akhbreed locked up tight. So long as they sit in the hub, there's no way the rebels can enter.''

"Yeah, as long as they sit in the hub," Charley echoed. "So the Storm Princess brings a Changewind right into downtown Covanti, the one thing they're powerless against. Maybe it gets them; at least it scatters them and keeps 'em from thinking much about defensive spells. By the time they got regrouped you'd have thousands of organized troops inside the hub against an army still running. Besides, this isn't the hub—it's the colonies. Jeez, I still remember from my high school history classes what a siege is. If they take the colonies and then put up a wall like this around the hub in all directions, the hub'll be cut off. It'll take a while, but no more raw materials, no more fresh fruit and vegetables. . . . They'll be eatin' their grapes before they crush 'em. The demon forces like the Stormriders will protect the rebels, and there won't be much of an army in there for a breakout.''

"Then the sorcerers would have to spearhead the breakout," Dorion pointed out.

"Uh-huh. And that means they got to leave the hub, right? So they break out of any side and the other three sides get invaded. Neat. They'd slaughter every Akhbreed they found and leave the sorcerers with nothing to come back to. I bet some of these sorcerers would make deals with them when that happened. Besides, who says the rebels don't have some sorcerers, too? Isn't that what Covanti thinks Boolean's up to? And isn't Klittichorn a full-fledged equal?''

Dorion thought about that. "Um. . . . Maybe I've got the same disease that those troops do. I can't see a hole in it, but you make this whole system sound so vulnerable. I can't believe that it's that easy to break through, or somebody would have done it by now.''

"They didn't have Akhbreed sorcerers on the rebel side before," Charley noted. "And they didn't have those sorcerers running messages and even troops between colonial worlds or coordinating things, and they *never* had anybody who could use the Changewind as a weapon before. No, it's gonna be a bloody, rotten mess now, and so many are gonna die it makes you want to puke just thinking about it. Still, if it wasn't for one thing, I'd just as soon see this rotten system fall.''

"What? Klittichorn?''

''Us. If the colonial races are all organized then the Akhbreed's outnumbered from a hundred to a thousand to one, and not a one of those other races has any reason to do anything but hate Akhbreed. If they win, bein' an Akhbreed is gonna be the worst thing you can be. And we're Akhbreed.''

That brought him up a bit short. "Um, yeah. I hadn't thought of that.''

They might have continued their conversation but there was the sound of a rider coming, and as soon as Halagar reached them and dismounted, Dorion could sense Charley vanishing before a wall of blank blandness. It was amazing how it happened every time.

"There's no problem moving through,'' he reported to them, "but there might be big problems on the other side. The word is that somehow large numbers of infantrylike units and mounted units appear to be able to move out from the worlds of colonial Tishbaal as they come up, and they are doing so. It's irregular, but no one can tell if the main bodies are moving in towards Tishbaal hub, or if they are fortifying in the null, or in some assembly world. The odds are pretty good we'll have to make our way through some kind of colonial force to make it into the kingdom, and probably an enormous force surrounding the hub.''

"But we've got to get in and out of the hub to go west,'' Dorion pointed out. "And if Tishbaal is that bad, imagine what Masalur will be. And just *what* we might have to get through as well.''

They had long ago dropped any pretense of assumed names for the women and Boday was able to speak freely under Dorion's very loose leash.

"Boday is ready,'' she proclaimed. "If it comes to a battle, she will do her part!''

Dorion looked over at her, then back up at Halagar. "Uh-

huh. So the three of us are going to take on a nurbreed army.
The odds at best may be only a few hundred to one. The pair
of you are mad!''

"There will be gaps and weak points," Halagar responded
confidently. "There always are in the best of formations, and
the border there is quite long, and the guards might be good
fighters but they have no experience. Come, my friends! It's
not as bad as all that. We shall have to forego our pack animal,
however, and that's too bad. Come—let us eat a little something and transfer what we can to our own mounts and get
some rest. I want to cross entirely in the darkness, when most
are asleep and guards are bored.''

"And jumpy and likely to shoot first and ask questions
afterwards," Dorion added grumpily.

Halagar shrugged. "There is grave risk from here on in,
but you knew that going into this. I would certainly prefer
being shot to being captured by these sort of people, though.
There is still time to call this off, if you do not want to make
the journey.''

Dorion sighed. "No, that's not really an option for us. All
right.''

"Well, then, is there anything in your magic that might be
of help? A spell to disguise us to look like whatever *they* look
like, for example, or to charm us against bullet and sword?''

"I don't think you can depend on magic," Dorion finessed
as carefully as he could. "For one thing, those that you ask
require much preparation and paraphernalia, long incantations, that sort of thing. Not to mention that I'd have to know
what we were supposed to look and act like. No, the odds are
I'll be far too busy dealing with any precautionary magicks on
their side to also handle us. You'd need a true sorcerer to do
it all.''

"Fair enough. I did not really expect much help from that
quarter," Halagar responded, in a tone that made Dorion
unsure whether he'd been insulted or not. "Very well," the
mercenary continued, "we improvise.''

The Klutiin guarding the extreme western sector were spread
thinly and certainly not expecting anything. They were tall,
thin creatures, particularly ugly to Akhbreed eyes, with mottled yellow and olive skin resembling that of an exotic snake,

a pair of deep-set black eyes, and a thin and very long proboscis that shot straight out from their faces and then angled down. They had forbidden, semi-automatic rifles slung over their backs, but seemed more comfortable and at the ready with their tribal spears, which they held in their hands.

The stretch of border was as mist-covered as the rest of the null, perhaps a bit deeper as the border range was nearby, but it wasn't difficult for Klutiin sentries to see and hear horses coming towards them. They were a good thirty yards apart at this point, walking back and forth, more a warning line than a barrier, with a company encampment back near the true and "real" colonial border of Tishbaal, whose worlds changed slowly but with eerie regularity behind them. Clearly they weren't there in strength or with intent to build and attack Covanti; they were, rather, a psychological deterrent, visible through the telescopes and binoculars of the Covantian Akhbreed soldiers far across the eternal mists of the null, and intended to be. A deterrent, and if need be, a holding action in case Akhbreed troops from Tishbaal's neighbor should come to the aid of their sister kingdom to the northwest.

When they heard the eerie stillness of the null broken by hoofbeats, the sentries were startled, and rather than raise an immediate alarm or go for their rifles, they went out of habit to their warrior stances with the spears.

"Riders!" one called out in the harsh guttural language of the Klutiin, but perhaps not loud enough. Almost instantly he heard a cracking sound and was gasping for air, pulled back and down by a leather whip expertly entangling itself around his neck, and he vanished beneath the mists.

The sentries on either side turned, unsure whether or not their comrade had been downed or simply had slipped on the spongy, soft, wet null surface. A moment later a figure wearing the sickly yellow tribal robes climbed unsteadily to its feet, shifted the rifle on its shoulder, and again assumed the readiness stance with its spear.

The one closest to the other frowned, as if sensing something wrong, but not being certain just how to cope with it. There was a sudden pull on his own neck from the back and he went down, a cry muffled by a knife swiftly and professionally cutting his throat.

Now, suddenly, the horses were visible, heading for the

spot right between the recently fallen pair. The sentries further on now gave the cry of alarm and began to hurry towards the spot where the horses would cross, but Halagar on the one side and Boday on the other swung their newly acquired rifles on them and cut them down with short bursts.

Dorion, riding Halagar's horse with its special saddle with Charley in front of him, slowed just long enough for Boday and Halagar to quickly mount the two riderless ones he led, and then they kicked the horses' sides into the fastest possible speed and headed for the true border as shouts and shots and flying spears showed up all over the place.

There was no way to choose or determine which colonial world they would enter, although they'd delayed their attack until a border came up that seemed relatively unfortified and smooth enough for the horses to make a clean run inside. It was a strange-looking fairylandlike forest of the deepest greens imaginable, with lush vegetation but with some clear openings, and, most important, only one border fence, set in from the null.

Halagar and Boday stopped after they reached solid ground, turned, and began shooting at the disorganized but very angry soldiers now rushing towards them from all directions. Dorion pulled up at the fence, saw that it was mostly just barbed wire like it had looked through the binoculars, and began hacking away at it with a sharp sword. He cut three of the four main strands away; the bottom one was just too low for him to reach and not also fall off or cause Charley to fall off. He urged his horse through the breach and it cleared it.

Boday turned, saw the opening, then broke off and headed towards it as well, leaving Halagar to lay down some fire. When she made a small jump through, he turned in the saddle and followed.

The null was out of sight in a moment, but the trio rushed on for a bit until they felt safe to slow down and await the others. Dorion in particular didn't want to lose Boday and Halagar in this stuff, and he certainly didn't want to have to yell to find them. There was no doubt in his mind that a heavily armed and very nasty patrol would be sent after them on the double.

Boday, still wearing the tribal robe, caught up to him and stopped, then pulled off the robe, and threw it away. "Smells horrible," she commented. "Like it lined the sty of a hundred sweating pigs."

Halagar joined them in another minute, a broad grin on his face. "Now, that worked rather well, didn't it?" he said with evident satisfaction. "Rank amateurs, even for colonials."

"Almost too easy," Dorion agreed, "although I did sweat a little right in there. Anybody hurt?"

"I've got a scratch where a bullet winged me, but it's nothing more than that," Halagar replied. "You?"

Boday was scratching all over. "Boday fully believes that the soldier was not the only one inhabiting that robe!"

That gave them a bit of a laugh, although it wasn't funny to Boday, and Halagar jumped down and examined the horses. "No shots—I doubt if they've trained much with those rifles, if at all. Not a single one put their weapon on automatic fire, which would have done us in but good at the fence. Still, we came through that one pretty well."

"Yeah, and, just think, we have three more of those to go," Dorion said grumpily. "If we were lucky this time, how many times can we afford to do that?"

"Not many," Halagar agreed. "But we'll have to take each one as it comes and solve it somehow. Best by stealth, I think, and trickery, rather than directly as here. We also have to get from here to there. If that was all the force they really are putting on the kingdom borders, then their main force must be elsewhere. It is inevitable that we will run into it sooner or later. I certainly wish I knew just what they were up to, though." He thought a moment. "Perhaps not so much holding off Covanti or threatening it as perhaps securing a vital area for other activities, like bringing in more troops by whatever method they've found for doing it. We shall have to watch our backs." He looked around. "Dorion—have you ever seen or heard of this colonial world before?"

"Beats me," the magician responded. "There's far too many to ever keep track of."

"I don't like being in these woodlands not knowing what might lurk here," the mercenary noted. "Let's find a reasonably open area and camp here for now. In the day, we'll head east towards the main road and follow it as much as possible without risking ourselves unnecessarily. I dislike moving by day, but in a strange world with an enemy about it is better to risk being seen, rather than not see what is lurking for you. From now on, though, everyone keep a watchful eye and ear at the ready. We want no surprises."

"You're going to camp *here?*" Dorion said nervously. "They'll be all over here in a matter of minutes!"

Halagar chuckled. "I think not. They can't know any more about most of these worlds than we do, and they can't spare many, if any, troops to go off into this darkness looking for us. Oh, they'll send a patrol or something that we can hear two leegs off, and they'll clomp around for a bit and make like they are doing a major job, but it'll be half-hearted and I doubt if those unlucky souls will really even want to find us. No, they'll just send a message forward that some folks stormed the line and trust to those further on to take care of us."

"Yeah, that helps a lot," the magician responded glumly.

It was amazing how quiet, almost dead, the place felt and sounded. But for the wind in the trees and an occasional sound of some insect or tree-dwelling animal flitting about, disturbed by their passage, there didn't seem to be anyone home at all. When they reached a shallow creek, the horses stopped to drink and didn't fall over, so they decided to make camp there. They set a rotating watch, of course, but if anyone was out looking for them, they missed by a country mile.

It was the quiet that got to them, both in the night and through the first few hours of the next day. This was not the kind of region where no one would want to live or work; the climate was at least subtropical, the vegetation lush but apparently not dangerous, and there seemed to be no predators lurking about anywhere. Still, there were no signs of paths or trails or large animal droppings anywhere about; nothing to indicate that this was a place that had ever seen any sort of man.

Dorion tried to use the daylight to good advantage, hauling out and paging through his *Pocket Grimoire* for any stock spells he was capable of throwing that might help them out. The invisibility spell held promise, but it was very limited and, being a basic public domain-type spell, was so easily countered that it would probably just trap them. It was strictly a one-person deal anyway, and transitory.

Let's see. . . . Love spells and charms, aphrodisiacs. . . . No, even if they might be useful, he couldn't see being fawned over by a love-starved Klutiian or something. The curses, too, seemed both too specific and too complex to be useful in a live or die situation, although they were fully half the book. Well . . . maybe. Here was blindness, deafness, striking someone dumb, that sort of thing. Fine if he had something organic of the subject's or was face to face with him, but otherwise next to impossible.

The hypnotic spells were a better choice, although they were simple and few and easily broken or stalled by someone with great will power. Those sentries back there, however, might have been easy marks—if he had the nerve to pop up near such ones and invoke the spell first. He didn't know what was best, if anything, but he was determined to keep looking.

They found the road without much trouble and followed it along the side, always keeping nearby cover in mind, and cautiously scouting every bend and every hill before venturing forth.

There was, however, no apparent traffic and no threats from either direction. At Halagar's insistence they kept playing it supercautious, which slowed their progress to a crawl, but they soon began to feel alone in a strangely desolate world.

Four days in, they came to a town center. Clearly established as a main support link on the road, it looked to have supported perhaps a thousand people in various forms of activity, but now the nearby fields stood untended and the streets seemed as deserted as the forest.

Halagar waited until nightfall and then went in on his own, looking over the whole of the town and taking his own sweet time about it as the others waited. He finally returned, shaking his head in confusion.

"No one! Nothing!" he reported. "It is strange. Almost as if everyone along here was ordered evacuated. Everything's been put away or carted away that was of any use or value, and the thing has been just abandoned. From the looks of the dung, feed barns, and the like, I'd say it's been this way for perhaps two weeks. There are some ugly signs, though. The government house had suffered a major fire—it's in ruins. A number of the Akhbreed houses and shops had been clearly

ransacked—not closed in an orderly manner like the rest—
and there were old, dried bloodstains in great numbers. I
think it's safe to go in there now, though, and even sleep in
those unused beds and perhaps work up something hot out of
what we've got. There's nobody left now. Besides, I'd like to
examine the town closer in daylight.''

They'd brought along mostly practical food, so there wasn't
much chance of a real cooked meal, but it was nice to be able
to brew coffee and tea at least. The real beds were comfortable, too, but both Dorion and Boday felt as if they were
somehow going to sleep in a gigantic grave; as if the place
were somehow haunted, tinged with evil.

The next day, Halagar discovered that their feelings were
somewhat justified, although nothing supernatural needed to
be involved. He brought them around to a place near the old
government house and pointed. ''Buildings weren't the only
things they burned,'' he noted.

Someone had dug large pits behind the government house
and filled them, then poured something flammable on the
piles, and lit them. But bones didn't burn all that cleanly or
well.

Halagar sifted through the charred and blackened remains
with a stick and uncovered some blackened skulls. ''This one
had his head crushed in,'' he noted clinically, ''but some of
the others appear unmarked. That doesn't mean much, but
there are a *lot* of remains here and they look almost all
Akhbreed in both pits.''

''What must have happened here?'' Boday asked, appalled.

''Not an invasion, certainly,'' the mercenary replied. ''They
would have just sacked the town and left the remains to rot.
This was orderly, organized. Only Akhbreed places were
burned or ransacked; only Akhbreed were thrown into the pit.
Whatever the natives look like here, they're certainly smaller
and different than Akhbreed, and there's none of their remains here. I would wager that if we looked hard we'd find
true graves for them. I think the inhabitants of this town—the
native inhabitants—awoke one day, or perhaps performed by
a signal what they had rehearsed for a long time, and systematically slew every Akhbreed in the town without regard to
who or what. Then their places were ransacked, their bodies
dumped here and disposed of, and they then very calmly

packed up all that they wanted or needed and every man, woman, and child went off.''

"They would not dare do that!" Boday protested. "They would know that they would be hunted down to the last survivor and tortured to death, and the whole province would be under military occupation.''

Halagar nodded. "That's the drill, yes, and it's worked for thousands of years. The Akhbreed colonials here surely thought that way, which was why it was so easy. But, who is going to look at this and vow revenge and hunt them down, Boday? By whose authority? By whose power?''

"Why, the Tishbaal, of course!''

He shook his head sadly. "I doubt it. They're probably withdrawn to the hub boundaries and fortified just like Covanti's. They're not coming in here now, not when they can't be reinforced from the hub. I think you're still thinking too provincially as well. Don't just look at this pit and this town—think about *all* the towns and colonial outposts and farms and factories and whatever on this world. All of them. The odds are there are a half billion or more natives on this world and maybe two, three million Akhbreed tops, spread out all over the place, all secure that their sorcerers and soldiers will protect them—taking it for granted. I should say that there *were* two or three million Akhbreed. Ten to one the survivors number in the thousands or less. They sealed the world off and then they rose up and claimed it for their own. I wonder how many worlds like this one there are where this has happened, and nobody knows? And not just Tishbaal, either.''

"But—they must be mad!" she maintained. "Perhaps things are bottled up now, but they can not crack the hubs, and sooner or later the Akhbreed sorcerers will come with or without the troops and make this entire race wish it had never been born!''

Dorion, also a product of Akhbreed culture, was as stunned by this as Boday was, but he understood what Halagar was thinking. "You're right," he agreed. "They wouldn't dare this knowing what must eventually come—if the hubs are in fact impregnable. Clearly the natives here think they're not. I wonder what convinced them? This isn't something you do on faith alone.''

"Perhaps we'll find out—further along the road," the mercenary responded, and they packed up and prepared to ride.

It was close to sundown when they reached it, just over a hill. Sitting on their horses atop the crest of the hill, they looked across a vast valley that was unlike anything they had ever seen.

The ground was yellow and purple, and strewn with tall, spindly plants growing from it up into the heavens with tendrils waving about—and not from any wind. The great, green weeds with thorny plates like bones thrashed like some alien squid half-hidden in burrows in the ground. Although planted, some were so close together that tentacles would occasionally touch and there would be a furious battle, ending only when the contacted tentacles of one were pulled out of their trunks by the other. The remains of dead ones littered the landscape as well, where two of the things had been too close for both to tolerate survival.

"Changewind," Dorion breathed.

Halagar nodded. "And note its symmetry. The storm touched down up there—you can actually see the start of it—then progressed in an unnaturally straight course along the center of the valley, stopping just at the edge of the fields up there. I've seen a thousand Changewind regions, and never one as regular as this. Here's the answer to our puzzle—and an unnerving one at that. A demonstration of blessing from the gods. Can't you see the effect this would have if it were announced in advance, through the high priests or whatever of the natives here? On such-and-such a date and such-and-such a time we will produce a Changewind just in this valley as a sign of our godlike powers. Word would get around fast—and if the Akhbreed were curious as well, or heard the rumors, or wondered where some of the natives were going and followed, what difference would it make? This would be a sign from the gods writ too large to miss. The uprising must have followed almost immediately. That's why there are still plants out there fighting for their space. There hasn't been enough time to gain balance as yet."

"Could Klittichorn actually have done this?" Dorion wondered aloud. "By the gods! If he can do that on cue and to such precision then what chance has *anybody* got?"

Halagar shrugged. "Who knows how they do it? I suspect

it's not as bad as all that, that they need the precise coordinates and limits at the very least. Otherwise they would have to be physically present—both a top sorcerer like Klittichorn and the almost irreplaceable Storm Princess—at each attempt. Too much risk there to them, and too much attention drawn. I doubt if this was done too many times—yet. It was practice at an ideal place of their choosing and with careful preparation that also was an effective demonstration of their power to the locals and perhaps visiting dignitaries and potential allies as well. But, think now how easy it would be to get the coordinates to the central government district of a hub, for example. They're fixed, unmoving amidst the constant world shifting around them.''

''Yes, but then why have they not just taken out the hubs one by one?'' Boday asked him. ''There must be more to it than that.''

''Maybe. Maybe not. You start taking out the hubs one by one, and you get two or three in a row all this precise, and you can't keep it quiet or quiet the suspicions of the remaining sorcerers. They'd get out of the hubs and fast, I'd think, and then they'd go hunting for Klittichorn as a group and that would be the end of this scheme. No, to get them, or at least most of them, you are going to have to attack all over Akahlar simultaneously, or as close to that as possible—before they can know what's happened to the others. The power is awesome here, but Klittichorn's had to tread on eggs none the less. He and his storm witch are still vulnerable and they'll only get one shot at this. That's what this is about. They're doing selective demonstrations to get sufficient rebel colonial forces to move to the hubs, so there will be an invasion and occupation force when the Changewinds hit. There will still be a hell of a fight. But this is genius. An all or nothing gamble for all Akahlar!''

''You sound like you admire the guy,'' Boday noted sourly.

''A professional soldier's admiration for a great strategic general, that's all,'' the mercenary assured her. ''I'm just beginning to wonder how we can ever hope to get through the forces inevitably massed around Tishbaal hub.''

Dorion looked back at the hostile, ugly valley with its monstrous plants. ''Even more immediate, I'm beginning to wonder how the hell we get across this valley.''

"We don't. Not with what we've got. But you can see where it begins and ends. I'd say we make an early camp here now and get some rest. Tomorrow we'll have to blaze our own trail around. It shouldn't be too hard—the people and animals of that village would have had to do the same. At least we know now why they have such a flimsy force at their rear and why the town would want to put themselves between the hub border and this valley rather than exposed behind it. At least I doubt if we'll have to worry tonight about guarding front and rear."

Boday looked back at the scarred valley and then at the peaceful and empty road. "Boday feels as if she is a horseshoe," she muttered, "with the smith's hammer behind and the anvil ahead."

· 6 ·

The Armies of the Winds

CHARLEY AWOKE SUDDENLY from a sound sleep and sat up, puzzled. It was still quite dark, and she was very tired, yet something had forced her awake even as the others, including the light-sleeping Halagar, slumbered on.

That was odd, too, she thought suddenly. There is Halagar right there and yet I'm me, I'm all here.

"Many men coming. You must wake and warn others," came a strange and eerie English-speaking voice in her head that seemed composed more of hisses and growls than human speech.

"What? Who?" she said softly aloud, startled.

"Hurry! Not much time!" the voice warned urgently.

Suddenly she saw a vision in her head through catlike eyes; an eerie, glowing scene without color or much depth, of creatures that were not quite human, riding animals that were not quite anything, either.

She frowned, puzzled. "Shadowcat? Is that you? You can *speak?"*

"I hoped to keep that secret, but hurry now! Wake guard, tell him, then wake others!"

She got up and looked around in the darkness. Dorion was supposedly on guard duty but she saw him slumped against a tree, dozing. She crept up to him and bent down near him "Dorion!" she hissed. "Wake up!"

He stirred, then jumped in reflexive panic and almost knocked her down. "Who? Wha—?"

"Shadowcat's out there and sees a small army moving this way, not far off," she told him. "You must wake the others!"

141

"Charley, I—*army?*" He was instantly on his feet if not quite fully awake. "Halagar! Boday! Trouble!"

Halagar was up and awake in a flash, Boday a bit more slowly and grumpily.

Halagar grabbed his rifle and quickly went over to Dorion. The automatic rifles they'd stolen from the sentries were very handy, but they hadn't a whole lot of ammunition for them.

"She can see through the cat," Dorion told him, nodding to Charley. "She says the cat's seeing a lot of armed men coming."

Halagar frowned and looked at Charley as if wondering how such a simple creature could even understand or convey such thoughts, but he was a professional. Such questions were for later, not when danger lurked close at hand. "Pack up what you can and quickly!" he hissed. "Dorion—get the horses. The three of you retreat into the woods a safe distance so the horses won't betray us. I'll come for you."

"Yes? And what will *you* be doing?" Boday asked him.

"I want to see who and what they are, if they are there at all and not one of Dorion's wet dreams. Hurry! And don't worry—I won't be seen. Which way are they coming from?"

"No way to tell, I think," the magician replied. "It's just visions from a cat."

They gathered up what they could and did as instructed. Dorion wasn't sure how far in they should go and wanted to continue a good ways, but Charley was adamant. "Just far enough! We want to be able to find him and him us again! Besides, I want to tune into Shadowcat again."

They stopped perhaps a hundred yards within the woods and Charley sat on the grass, cross-legged, and concentrated while Boday and Dorion held the horses nervously.

"Yes, I see them!" Charley told the others. "Shadowcat's up in a tree or something, looking down at them. Big, ugly sorts. Hideous in some ways. No hair, it all looks like bone. Sort of diamond-shaped bony heads out of which eyes peer kind of like, well, maybe a turtle or something. Just slits for noses, and the mouth looks more like a short beak. Bony plates down their backs, too. Mean-looking mothers. Riding what look like baby dinosaurs or something, with the same kind of bony plates and heads."

"They sound too big to be of *this* world," Dorion noted.

"Well, they got like machine guns or something. All of 'em," Charley reported. "Jeez! It's like a small army!" To Shadowcat she shot the thought, *"Why didn't you ever tell me you could communicate?"*

"Quiet!" came the eerie-sounding reply in her head. *"I have enough problems just keeping balance. People do too much talk, say nothing."*

"Listen!" Boday hissed. "You can hear them even this far back!" The horses stirred a bit, getting an unnerving scent and strange sounds in the darkness.

They were past in a few minutes, the sounds slowly vanishing in the night, and things were suddenly quiet once more.

There was a stirring in the dark forest to their left and guns came up, but Halagar said, "Hold it! Know what you shoot before you fire!" and stepped out.

"What were they?" Dorion asked him.

"Galoshans," he replied. "About fifty of them, all heavily armed with weapons of a kind I've never seen before, although I can imagine what they can do. They're a particularly unpleasant group and I'm not surprised to see them in this. They live mostly on a mixture of beast's blood and milk, and their skins or whatever are hard as rock. You've got to practically hit them dead on with a bullet in the face to stop them. They're tribal nomads from a world that could stand a lot of improvement. I was once part of a detachment who had to hunt some renegades down. The idea of them with mere rifles, let alone any kind of repeating weapon, is chilling."

"They were heading towards the Tishbaal hub," Dorion noted. "So they're between us and where we want to be."

"Well, there'll be that and worse," Halagar assured them. "Make what camp you can here, just in case they have a rear guard or are only the first wave." He stalked over to Charley and pulled her up roughly by her arm and off to one side, away from the others. He pulled her to him and slapped her face so hard that her head snapped back and the resulting pain that came a few moments later brought tears to her eyes.

"You listen to me," he hissed. "You are *mine!* If you need to warn anybody again, you wake *me* up and tell *me*, understand? You're *mine*! The next time you forget that or fail to please me, I'll break your damned arms! And you tell neither of them about this, understand? You just tell them you worship me and want to be mine always. And if anybody should ask if I beat you, tell 'em you love it.'' Then he grabbed her by her hair and almost dragged her back to the camp.

She was shocked by his reaction, and confused. He'd given no orders before that she had to obey on this, and she would have found it next to impossible to tell him in Short Speech what was coming and how she knew it. This was a side of Halagar she'd not seen before and one that frightened her. She began to wonder for the first time just what things would be like if Dorion and Boday weren't around to keep him in check.

"How did the girl know?" he asked Dorion, seemingly calmed down. "How did she tell you with the air she has for brains?"

Dorion sighed, wondering how much to tell, and deciding to tell as little as he could get away with. "Like most of her type she comes from someplace else and she has her own language. I understand the tongue, but few others do. When there's danger she reverts to it, knowing only the Short Speech.''

"*Hmph!* I thought the potions took all that from them."

Clearly Dorion hadn't heard the altercation in the woods and it was too dark to see any effects. "What's got the bug up your ass?" he wanted to know. "If she couldn't do it, she couldn't have warned us, and we'd have been spotted by their forward scouts. The girl and the cat saved us!"

Halagar did not respond, but stalked off to prepare his own bedding once more.

Charley felt scared and confused. What the hell was going on now? It had been going about as well as she could have hoped, and then *this*. She needed to put this out of her mind, be Shari again, but Shari, who was almost automatic, wouldn't come. Her face still stung, and when she touched it, it hurt a bit.

"*Shadowcat? I need somebody to talk to. Are you there?*"

"*Go sleep, stupid girl!*" came the response. "*You wanted him, you have him and he have you. You want furry friend to talk to, next time pick dog.*"

She didn't get much if any sleep that night, but in the morning Shadowcat returned and took his accustomed berth in the saddle blanket having refused to say another word to her. She did not revert to Shari at any time then or during the next few days, but she acted as if she had to Halagar, who seemed both rougher and more callous towards her than before. She wondered if this was just his ego at not awakening until a rather noisy force was almost upon them when he'd convinced all of them, even himself, that he was nearly infallible in these situations—or whether that was simply the catalyst for the real Halagar to appear.

Still, as they neared the null border and had to stop and make camp well off any roads or paths, she found herself left alone with Boday as Halagar decided to scout what lay ahead and wanted Dorion's magical eye and experience with him. Boday came over to her and bent down and examined Charley's face.

"Boday thought so," the artist muttered. "The dark skin dye hides the bruising but the eye shows it still. So Halagar beats you, does he? Boday noted the resemblance to her late and unlamented second husband."

Shadowcat crawled out of her perch, stretched, and as if on cue crawled into Charley's lap. Although she wasn't too certain about the cat, if it really *was* a cat, at this stage, Charley had reasoned that at least the thing was on their side. If not, why warn them at all at the cost of betraying just what intelligence lay behind those feline eyes? She began to stroke the cat, and, thanks to Yobi's spell, her thoughts became audible to Boday.

"I do not mind the beating. In fact, I enjoy it," she said to the artist although those weren't the words she meant to send. That damned slave spell!

"Ah! He commanded you to say that, didn't he? And that you're a masochist, and you love him, and would die for him, and all that crap. Yes?"

"Yes," she responded, at least thankful of Boday's worldliness.

"Ah! My little butterfly, how you are still having your education, even if you do not see all the truths or understand the values, or learn all the lessons! Back in the long ago you were a courtesan, a cultured creature pampered and kept with only the best sent to you and you thought that was what it was all about. The romance of the erotic, yes? But there you were

protected from the average by Boday and her procurers. The
girls on the street, they must take what comes, and those who
are out there are not simply poorer but far stranger. The men
who love to beat up women, the mutilators, the fetishists—
the men who are sick in the head. Anyone who will pay. That
is where you would have wound up eventually, as courtesans
are prized for being young and even the most pampered grow
old too fast. That is why the memory potions or happy drugs
are so necessary. In so many ways, after all this, you are still
a child, relishing no responsibility, seeing the world not as
the cesspool it really is, but as a playground.''

"I've had a choice?'' Charley retorted.

Boday shrugged. ''Life deals mean cards many times—
most times. The point was not what you were forced to
become or do, the point is that you enjoyed it, relished it,
embraced it. Boday should not have made you so beautiful.
Boday should have made you walk the streets. Then your
brain would have been plotting and planning escapes and
working against your lot. You have been a fighter, but only
when you had to be, and only so long as the danger was
imminent. Then you quit and retreat into this oh, so comfortable shell.''

"What can I do? I'm blind and I'm weak and I must obey
him. You know how the spell works.''

"Indeed. But your blindness isn't just in your eyes, it's in
your heart and soul. Do you believe for one minute you
would have been given as some kind of payment to Halagar if
you had raised even the smallest objection to Dorion? We
survived this far without him, and if we survive, it will not be
because of him. But, no. You *wanted* dear, sweet Halagar,
Mister Muscles with the perfect cologne and the granite prick.
When you begin to think of yourself as an object, a thing, a
pretty flower and nothing more, then you start judging everyone else by that as well. Very well, you have his outside—but
you must take his dark inside with the rest. He is an evil,
twisted man. His kind, who choose killing as a career, usually are, and Boday has seen many in her life.''

"But he's on our side!''

"So? He is an evil man who is on our side. There are
probably countless good men, holy men, on their side. Whose
side someone is on only matters when someone is attacking

you, but no matter how dangerous the situation, you are rarely under attack. The rest of the time you must co-exist with swine. Not that all men are swine, but the ones who are attracted to girls like you—or women like me—tend to be. That is why Boday found her darling Susama such a joy and a relief.''

Charlie was suddenly struck with a revelation. ''You could reverse that potion, couldn't you? A top alchemist could always figure an antidote.''

''No, it is a good one, but love potions are very simple, really. To counter it you need only take an overriding potion that redirects the fixation to something neutral and harmless. More commonly, and with fewer side effects, one just finds a good magician and uses magic to overpower and neutralize the potion. That is what some of my friends and associates did back in Mashtopol a few weeks after I took it, when they recognized the symptoms.''

''You mean—you *haven't* been under a love potion all this time?''

Boday laughed. ''Darling, Boday has had nine husbands, and the only one who was any good died of heart failure after a night of passion. The rest were rich or intelligent or sometimes handsome but they were rich, intelligent, or handsome scum. Boday murdered three of them herself, although if the facts were fully known and she was not such an expert at alchemy, she would still have been freed. Those weeks with the potion, she realized that she did not, never had, needed a husband—she needed a wife. Boday had to live a long time and fight the world before she learned why she was so miserable and what she really needed, and the difference between love and lust.''

''And you gave all that up—voluntarily? For *this?*''

''Well, not for this, my little darling, but she gave it up, yes. To tell you the truth, Boday was at a creative dead end and no longer expanding inside as an artist. It was all too easy. No offense, my little creation, but Boday was trapped in the comfortable but sterile world of the purely commercial artist and in serious danger of becoming a hack. It all had become so—*boring*. This—the challenge, the adventure, the dangers, the horrors—this has energized her. If she survives she will become the greatest artist of her age! If not, well, she will have died for love and for her art. But you, little butterfly—you will have lived and died for nothing. Not love, not art, not for a cause, or friendship, or even ambition. Royalty and sorcerers are born to their destinies; the rest of us must carve out our own with courage and will, or we will not matter at all. You have given up your ego and your dreams, and, frankly, the only difference of late between Shari and Charley is that Charley has a better vocabulary. I—''

Boday suddenly jumped up, her rifle swinging around to cover in one motion, but it was only Halagar and Dorion returning. Shadowcat looked up, climbed off Charley's lap, and went back to the bedroll.

Dorion was breathing so hard that it sounded as if he was going to drop dead any second; Halagar had barely a whisker out of place. "We've got it!" said the mercenary triumphantly.

"Got what?" Boday responded.

"This," he replied, bringing a small pendant and chain from his shirt pocket. The stone hanging from it was undistinguished and ugly; it looked like a pebble picked up from the side of the road.

"You stole a rock?"

"Uh-uh. Better. Had to kill for this one, but it was worth it. I got the idea when those Galoshans trooped by the other night. There were two Akhbreed with them, riding those big lumbering beasts of theirs like natives, dressed in black uniforms with unfamiliar insignia. Of *course* there were Akhbreed involved on the other side, from Klittichorn and the Storm Bitch to the men who worked the hubs for them! I had to wonder—after seeing the remnants of that massacre, how could they tell *their* Akhbreed from the rest of us? Most of those colonials can't even tell us apart. That's why I wanted Dorion along. I was certain it had to be some kind of spell or charm.''

Dorion was still breathing hard and sweating like mad, but with a few interruptions for coughing spells, he managed to join in.

"Yeah, that's it. A real simple thing and they all wear them, colonials and Akhbreed traitors and mercenaries alike. I know it doesn't look like much, but it doesn't have to. It's a generic spell but fairly complicated, so they can be mass-produced but not easily neutralized. Anybody wearing one instantly knows friend from foe.''

Boday frowned. ''So how does this help us?''

''Don't you see?'' Halagar responded. ''It's just a stone on a chain. Almost anything will do. We got two—courtesy of a couple of very careless guards who will be careless no longer. We got rid of the bodies—I doubt if they will be easily discovered. But with these on, Dorion and I can ride right through that line and encampment and be recognized as friends. I'm a known mercenary, so even if somebody recognizes me, it's not hard to believe I'm working for them now, and they've got dozens of Third Rankers down there, so Dorion won't even be noticed.''

''Mostly magicians who ran into trouble along the way and blame the big-shot sorcerers,'' Dorion added. ''I'd bet on it. There's lots nursing grudges. And if any of them should happen to know me, unlikely as that is, they'll also know that I'm the *last* guy to be working for Boolean these days, and the first with a grudge.''

Boday thought about it. ''It seems a bit too easy, but even if it works there is still a problem. Where does that leave Shari and Boday? We have no such charms.''

''Thanks to those rings in your noses it's not as much of a problem as you might think,'' Dorion told her. ''They didn't kill all the Akhbreed colonials after all. The ones they captured—men, women, children—they hauled in to the magicians they had where available and fitted them with slave rings. There are hundreds, maybe more, Akhbreed colonials down there, all slaves, all doing whatever their former subjects and now their masters want. I'm not sure you're gonna like what you see down there—I sure didn't—but just keep very quiet and very obedient and prepare for some rough talk and treatment for a little while, and you'll fit right in.''

Boday didn't like the sound of that. ''How many are there down there, anyway?''

''It's indescribable,'' the magician replied. ''You'll have to see it for yourself, and hold your stomach.'' He paused for a moment. ''But first I'm afraid the two of you will need a little preparation. Uh, this may seem odd, but I'm afraid both of you will have to take off everything you're wearing and, ah, maybe roll in the dirt a bit.''

*   *   *

This was one time when Charley felt her blindness particularly frustrating, but Shadowcat was peering out as curious as she was and giving her at least a cat's eye view, which was enough.

It was like a cross between a giant city and a massive armed camp. Coming down the last hill to the null, people—or sort of people—and animals and tents and even temporary buildings seemed to stretch along the border as far as the eye could see in either direction. While it extended a ways into the null, the bulk of the encampment, the people, and supplies seemed to remain on the world they had just crossed; one of several, it appeared, that was being used as staging areas. "Probably any world where they had a successful revolt," Halagar guessed. "They probably have sufficient navigation to bring in forces at will from several worlds—totally protected reserves that can be almost instantly brought to bear. It's brilliant."

Less brilliant was the organization down below, which was close to nonexistent. Most of these races had never seen each other before and appeared as strange or exotic or monstrous to one another as they did to the Akhbreed themselves. They spoke a dozen languages and a hundred dialects, and the only thing they really had in common was that they and their ancestors had been kept under the rule of a single race and subject to the tyranny of an absentee king and his own requirements for thousands upon thousands of years.

Nor had they slaughtered all the Akhbreed in their regions. That would have been too easy and not very satisfying. As with most former subjects suddenly liberated after so long under a cruel system, they found less wrong with the system itself than with their own people's place within it. Those Akhbreed who had been taken alive and unhurt, who had surrendered, who had not gone down fighting or committed suicide, were brought here, packed in wagons like pigs, and in an almost assembly-line fashion were fitted with slave rings by busy magicians working in crowded tents. Stripped of all they had, broken and naked, these people were then given over to the rebels to do whatever bidding was demanded of them.

Filthy, beaten, driven to exhaustion, suffering every degradation, they hauled stuff, waited on their former workers, shoveled dung, dug field latrines, all the worst stuff, while others suffered the depths of public degradation and humiliation for the amusement of the crowds. They looked empty-eyed, the walking dead.

The bulk of the natives were of three groups—the Galoshans, of course, and the Mahabuti, whose world Charley and the others had just crossed, revealed for the first time as short, squat little people with wrinkled hides of the dullest grey, with broad bearlike clawed feet and hands that matched and short, barren, ratlike tails. Here, too, were the bulk of the Klutiin, in the wrong political jurisdiction but not seeming to mind a bit. Clearly it was not Covanti that was threatened, at least not yet.

Although they had all tensed when they crossed the first line of pickets, and hadn't relaxed much when they reached the beginnings of the camp itself, few paid them much attention. Clearly the stones were working, although neither Halagar nor Dorion believed that they alone would solve all their problems. Such a generic sort of badge was necessary because of the sheer numbers involved, but the masterminds of this rebellion were far from stupid. The more generic you made something, the easier it was to steal or copy. It served as a uniform, but there must always be a wariness for spies.

Somehow, in the bedlam, Halagar heard gruff, guttural Akhbreed being spoken and headed for the source. It was one of the crested Galoshans barking orders to a number of Akhbreed slaves. It looked up more in curiosity than in fear as it saw Akhbreed approaching fully clothed and on horse-back. Halagar halted just in front of him and saluted.

"Your pardon, sir!" he shouted above the din of the mob. "Captain Halagar of the mercenary militia. Where's the command center?"

"Why?" the creature shot back with a roar, making it very clear that he didn't like Akhbreed as allies at all.

"I have orders to report to the commanding officer," the mercenary responded smoothly, ignoring the tone. "Orders directly from Colonel Koletsu of the General Staff."

"Field command is out *there*," responded the Galoshan, pointing towards the null. "But you'll need passes to get out of here."

"Well, who do I see to get them?"

"Commanding officer. But, yes, you wouldn't *have* a commanding officer. All right." He turned and pointed up the border. "See that big red tent about a leeg north? That's combat support. Somebody there can help you." And he turned and went back to making the lives of several Akhbreed men and women miserable.

It was their eyes; the eyes of the Akhbreed that were otherwise so vacant, that haunted them. Those eyes came alive, if only for a few seconds, as the quartet passed them, as if searching for help, for allies, for some sign of kinship or hope. They all regretted that they dared give none, nor did they have much to give.

Going through that mob was difficult not just for the sights but because of its overall atmosphere. It stank of strange and unpleasant scents; it was a cacophony of noise, with everybody seeming to speak at the top of their lungs all at once and constantly in a tremendous number of strange dialects, and it was also dicey, since all four were Akhbreed and these people were united only in their intense hatred of the ruling race. Dorion was fairly safe because they depended on the renegade magicians and because they still feared the magic, but even Halagar had to watch it, since, ally stone or not, rank or not, it would take very little provocation by this kind of mob to bring him down.

In fact, both Charley and Boday had felt stupid and ridiculous after being ordered to roll in the dirt and some man-made mud until they were satisfactory to the two men; Boday had bitched loudly, and both had wound up feeling ratty and gross. Now, both women wondered if they were ratty or gross enough for this crowd.

For a measure of protection, Boday was riding double behind Dorion and Charley in her usual spot in front of Halagar. The third horse, riderless, was being led, with the bedrolls and other supplies. As they went through the crowd, though, creatures of the various races would come up to them, some shouting epithets or spitting on the ground or towards them. Some struck, and Halagar had to caution them it ignore it.

Less was directed at Dorion, for they still feared magic, but his cherubic face and stocky demeanor simply was not the sort to inspire awe and fear no matter how grim he looked or how much he glowered at them, and some were bold enough to come forward and attempt to grab Boday, perhaps pull her off the horse.

Dorion wasn't the world's best magician, but he wasn't *completely* powerless; a mild shock was enough to discourage.

That had the effect of turning the various natives' attention to Halagar and particularly Charley, who, it had to be admitted, looked pretty good even with dirt and mud. She looked somewhat like the idealized Akhbreed woman, and for colonial races raised as inferiors on their looks and held up to Akhbreed standards of what was beautiful or handsome, the pair in front drew much attention. Halagar quickened the pace, but more than one native got a hand or claw or something on her with intent of dragging her off, and a bit of Halagar's leather uniform was torn as if it were paper. He simply had to bear it and do his best; not the greatest of skilled mercenaries nor any great rebel rank, real or not, could have defended against a mob.

Now, for the first time since seeing the system of Akahlar, Charley began to have doubts about the wisdom of rebellion. This was the future they were seeing here; a future of confusion and brutality, in which revenge rather than just freedom was the primary motivator. Take away the Akhbreed authority, and these people would quickly be fighting among themselves for what was left. Revolutions, particularly when they had a self-evident just cause, had always seemed romantic affairs, the morality all black or white, the rights and wrongs perfectly defined. For the first time she began to wonder if things really were as simple as all that.

The combat support tent was guarded with better, more experienced troops; obviously the hard core of the mostly disorganized irregular army building here. These, too, were the tough, diamond-crested Galoshans, but they had a different bearing that was all military. Again, Halagar gave his spiel, which, to Charley's ears anyway, sounded a bit too pat and convincing. She began to wonder how he knew all the right names.

"Captain Halagar of the mercenary militia, on direct orders from Colonel Koletsu of the General Staff. I must get permission to pass into the null."

The Galoshan stared at him. "Why? What orders do you bear?"

Halagar sighed, aware of the innate hostility and also of the vast potential mob behind. "With all due respect, soldier, I can't reveal that to you, any more than you would to me. If I could just see the commanding officer, though, I'm sure we could work this out."

The sentry thought a moment. "All right. Just you, though, Captain. The others remain here, along with your weapons and horses."

Halagar nodded, dismounted, and the others did likewise. "Just stay here and say nothing," he whispered to them. "I know it's a nervous situation but consider that the alternative is trying to fight or sneak through all this. At least you're safer inside this picket line."

There was no arguing with that, so they sat, Boday and Charley sitting together and keeping very quiet and very still. Dorion tried to look unconcerned, but he wasn't at all thrilled, either. At any moment, the slightest hint of anything suspicious would make things instantly unpleasant.

The nearest sentry came over to him and gestured at the two women. "They his, magician, or yours?"

"Personal slaves. They were slaves even under the old order, so this isn't much different for them." The conversation was making him uncomfortable. Too much chance of a slip of the tongue here.

But the guard just nodded. "That explains it, then. I thought I noticed a different look about them. They say they're going to be pulling the women out of these camps soon. Going to start a breeding program. Some of the animal husbandry experts are opening up a whole new business in slaves. Akhbreed, mainly, but some of the other races who won't join us will wish they had, too. That bother you, you being born Akhbreed and all?"

It did, more than this sentry could know, but that wasn't the required answer.

"The system's been just as bad to some of us as to most of you," he responded. "You don't know what some of those big-shot sorcerers are like close up. I do. I've been a refugee in the wilds for many years, seeing little of my own kind, living and dealing mostly with halflings and changelings and the like. The system's done such horrible wrongs that it's only to be expected that setting it right will cause suffering as well. I had a mild brush with a Changewind anyway, so I'm not wholly acceptable to them any more, either.''

The sentry nodded sagely. "Most all the magicians working on our side have some problems like that, either from magic backfiring, curses by higher-ups, or occasional Changewind problems. Nobody ever knew how many like that there were until this.''

And, with that, he slowly wandered away. Dorion allowed himself a nervous sigh, and Boday caught his eye and seemed to understand.

It took Halagar almost an hour, but when he came back it was with an escort of soldiers. "Come, Dorion! The General was most understanding, and we're getting a security escort to the border. All I had to do was mention Masalur and all barriers dropped. You two—take the third horse, double up, and ride between us!''

Boday was immediately on her feet and lifted Charley into the saddle and then climbed on behind. They both were thin enough that a common saddle wasn't all that cramped. It wasn't until they were on their way that either could wonder just how easily Halagar seemed to have managed all this. Was he working both sides or not? Or was this some kind of trap for all of them?

The guard parted the ways of the crowd down to the null border itself, and then took them in, past the equally professional picket line. Out here was no colonial rabble; the soldiers of the rebel forces holding the colonial side of the null looked tough, efficient, and businesslike. The commanding general, a rough-looking creature with mottled rust-red skin and a serpentine face, who was of no race either Halagar or Dorion had seen before, was crisp and businesslike. This man was a pro, trained and prepared for this point in time.

He pointed a long, clawed finger out into the null. "That's the enemy, about twenty leegs beyond. From my front line here, it's a no-man's-land until their frontier line. They're established quite well—their commander seems to know what he's doing—but when we're able to move they will be vulnerable with little or no cover.''

Halagar was the professional military man all the way.

"You really think you can take them? Your troops here look excellent, but there are not enough of them, and the bunch back in Mahabuti, if you'll forgive me, would be cut to pieces by any good defender, and not inclined to obey your orders."

"Well, we're doing what training we can with them, but you're right. They're strictly a rearguard force, or cannon fodder, depending on the situation. I have sufficient forces, though, both in reserve in other colonial worlds and more coming all the time. I'll need more time than I have to whip that rabble into shape, but I have enough time to get sufficient forces for the real fighting together." He paused a moment. "So you're on a special mission from Colonel Koletsu. How is the Colonel?"

Halagar was unfazed. "I'm afraid I've never met him, sir. My instructions come by courier. I've never actually seen any of the people I work for."

That was the right answer. "Well, neither have I, although I saw this Klittichorn once and he impressed me as one nasty character. I confess I'm uneasy about building his power so much, but if you're going to have to deal with the power of sorcery you're going to have to deal with the devil, and if that power's on my side I can't quibble about it not being perfect. I assume that you're going to pass into the hub as refugees? If so, don't get shot by a nervous sentry over there."

"We'll be as careful as we can. I'm hoping to pass us off as double agents. Get a convincing story and pledge allegiance to the king and like that. Enough to get me through, anyway."

"Like you did here," the general muttered. "But I don't care who or what you are, Captain. If you're truly with us, then you'll wind up rewarded and living in the only remaining center of Akhbreed freedom in Klittichorn's immediate domain. If not, then you'll join those wretches you saw back there, if you survive. Pretty soon the last obstacle to us will be removed and then it will be time to strike. I've grown old waiting for this; I'm not about to fail."

"Well, I'm counting on us all being evident Akhbreed to tilt any doubt on their side in my favor," he told the general. "Am I going to have to go through all this on the other side as well, though?"

"Not much. There's just enough force against the west border to secure it so we can bring up our own forces as need be, nothing like this. But when you get near Masalur hub, it will make this look like an unpopulated desert. If all goes well with you, though, then you ought to reach there just in time for the fun."

Halagar didn't know exactly what that meant, but he responded, "Well, that's when and why I'm supposed to be there. Those of us with combat experience need to evaluate what's what."

The general nodded. "Yes, indeed, we do need that. We will win, but the casualties are going to be a hundred times greater than they need to be because we're using, of necessity, all green troops. Very well, Captain. I'll give the orders for you to pass."

And, like that, they were through the line and out into the middle of the no-man's-land of the null.

When they got far enough out that the others felt free to speak, Boday said, "You were very chummy with those slime, and very free with the right names. One might wonder with that general just whose side you're really on."

Halagar chuckled. "I'm a mercenary, and I'm on the side of those who pay me, which in this case is Dorion. As for the names, I picked Koletsu because it's a fairly generic name. I have no idea if a Colonel Koletsu exists anywhere, let alone in the rebel general staff, but I took the gamble that those people wouldn't, either. A military command is a vast bureaucracy; nobody knows all the players, particularly those on the operational level. I wish, though, that I knew what the general meant by getting there just when the fun begins. My best guess is that they are going to move for practice on your friend Boolean, and quickly, to test out their system."

Dorion looked ahead at the slowly appearing hub border on the horizon. "He was right about us getting shot coming in, though. Shoot first and ask later, I'd say, particularly if these guys are as nervous as the ones back at Covanti."

"Well, I picked up some yellow cloth for a pennant when I was back in combat support," Halagar told him, the yellow pennant being Akahlar's symbol of truce. "I'd say we hold it and come in openly, slowly, and wait for the challenge. If we talked our way through back *there*, we should be able to talk our way through here, surely.''

None of them talked much about what they had seen back at the border, but it was on all their minds. For Charley, it had always been a cut-and-dried situation: the Akhbreed should give the colonials and natives their independence and deal with them as equals and everybody would live happily ever after. Happily ever aftering, though, wasn't the result. Oh, you could argue that the Akhbreed had brought this on themselves by maintaining such a system for so long, but did anything excuse what she'd seen back there? Did mere oppression warrant genocide? Or would she think it did, if *she* had been one of the oppressed? And what were those people going to do once they had totally destroyed the Akhbreed culture and its knowledge and skills? They knew the basics of getting raw materials, but did any of them know how to build the buildings and repair the machines or engineer even a sanitary system? Who would keep them from fighting each other in constant wars? Were they in fact anticipating something that was going to wind up reverting thousands of civilizations back to the Stone Age?

It was much too heavy for her; there shouldn't be situations where all the solutions were bad. All this war and hatred and savagery was so unnecessary and so tragic for all of them. Things had been so much simpler back home—or had they only seemed that way?

Well, the bottom line was that she couldn't do a damned thing about it, and that fact, instead of frustrating her, made her a little happier. God, she'd never want *that* kind of responsibility. . . .

"Did you *really* have a brush with a Changewind?" Boday asked Dorion.

"No, I was making that up as I went along. All my life my best asset has been my voice. One on one, anyway, I've always been able to talk my way out of just about anything. It explains why there were so many magicians there doing their bidding and yet getting along in that crowd of hate, though. Changelings and those somehow deformed by delving into forbidden magic way beyond them—that's who those guys are. Now their differences, their deformities, become an asset and not a curse. Hounded out of the hubs, made to feel like monsters—the kind of folks like we saw back in the Kudaan. Now they got a chance to get even with all those fine Akhbreed types who looked down on them before. You know, until now I never could figure why somebody like Boolean, who never missed a chance to knock the whole Akhbreed system, would risk his neck to defend it. This is the first time I think I can understand. It's all hatred and revenge. This whole revolt is all hatred and revenge, from Klittichorn and the Storm Princess on down to those people back there. That's what their whole new society is gonna be built on—hatred and revenge. Makes a society built on callousness and indifference seem downright nice by comparison."

It took several hours of slow, cautious travel to reach the outer defense line of Tishbaal hub, and when they did, in spite of their pennant and their precautions, they still got shot at.

"Hold your fire, damn it!" Halagar shouted. "We're Akhbreed and we're not with *them!* Let us talk to your officers!"

There was no immediate reply and he grew impatient. "Damn it, look at us! If you have anything to fear from the likes of us, then all the guns in the world won't save you!"

Suddenly an entire squad of uniformed soldiers rose from the mist, guns pointed directly at them. "All right, sir," said a nervous sergeant. "You just keep those hands free—all of you—then dismount and follow us."

In a stroke of luck, the intelligence officer of the forward defenses knew Halagar. Not personally, but they had met in the performance of the mercenary's old duties as a Covantian courier. After that, there was no question that they would be admitted, although first they had to be thoroughly debriefed on what they'd seen back where they'd come from, and how the hell they'd gotten through.

Without identifying the two women and letting the officer's mind assume the obvious about them, Halagar gave the basic story flat out.

"Perhaps we should hire you on," the intelligence officer, whose name was Torgand, remarked. "We've tried infiltrating people over there regularly and none of them ever get back to report."

"The Akhbreed they have working for them keep well

back of the border and in their own camp," the mercenary told him, "as would I in their place. I'm not certain any Akhbreed will be safe once the fight begins."

"Yeah, well, we're still trying to figure out how that can be. Our shield is strong; they can take out our forward element, of course, but even our picket line is within range of hub artillery. And even if they send that rabble in wave after wave, they're not going to break the psychic shield that prevents any non-Akhbreed from entering the hub. They've got a bunch of magicians, maybe even a few real sorcerers on their side, but all of them together couldn't break the kind of shields the hubs have."

"I thought so, too, until I saw that Changewind valley. Those shields, like all magic, are as nothing to the Changewind, and I am convinced that their bosses can drop one wherever they want it. Right in the center of the capitol if need be. No sorcerers, no shield. Or even a Changewind that simply sweeps from inland to the border, breaking it in a wide swath. An avenue in. I'm not certain what they plan, but I am certain that they are confident of success."

"Nobody has ever been able to influence a Changewind, you know that," Torgand responded. "That valley might seem impressive but I've seen the winds do things just as regular and just as odd. They follow their own rules but they do follow rules. And even if there was somebody who could do it, they'd have to do it one at a time, and it wouldn't take much to find out who and from where and all the other sorcerers would track them down and destroy them out of sheer self-defense. No, it just doesn't fit the way the universe works."

Dorion was having none of this. "Then why are you holed up here in fortifications, shooting at yellow pennants, and scared out of your skulls? Those poor people we saw being abused are *citizens*, damn it! They have *rights*. And the right of any citizen is protection and defense from his King and all the power at the command of the Crown."

"He's got a point," Halagar noted. "Why wasn't this nipped in the bud in the usual manner, with massive force, even big-league sorcery? That's what the damned army's for—keeping order and law in the colonies. Instead you withdraw everybody to the hub and let it spread."

"I know, I know," Torgand agreed. "You think it hasn't gotten to us, either? Complacency, mostly, I think. The Chief Sorceress here has been cracked in the head for more years than I can remember. Senile, batty, and mean as hell. She no longer emerges from her quarters at all, and nobody can tell her anything she doesn't want to hear. She ignores even the King's commands, and she's powerful enough to zap even some of the strong adepts who'd normally take care of this. You know how nuts she is? She keeps calling His Majesty King Yurumba, and Yurumba died over two hundred years ago! She insists that this isn't happening and seems to really believe that she was on a tour of the colonies only weeks ago. She's completely lost, senile, and mad, and nobody dares cross her since she's never allowed any of the adepts to live who came close to approaching her power or threatening her position. She's the only one we have who can keep the shield up, and since that's the case we had very little choice. We can't go against them without sorcery to back us up, not on this scale, and not with those damned illegal automatic weapons that are better than anything *we* have. All we can do is pull back and rely on her to at least keep up the shield."

Dorion nodded knowingly. "I thought as much when I saw this. They're all too old or too lazy or too incompetent at this stage to really do the job. I wonder how many centuries we've been running on sheer reputation? How long we've kept the colonies in line with fear of sorcerous power that in many cases just isn't there and hasn't been for some time? The best Second Rankers don't want to be Chief Sorcerers— they want to experiment or specialize or pursue their art to the bitter end. They retire and separate themselves from politics, or they get into territory too dangerous even for them, and they wind up malformed creatures—or they wind up summoning the Changewind and vanish into the Seat of Probability. That leaves mostly mediocrities as our defenders. Damn! That's what the enemy saw. He wined and dined and socialized with them and he saw what frauds our whole way of life, our whole world, was built upon."

"That's water under the bridge," the mercenary pointed out. "I am far more concerned with the rebel general's comment on the forthcoming 'fun' at Masalur. You have any information?"

Torgand shook his head. "None. We've been pretty much pinned down here for weeks. Right now, you know as much or more than we do about all this."

Boday caught Dorion's eye and he went over to her and bent down and she whispered, "Ask him if he has any knowledge of a short, fat girl about the age of our own coming through here."

Dorion nodded and went back to the soldiers. "Any sign of a girl, maybe twenty or so, pretty fat with a deep, almost mannish voice, who might look like the overweight sister of the pretty one there?"

Torgand shook his head negatively once again. "Sorry, no. At least, if she did it was before we were set up here. You might check with Immigration and Permits to see if she cleared before that, but since we've been here only a few refugees have made it across and none of them sound like somebody like that—and I've had to interview them all. Why? Somebody else trying to get through here that got separated from your party?"

"You might say that," Dorion responded carefully.

"Well, think about what you went through to get here. If she didn't make it by now, my guess is she either can't or she's dead or she's some colonial's slave over there. You were damned lucky. It'd take a full-blown sorcerer to get as far as you have at this stage."

They had spent several days in Tishbaal hub, like the other hubs a relatively compact city-state, but, unlike the others, one that had been under siege for some time. At one time it must have been a bustling metropolis, and exciting place to be. As they had progressed north and west, the kingdoms had seemed to be looser and far more liberalized than the more conservative Mashtopol. Here the women had some fashions, the dress and moral codes seemed loose, relaxed, sort of the way Charley remembered things back home. Now, though, it was looking like a fading shadow of its former self, its factories and distribution centers closed both for lack of raw materials and for lack of ability to deliver anywhere. Shops were running out of many things to sell; electricity was rationed due to the lack of coal and other fuels that kept the plants going. Nearly half the city was unemployed and mad as hell about it and about the government's seeming impotence to deal with it.

And it was incredibly crowded and dirty, with far too many people living in quarters barely large enough for two or three people and many more sleeping in parks or tent cities. The refugees and the panicked, come to the hub for protection, and further straining its resources.

About the only thing that had kept the lid on was that the layout of the hubs included managed truck farms that produced an adequate supply of food for the population. Still, meat was rationed and there was a lot of hoarding. People who were used to thinking of themselves as the height of creation and masters of all, were now forced into decisions between their pride and the government handouts of food and other supplies that kept them going on a basic level. Although a fair number of colonial populations had remained loyal (or so at least was the word from a few brave folk who made it across the null from the other, less defended, border points), no colony was truly safe for Akhbreed or the great wagon trains the Akhbreed had depended upon for so long. Loyal colonists simply could not enter the hub to deliver things themselves, for to drop that prohibition would have invited the rebel forces in as well.

Leaving the hub, they entered what was supposed to be a friendly colony named Qatarung, their identity stones and Halagar's glib tongue giving them few problems in getting by the paper-thin rebel line on the Masalur side. The rebel force was there merely to enforce the siege; it was clearly not ever intended as an attack force, although if Tishbaal in its desperation overran them, their commander was confident that reinforcements sufficient to crush such an attempt were easy to bring up. Halagar did not disbelieve him.

Qatarung was vast fields of sugar cane and palms and other tropical agriculture. The large, apelike natives seemed mostly ambivalent to all that was going on around them, more than truly loyal. It was easy to get the impression that they would love to join the revolt if they could believe even for a moment that it had a chance of long-term success. In spite of their brutish appearance, they weren't at all stupid or even naive; if the hub could be broken that was the end of it and they would be overjoyed, but they were as convinced as Torgand had been that the hub could not be broken and overrun, and, if it could not, eventually there would be vengeance of the most horrible sort, no matter how batty the chief sorceress was or how dismal the conditions were in the hub itself.

In the meantime, they were exactly what the rebel sentry on the other side hated—the ones who, by taking no side, had profited the most. Tens of thousands of Akhbreed colonial families had moved into the hub for safety or, after the troops had closed the hub because it simply could accept no more, had moved well away from the intersection points, in many cases thousands of miles away, where there were neither natives in any number or rebel troops on the march.

The Qatarung, in fact, were for the first time running their own place, pretty independently of the Akhbreed and under their own tribal rules, and they seemed to be coping just fine. If the hub held, their loyalty would be remembered and their relative racial position vastly enhanced; if it did not, they would cheer the victorious rebels. Dorion and the others suspected that most of the colonies were really like this, with only a few totally committed to the rebel cause. Still, those few would outnumber the Akhbreed by a fair amount, and the level of weapons they had made up to some extent their lack of real training.

Not all Qatarung were playing both sides, though. The rebellion still had a good deal of emotional appeal, particularly to the young, and there were signs of looted plantation houses and even uglier events here and there.

They were three days in when they were set upon by a gang. It was on the quiet road going between endless tall stalks of sugar cane, in the middle of the day, with the sun shining brightly. Shadowcat was napping, and while he heard something rustling it was far too late to give a warning by the time any of them, including him, realized it was danger.

They emerged from the cane with shouts, panicking the horses, and surrounding the quartet of Akhbreed in a flash. Their weapons were two single-shot stock rifles, a shotgun, and three enormous machetés; a half-dozen young Qatarung males showing solidarity with the rebels and contempt for their clever elders.

Through Shadowcat's eyes Charley saw them—round-faced, barrel-chested, with muscles on their muscles and thighs bigger than watermelons, nearly covered with brown hair, kind of like a cross between Bigfoot and Alley Oop.

"What do you want?" Halagar demanded to know in his best command voice, which really was impressive. "Why do you greet us this way?"

"Get off your horses, Akhbreed—all of you!" growled back one of the thickest, if not the tallest, of the natives and clearly the leader of the pack. "Your days of arrogance are past. Qatarung is *ours* now." He turned to his gang. "Five seconds or you shoot both the men. And shoot the magician if he so much as raises his hands. Shoot him in the head."

· 7 ·

A Little Practical Treason

"You MISJUDGE US," Halagar told the gang. "We're not with the kingdom; you can surely see that just by looking at us. I'm a mercenary in the employ of Lord Klittichorn's general staff, charged to go to Masalur in advance of, well, what will happen there, to evaluate it for them."

"Shut up and dismount!" the leader barked. "We're not as cut off as you think. We know who you are. You match the description perfectly. We want the woman. The rest of you might live, if we feel like it; the woman's our only concern."

Halagar put his hand on Charley's head and jerked it around a bit. "Her? She was wanted once, but no more. Didn't you get the word on that?"

"Not her," the Qatarung gang leader responded. "*Her.*" He pointed to Boday, whose mouth dropped in sheer surprise. "No more questions! Get down! Now! I'll count to five! One—"

Halagar judged their position and the position of his own party, then nodded. "Everybody do as he says," he said calmly, eyeing the leader, who held the shotgun.

The four dismounted, Halagar helping Charley down. *Clearly not professionals*, he decided at once. *Otherwise they would have realized that we were better targets and easier to cover up there than down here, on the same level as the horses.* There was no time to alert or prompt the others; they would just have to follow or get the hell out of the way.

"All of you up here where we can see you!" commanded the leader.

"Yes, right away, sir," responded Halagar, taking out the

pocketknife he carried in his pocket and then sticking and slapping his horse.

The horse whinnied in shock and pain and reared up; the other two backed up, startled, and at least Boday got the idea, grabbed her whip, then slapped her own horse hard on the rump and leaped into the fray.

Halagar went right for the leader, grabbing him and spinning him around, so that the shotgun discharged into the rifle-toting gang member nearest him. Dorion, knocked back when the horses unexpectedly bolted, recovered quickly and rushed the other man with the rifle. The gunman was twice his size and four times his muscles, but Dorion was able to discharge his shock spell, which also had the effect of firing the rifle harmlessly.

A fourth was bringing his macheté down on the magician when there was a sudden *crack!* and it was plucked from his hands with a whip that left a bleeding wound. Dorion was startled for a moment as the big knife fell narrowly missing his head, but he rolled, picked it up, and plunged it into the nearest abdomen.

It was still an unfair fight; the two remaining ones with the machetés, plus the leader and the rifleman recovering quickly from Dorion's shock were more than enough in muscle and bulk to take the others on, but by this time Halagar had the leader in a viselike hold, one arm twisted back and his head pulled back with the knife at this throat.

"Everybody freeze or I'll cut his damned throat here and now!" Halagar bellowed, and it caused enough of a pause for the others, except the two writhing on the ground from wounds, to see what the situation was with their leader. It was too much for two of them; they dropped their weapons and fled into the cane. That made the score one leader with a knife at his throat, one rifleman with an empty gun, and two badly wounded on the road. The rifleman muttered a curse in his own language, threw down his rifle, and made for the cane himself. They let him go.

"Your friends aren't very loyal or supportive," Halagar taunted the leader, who struggled but not only couldn't free himself, he didn't seem to believe it was possible for a mere Akhbreed to hold somebody as big and strong as he in any kind of grip at all.

"They will fry in the netherhells for this!" the leader grumbled. "I will chase them for eternity!"

"Never mind the regrets. Who put you up to this? And what's so special about that woman?"

"Courier from the Masalur border," the Qatarung responded, giving up his struggle. "They bring us news and link the cells together. They gave us the descriptions of those three and at first said to let them pass if they came by. About a week ago we had that changed. They didn't care about the magician or the little one, but the tall, skinny one was to be taken at all cost and whoever brought her to any active border post would be rewarded beyond their dreams. That's what it said."

"Why?"

"How the hells should I know? First they said find a thin, pretty girl and a fat one. Then they said never mind the thin, pretty girl, just kill the fat one if you see her and bring something of her for a reward to prove you did it. Then they say they want the tall, skinny one, but *alive*. We just try and keep the orders straight and follow them. Fellow saw you all and recognized you a couple days back. He contacted us last night and we came after you, that's all."

"Are there more of you ahead?"

"I dunno. Maybe. Probably. Most of our side's gone to Masalur, together with some of the tribal chiefs, to see the demonstration."

"What demonstration?"

"I don't know! They don't tell people like me stuff like that! Just that anyone who wants proof of rebel victory should be at the border of Masalur hub by the evening of the Feast of Glicco. That's eleven days from now. It was supposed to be last week, but they had to postpone it for some reason so they say then for sure. Most have already left, 'cause you need big-shot magicians to get into Masalur and most of them on our side'll be going to the hub border as well."

"Thank you, my friend. You have been most helpful, in your own crude way," responded Halagar, and very cleanly and neatly slit the Qatarung's throat and left him gurgling and writhing in the road, choking to death on his own blood, next to the other two, one of whom had stopped all movement.

Halagar ignored them. "Damn! The gods know how far the horses have bolted, but at least they bolted our way. Dorion, pick up the guns. Boday, search those pouches on their loincloths for ammunition. We may need these." He looked up at the sun. "We will also need all the light we can get."

Boday came up with about twenty rifle bullets and six hand-loaded shotgun shells. It wasn't much, but it was better than being almost totally defenseless.

Halagar held one rifle in his left hand and took Charley's hand with his right and began walking down the road.

For Charley, the attack and the brutal defense had been a mixture of sounds and long-term fear, but she'd simply fallen back and hoped that it would all miss her and it had. She still wasn't very sure of Halagar, but at least today he'd earned his pay.

"Surely they must have mistaken us," Boday insisted as they walked. "It is insane. Why would they want Boday? Perhaps, within tall, short, fat, thin, man, woman, we all look alike to them."

"Uh-uh," Dorion responded. "They knew who we were. Magician, pretty little one, tall skinny one—and even that reference to the fat one. And their news was recent, too, because they knew the hunt for Charley had been called off, and were apparently ahead of the gang back at the borders or they'd have taken us. That means the word is going back from Masalur's border where the bigwigs are. No, they weren't very good at being a rebel band, but they knew a jackpot when they saw it and went after it, and apparently you're it. The question now is why? As near as I can figure, you just came along for the ride through all this. Something you know? No, that can't be it. You've been with us since the Kudaan, so anything you know we should know, too."

"Boday came along because her darling Susama needed her and needed to be protected," the artist pointed out. "And to find new inspiration."

"Beats hell out of me," Halagar agreed. "I can't figure it, and I sure didn't figure it. It means we're going to have to find some kind of disguise for you at the next and last border crossings, though, and stay out of real visibility."

But as they walked it kept going through Dorion's brain, again and again. Why Boday? Why particularly Boday? The only thing she'd done that in any way linked her to this was that she'd made that rather bizarre marriage to the missing Sam, and. . . .

He snapped his fingers. "Yeah! That's *it!* It *must* be it!" He turned to Boday. "I knew you were married to this Sam, Susama, or whoever, but I figured it was kind of a love match. I never really connected. . . . That marriage spell you got—that's a real civil Tubikosan marriage spell? To her? They actually let you do that?"

Boday nodded. "Indeed yes. It is considered immoral, true, but it is not illegal. In fact, it is actually mandatory if one is going to do it, since they wish their—ha!—deviants known and registered and classified instead of hidden, so we can be kept in our own place and not sully the temples or be mistaken for polite society."

"It just never hit me before," the magician told her. "Look, so this Sam, or Susama, is still missing, and she's another incarnation of this Storm Princess—without whom Klittichorn can't control the Changewind, right?"

They were all three all ears now. "Right," Halagar responded.

"So now they're gonna do their big demonstration, which might be screwed up if another Storm Princess pops up—and *maybe* they're gonna do the whole rebellion not long after that. Maybe she's no threat. Sorry, Boday, but maybe she's a slave or under a tight spell or something like that and is safely out of the way. She's not dead—now that I look I can see the thin marriage spell thread still running from you off and away in back of us. But they don't know and they're nervous. It's like a random, loaded gun pointed at them, the only thing that can queer their deal. Nobody, not the greatest sorcerer in all Akahlar, can find her on his own. Nobody thought of this before, just like we didn't, but somebody now has. The only way is to have you and then follow that magic thread all the way to her. A good enough Second Rank sorcerer could do it. Hell, Boday—that makes you the second most wanted fugitive in all Akahlar."

That sobered them all up fast, and made all but Halagar feel rather stupid that it had been there all the time and had occurred to none of them. To Halagar, this whole business of the marriage thread with another woman was news. It was also unsettling to him, evoking the same emotional sensation as, say, vomit. The fact that, to him, this whole thing suddenly turned on a legalized perversion somehow changed things, although he wasn't quite sure how yet. There were certainly humorous elements to it, but, somehow, after seeing all that he had seen, it didn't seem very funny. He had begun to attempt to think this all through almost from the start, in a mental battle of honor versus pragmatism, and he still wasn't quite certain he'd resolved it. He had never feared death in battle, but it was beginning to feel more and more like death in the service of a lost cause and lost ideal. He had never had any causes beyond his own self-interests not any ideals beyond his sense of personal honor.

He had never yet betrayed a commission undertaken, but he *had* failed a few times because the commission had proved impossible. Even if these others hadn't yet made the connection, he knew full well what was going to happen in only eleven days. It was obvious. As obvious as that marriage spell should have been to the likes of Dorion, who could not only be told of it but actually *see* it. If they actually found the horses today and they were all right, and if they made good time with no more major problems and delays, they might make the border of the Masalur hub in about eleven days. The odds of that were very slim indeed. The odds of bluffing their way through that horde of soldiers, of who knew how many races as well as major tribal leaders on the fence and probably bigwigs from Klittichorn's headquarters as well, were nearly nil. He began to wonder if there was perhaps a single logical course to take.

Boday, however, had a less troubled reaction. *Boday, the key to history! The entire future of the Akhbreed and all Akahlar revolved around Boday and her fate!* How simply *marvelous!*

It had taken the whole of the day to eventually find the horses, thankfully not stripped of supplies, although they lost a few things in the scramble. The stuck horse seemed no worse for wear, the wound superficial and healing well, and Halagar was much relieved at that.

Charley, too, was relieved to find a very happy Shadowcat, out of his perch now where he'd ridden on the runaway horse, but absolutely overjoyed to see her. The only thing he commented to her, in spite of all her prodding, was "*About time!*" but the purring seemed to be genuine and indicated a bit more softness inside than he wanted to admit.

There were some nervous moments and narrow escapes on the remaining three and a half days to the null and the border with Masalur, but by being quick and cautious they managed to have no further cause to fight.

The most surprising thing about the Tishbaal-Masalur border was that there were practically no colonial troops there at all. Oh, there were signs that at one time not long before there had been massive movements of men and supplies through the region, with a long camp, but they were gone now—inevitably into Masalur. So confident were the rebels at this point that they had only a few roving patrols going up and down the border on the Tishbaal side, and those were easily avoided. The Masalur side, however, looked like trouble.

They stood in the mists of the null and surveyed the scene with binoculars. Finally Dorion sighed and put them down. "No doubt about it," he told them. "There's some kind of shield prior to the boundary. It's not strong like the ones the Chief Sorcerers do for the hubs, but it's stronger than *I* can handle. From what I can see of it, it's not specific to any particular race or kind, just a real barrier to everything. Any second ranker could knock it over in a moment, but there don't seem to be any second rank sorcerers around—at least not on our side."

"So you mean we're stopped?" Halagar asked him, actually feeling a little relief at the news. "We can't get in?"

"Not exactly. There's a single point where the two halves join that looks designed as a passage, but that's the only place. It means everybody and everything has to go through just that one point. There'll be no sneaking in to this one, and the only way you can maintain something like that is with a top magician actually present to control it. If we go in at all, we go in there—and that means right up to a very good magician at the least, into the colonial world *he* wants us to go into, and that's that. We have to assume they have the wanted posters on us there, too. I don't see how we can do it."

Halagar thought a moment. "Well, they're looking for two female slaves of a certain description travelling with a magician. They don't know about me and they don't really want Shari. With my stone, the two of us are as likely to get through here as we were at the other places. If we tried it, say, several hours apart, and if you somehow could manage to not look like a magician, then they might not even connect us. It's either that or you two wait here and we'll try and make time and reach Boolean somehow and then come back for you."

"No. We should still travel the last road together," Boday responded. "There are too many chances for one as valuable as Boday to be lost skulking about in these regions for days or weeks. Boday is both artist and alchemist, and she has her small kit taken from Covanti. With a few hours, she might be able to make sufficient changes not to be recognized during that brief crossing. In fact, perhaps she should go first, since it is the greater risk."

"No," Halagar replied firmly. "If you go in first and are still recognized, and we don't know what sort of powers we're dealing with there, then there is no way we can help you or hope to get close. If we get through—and you can probably get close enough to watch it all through binoculars, Dorion—then we can take up a position over there and cover you just in case you have problems. And if we don't get through, for some reason, you'll know that there was no way for you to get through in time to avoid capture, which is all that's left."

"Sounds reasonable," Dorion agreed. "All right—let's try it."

They found a position where Dorion was still reasonably out of view from the entry station but could observe fairly clearly not only the station but perhaps a quarter of a mile into whatever colony was coming up as well. It wasn't until they were set and Halagar and Charley were on their way and pretty much beyond recall that Dorion was suddenly struck by the idea that they might not be admitted into the same colony! Well, he knew Masalur very well, and the barrier was a good distance inside the null. If need be, he'd just see which one Halagar went into, go where he was directed, then slip down and back out inside the barrier and call that one back.

It was likely, though, to be the same one. This bunch liked crowds.

Halagar approached the entry station slowly but confidently. He held Charley tightly and whispered, "I know Dorion or that cat creature or both have probably put checks on my authority, but listen to my orders. You will say not a word, and do nothing, no matter what happens, and if that won't remain a valid command then I will take my knife and slit your tongue and break your legs. And if that cat creature so much as moves from his comfortable pouch I will destroy him. Now, put your hands behind your back."

She obeyed, wondering what the hell he was talking about, and was surprised to feel leather straps tying them securely behind her. Jeez! She was blind, stark naked, and a slave. What the hell did he think she could do?

Shadowcat remained still, not because he feared the big man, but because of the big man's will and position and what he might do to Charley if anything was pulled. Besides, it was better to find out what the hell the bastard was planning first.

The soldiers guarding the gate were Hedum; he'd seen them before in his travels, and they no less impressed him now than when he'd first seen them as a young soldier of fortune. Over seven feet tall, with long, spindly-looking arms and legs, a glistening coal-black skin, totally hairless, and all the more intimidating for it. Still, they looked basically human, until you got to the head, which looked like a coal-black sunflower, only the petals were not petals but thick, tubular tentaclelike shapes that were in constant motion. Some terminated in eyes, some in hearing or other sensory organs, and two were mouths. Of all the races of Masalur they were the strangest and also the meanest and most incomprehensible to Akhbreed. Just the sight of them with automatic rifles and a criss-crossed set of ammunition belts across their chest was intimidating.

The Hedum also quite literally talked through their nostrils; the effect was eerie, unsettling, and about the most inhuman around. Two flanked the theoretical opening in the shield, and the one on his left stepped forward.

"Who are you and why do you come here?" it asked, in that mixture of honking and wheezing that was the way they could manage the Akhbreed speech.

"I am Halagar, a mercenary. I answered a call for men

with past military experience and was told that if I got to the Masalur hub border in the next week or so I would find a great deal of work.''

''An Akhbreed slave girl. Not mine, although responding to my commands at the moment.''

Eyestalks leveled themselves on her. ''She does not look as though she is responding well to your commands,'' it noted. ''Still, wait here. I will summon the magician of the gateway.''

The Hedum turned, faced the barrier, and placed both enormous hands on it, one on either side of the theoretical opening. There was a chilling, ringing sound and an almost immediate response from inside a tent in back of the gate. Presently a middle-aged man in black robes appeared—an adept! High power indeed. Klittichorn couldn't have too many adepts on his side or he'd not have waited this long nor been this cautious. Adepts were essentially Second Rank themselves, although not as powerful as full sorcerers—yet. Basically they had the power, but not yet all the skills and experience. Still, they were formidable.

The adept stood there, looked at both of them, frowned, then said, ''Dismount and walk through. We'll bring your horse through after you.''

Halagar slid down, then picked Charley off and virtually carried her through. He was not blind to the fact that several more Hedum within the barrier shield were pointing guns right at him.

The adept went up to Charley, seemed to examine her top to bottom, then put his finger on the tiny slave ring in her nose and stepped back. ''She's bound to Boolean,'' he noted. ''Not *by* Boolean, but definitely *to* him.''

Halagar nodded. ''I know. I know of no one capable of removing the spell.''

''I could, but it would be a lot of trouble and time. However, the fact that she is not bound by him makes for an easier remedy. Has she ever been in his presence?''

''As far as I know, no.''

''Then it's easy. Now tell me why I should bother.''

Halagar hesitated only a moment. ''My name is Halagar, a mercenary most late of Covantian service. I was hired by a two-bit magician named Dorion who's working for Boolean

to bring her and another woman to him. The other woman is
Boday, wife of Susama. Interested?''

"Very. But if you betray them, why should I believe you
won't betray us?''

"No percentage,'' Halagar told him. "I know what you're
going to do and that will make the whole mission moot
anyway, since there's no way I can practically do it from this
geographic point and I know it, and since in less than a full
week the spell would dissolve of its own accord, wouldn't it?
I keep my commissions, but not when they are obviously
beyond my ability to perform.''

The adept smiled. "Now I am very interested. Where is
this Boday?''

"Not so fast. First, I want that slavery spell transferred to
me. Second, I want an officer's rank in your forces, and
protection and safe reward at the end, if I serve loyally and
honorably and survive.''

The adept shrugged. "Sounds fair enough. Very well, as a
demonstration.'' He walked over to Charley, who was now
livid and suddenly felt no loyalty or attachment to Halagar at
all and a very strong urge to warn Dorion. The adept knelt
down and made a few passes with his hand, however, and she
suddenly stiffened and went into a deep trance.

"Fascinating,'' he said aloud to himself. "She's got a
regular bundle of stuff in there. Even demon spells. She's got
a familiar, too! Where is it?''

"In the saddle roll,'' Halagar replied, but even as he turned
to look at the horse he saw the shape of the cat leap from the
bedroll and run like hell through the startled soldiers and out
of sight. Attempts by the Hedum to catch him proved more
comical than effective, and he was soon well away into the
countryside.

"Forget it, then,'' the adept told him. "Just make sure it
gets no more of her blood. That's the way to kill them. If it
shows up, don't kill it—that'll only cause problems. Trap it
and let it starve. They're devoted but generally not very
bright. All right.'' He turned back to Charley. "Girl, what is
your native language?''

"English,'' she responded dully.

"All right,'' he responded in clear but heavily accented
English, "now listen to me. I am telling you a secret and you

will believe it. Now I tell you that Halagar is Boolean. Boolean and Halagar are the same. He chooses to use the name Halagar for now and so should you, but only you and he and I know that he is really Boolean, your lord and master. You know it, you believe it to be true, and nothing, no one, no evidence, no thing, shall convince you otherwise. He is your lord, your master, and your god and you belong to him and must always obey him. You are his to do with as he wills. When I snap my fingers you will not remember that this has happened but you will suddenly know and realize this as if it were divine revelation and you will believe and act accordingly. Also, your cat familiar is an evil creature, a demon who wants to harm your master. If he tries to contact you, you will shut him out and never seek him out, and you will never let him feed upon you. If it tries to contact you, you will not understand what it is saying nor obey, but you will tell your master. Now . . . three, two, one. . . .'' He snapped his fingers, then got up and turned to Halagar.

''It won't hold if she actually meets the real Boolean,'' he told the mercenary, ''but in a few more days that won't be a problem. In fact, upon Boolean's demise the spell will be permanently affixed, replacing the original, until your own demise. Now, what about this Boday?''

''If we're seen to be safely leaving, in no more than a few hours she will try and walk right in here with Dorion,'' he told the adept. ''And she has the same slave spell Shari has, so she'll be easy to lead away and very cooperative.''

''I see. Now about how powerful is this Dorion?''

Halagar smiled. ''I seriously doubt if Master Dorion can successfully palm a card or make a coin vanish. He used to work for Boolean but the old boy exiled him to Yobi in the Kudaan, apparently for incompetence. This was supposed to be how he'd get back in.''

The adept suddenly reached up and Halagar felt a tug on his hair. ''Hey! What—?''

The adept took out a pouch and put a lock of the mercenary's hair inside, then put away his small clippers. ''Just a bit of insurance that you will have no second thoughts and will stay on our side,'' he said lightly. ''With this, I can curse you anywhere in Akahlar.''

For Charley, sitting there, things became momentarily confused and then suddenly there was no confusion at all. When things had been going wrong the Master had suddenly revealed himself and his power to her and all was suddenly clear. Now she understood that Halagar was Boolean in disguise and thus her true master. It came as a complete shock, like a bolt from the blue, that revealed his power, but now everything was in place. She did not understand what he was doing or why, but it was not her place to do so. Such powerful beings were more than human; she could no more comprehend them or truly question them than a pet could comprehend or question the actions of their owner. In fact, that's just how she felt—like a pet dog, there to serve and obey, unquestioning, dependent, too low to comprehend.

Halagar was none too pleased about an adept having a part of him but it was a small price to pay to resolve his future. He came over to her, untied her hands, and saw in her face and demeanor the great change wrought within her. "This will be our secret," he told her, "to be revealed to no one. From now on you are Shari, slave girl of Halagar. That's your only identity and your only loyalty. Now, come—give me your hand. We must ride. We must not be late for their big show."

"Yes, Master," she responded, and that was all there was to it.

Dorion had been watching from the null, and while he had some bad feelings when they were held up by the adept, seeing them mount up and ride off made him feel relieved. Maybe they were going to make it after all!

Boday had used her kit to paint elaborate and colorful designs on her face and upper torso. She certainly looked—different—like some primitive savage, and maybe it would do. Dorion played with a simple by-the-book illusory spell that would make his robe appear to be some uniform, but when he saw the adept he knew that his simple and stock tricks would be of no avail. The hell with it; he would wing it as he was.

They mounted up and headed for the gate. The Hedum challenged them as it had challenged the first two, but the adept came out from his tent quickly and bade them come inside. The magician was just beginning to feel confidence returning when the adept said, "Well, brother-in-magic, I thank you for bringing us that which we have long sought."

Dorion frowned. "I do not understand, brother."

"Sure you do. You are Dorion and this is Boday, mate of the one we have sought for so long. Don't look so shocked or come up with any denials—your comrade betrayed you. And don't try anything unless you wish to test your own powers against mine."

Dorion hesitated, but he had too much respect for what it took to get that black robe, and too much understanding of how little power he himself possessed to do it. "No, brother, it's your game."

The adept smiled. "Let me make a bit of adjustment in our rather colorful slave here so that she believes me to be her true master, and then we can depart."

"Depart—for where?"

The adept smiled. "Why, we are going where you wanted to go. To Masalur hub! There we'll watch the final demonstration of My Lord Klittichorn's power and then meet up with some more of my brethren, and then together we will reunite this woman with her lover—an all too brief and sad reunion, I fear. And with those two steps we will erase forever the last hope of the old order in this world."

Out in the woods, Shadowcat had no luck in contacting Charley; she had shut him out entirely, even to the visual link, and now, with just she and Halagar on a single horse, it was clear that he could not hope to keep up with them. It was time to think it out.

The imp was a minor demon charged and bound to Yobi, who had no true existence in this dimensional level without inhabiting a body. Yobi had placed him inside the cat when Charley had selected it, and since then the imp had maintained himself through her blood energy while maintaining the cat body in the usual way.

Trapped in the body, which he needed to have corporeal existence on this plane, he needed her blood to survive, to replace the type of energy that was part and parcel of the very atmosphere and makeup of the netherhell to which the imp was native. By preying upon locals he might sustain himself for some weeks, but the link was to Charley and the energy level would be down at the very time he needed it the most. Worse, the locals here would probably not be Akhbreed and their blood, let alone blood type, was probably unsuited to his needs. Without Charley, he would die.

He cursed himself for not simply tearing Halagar's throat out one night as he'd been sorely tempted to do. Instead, he'd kept her in the courtesan mind-set, having learned of the spell from her own brain, so that she could not betray the full facts about herself to the man the imp had never liked or trusted. He could not destroy the cat body deliberately; that was against his nature and the rules here. He could provoke a killing, which would free him, but that would only take him back either to the netherhell or perhaps to Yobi's laboratory in the Kudaan, very far from here. It was a last-chance option, but it might well be too late if they killed Boolean.

Looking out from the bushes, he saw the Hedum bring up a sleek coach with six fast horses. To his surprise he saw the Hedum driver get down and Boday climb up and take the reins. Bewitched, certainly, and under the control of the evil ones. Two Hedum put large chests and blankets and bedrolls on top of the carriage in the luggage rack and secured them, then jumped back down, and Dorion emerged from the tent with the black-clad adept and both got into the coach. Dorion looked unhappy but not bewitched, which might or might not be some advantage. Shadowcat wondered what blood type both the magician and Boday were.

He eyed the luggage rack and judged where the coach had to pass and the probable speed of it when it did, then looked around for a convenient and climbable tree. It might be for nothing, he knew, but it seemed the obvious thing to do.

The rebel forces around Masalur were so confident that they even had bleachers erected for the big shots.

It was a far thicker but better organized crowd than the one back at Tishbaal; only the best rebel troops were here, all well-trained and eager to see some real action. They, and their support troops, remained relatively apart from the others, who seemed to be of all races, shapes, and sizes. Here, too, were large numbers of robed magicians and sorcerers of all ranks, although Third Rank types dominated with a smattering of black-clad adepts, and there were very few with the colorful robes of the Second Rank. The fact that there were any at all was impressive to the observers. The one thing they all had in common was that they were on the outs with their own establishment, either having been changed or malformed or having committed some political or ethical violations that had at best estranged them from their own kind and at worst embittered them towards it.

Here, too, surprisingly, were a fair number of distinguished-looking and not so distinguished-looking Akhbreed; men, and some women, of obvious wealth or power in key areas with their own axes to grind, hoping to carve out wider niches in the wreckage the new order would leave, and very useful to ones like Klittichorn. Men like Duke Alon Pasedo, whose family was barred by Akhbreed law and spells from coming this distance, but who had many grudges against his kingdom and many friends among those who sought to inherit this world. There were a lot of Pasedos about, although they were dressing plainly and keeping a low profile. There was no use in giving any of the colonial troops who would have to fight in this, any idea that they might also be serving the interests of some Akhbreed types.

Most of the Akhbreed on hand, however, had gotten the slave treatment. Much of the stands, the temporary buildings, field kitchens, and pit toilets had been built by them, and vast numbers continued to do the manual labor and dirty work of maintaining the whole place. They weren't really needed to the extent they were being used, but the rebel command staff guessed rightly that the sight of them in such low situations and so debased would keep morale among the native troops high.

The Hedum acted as the traffic cops, keeping the various factions separate and out of each other's way. They were polite but very firm and imposed a sense of order and strength on the vast assemblage.

One look at such a mighty, organized, and confident force and Halagar knew he had made the right choice. Any Chief Sorcerer who would remain bunkered inside his hub and allow this so close to him was another who was more smoke than fire, a sure sign of the system's rotten core.

Somehow, this Klittichorn had stumbled onto the great power that the Storm Princess possessed. He probably wasn't the first, but he was the first to realize the weakness in the center of the system after so many thousands of years; to realize that he might get away with using that power simply because his colleagues in sorcery could not believe that they were not impregnable. To have godlike power means nothing in the end if you have not the wisdom for it.

The Hedum traffic director pointed him towards a small three-sided tent pavilion. Sitting there were three officers, a senior and two juniors. One had pea-green skin and bug eyes and looked more like a giant lizard than a variation of humanity; another was bald, squat, with an incredibly wide face and hairless skull from which protruded two bony horns like great but misplaced carnivorous teeth. The third was a tiny, gnomelike creature with huge upturned pointed ears, a rather stupid expression, eyes like dinner plates, and who looked like he had been born old. None were races he recognized, and the quality of their uniforms—and the sameness of them in this vast jigsaw army—indicated that they were probably from Klittichorn's own staff.

"Yes, name?" the gnome asked him.

"Halagar, sir. A mercenary officer by trade but a volunteer to this cause. I have proved it by capturing the fugitive Boday and turning him over to the adept at the Masalur border."

"Indeed. Well, welcome, then, sir. We have no billeting for such as you—unexpected, that is—but you are welcome to set up anywhere over there near the tree line where you can find space. There's a cold field kitchen there and pit toilets just in the woods. I would suggest, to avoid problems, that you remain in that area. You'll get as good a view as anyone from that camp." He looked over at Charley. "And this, I take it, is a prize of battle?"

"My personal slave," he responded.

"Well, the rules here are that all slaves are put in the pens and assigned work and cared for en masse, so to speak. It avoids, ah, nasty situations."

"I understand, but for practical reasons she should stay with me. She is blind."

"Indeed? Then why keep her, then? What good is she?"

The horned giant looked at Charley and then over at the gnome. "Stupid question," he rumbled.

"I, uh—oh, I see. Yes, *ahem!* Well, she'll have to be with you at all times, even when taking a leak, and because she's blind I suggest you see one of the smiths and get a collar and chain for her so you can stake her and not have to constantly be watching out for her. Just see one of them along here—they'll do it.''

He nodded. ''Thank you, sirs. I believe this is going to be a most interesting new time for me as well as Akahlar.''

The green-skinned one looked over at him and said, in a surprisingly pleasant and mellow upper-class accent, ''Tell me, as a soldier of fortune and professional, what do you think of the operation so far?''

Halagar shrugged. ''To be frank, sir, it shows the other side as stupid, dry-rotted, and impotent. If I were this sorcerer over there, I'd have waited until everything was in place over here, then sent my entire army in with everything they had backed by all the sorcerers and sorcery at my command. As cramped and exposed and backed up as you are here, your automatic weapons would shoot as many of your own people as them, and you would be broken and destroyed. The fact that he has not done this shows that he must lose, and he's supposed to be one of the smarter ones.''

''You are not alone in that line of thinking,'' the gnome told him. ''Many of us recommended a low-key and covert build-up even with the organizational problems that would cause for that very reason. However, we tried build-ups of this kind in a dozen areas where we could bring a concentration of forces, and the reactions were always the same. If they will not help one another, our sorcery is at least the equal of their sorcery out in the open like this. You do them an injustice when you think them stupid, however. Think of the cost in lives and materiel to put down something like this. Their militia is designed to hold and maintain the colonies, not fight a frontal war. Far easier to endure, and allow our own weaknesses to consume us.''

''The only weakness we have,'' the horned giant picked up, ''is that the basic compactness and circular shape of the hubs makes them ideal defensive positions both from a military and magic point of view, and we have a less than cohesive force. They can reinforce from the center as needed, either power or men or both. They know it, and that's why they sit, waiting us out, believing we'll not be able to keep our forces together for a long siege—and it might even be the correct strategy under the old rules. This is a collection of independent races not used to dealing as equals with anyone other than themselves. Different, squabbling, with little in common except the thirst for freedom. But you remove that center out there, before your own forces begin to fall apart, and you have them. Tomorrow, at three in the morning, we will remove that center and attack from three sides. Tomorrow night, we will turn that center from enemies into automatic allies."

"Uh, do you have a Mandan cloak?" the green one asked him.

"No. We lost most of our supplies early on. Would there be a problem from this point? I know Changewinds never cross nulls."

"That's true, but it means you should wait a day before going in yourself and seeing the aftermath, just in case there are spin-offs. With a storm of this concentration the weakness down to the Seat of Probability remains unstable, and in spite of buying, begging, borrowing, or stealing every Mandan gold cloak we could lay our hands on for several years we haven't nearly enough. Well, just watch from here and wait. When it's all secure, we'll see if we can spare some for people like you. Thank you—that's all."

Halagar set up the bedroll in an area that had a fair number of Akhbreed, including some of his own kind who he recognized and who recognized him. Some were men like himself, who saw this side as the winner and thus the more profitable to be on; others were pirates, bandit chiefs, and other very tough customers, some of whom he'd gone after as a lawman.

To Charley, the collar and chain was the ultimate in degradation. The metal used was light and thin, but the collar was welded around her neck and the chain, maybe six or seven feet of it, was welded to it. Very quickly she had been reduced to being paraded around, filthy and naked, on a leash, like a trained dog, and Halagar wasn't above having her basically do tricks as well. In fact, he bragged and showed off so much that eventually he yielded to the social pressure and new comradeship and actually loaned her out to them. She had always liked anonymous, uncomplicated sex up to now, but these men were filthy, brutish, and a little sadistic, and she had no choice but to go through her entire vast sexual playbook with them on the grass for hours, unable to put her mind on automatic because of their nature, feeling at the end bruised, battered, and utterly defiled, and she was commanded to act like she enjoyed it and beg for more.

And some of them were only nominally Akhbreed, and many had very bizarre turn-ons, and those caused her both shock and disgust like she'd never known.

And they were in no mood to turn in. They were all killing time until three o'clock when the major battle would begin, and that seemed like forever. When it finally ended, about an hour before Zero Hour, she was so battered and so exhausted that she just lay there, unable and unwilling to move, but she couldn't stop thinking, even in a state of shock, trying to hold on to her sanity. Boday had been right; she'd still been a child, naive and stupid about this kind of life, romantic in a world that was truly a cesspool. She was property and treated worse than his horse, and it would continue to be this way, over and over, because that was all she was good for, the only use she was to the master. And it would go on like this, day after day, week after week, year after year.

She couldn't stand it, she knew that, but she also had to obey, had to do it, without choice, without thinking, with no hope of rescue. She thought of those hollow, dead expressions on the slaves back in Tishbaal and knew that she would be as shriven and without hope inside as that in very short order. The time had come, now, here, tonight. She knew she had to do it before she was commanded to speak only Short Speech or to never use English. "Charley, be gone!" she said aloud, firmly, and slowly her expression changed to one of dull acceptance, her manner relaxed, as one who thought only in the most limited ways and matched her situation.

The slave spell was not gone, but Charley was, and little Shari actually managed to drift into an exhausted sleep.

Masalur was an almost fairy-tale land; its central castle and government offices, with their many spires and minarets shimmering in their Mandan gold sheathing, were known far and wide as the most exotic and distinctive such buildings in all Akahlar.

Beyond the government center with its architectural beauty

and landscaped gardens and parks was a ring road, and just beyond on all sides was the commercial heart of Masalur, with its shops and bazaars and business centers for everything from commodities to insurance. One actually had to go about three miles from the center to hit the first all-housing areas, and these were densely packed, multistory apartment buildings containing hundreds of small flats. The final ring was the region of wealthy merchants who outdid each other with lavish homes and grounds. Only beyond that, perhaps an eleven-mile-circular city, did the land become rolling hills and farms sufficient to feed the city population, more than two million in normal times, perhaps double that now with the refugees inside.

Although it was in the early hours of the morning, after even the last of the clubs and night spots had shut down, there was no mistaking that a major storm was rolling in. Clouds seemed to rush in and thicken around the government center itself, the storm center appearing to form almost directly atop the royal castle. Those with the magic sight might have seen a glow in the clouds and wondered, and also seen the outer edges of the storm appear to take on the looks of strange beasts whose eyes and mouths were illuminated whenever lightning discharged inside the storm. The better magicians and Chief Sorcerer's staff would have recognized them as Sudogs, more here than could be remembered to be in any one area before. The Sudogs were weak and minor imps attracted from the netherhells by the conditions of great storms, but they were generally harmless and could not sustain themselves in Akahlar without the cloud "bodies" which would dissipate with the storm itself.

It would have taken an expert in both demonology and military tactics to recognize that the Sudogs were not merely using the storm for a brief reality but were moving around purposely, cautiously, almost as if directing the storm's shape and makeup. This they could not really do, but a sorcerer with contacts in the netherhells could use them to "see" from their unique vantage point, and if that sorcerer had power over storms, this information would allow very precise targeting.

For the first few minutes, those who were awake below ignored the storm as just another inconvenience; subtropical regions were used to being rained on at all hours. Now, though, the storm seemed to exude a strange sensation to those with the magical talent, as if those below it were descending in a fast elevator, and men and women in various places suddenly woke up, grabbed their robes, and headed for the alarms.

Changewind! A Changewind coming, in the hub itself!

Hub cities were far too dense to allow for full shelter and warning, but the alarms rang anyway all over the place, and sleeping people were roused and headed for what shelters there were if they believed that they were in any real danger. The government centers, of course, were sheathed in Mandan, the only substance that would deflect a Changewind. The royals, the permanent staff, the nearby senior bureaucrats, and the military command began quickly shutting the windows, pulling the shutters, fixing the seals to keep even the breath of Changewind out, then going down to the below-ground shelters where the winds, if the shields held, could not penetrate at all. A surface covered by Mandan gold was also safe below it; that was why, even out in the open, a pit or trench and a cloak of Mandan on top might well save you.

Particles no larger than small stones broke free from the great mass known as the Seat of Probability on a dimensional center far "below" Akahlar, which was only the closest-in point where carbon-based life could exist and did. The small particles immediately shot out, breaking down, colliding again and again, gaining speed and momentum, breaking free of their parent block, and shooting up through the Lower Hells, punching through one after the other, their explosive reactions widening more and more and attaining a circular, cyclonic shape, remaining in the Lower Hells only until they found a weak spot to continue through their outward, upward journey towards the dimensions and realms of men.

Klittichorn and his associates, through the "eyes" of the Sudogs who were too dull to realize their own danger, were providing that weak point, and the Storm Princess in full possession of her powers was holding and shaping the resulting storm center, waiting for the Changewind to break through.

Since the Changewind was supposedly random, and Mandan gold scarce, not even the richest of kingdoms nor the greatest of sorcerers ever lined the below-ground shelters. Mandan would protect you from a Changewind bearing down upon you, but the odds of one breaking into Akahlar under your very feet were so small as to not be worth calculating.

From their aerial vantage points, the Sudogs watched in fascination as the very ground of the government circle and into the business circle seemed to glow with a dull, white magical fluorescence, then grow stronger and stronger, more and more brilliant, until suddenly there was a tremendous rush and a great, swirling, tornadolike maelstrom broke free and reached for the storm clouds above.

Buildings, grounds, trees, streets, and all upon them seemed to shiver and melt at the touch of the white cyclone; the Mandan gold sheathing on the government buildings turned dark but held, yet began to crumple inwards into a heap as the supporting structures under them were melted away by the power from below; blackened gold foil that protected now only itself.

The maelstrom and the gathering storm mated in a dance of power, obliterating the Sudogs and all else and widening the regular storm into a monster of wind, rain, and local tornados which, while not Changewinds, were nonetheless black angels of death in the dark.

The mass now covered almost the eleven-mile radius of the city proper, with the white whirling maelstrom at its heart the center of its own meteorological solar system. Its energy partly expended on what it was touching, it could not remain still, and instead began to move with the storm itself. The core maelstrom widened, becoming less powerful only in degree, touching and changing all that it contacted, and moving now, out of the center, with the great storm.

Normally its passage would be swift; fifteen or twenty minutes and the white maelstrom within would find its weak point and travel upwards once more leaving the lesser but still devastating storm to blow itself out in the null, but this was not the pattern here.

The storm took a turn and began a slow, steady march around the city, dragging the Changewind at its core with it, as if somehow orbiting the center of its birth and unwilling or unable to break free. In less than an hour it had made an unprecedented, impossible three-hundred-and-sixty-degree circuit in a widening spiral, obliterating, then reforming all out into the farm belt itself. Masalur was not merely to be devastated or decimated, it was to cease to exist.

Across the null border between the colonies and the hub, from three sides, whole divisions of rebel troops began to move briskly across; thousands of men on foot following lines of calvary that seemed to stretch from horizon to horizon, bearing down on the armies of Masalur, who were now caught between the oncoming force and the Changewind at their backs.

Even with the strongest telescopes, it was nearly impossible to see just what was going on at the hub border, but, unaided and without even magical sight, the entire horizon seemed to be glowing and the enormous booming claps of thunder rolled across the null and mixed with the distant sounds of artillery opening up.

Halagar stood on the ridge and watched from afar. He'd given up on the telescope, but just the fact that he could hear so much rumbling from so far away and see the whole horizon apparently ablaze awed him and his companions. They watched, too, open-mouthed, as great, demonic stormriders came out of the null clouds and right into the command areas of the rebels with reports and information, and carried instructions from the general staff back with a speed that nothing else in Akahlar could match and that no defender could slow or even effect.

Less than a half a mile from Halagar, Dorion stood atop the coach that had brought them here only an hour before, open-mouthed and with heart sinking. With his magic sight he could see and psychically *feel* the power out there, the finger of white barely glimpsed now and again as the spiral widened outwards. There was nothing else to see, of course, and no way to know just what it was like over there; Boday, exhausted from driving much of the past few days and through some of each night, had watched for a few minutes, then curled up and went soundly to sleep on the driver's seat.

But, somehow, even with nothing really to see, he couldn't stop watching.

He had actually been treated with the utmost respect since being captured. The adept, whose name was Coleel, proved a rather pleasant, even interesting fellow, with enough power and skills to be totally confident of himself; second rank in all

respects save having successfully stood the examination by a
committee of full Akhbreed sorcerers—something that, shortly,
might be a bit difficult to assemble anyway.

His fall had been dramatic, although not for the usual
reasons. As an apprentice to a sorcerer far to the east, he'd
been posted as a magician in residence in a colonial capital,
where, because he was already so powerful—a natural, as it
were—he'd spent some of his copious spare time studying the
natives and their culture instead of working all the time on his
skills, and he had regaled Dorion with tales of these people,
the Grofon, on their trip to this point. To hear him tell it, they
were a particularly beautiful people, inside and out, almost
angelic, and very similar to Akhbreed in appearance, but they
were hermaphroditic—their whole world had developed
unisexually—and had some "trivial" and "beautiful" differences like multicolored hair and bushy tails. A city boy and
true believer, he'd expected to be posted to some primeval,
primitive world with monstrous creatures more animal than
Akhbreed, and instead he'd found a beautiful folk with a
gentle culture. He'd become quite close to them.

Then there came a ritualistic period in a local tribe's life, a
period of just four weeks that came only once every twenty
years, which fascinated him, but which had the inconvenience
to come during the peak harvest time. The Imperial Governor,
a royal relative on his first assignment, had blown his stack at
having all the natives cease work for so long a period during
so critical a time, and he ordered them back to work. When
they ignored him, he ordered troops in, only to find that in
the one matter of religion, they would rather die than work.
Infuriated, the governor had declared a civil insurrection although none really existed and ordered mass executions in
public—children as well as adults, randomly. Coleel was
ordered to protect the troops; when he refused, the governor
threatened to bring him up before an Imperial Court of Sorcery for violating his oaths. The governor had too many spells
of protection from the Chief Sorcerer for Coleel to do anything to him, so the magician had done the most pragmatic
thing available and shot the man in the head. He had then fled
and lived with the natives in a far region of Grofon, for
sixteen years a fugitive, until word of the rebellion had
reached him and Klittichorn's cause and protection was offered.

Dorion thought it was too bad the guy was screwed, and wished he'd known him under more pleasant circumstances. Now an act of compassion and self-sacrifice was being turned into complicity in the greatest butchery in the history of Akahlar.

It seemed it wasn't nearly as hard for Klittichorn to get good recruits with high magical skills as it would have seemed.

Dorion had no idea what they were going to do with him, but, although no spells had been cast on him and no guns were leveled at him, he had no more choice in that than did Boday. He looked back across the great null, and wondered what hell was going on over there. If Boolean still lived, he surely had been transformed into something far different than a sorcerer, and that was as good as being dead.

· 8 ·

The Fugitives

HALAGAR FINALLY DECIDED that he had to get at least a little sleep or he'd be shot to hell when anything interesting happened.

For a while, he and his new comrades had watched and received relayed battle reports and wished they were in it somehow, but after a while came the realization that this wasn't his fight, not this time, nor would there be much to see before perhaps a day or so later. Better to be at your best than to waste yourself on this, and then look lousy just when you wanted to impress somebody.

He went over to where Charley had passed out a few hours before and frowned as he thought he saw some smaller shape, like an animal, dart from her still form and off into the darkness. *If I didn't know it was impossible, I'd swear it was her damned cat,* he thought to himself.

He went over and looked at her, and it *did* seem that she had a wound on her right breast, but that might well have been from the earlier night's play. Probably was, considering the location and considering it sure wasn't bleeding. *Over tired,* he told himself, lying down on his sleeping bag and stretching out.

The boys had been a little rough with the girl, but, hell, that was all she was good for, and she'd survive. Besides, she'd paid off already. Letting them have their fun with her had turned a bunch of mercenaries and misfits into a kind of comradely unit with them all feeling kindly towards him. She was unique; the only one of her kind in captivity, maybe the only one anywhere if they did to other hubs what they were

192

doing to Masalur. Hell, she'd be real useful in keeping a unit happy out in the bush and a real inducement to ride with him.

He shut his eyes and relaxed and tried to get to sleep. With Boolean dead and the rest lining up for the slaughter, and with him and his pet and his new comrades and position, things were about as good as they could be.

Suddenly his eyes opened wide in sudden shock and pain; he tried to yell out, tried to scream, but nothing came. With tremendous force of will he reached up and grabbed onto whatever *thing* was tearing into his throat and came down on a small, furry body. In desperation, unable to breathe, hardly able to think, he grabbed the animal's torso and squeezed with all his might, trying to crush it, pull it away.

It was a death grip, and he knew it, even as he pulled the creature off him, its gaping mouth taking much of his throat with it and threw it with all the force of his command down to the ground. He sat up, trying to talk, pointing at two glowing eyes in the dark, then sank back for the final time in death. The last thing he heard before darkness fell upon him was an eerie, gruesome voice inside his brain.

"Bad man! Evil man! Die! Die!"

At the moment Halagar died, Charley woke up and sat up. She was feeling sore and bruised and very frightened but she was suddenly very wide awake. She was also not Charley, but Shari, making any conclusions or decisions nearly impossible.

Shadowcat was hurt, badly hurt; Halagar's will to live and his dying strength had been unexpected and particularly brutal. Most of the familiar's ribs had been crushed in the death embrace and he could barely move. He was bleeding inside, and he knew he didn't have a whole lot of time left. He reached out to Charley's brain and found only Shari there. It confused him, but he knew the trigger and sent it.

"Charley return," he managed, glad that it required only mental contact.

Slowly, and with some horror, Charley felt herself once again, and she didn't like it a bit. *"Oh, god! It didn't work! I can't send myself away!"* But there was something odd, something different. Halagar—that bastard! Somehow she'd been tricked into believing he was Boolean. What in hell was happening to her now?

"Charley," came a familiar voice that both startled and frightened her.

She looked around and finally spotted a magical aura of lavender fuzz about ten feet from her, although it didn't look right, somehow. It was constantly changing shape, and the whole center seemed the deepest black.

"Shadowcat?"

"Quiet! You want to bring the others? You know what they will be like. You can do nothing for me. Halagar is dead beside you, but he has had his revenge. Do not weep for me; only the cat dies. I return home free and clear. You must get away. They will think you did it and what you have suffered will be nothing in comparison to what they will do to you. Go directly back, away from the null. This is cover and no one left."

"But—I can't leave you! And what can I do back there? I'm blind!"

"Trust your instincts. Survive. Use what you have. You must believe me, and in yourself. I do not know how long it will take, but if you survive then help will come, and if you survive then there is still hope. I can say no more. Now, leave me. I die now, and I prefer to die alone."

"No!" Then, "How will I know the help when it comes?"

"You will know. Farewell, Charley Sharkin. And, next time, pick the dog."

The blackness inside the lavender fuzz grew and engulfed the color until there was nothing left. No—not quite. A tiny ball of twinkling crimson, a jewel or starlike thing no bigger than her thumbnail, burst forth from the blackness and came towards her, then touched her for an instant, and then was gone.

She got up and almost immediately stepped on and almost tripped over her chain leash. She grabbed it, followed it, and found where it was pegged with a tent stake in the ground. With both hands she pulled the stake out and then gathered up and coiled the chain over her shoulder. There was a lot of noise around so she wasn't worried about that, and if those foul creatures were around she couldn't tell. Made no difference now; she had to act as if it were still dark and everything unseen. What she *could* see was the null, and that meant she knew the direction to go. She got up and walked away from it, and within no more than eight or nine steps she walked into a bush. She worked around it, met another bush, then a tree, and, using one hand to feel ahead of her, she continued on back.

She didn't know how far she was going, or even if she was making any progress, but using the sounds of the throng on the border as a guide she thought she was going well away from them. She wanted to hurry, but every time she did she tripped and fell. Several times the chain slipped, and she had to pull it back and wrap it, often tugging to free it. After that, it was very slow and cautious, using her hand and a lead foot. She suddenly stopped and thought a moment, then uncoiled some of the chain and began waving it back and forth in front of her. It wasn't a white cane, but it did help.

Suddenly she felt herself step into mud, then she slipped and fell into it and down a short embankment and into cool running water. She lay still for a moment, afraid that the chain had hung on something, afraid that this was a broad river, but after a while she got confidence and pulled on the chain and it came. Getting to her knees, she cupped her hands and put them in the water, not knowing or caring if it was fit to drink or not. She tried it, it tasted okay, and she drank.

Feeling a little better, she got to her feet and wondered what to do next. Was this a little wadable creek or a broad river with slippery rocks and deep spots? If she tried to cross and slipped, then the chain would most certainly be the death of her.

But—back there, it probably was light by now. They probably had discovered Halagar's body and that she was missing and they might even now be looking for her, figuring she couldn't have gotten far. If they found her, then the horror would begin again, only worse, and eventually they'd drag her to one of the big-shot sorcerers there and. . . .

No. She was going to die, almost certainly, probably by stepping where she shouldn't or victimized by insects or wild animals or maybe by accident or drowning, and certainly eventually by starvation, but she would die free. For the first time since she'd fallen into Boday's clutches, she was really free, with nobody to rescue and nobody to obey. Compared to that, somehow, none of the rest mattered. Being on her own, being free, even if for a short time with death the only

reward, suddenly seemed the only thing that was important
any more.

She walked into the creek, carefully, and found it shallow,
no more than hip deep at the center, the bottom a mixture of
mud and tiny rocks or pebbles. When she realized that it was
getting shallower again, she stepped back a bit and knelt
down, so that the water came up to her neck, and she
splashed it on her face and even immersed and wrung out her
hair. Somehow feeling much better, she got back up and
continued to the bank—where, of course, she found more soft
mud. Somehow it didn't matter. It was *new* mud.

She knew, though, that she was spent. The hair weighed a
ton as wet as it was, and she'd had a horrible night and very
little sleep. On the other side, she decided to follow the
stream for a bit, checking, until she found an area that
seemed to be an irregular row of bushes almost as tall as she
was. Wishing she knew how much, if any, cover they really
provided, she sank down in the grass or weeds or whatever,
stretched out, and more passed out than went to sleep.

It was six in the morning; the sun was not yet up, but false
dawn gave a gray and colorless beginning to the day, and
allowed the whole scene to be visible.

Dorion was dead tired, but he still resisted sleep. Just from
hearing various people talk as they passed nearby, and checking occasionally with anybody who looked like they might
know something, he had a fair picture of what was going on.

Before the Changewind had exited, it had covered perhaps a
third of the hub, including the entire capital and center and
touching probably eighty percent of the swollen population.
The land was now a swampy region with thick, bizarre
vegetation, and most of it was under a thin layer of water; a
shallow sea dotted with countless hundreds of tiny "islands"
of thick growth that rose no more than a few feet above the
swamp. The water area, too, was covered with vegetation,
although, as usual, it was of types and kinds that hadn't been
seen before.

Mandan hadn't saved the city center, and it hadn't saved
those in the public shelters, few as they were, or the private
ones of the wealthy further out, either. True, unlike the center

they had received only the Changewinds the shelters were designed to protect against, but the changeover in topography had opened up the regions around them, and the swamp water had come flooding in through the air intakes and flooded those shelters. It probably would never be known how many drowned that way.

The first rebel units into the transformed region were using loudspeakers during the inhabitants of this new land to come forth, assuring them that they would be well treated and welcomed and would not be harmed in any way, let alone killed. That because Akhbreed rule was dead not only in the hub but in all of Masalur, they would be helped to rebuild, to grow, as a new race among the many—equal now, but no longer superior or masters of all. First reports told of the appearance of "very large women" with deep green skin, long, purple hair, with four arms and four breasts, one set atop the other, and long, thin, prehensile tails coming forth. So far, no males had been seen, and all of the "women," at least to the eyes of the colonial forces, looked to them to be exactly alike in appearance.

The new Masalurians, Dorion thought. And possibly Boolean among them, although nobody really knew what happened to anyone who was sitting on a Changewind when it broke through. He and the others might now be just part of the energy of the storm rising through the outplanes.

Although the rebel forces were jubilant that it had all worked as they'd planned and dreamed it would, there were some sour notes and long faces among the celebrants. The Masalurian troops, who'd not been touched by the Changewinds, had fought with exceptional skill and ferocity and, with nothing to gain or lose but revenge, near suicidally. The rebel forces, who had never actually fought before and had neither the training nor the discipline of the defenders nor the defender's knowledge of the land from the hub to the transformed region—divided as well by racial loyalties, conflicting generalship, and language barriers—had been cut to pieces. Losses among the victors were not merely high, they were astronomical, and the remnants of the broken Masalurian army were still fighting guerrilla actions in the hills and might take weeks or even months to completely dislodge. The top generals here and the members of the General Staff were conferring in secret in the command center now.

When word inevitably got out about Masalur to the Chief Sorcerers of the other hubs, there would be much consternation and concern, but they would still not accept the truth—not enough of them, anyway. Although a Changewind had never broken through in a hub center in recorded history, it was not impossible. The whims of chance, really. The odds of it happening again—billions to one, old boy. Why, no one can or would dare summon a Changewind—you'd have to be right on the spot to even try and you know that would be the end of you. As for controlling and directing it—impossible! Why, in thousands of years of study and experience nobody had ever. . . .

Well, so it would go. Klittichorn got this one for free. But if it happened a second time, and in the same manner, reality would shove aside dogmatism. They'd know that indeed somebody *could* do it, and then they would remember Boolean's words and warnings. They'd be watching, they'd track down the horned one, and they'd burn him to the netherhells no matter what the cost, just for insurance.

Next time, Klittichorn couldn't stop until he got them all. Never mind Boolean's worried questions about the effects of so many Changewinds all roaring through at the same time; did Klittichorn in fact have enough rebel armies for it? And after the inevitable word of the massive losses and gross slaughter suffered here, would he still find enough eager volunteers?

Dorion looked over and saw Coleel walking quickly towards him. *Never mind the philosophical questions,* he thought apprehensively. *The question now is whether I'll be around to find out and, if so, just what condition I'll be in.*

"You're still awake, I see," the adept said, sounding not very cheery. "Good. Saves me time. Come with me. There's something I want you to see and comment on."

Dorion got down, feeling a bit dizzy and light-headed from the lack of sleep but still too worried to do anything else. "Yes?"

"Follow me. It's some walk up this way, but I think you might be able to answer some troubling questions."

They began to walk, and Dorion asked, "You're not going to tell me any more?"

"Wait until we get there. You can see it, about a leeg up and towards the trees, with all those people around."

Dorion shrugged, puzzled but intrigued, and continued walking. "Well, can you tell me if it's true about the new Masalurian being a green woman with four arms and four breasts?"

"Yes, it's true. And it seems that they're all like that and all really do look alike. They have some sorcerers going in now to examine them more closely—I was supposed to go with them but this took precedence. Right now the preliminary word is that they're some sort of plant-animal hybrid, unisexual, possibly capable of photosynthesis but bearing and nursing live young. Of course, we don't know that for sure, and we're guessing about the latter, and will until we see some live young in who knows when? I mean, those people don't even know themselves yet. The breasts indicate live, nursing young, of course, which poses the question of why a photosynthesizing species needs mammaries, and that tail—the end of it resembles, well, a male sexual organ. They're like nothing anyone's ever seen before. They're in shock, of course, and most will need our psychic help to adjust, but it should be fascinating to see how they develop as a species. It's never been done before with civilized people—they've always gone in and wiped them out. Only among primitive colonials who weren't found earlier, and even then the number was small. This could be a species that begins in the *millions*. Ah—here we are."

Coleel parted the crowd and Dorion followed, then stopped short when he saw the scene, being kept clear by Hedum sentries.

It was Halagar, all right, his eyes wide, his expression one of stark terror, frozen there now until the elements ate it away, his throat a bloody mess. Dorion felt a mixture of revulsion and satisfaction at the sight. The bastard had gotten what he deserved, and quickly, too. Maybe there *was* such a thing as justice in the universe after all.

"The girl?" he asked. "Where's the girl?"

"We don't know. Gone, that's all."

"Charley wouldn't—couldn't—do *that*. Not like that. And she was under your spell. . . ."

"That spell was broken the moment he died, so right now she's free meat, with a slave ring and no master. She'd become the property of the first person who touches that ring, and that might have been what happened, although nobody else nearby seems to be missing or unaccounted for according to the group here. But, no, she didn't do it. *That* did."

Dorion looked where the adept pointed and saw the still form of Shadowcat, eyes also glazed in death, caked blood on the side of its mouth and in a pool beneath its head in the dirt.

"Well, I'll be damned," Dorion sighed. "I didn't know a cat's mouth could open that wide. Remind me never to have one if I need a familiar. But how did it get here?"

"The only way short of very powerful magic is embarrassing, I'm afraid," Coleel commented, "and will do my standing no good at all. It had to come with us, maybe even feeding off you or Boday. It wouldn't have dared touch me, but have you noticed any small wounds or punctures on yourself or Boday?"

Dorion frowned, lifted up his robe, and there was a large, bruised area on his thigh and tiny puncture wounds. "I'll be damned! It's been itching like crazy, but I just figured it was a bruise."

The adept nodded. "That's how it kept going, although it wouldn't have had full strength. It must have made psychic contact with the girl, came here, waited, somehow fed on me and gotten strong again even though my spell would have her reject it so she must have been asleep, then waited for its chance." He sighed. "There's a lot of loyalty and a lot of guts there in that little form. I disagree with you, Dorion. I think a cat like that is *exactly* what I'd want for a familiar."

Dorion walked around the site, wishing he wasn't so tired so he could think more clearly. Suppose, just suppose, Coleel was wrong about Charley. Suppose the cat had used her for strength, and by killing Halagar, had broken Coleel's spell. If Shadowcat did his job, and made certain Charley had all her wits about her, she wouldn't just wander into the crowd. These other tough mercenaries would have been sleeping on both sides and she'd have walked into one of them, who would have grabbed her. She certainly wouldn't have walked towards the null, even though she could see it, because it would have meant going through more masses of sleeping bodies and guards. No, she'd go back into the woods and try and get as far away as possible. That *had* to be it. Otherwise she wouldn't have gotten far enough to be lost in this mob.

It wasn't certain, but it was the only possibility with an out for him or her. But if she did go back there, then she didn't stand a chance of survival. Not blind.

He went back over to Coleel. "Well, there's nothing more to be done here. Can I ask what's going to be done with me now?"

"Just hang around. Go to sleep—it looks like you need it. We have the Boday matter to handle yet as well as mopping up here. When they can spare the people and time, a board of magicians will be convened on you in accordance with our oaths, and you'll have a chance to justify your continuing existence. If you fail, you will be stripped of your powers, cleansed of your spells and geases, fitted with a ring, and thrown in the slave pens."

That was a chilling end to all this. "Considering that, you've been pretty generous with my freedom."

Coleel shrugged. "What can you do? Forgive me, but I can tell your relative magic strength and abilities, and they are not threatening. You haven't the proper spell and charm to be authorized past the borders of this camp, so all know you are a potential enemy. If you tried anything foolish, you would simply lose your right to the board hearing, and it would save everyone time and trouble." He looked out at the null. "Besides, what would be the point? You no longer have a master or cause to serve. Now, forgive me, I must get this mess certified and cleaned up and tend to my regular duties. You can find your own way back, I trust." And, with that, he walked off back down to the tent city.

The crowd was dispersing now; there wasn't much left to see, and the gory sights being hauled back in wagons from across the null provided more prurient interest to those who loved to gawk at such things. Dorion walked slowly away, trying to think about what to do.

If only there was some way for him to slip away. He wished he had the nerve even if there was such a way, but he was between a rock and a hard place as it was. They'd give him his board, but they couldn't trust him or what he said and, frankly, he wasn't powerful enough to warrant their attention.

With power, even solid Third Rank power, they might purge his mind and "turn" him to their cause because they needed more magicians than they had, but he was nothing, almost a fraud.

He watched as four Akhbreed slaves, looking exhausted and drawn, walked through the crowd towards Halagar's remains, there to get rid of the body and clean it up. Everybody just, well, ignored them, and why not? They could only obey, after all, and there were tons of them doing the shitwork around. . . .

Almost a fraud. . . .

He walked down towards the small tents where the prisoners from Masalur were being fitted with slave rings. He stayed there a bit, talking "shop" with the overworked magicians, who knew he was not one of them in all respects but who just didn't give a damn, and, after a while, he wandered away again. The rings had been there by the carton load; sensitized, but "raw," waiting for the binding spell and the insertion. It was no big trick to palm one, which he now fingered loosely.

In here, the tents were so packed it was difficult to walk between them. He went over to where the VIP horses were informally stabled, ducked between two tents just before the stable area, then kicked off his boots, leggings, robe, undershirt—everything. He looked at the ring and let the simplest of slave spells flow into it, the kind they were doing out of necessity. He wished he could totally fake it, or make the owner tag his own, but that would be seen through very quickly. He therefore sensitized it to Charley and, taking a deep breath, invoked the final spell that caused the ring to pass relatively painlessly through the bridge of his nose without breaking skin and lodge, hanging, inside.

Waiting until it was as clear as it could be, he slipped around the back of the tent and into the rear of the stable area. The water troughs there had splashed all around, causing a nice mess of red mud, and there was other dirt around as well, although he decided to pass on the most obvious scent. Now, filthy, ringed with a spell that wouldn't read false, and looking lousy from his lack of sleep in any case, he got up and simply walked out into the mass and back up towards the tree line.

There were loads of people around, Akhbreed and colonial alike, but none gave him more than curious glances and then ignored him. A couple of brown-robed magicians walked near and he felt their automatic probe for anything unusual, but he read true to them and it probably didn't even register in their minds that they'd done it.

Normally his nerves would have given him away, but since the first activated items in the sensitizing spell for the rings was a compulsion to present yourself to your master, he had no choice. He *had* to find Charley, and that quieted all other fears and replaced them with wariness.

He passed quite close to where Halagar's body had lain, and close, too, to many of the people who'd been there when he was, but, as usual, they had seen the brown robe more than him, and he looked quite different now. Before they had seen a magician; now they saw a slave moving with purpose and obviously carrying out a command. Not even the Hedum guards gave him a second glance. He headed for a likely spot—the field latrines just in the woods—but as soon as he was close to there he veered off to the right and doubled back behind the death scene.

There were no obvious signs immediately behind, and he paused a moment. *Think, Dorion, tired as you are! You're blind and you have to get away and be sure you do. You can't see, and you don't have the null reference after this point, so how can you be sure?*

Hearing. That assemblage out there made a constant, terrible racket that he'd gotten used to through the night. So you walk away from the noise. Well, that gave him a place to start.

After several hours, he was beginning to panic, fearing that he'd made a dreadful mistake. The area, even assuming walking generally away from the noise, included a wide triangle, and there was almost certainty that she wouldn't have managed anything close to a straight line. Might there be something up there that would stop her? A wall or steep drop, perhaps? Go directly away and see—it was the only thing he could think of that he hadn't already tried.

About a third of a mile in the woods, he hit the creek, meandering peacefully through the forest. At first it was only welcome water, far too small and too shallow to be the kind of barrier he sought, but as he went down to it to drink, he lost his footing in the soft earth, and slid down into it. Now a bit bruised and mud-caked, he sat there in the water suddenly feeling like a fool and hoping it was only exhaustion. Sure—he could see this thing and know it wasn't much, but she couldn't! To her this might be nothing, or it might be a great, wide river or sea. He drank, then picked a direction, and started walking.

Now, for a change, the fates were with him. Less than a hundred yards from his starting point he found a part of the bank given way and signs that someone had done pretty much what he'd done. It was so broken he thought she'd fallen down and then clamored back up, and he did likewise and searched the area but could not find her. He returned to the break and looked across the stream and now could see what might be signs of somebody getting out the other side. That was discouraging, since it meant the creek hadn't stopped her after all, and he might have an even wider area to search. Driven by his self-imposed compulsion and against the protests of his body, he waded across to the other side and climbed up on the other bank, telling himself that no matter how wrecked he was, he was still in better shape than those poor wretches back at the border.

Still, he knew that even to complete his compulsion he'd have to get *some* rest. He was feeling dizzy, had a hell of a headache, and was seeing things all blurry. He began searching along the creek bank for some kind of decent cover he could use to lie down just for a little bit, to get himself back into some kind of shape.

And suddenly he saw her, lying there like some dirty, limp rag doll, unmoving behind the bushes. He ran to her, fearing that she might be dead, and knelt down beside her. He took her, shook her gently, and said, "Mistress! Mistress! Are you all right? Wake up and speak to me!"

She stirred, mumbled something, then suddenly her eyes were open and she was aware first that she was in someone's grip and began to scream and push away, but then she *saw* him. Not Dorion, of course, but that magic aura whose distinctive shape she'd shared most of a long journey with.

"Dorion?"

He felt like crying. "Mistress, you live! You are all right!"

She frowned, unable to see the shape he was in, reached out, and began to run her hand over his body. "Dorion—why are you—oh my! Sorry!—naked? And what's this mistress crap?"

He lay down beside her and tried to relax, then told her the whole story. She had slept so hard that, while still exhausted, she felt wide awake and clear-headed, although her head was killing her when she moved. She listened, fascinated.

"Let me get this straight. To get out of there without getting noticed, you made yourself *my* slave? Jeez! All the time I been here, I been somebody *else's* property. Will it wear off?"

"No, Mistress. It can only be removed by *two* magicians of some skill, Third Rank, or a Second Rank sorcerer with some time and a lot of work. It's not supposed to be easy to undo."

"Even if I gave you freedom?"

"No, Mistress, that would be worse. Then I'd be a slave with no master, and the first free person who touched me would be my new master."

"Well, I wouldn't, if I could. I don't want you away from me from now on, and this'll keep you close. You made your bed and you're stuck with me, but cut that Mistress crap. It sounds wrong when it's addressed to me. Just Charley is fine."

That pleased him. "As you wish—Charley."

She suddenly came over and gave him the hug of his life, clinging to him, breaking out into tears. "I need you, Dorion. I need your eyes, your strength, and, most of all, I need your company."

"Whatever you want, I'll try to do, Charley," he told her sincerely, "spell or no spell."

"Just hold me," she sobbed. "Just hold me close until I can believe you're really real."

He did so, and felt better and more important than he ever had in his whole life. It wasn't until much later, lying there, her head in his lap and him stroking her hair, that he suddenly was struck by a wrongness. Not from Coleel or that bunch, but something wasn't quite right. Looking down at her still angelic face, as dirty and scratched up as it was, he suddenly realized that he'd been looking at it all the time.

Like Coleel, he'd assumed that the slave spell had neutralized when Halagar had died, making Charley temporarily free but only until someone, anyone, else touched her ring. Anyone but him, of course, since a slave could not be a master of his own mistress. But there wasn't just the sensitizing spell in her ring; it was complete. It was still Yobi's original—he knew her handiwork well enough. But that spell bound her not to Dorion—that was only temporary and had been neutralized by his own actions—but to Boolean. If Boolean had died, or been swept away, or had even been transformed into some four-armed, four-breasted plant girl, the spell would have been negated the same as Coleel's had been when Halagar died. The spell, however, was intact. Although Charley didn't seem to realize it, she, too, was still a slave.

His own excited start bumped her head a bit and frightened her for a moment. "What's the matter? You hear something?"

"No, no, Charley—your ring! Yobi's spell's still on! Don't you see what that *means?*"

She sighed. "You mean—I'm still a slave after all?"

"Yes, but it means a lot more than that. Charley—it means Boolean's still alive! Still alive and still unchanged." He gave a low chuckle. "It means either that he was as smart as I thought he was, or that, for all that, the bastards missed him!"

She frowned. "That explains it, then. Just lying here, feeling a little safe for the first time in a long time, I suddenly had this thing in the back of my head whispering that I should go to Masalur hub and find somebody. But—if you're right, Boolean couldn't be *there*, not *now*. Jesus, Dorion! I'm gonna wind up with a full-scale compulsion to find Boolean, and I no longer have his address!!"

"Then you must use your head to fight it. You know he can't be in Masalur, so going there does not fulfill the command. You can not find him, not with things as they are. Your duty, then, is to simply remain free and alive and out of anyone else's hands until he can find you—or until some clue presents itself."

She thought that one over. "I—I guess you're right. I guess that's why I *can* fight it, why it's not overriding everything. Why I didn't really know until you told me. But that means it could be a real long time. Out in the woods, naked, savages, really. Sort of caveman and cavegirl, only without the cave or the skins. And fugitives, too. We can never be seen or mix with others. Around here, Akhbreed's gone from being the highest to the lowest of the low."

"I know. But it's a big world, a whole planet, and it's real warm here all the time, and it's thick forest around here. We'll be hard to spot or catch. If we can only find a source of food and water, we could make out okay." The fact was, Dorion didn't feel hesitant about it at all. Except for the food problem, which would have to be solved and soon, this came about as close to his private fantasies as he could ever come.

She frowned, still thinking, although this wasn't one of *her* fantasies. "Dorion? How can you be my property if I'm still a slave to Boolean? Property can't own property."

"That's what fooled me for a while. Because I wasn't bound to you—that would be beyond the spell—but because I bound myself that way, freely and of my own will. It's the only way possible."

"And you gave the magician's life up and came after me to live like this—for me." She said it like she couldn't get over it.

"Yes, Charley," he replied, not adding that it was certainly the best of his possible alternatives.

It was well past noon when two high rebel officers and a sorcerer of the Second Rank sought out Coleel, who was beginning to think that the mop-up work from the night would be never-ending.

The Second Rank sorcerer was one of only two on site during the whole battle; the rest had participated, somehow, remotely in a way only Klittichorn knew. The rebels had a large number of acolytes, magicians, and adepts, but very few of the Second Rank. Their powers and egos did not in the main make them terribly cooperative with one another nor willing to be under one of their own.

This one was a mean old fart with a face that looked like he'd died about three centuries past and refused to recognize the fact, but he had a fairly strong walk. His name was Rutanibir, and he was short-tempered, mean, and pissed off at the universe in general. What his motives were for working with Klittichorn wasn't known, but he was a key man in the field.

"You have this homosexual woman?" Rutanibir asked him in a shaky voice.

"Yes, Master. I—"

"Silence! Why wasn't I notified immediately of this? Take me to her at once!"

Silence was one thing he didn't want to concede. "Master, this *was* reported, but so close to the start of the battle that word did not apparently get to you. She's under my control as a slave, though, and she was commanded not to move. Come. I will take you to her."

They walked briskly along, the throng parting rapidly and averting its gaze from the wizened old man in the silvery robes. Because of the fear he generated, it took only a few minutes to find the coach and go up to it.

"Boday!" Coleel cried out. "Come! Attend me!"

There was no reply, and he frowned, suddenly nervous. He jumped up on top and saw that she wasn't in the seat or foot well, nor under the tarps. He climbed down, looked inside, under, and all around. She simply wasn't there anywhere.

"Incompetent idiot!" Rutanibir snapped. "No wonder you never made Second Rank! Whoever gave you those black robes should be drummed from the Order! You *knew* she was important, even vital! Yet you let her sit here, unattended, all night, with all hell breaking loose, and didn't even *think* about her! Didn't think at all. . . ."

"Master, I—" Coleel suddenly stopped and stood straight up, a tremendous look of confusion on his face. "Why in the name of the Seven Sacred Words *did* I do that? You are correct, Master—it makes no sense at all. And that magician—Dorion. I gave him free run of the place! And parked right here, not two leegs from the rest of his party. And I spent five days in the coach and never even *sensed* the presence of an unwanted familiar. I admit to abject incompetence, Master, and throw myself at your mercy."

Oddly, his talk calmed rather than enraged the old sorcerer, who waved off the comments with a casual hand gesture. "That son of a bitch," he muttered under his breath, more to himself than to any of the others. "Sixty-one-percent casualties and we still missed the old bastard. It *has* to be. All that—and he wasn't even home! He's been standing *here*, next to all of us, playing games with us and laughing at us all this time!''

The two military men turned and stared at him, and it was finally Coleel who asked, ''Pardon, Master, but do you mean I was bested by superior power? Who? Who would have such power and such audacity?''

''Boolean, of course, you idiot!'' the sorcerer snapped. ''Son of a bitch!'' He turned to one of the generals. ''You said you had a man back in Covanti who thought he'd tracked the girl. At the time it didn't seem worth pursuing, but if Boolean's *here* then we still have a chance.''

''Yes, sir. Fellow's name is Zamofir, one of our best agents. He thinks that she got caught up in a move to give brides to a bunch of ex-convicts developing a valuable business in one of the Covantian colonies. He's got a band of men with him, loyal to our money if not to us, and he's willing to go. He's in Covanti still.''

''Good, good. It's no mean feat even for one of Boolean's skills to follow such a slender and nebulous thing as a marriage thread over three kingdoms and into colonies. It'll take time. Lots of time. I can reach some of my people planted in Grotag's office in a matter of hours. All I need is my kit and someplace quiet. Your Zamofir and his band can be riding to her before Boolean is even clear of Masalur.'' He put one wizened hand into a fist and gently struck his other palm with it. ''Yes, indeed. So he's outsmarted us, has he? Escaped and all that. Well, precious little good it will do him if your man's right. And he'd *better* be right, General. He'd better be right. . . .''

He was a small, thin man with long, thinning black hair just starting to turn gray; the most outstanding feature of his sharply angled face was its long moustache, which he usually, as now, kept waxed and perfectly shaped so that it stuck out from both sides of his face and curled up nicely. He would never be considered handsome, but he could be charming if he wished; still, no matter how he dressed or where he was, he always looked dapper and out of place beyond the casinos and social gatherings of the business set.

Now he was dressed in casual riding clothes; a simple cotton shirt and tough denim pants with boots, all of which looked new and had some unnecessary fancy stitching. He took out a long, thin cigar from his pocket but did not light it; it was just a pacifier at this point. You didn't want to smoke, not in *here*.

Several large, burly men dressed in the sort of clothes one knew instantly were not bought special but were the ones in which they lived and worked, entered the cave as well, all illuminated by magical hanging lanterns that had plenty of light but no heat or flame to speak of.

Zamofir, their leader and employer, pointed to a carton. "There. Use the crowbar behind that box and get the lid off that one."

One man got the crowbar and another assisted, and the lid broke open revealing a box full of large metallic guns packed in straw. One of the men reached down and picked one up and looked at it quizzically. "Looks like a rifle of some kind, but it's too fat to steady," he noted. "And where do you put in the bullet?"

"Idiot!" Zamofir snapped. "Let me have that. This, gentlemen, is what is known as an automatic rapid-firing gun, known where it came from as a submachine gun. These, and the cartons of ammunition around, were gotten with great skill by Lord Klittichorn using his powers to extend to the outplane. They use these big, fat clips, like this. You turn it over, press here, insert the clip so until it clicks in place, then throw the safety here and it's ready to fire. To reload, you just press here, the clip drops out, and you shove another in. Clear so far?"

They all nodded, crowding around. "But how do you hit anything with it?" one asked. "I mean, it doesn't even have any decent sights and it's too square."

Zamofir sighed. "Follow me, gentlemen. I do not want to demonstrate in here."

They went outside with the loaded gun, and Zamofir picked a small, thin tree about thirty yards away. "Watch the tree. Each one of these clips holds a hundred carefully packed rounds. You just point the gun in the general direction, then pull the trigger. Even *you* can do that." And, with that, he demonstrated, and the rattling filled the air and smoke poured from the top of the machine gun, although nobody noticed.

They were all watching as the tree was sliced almost in two and much of the surrounding area was also pockmarked.

"The shells are ejected automatically. Don't bother with them—we have a sufficient number of clips here. Each man will take one of these and as many clips as is practical for him to carry. We'll practice on the way, although little is really needed once you learn how to keep the gun reasonably steady. Now, there are twenty-one men and four women there at the camp, but it's unlikely that more than half the men will be there at any given time. Their big product is a key mineral found in certain kinds of ocean fish in that world, so they're out in shifts for days on end on small boats trawling, while the rest work the refining process back at the village. Twenty of us, with *these* should be more than enough."

"How far is it?" somebody asked.

"We are riding hard and light, but the village is out of the way and far outside the intersection point. Once we turn off the main road, it is unlikely that there will be any people at all between us and the village, so we'll be on our own but unimpeded. If we *do* meet anyone, kill them and go on. With consideration for the horses, it might well be seven or eight days to the village, depending on conditions. Once we get there, there is to be no quarter. Men, women, children, livestock—if it moves, it dies. *Particularly* all the women. If they surrender, we take their surrender, and then execute them. All are to die and all buildings and structures burned, and any boats, even so much as a rowboat, also burned. We want the place devastated, so that even if someone should escape, they would have no place to go and nowhere to turn."

"Aw, can't we even have some fun before—" somebody else started, but he cut them off.

"Listen! We're working for a big-shot sorcerer who can reward us all handsomely or punish us beyond our wildest nightmares. If we fail, then killing ourselves before he gets the word of our failure will be the only way out. Likewise, we're in a race against another, equally powerful sorcerer. The only good thing is that he doesn't know exactly where our girl is and I do. He's got to do things the hard way, and that takes time. If we're not out of there, and I mean *well* out of there, before he finds the spot, then we'll get it from the other side. For almost the last two days' ride there's only a single road, in some places too narrow for two horses to run abreast, for most of the length, shut off on either side by a wall of dense and nearly impenetrable jungle. If we don't get in, do our job, and get out past that trap, we'll be caught in it. Understand?"

They nodded soberly, and clearly a few were having second thoughts about this. Zamofir was quick to sense this and counter it.

"There's only one reason for any of us doing this—the price. We go in, do it, get away with it, and get back safely, there *is* no price too high. Name your own ticket. Your own little kingdom with all the wine and honey and slave girls you want—and I mean for each of you. This is the first job I've ever had where the prize was worth any risk, and I've worked for these people a long time. They pay off for success. Nobody, however, fails them twice. Now—get your weapons, ammo, and gear and saddle up. We ride *now*, and go as far as we can, then get as short a sleep as we can stand, and ride some more."

"What about the border?" one of the men asked. "Between the soldiers and the rebels it'll be hell getting through."

"Not *this* one. The rebels are on our side, dummy—they won't block us. They have their orders. But there's no army, no pressures, on this side. We've drawn them all to the south and west. The most we'll have to deal with are a few officials and the usual border guards, and under these conditions we can dispense with the niceties and just blow them to hell."

That didn't prove necessary. The border personnel weren't at all concerned with anyone going *out*; they were much too harried with the refugees and nervous ones from the colonies wanting *in,* and were more than glad to wave twenty Akhbreed through who wanted to go the other way.

Even Zamofir was impressed with the huge numbers of people along the road, even the main road across the colony he and his men wanted. The crowds slowed his progress considerably, and in some cases stopped them dead for some time. They were in no mood for that sort of thing, but the fact was that, in this case, they were twenty against an endless stream, and many of these colonial types, even with their families, were tough and hard-looking people with plenty of fight in them as well. You could machine-gun a whole mob, but they'd just keep coming, and then there'd be a ton of folks after them and blocking the only exit. Even with all that firepower and the clock ticking, Zamofir's group simply had to wait and cope.

The eastbound road was only slightly better, and it took them almost a week to finally make it to the final cutoff over to the sea. It was less a road than a tunnel through the jungle, dark, narrow, and forbidding, and they had better than two days on it to the settlement. At least, here, there weren't any crowds or refugees; indeed, there seemed to be no people, no habitation, at all.

There was the sudden crack of a rifle shot, and one of the men fell backwards out of his saddle and onto the ground, where those behind trampled him. A second shot came and another man fell, and now they suddenly all pulled up and dismounted fast. The dense, forbidding jungle was the only cover available aside from the horses, and none of the men really wanted to go into the jungle. It might be just what the shooter or shooters wanted them to do.

"Where did it come from?"

"I dunno! Over to the left, I thought, but the echoes made it hard to tell for sure!"

"Is it many people or just one guy?"

"One guy, I think. There were only two reports, both sounding the same and just about the time it would take to shoot and reload. We're like fish in a barrel on this damned road!"

Zamofir hunched behind the horses and cursed. "Well, if you hear anything, you open up with the machine guns," he told them. Spray the whole damned area if you have to."

"Who the hell's shootin' at us, anyways?" one of the gunmen asked him. "And why would anybody do it? They don't know who we are or what we're fixin' to do."

"It's that damn' sorcerer, that's who!"

"Don't be an ass," Zamofir told him. "Sorcerers have better ways to deal with us than shooting high-powered rifles. Maybe somebody who's working for the other side and is paid to delay us. But how'd he beat us here? Shit! More delays. . . .''

"Yeah," the man nearest him grumbled, "and we got at least another day and night in this trap of a road."

"Well, he *can't* dog us all the way," the little man maintained. "There are no other roads, and even the natives here can't fly. I say we can get pinned down here and picked off one by one or we can ride like hell and leave him in our dust. When we're well clear, we'll drop one man and he'll give our pursuer the same treatment."

"Yeah? Ever think that maybe his horse is *ahead* of us? That he's already gone, and maybe even now is mounted up and riding maybe an hour on and settin' up the next ambush? That's what *I'd* do."

"Fuck it!" Zamofir snapped. "I'd rather be shot than face either Boolean or Klittichorn. I say we spray all around, three-hundred-and-sixty degrees, then we mount up, and ride as fast as we can. Either we outdistance him if he's behind or, if we're fired on again, we *keep riding* no matter what. If he had more than a rifle he'd have wiped us out by now. Our only chance is to get ahead of him, and if we overrun his horse so much the better. What say you?"

"Beats hidin' out here," somebody muttered, and flicked off the safety on his machine gun.

After two days of being rained on, bitten by insects, and weakened by lack of food, the primitive life had lost its romantic appeal, even to Dorion. For Charley, it was about as bad as she could imagine, short of another round with those bastards back at the camp, but something that had to be endured.

"Dorion, we will have to take chances while we're still strong enough to move," she told him. "We need food to survive."

He nodded. "If we have to, we'll head back up towards the camp. It should be breaking down now as troops leave and as the rest move into the unchanged areas of the hub. And, if I remember rightly, there used to be a small town a few leegs in from the border, as usual. It's probably not much now, but they had orchards and stuff. If it wasn't picked clean to feed all those troops, there might be *something*.''

"Let's go there, then. We haven't much choice.''

It took them two hours to reach the road, and then they had to parallel it within the forest. There was a lot of traffic there, mostly wagons and such, almost all going away from the hub in steady streams. The conquerors were leaving the scene of victory now, taking what remained with them. For a victorious army who'd just done the impossible, they looked pretty damned grim.

Much of the town had been destroyed; cannibalized for the wood and other materials to build the structures at the border, but some of it remained. A small group of colonial natives remained; small, hairy humanoids with short, thick snouts and shiny yellow eyes the size of egg yolks, but it was hard to say whether they were the remnants of those who had lived there or if they were part of the force. Dorion did not remember seeing any of them at the campsite.

A couple of hours reconnaissance convinced Dorion that they probably weren't part of the attack force or anybody official. Apparently they were scavengers; opportunists there at battle's end who made forays into the campsite and came back with whatever wasn't nailed down that they could get away with. There were only a dozen or so, but they were tolerated because they were the "host" race and this was, after all, their world and their region now. Too many to take on, particularly when one good yell or scream would bring some of the passing "allied" forces to their aid. And, as expected, the orchards and such nearby had been picked clean.

There was, however, a mounting pile of discards out back, including a lot of soldier's kits—cold rations and the like. They were either quite choosy or quite wasteful, and Dorion was too hungry and in too much need to quibble. When it grew late, and the inhabitants of the town ruins bedded down and the procession halted or at least slowed to a trickle, Dorion led Charley across the road and to the back. They were not particular, and Dorion didn't give Charley the exact details and she didn't want to know. It was enough that the food was edible, that it filled, and that it wouldn't harm them.

The fact that it was somebody's half-eaten garbage showed just how low they'd fallen so fast.

"If we can get enough for a little journey, we'll head south again and off towards the west," he told her. "There's a bunch of groves and orchards down there, maybe two- or three-days' walk, that I'm sure the locals would have protected. They were parts of old plantations here, as I remember. I'll rig up some kind of shelter in the bush nearby there, and every night I'll go down and pick what we need so that they won't notice. We might be able to survive almost indefinitely."

She sighed. "Indefinitely. Like animals. And how long would it be before we crack, Dorion? How long before we talk each other out and stop? How long before survival becomes the *only* reason for living? Maybe it's different with you, but you can see. The sheer boredom would kill my mind in weeks once we got set up and got a pattern established. I'd flip out, be nothing more than a naked chimp in the wild. We're not living any better than that now. No, I'd rather die than that."

He shrugged. "What other choice is there?"

"Dorion, we have to get out of Masalur. We have to go where they don't control things yet. Not back, though. Not where *they're* going. You lived here in the glory days. There must be decent colonial worlds that aren't a part of the rebellion. Ones with gentle people we might find some help from. You told me yesterday that Coleel hid out from his king and sorcerer and all for like fifteen years. We got to do that, too. You can still navigate, can't you?"

"Yeah, sure, but. . . . What if I pick wrong? The only places that might be likely, and that's just by reasoning it out, are ones to the east. That was the side that they didn't attack from, probably because they didn't have enough allies there. Or we could guess at one right here—if they had to import folks from Covanti to fight, then there's got to be a lot of colonies who didn't want to join up."

"Yeah, but you'd have to call it up from the null. I kind'a think that would draw attention. No, that east is best."

He stared at her. "But that means going right through the camp, across the whole null, and through part of occupied Masalur hub!"

"Yeah," she agreed, "but it would scratch *that* itch in my head. It's gotta be a mess over there, and I can fend for myself in the null. Sam once did something like that. I say try it. If we're caught, we're caught. If not, we at least got a chance at some kind of *life*."

"All right," he sighed. "Then we'd better eat good and cross in the dark tomorrow. And pray to whatever god you have that all the Stormriders are gone and that there are no magicians in range. Otherwise you'll go back to being a pet, and I'll be at hard labor until I drop."

· 9 ·

Boolean

THERE WERE STILL a *lot* of people at the border, but a fair
number seemed to be male Akhbreed slaves doing massive
cleanup and even more massive burials. Apparently, with
their furious working, the rebel magicians had created literally thousands of Akhbreed slaves out of both the survivors of
the defending army and the locals who lived in the nearest
unaffected hub areas. The slave spells were generic, and thus
easy to do. They had to obey *any* order by just about anybody
who was not Akhbreed, subject to the hierarchy of rebel rank.

Clearly some order and better treatment was already initi-
ated. Large numbers sprawled, asleep, on the grass where not
many days before armies had waited, while others seemed to
be feeding on the leftovers of the invaders.

They appeared to be mostly males, and although some
were very young, they all seemed at least past puberty. What
women there were looked old, at least past menopause. Where
the younger women and all the children were, Dorion couldn't
guess, but he remembered the sentry's comments about breeding programs. The Akhbreed had never done much enslaving
of the colonials, primarily because there were far too many of
them and far too few Akhbreed, and that required subtler
means. But if you could pick out just one race, known on
sight by every intelligent being in Akahlar, you might well
enslave it and breed it to serve. And all in the name of
"justice."

Charley shivered. "This place, this life, isn't fun any
more. Thank god at least I can't have kids. Boday's potions
killed off my eggs or something."

"Sorcery can always undo alchemy if anybody takes a real

218

interest,'' he responded. "Remember, the way you look was
only streamlined by Boday; it was a product of sorcery at the
start. Unravel that spell and the alchemy ceases to exist, like
it never was. Don't feel too sure of yourself. You still want to
go through with this?''

She nodded. "It's just something I feel I have to do. Or, at
least, try.''

"I can not disobey your wishes," he noted literally, but
without any real enthusiasm.

Getting across the almost half a mile of open area before
the null wouldn't be easy; still, Dorion reasoned that the
center along the main road was probably the really dense and
active area and would remain so; further down, well down,
there might be nobody at all.

Indeed, they'd gone no more than a mile in the woods just
off the border region when they were out of sight of apparently everybody. Oh, there were some tiny little dots very far
off, too far for him to even make out what they were, but he
wasn't as concerned with that. Taking her hand, and a deep
breath, he walked her out into the open and down towards the
null. He didn't rush or run; that might have attracted some
attention from folks to whom *they* were just little dots, but
his forced walk was brisk and steady and, to her credit, she
kept pace with his reduced steps.

Even so, it was about as tense a few minutes' walk as he'd
had yet, and he felt tremendous relief when they reached the
edge of the null itself. There appeared to be no super alarms,
no complex spells or shields, along the border; why bother?
The only place you could go was the hub, and that was by
now crawling with rebel troops and magicians and would
probably be next to impossible. It was something he preferred
not to think about until he got there.

Charley felt odd in the null mists; it gave her a sort of
limited vision that was quite welcome, and it felt a bit cooler
and cleaner, somehow, than the forest they had left. More,
her presence in it had a certain *rightness* to it she couldn't
explain, not to Dorion, not even to herself. Like, well, that
she *belonged* here, doing this. That it was the proper thing
to do.

They were too weary and too apprehensive to hurry the
crossing, though, taking it nice and leisurely. It was a good

twenty miles across, and, while they'd slept, eaten, and drank, they had nothing with them.

They were well out in the null, more than two hours out at least, with the fading "shore" of the colonies behind them looking far off and, now that they were within the hub, shifting and changing every few minutes. They finally decided to rest a bit. She was very tired, but had been waiting for him to call a break. It was only when she realized that he wouldn't call one, carrying out her command, that she called one herself. This mistress stuff was complicated.

"Have you been thinking about where we might go, assuming we make it through?" she asked him.

He nodded, although it was meaningless to her. "There are a couple of possibilities over on that side. Warm, good cover, and natives who didn't have as much of a grudge as many did. Boolean did a lot for Masalur—that's why they had to import troops from Covanti to supplement. He couldn't break the system, of course, but he introduced a large measure of self-government and administration in many of the worlds that had more advanced types, and even allowed colonial ownership on a limited basis of many of the commercial enterprises there. Most colonists hate their Chief Sorcerer; Boolean's probably the first to be more disliked by his fellow Akhbreed than by their subjects. Not that there weren't a few who spurned everything—you saw that type here. The Hedum, for one. But not many, out of hundreds."

"I'm surprised the kingdom let him do any of it."

"They didn't want to, but his power was *enormous* and they wanted to tap that. They let him try it in a couple of places just so they could prove to him how wrong he was, and, in the year or two after he allowed the natives to set up their own shops and keep a lot of their own profits, even from the quotas they furnished to the Akhbreed, productivity increased and unrest went down. When they all worked for the big companies or the government they worked the minimum; when they began working for themselves, on their own land, they worked like demons. They still fought extending it, but he was making headway. Now . . . well, I guess every colonist owns his own, huh? And all quotas abolished."

She nodded. "He sounds like an interesting man."

"Well, interesting has several connotations. He's as nutty

as they come, only in his own unique ways, and sometimes he's not at all easy to take, but. . . ." He stiffened and she sensed it.

"What's the matter?"

"Head down and quiet! Somebody or something's coming this way and I can't tell who or what it is."

They hunched down so that the mists covered them and almost held their breaths. Charley could hear now what Dorion had heard, but it sounded odd, like muffled footsteps rather than the steady beat of horses or other beasts. Just a couple of people, very close, although she was certain there had been no one near only minutes before.

The footsteps stopped, and a man's voice, very near them, said, in English, "Well, it's about time! A few more hours and we would have been forced to give you up. I was beginning to doubt Yobi's competency, or yours."

Dorion knew that voice; even in English it was hard to forget it. He poked his head up and saw a man standing there wearing the buckskin outfit of a Navigator and for a moment it threw him. Then he saw the face and said, "Holy shit!"

"And the same to you, Dorion. Get up, Charley. You've been itching to meet me for quite some time so you might as well do so. You can't run from me."

She felt herself rise and turn towards him even though she hadn't really willed herself to move, sort of like a slave spell interacting, and then she saw the speaker with her magic sight, all deep crimson, but not like Dorion's rust-red aura; this was intense, and a churning, throbbing mass. All but a little blob of emerald green that seemed to be perched on his shoulder or someplace like that, and move a little on its own. That part confused and bothered her.

"Come on, you two. Why, Dorion! That's the filthiest I think I've ever seen you, and out of uniform, too. Come on, you two. Boday is waiting for us and we have wasted too much time now. Also, I don't want to run into old Rutanibir, who's lurking all over here of late trying to find me. He's the same old incompetent asshole he always was, but I can't afford any more delays."

Charley found herself following the man and yet terribly confused. Dorion sensed her total befuddlement and said,

"Charley—we don't have to go any farther into the hub. That's Boolean. We found him—or he found us."

Boolean! Here! Alive! And with Boday! It seemed too good to be true, coming out of the blue as it was. And yet, after this, *this* was the great Boolean, the wizard of wizards, sorcerer of sorcerers? He sounded so, well, *ordinary*, more like her old high school English teacher. She wondered just what he looked like. Then an unsettling thought hit her, and she whispered to Dorion, "Are you sure? Remember how the adept fooled Boday and me."

Dorion shrugged. "Fairly sure. Might as well accept him, anyway, since if it isn't him, then there's nothing we can do about it."

"You're going to have to tell me how you wound up a slave with a ring in your nose without first being defrocked, Dorion," Boolean said as they walked. "You know the rules of the Guild. You defrocked yourself when it happened. Can't have anyone with the power enslaved." He paused. "Save it for now, though. We have a long journey and a lot of time for stories once we're under way."

Dorion hadn't thought of that angle to slavery. No wonder nobody had spotted him as a magician back at the camp. He wasn't one any more. It was a small loss, but it stung his ego greatly. Still, he wasn't going to admit *that* to Boolean, particularly within earshot of Charley. "H—How'd you find us? And why not sooner if you could?"

Boolean chuckled dryly. "Same old impertinent little twerp, aren't you? Well, you know it was kind of a crowded mess over there, and it was no mean feat keeping myself out of sight and undetected as I watched their little show. I knew where you were and I figured I could just pick you up when I was done. I knew you were there because my spells at the kingdom's borders told me so, and I had one of my associates unobtrusively there to sort of invisibly suggest to Coleel a few courses of action. But Charley vanished in that mess, and then you vanished after her while I was over surveying the damage, and I barely got Boday out of there before Rutanibir was called in. So, with all hell breaking loose and our appearance urgently needed elsewhere, I had to cool my heels and pray that Yobi's spell—which mandated that if anything went wrong Charley was to come to the capital and find me—

would lead you into the null. Glad I got you, too, Dorion, but, frankly, you weren't on my priorities list. Once Charley got into the null, though, she was in my element, so to speak. I knew immediately and got here as fast as I could.''

"Damn it, she'd just been raped! You expect complete recovery and cold logic from somebody who'd just been through *that?*''

Boolean sighed. "Well, no, but I'm not omniscient, Dorion. I really thought that fellow was far too possessive to allow it. All right, score one for your side. I apologize to the lady, but things were getting critical fast.''

Dorion's anger was mollified somewhat by the unexpected concession, but he was still confused about the details. "But—how could you know? That she was in the null, that is?''

"The spell, you poor excuse for a magician! She's keyed to me! That ring makes her mine, right? I sensed it as soon as she entered. I've been looking for it for a couple of days now. Oh—I'm sorry, my dear. Feel free to speak your mind and say what you please. Sorry for the lack of nice introductions, but time is wasting. I'm James Traynor Lang, Ph.D., although here I call myself Boolean. It's one of their silly customs that sorcerers have to have ridiculous trade names.''

"I—I hardly know what to say. *What* name did you say?''

"James Traynor Lang, winner of the Nobel Prize in physics and formerly a full professor at the Massachusetts Institute of Technology. You've heard of it?''

"Of the college, yeah. Of you—I'm sorry.''

"Well, I'm not surprised. I don't think I won the prize in your world, just in mine. Our worlds are close by, but they're not identical.''

"*Your* world! Then you're not from here?''

He laughed. "My dear, almost *none* of the Second Rank sorcerers who amount to much are born and raised here. You've got to be a genius to be a native and a power. No, we're mostly mathematicians, a few physicists, even one engineer, god help me! Different worlds, of course, but all from the upper outplanes. For a while, most all of 'em here had German accents, but in my time English has been the language where much of the big work in math has gone on and it's displaced German as the dominant tongue of the Second Rank—thank heavens. In English we just appropriate whatever local words are handy and invent new ones if needed. In German you have to run together old words to make new ones and it gets unwieldy as hell in this environment. We still have a smattering of old Germans, plus a couple of Italians, a Dane or two, a couple of Russians and even one Japanese—he's the engineer. Ah—there's Boday!''

So that's why English was so popular among the sorcerers! she thought excitedly. Suddenly she didn't feel so alien and alone any more.

"Charley!" Boday screamed—her only English word, really—and ran to her, picking her up off the ground and hugging her. "Boday is so happy to see you! That you are all right! We were afraid we would have to desert you here in this desolate place!"

"All right! Calm down!" Boolean shouted. "I wish I could give you time to sleep and feed you filet mignon and get you bathed and rested and all that, but, first of all, my old quarters have been kind of blown to heaven in little particles or changed into tree-lined swamps. Second, in spite of my getting to Boday first, they know where our missing Sam is. She's in a Covantian colony and the only lucky part is that she's stuck in the middle of nowhere in a place that's damned hard to get to, and I had somebody there to slow the bastards down. But time is wasting and it's a long trip, and we still have to beat them or she's dead and probably this was all for nothing. Crim can't keep a whole horde down forever—he's got the same problems with geography they do.''

"They've got Second Rank sorcerers," Dorion pointed out. "How come they can't get there by the quicker routes that only sorcerers use well ahead of us?"

"Because they don't know where she is. Without Boday, they're at the mercy of a mercenary bastard free-lancer named Zamofir who's been dogging her the whole way. He found her the same way Crim did, but Crim can't break that damned spell she's under so there was no use in him rushing to her first. He was better used guarding the door. Zamofir's going for the big payoff, biggest of his career. He tells them where and they don't need him any more. Of course, if he fails, he'll be enslaved to the demons in the netherhells for a few thousand years of torture, but he's going double or nothing for the big payoff and he knows it."

"Zamofir," Charley repeated. "The little man with the moustache? The bastard who joined up with the raiders on the train?"

"That's him. He's very good at what he does, which is anything at all that pays handsomely. No morals, no scruples, nothing. This is a rare time when he's doing his own dirty work instead of hiring it done, but since he took responsibility he also takes the blame or the reward. Now—Charley, you can ride with Dorion, since you make such an interesting couple. Dorion, lash her down and hold her tight. We're going to have to make real speed here. Boday, you take the point in front since you're my confirmation that we're going correctly, and we'll take the rear. Don't worry about guidance—I'll be handling things."

Dorion took Charley over and guided her foot into a stirrup. She started to help herself up, when she realized it was a pretty low and fairly shaky saddle and froze. Then slowly, she felt *under* the saddle.

"Dorion—there's no horse under this saddle!" she whispered through clenched teeth.

"Yeah, I know. You get used to these things with real sorcerers. You think we could make it by *riding?*"

He hoisted her up, secured her as best he could, then climbed on in back of her. "Hold on," he warned her. "I have a sinking feeling that we're going to go very fast and maybe very high."

"All right," they all heard Boolean's voice as if he were right next to them, "let's get going here. Hang on and don't fall off. We've got close to a thousand miles—two thousand leegs in the local parlance—and with breaks for stretches, food, and drink, and one sleep, it's going to take us two or three days to get there. It's going to be *very* close as it is."

And, with that, the saddles rose straight up in the air, lined up in his predetermined pattern, and paused there for just a moment. Boday was muttering very nervously and Dorion wasn't too thrilled himself. Charley could only imagine the sight, but she could see just how far down the null was.

Boolean sighed and looked back at Masalur hub spread out before him. "It used to be one hell of a town," he muttered, and suddenly the saddles were off like a streak, back across the null, across an unfamiliar colonial boundary, high above the trees and roads, heading back to Tishbaal, back to Covanti, and, eventually, to Sam.

Dorion held her tightly, but Charley had the distinct feeling that he was holding on to her just as much for his own sake as for hers. As for her, her head was still spinning from this rapid and dramatic turn of events; she hadn't had time to collect her thoughts and emotions or even catch her breath.

"Dorion—how is it possible? Are these some kind of saddlelike vehicles or something?" she asked him.

"No, just saddles. They look like ones off army horses."

"Then how—?"

"It's fun to be a sorcerer, Miss Sharkin," Boolean's voice said to her. "Don't worry—you'll get used to it. Besides, it beats broomsticks, even if it is the same general principle."

Charley had met some magicians, and Yobi, of course, but she had not until now experienced the real power that these high ones possessed. Even after all this time in Akahlar, and with all the demons and charms and spells, somebody who could do this, apparently with a wave of his hand, was as shocking and inconceivable to her now as it would have been on the streets of Albuquerque.

And yet, in many ways, it was power from a man who seemed both very friendly and ordinary and yet so callous of lessers, too. He'd lived and done his work in Masalur for many years; he had to know its people, really like both those people and the place itself. All that had been destroyed; whether or not he'd had the power to stop it was not the issue. What *was* the point was that he didn't seem very broken up about the fact that everything and everybody who meant anything to him in Akahlar had just been totally destroyed, and all he could do was make light conversation and comment that it used to be a hell of a town.

Dorion had warned her that Boolean wasn't quite right in the head, but she couldn't help being disturbed by the man's reputation on the one hand as a social critic and reformer and the most vociferous battler of Klittichorn with somebody who could be like that, and she said so to Dorion, not caring if the sorcerer could hear her or not. He *had* given her permission to speak her mind.

"He's always been nearly impossible to figure out, like the other Second Rank sorcerers," the magician responded. "But he's always hidden a part of himself from even his closest associates. I think he feels it, though. More than he'd admit."

"No, not more than I'd admit," Boolean responded to them. It was eerie how, even with the wind rushing by and them whooshing along at a good clip it sounded like he was right next to them. "This was the most agonizing time I had since I learned how to do miracles. When I first wound up here, I apprenticed in this region and they were all good to me. I was fascinated by the place and by the possibilities. I had a lot of close friends there, and there were a lot of good people rolled over in that mess."

"Well, you knew it was coming," she responded. "You weren't just not at home when it came by accident. Why didn't you warn them to get out?"

"To where? If I started any major evacuation or gave them much warning at all, it would tip Klittichorn that I was on to him. He'd have come in with everything he had right then and there and it would have been far worse even than now. They're in shock, but they're not dead, and a fair number have kept their wits about them. I went back in and sought some of them out—after. Not that easy to do, by the way. They really are absolutely physiologically identical. Fortunately, I knew where to go and what names to call. There will be a ton of mental breakdowns and some suicides and perhaps other problems we can't imagine, but there are enough folks there with level heads and strong personalities to pull it together with hard work. It's better than the alternative."

"Alternative! You sneak out and leave them to be turned into—whatever it is they are. What we heard about them makes them total nonsense."

"Green French porn queens who have been double exposed is about the best I can give it," the sorcerer replied, chuckling a bit at the description. "Yes, I agree, a species that is apparently born animal and becomes plant doesn't make sense, and I have no notion as to what the extra set of arms, let alone breasts, are good for, but we aren't exactly well designed, either. We only make sense because we're the norm to our own selves against which we measure everybody and everything else. We could be designed far more efficiently, I'll tell you. But it's only form, and it's not a bad one considering that many of the results of Changewinds I've seen have looked like refugees from a bad Japanese horror movie. I expected far worse. I *did* get as many members of my own staff out as possible, since I didn't want them to lose their power, but some volunteered to stay, both because it was their home and because somebody had to maintain that shield while I was gone for a sufficient time to convince old Rutanibir and his flock that I was still home. The rest I couldn't help. They would have been chewed to pieces in a panic evacuation, and, frankly, the majority are far better off as a new race than as millions of slaves of the new administration.''

She hadn't thought of that. "You said it was better than the alternative. You mean total slavery?"

"Oh, no. Klittichorn's been getting very good at using the maelstrom effect of the practice Changewinds his princess has been calling up all over the place. In between the outplanes, dead center in the storm, it's a calm, almost a sort of vacuum cleaner effect. She's been quite good at putting it where he wanted it and he's been very neatly scooping up what he needed and dropping it down to him here. The effect is hard to explain, but you have at least experienced it. It's what he used to pick *you* up. You remember dropping through the maelstrom to Akahlar. It's a natural phenomenon of the wind, which has picked up and dropped a ton of stuff on Akahlar and the colonies and the lower outplanes over the millennia, including probably the first Akhbreeds. There's some evidence that nothing is actually native to Akahlar; this is, as I once told you, the ass end of the universe. Among the things he's picked up, other than people, are heavy weapons and ammunition and, among other things, a few thermonuclear devices.''

She was shocked. "You mean atom bombs?"

"They're primitive. They are hydrogen at least. And it didn't take him long to figure out how to bypass the fail-safe mechanisms and replace them with his own, either. He didn't wind up down here with just the shirt on his back, you know. Among the things that came with him because they were caught in the same vortex was his portable computer and much of his current notes and fancy mathematical programs. That's what's made him a top dog so quickly. Once he grasped the basic mathematics of magic here, he was able to build and solve enormous equations with the thing, far beyond the abilities of even the greatest mathematical minds here. Once he had a little experience, he could work out how to do just about anything and knock over any big-shot sorcerer who stood in his way. And, of course, he *is* a genius, one of the rare true ones. Another Einstein, da Vinci, or Fermi at least.''

"Smarter even than you?" she asked him, wondering about his reaction.

"Oh, my, yes. Certainly. Although I am one of the few minds capable of not only understanding but using and perhaps refining his work. I, for example, never dreamed it was possible to enter the Maelstrom through the weak point after it had passed, but once I saw that he could, well, I figured out the way. That relative intellectual position, alas, is why all of this came to be. In a way, it's all my fault, although I have days when I wonder if that is entirely true. Certainly some basic defects in my character helped shape this crisis. You see, I'm a very good wizard, my dear. I'm just not a very good man.''

And slowly, as the miles passed far beneath them, Charley learned what lay behind all this mess, and it was sadder still for being so, well, petty.

Lang had been a professor at Princeton at the time; a boy genius—he'd had his Ph.D. and his voter's card at about the same time, and had already accomplished a lot by the time he first met the man who was to become his enemy.

Lang's interests lay in the far edge of theoretical physics; the kind of pure intellectual activity in which men still sat in small offices and thought deep thoughts and imagined the unimaginable and then built mathematical and computer models to illustrate various principles that, in fact, probably had no practical application ever, and in which only the mathematics would ever indicate whether or not they were right, or had wasted their whole lives on a falsehood.

He became particularly attracted to a relatively new field called Chaos Science, which sought to really explain the unexplainable. How could a random explosion of dense matter from the monoblock that created the universe form into such a useful and beautiful pattern, with its own very comfortable natural laws and limitations? Why did the freezing of water vapor form such complex and beautiful crystalline structures, and why were no two apparently exactly alike? Order, often highly complex order, almost always resulted from the most random events. There had to be a law, or a set of laws, that explained it, at least to a degree.

Doctor Lang became a leading theoretician of the relatively new science, and, as such, those also interested in it wanted to study under him. Among them, and the best of them, was a young Cambodian refugee born Kieu Lompong, who adopted the Americanized first name of Roy, a combination he joked he'd gotten by playing with numerological tables. He was young, intense, brilliant, but with no social life and no outside interests and, most of all, Boolean noted, no sense of humor at all.

Little wonder. As a child, he'd already been to hell, having seen his parents slowly hacked to death in front of him while black-clad revolutionary soldiers held him and made him watch, then put into virtual slavery in the rice paddies where he had to pretend to be a peasant and disguise his genius at all costs, for the new rulers killed the whole intellectual class.

He had finally escaped, and his genius had been recognized in the refugee camp, and he was made one of the exceptions to be brought to the United States under foster care of distant relatives who now lived there. His now unshackled brilliance produced an even greater rise in academic achievement than had Lang's; he was, under Lang, a Ph.D. candidate at the age of seventeen.

Under Lang's tutelage, and with access to the big university computers, Roy Lompong, in just a few short months, was able to come out with something that apparently had been percolating in his head for years: a unifying mathematical principle, a single equation, in its own area as significant as Einstein's in his, that unified and revolutionized the whole chaos science community. The thing was, he was in such a pure intellectual area that he didn't realize what kind of a breakthrough he'd made. To him, it was just a tool to use in studying specific phenomena. It was a whole new mathematics that made work in the field really amount to something in much the same way as Newton had invented calculus just so he could do the mathematical proofs of the theories he was interested in. Instantly obvious to Lang, it nonetheless would never have occurred to him. And yet, only the Princeton team knew it.

"He was so wrapped up in his projects on the creation of the universe, already with the best minds in the field, and he simply never got around to publishing it. He'd stopped reading the literature anyway; it was all beneath him, in the same way that Hemingway wouldn't bother to ever read Doctor Seuss. But I was his advisor and the head of his doctoral committee. And it *was* published, under my name, with Roy and three others credited with assists, just a few months after he got his degree and accepted a chair at Cal Tech. I doubt if he was even aware of the furor the article caused—his head was always in the clouds. In fact, I think it wasn't until three years later, when I got the Nobel for it, that it really hit him what I'd done."

Charley gasped. "You *stole* his idea? And took full credit for it?"

"Yep. And the money and the worldwide acclaim and all the rest. I mean, they looked at me with my reputation, and they looked at this twenty-one-year old who was my 'protégé,' and drew the obvious but wrong conclusions. It wasn't the first time it was done. In fact, it's done all the time—it's just rare to win the Nobel for it, and particularly in so short a time. I did, and he flew into a rage about it. It was his life's work to date and it was all his, and I'd taken it from him. More importantly, I'd hit him right in his Asian sense of honor. The fact that it was done fairly often didn't mean that he knew that. That the young discoverers often get professorships and posts elsewhere as rewards by their tutors who take the credit. It's not science, it's a crooked way of getting ahead in money, power, and prestige in the university environment. And he had no forum. Oh, the news was interested in his accusations about me, for about three days. But when the newsmen discovered they couldn't even comprehend the basics of what I'd stolen, it was old news fast. And the scientific and academic community, well, they were more comfortable with good old establishment me than with young firebrand Lompong, whom they'd hardly heard of. What he was doing just wasn't done—not cricket, old boy. You'll get your turn later. You see where it got him."

"Yeah. Nowhere. So Klittichorn's from the same world as

you, huh? You must have a pretty nasty home world from what you say about those soldiers and his parents and all that. I never even heard of the country you said he was from.''

"It's irrelevant. Your world's history and ours diverge quite sharply because of various key assassinations and a major nasty war we lost that yours didn't fight, but yours had its share of misery as well. All of them do. At any rate, I went from obscurity in an obscure field to department head at a quarter of a million bucks a year at M.I.T., and I was on top of the world. He was a bad boy, bitter at his colleagues as much as at me, bitter about everything. He became unglued and started thinking about some practical applications for his theories. He went up to Livermore Labs, which is a think tank run by the university for the government, it's where they sit around and invent new bigger and better terror weapons. They have a hell of a budget, though—as close to bottomless as you can get—and among the most sophisticated computers that world ever dreamed of. I'm not sure what led him to it, but he got real interested in crazy phenomena. The wolf boy in Germany, people disappearing in full view of onlookers, spontaneous human combustion, rains of frogs—all sorts of weird stuff. A fellow named Charles Fort used to write books on it. Unexplained appearances and disappearances and odd-ball phenomena of every sort.''

"Flying saucers and stuff."

"That, too, but there's a lot weirder and more substantiated stuff as well. Somehow, in trying to explain it, he hit upon the theory of the Changewind and its key maelstrom. I don't think he was prepared for the Changewind effect, but the multidimensional effect, the worlds over worlds, tied in with other areas of new physics. He wanted the primal cause, the mechanism, for random events, both major and minor, to tie it in with overall chaos theory. He needed Livermore's computers to finish the work, and somehow he managed to convince some politicians that it had weapons potential. Maybe he *had* a weapon in mind from the start—I don't know. But it boiled down to a practical experiment many years ago out on the Nevada test ranges, where they blew up the atom bombs. Some kind of device, maybe part Tesla and part Lompong, that would create a weak spot in the dimensional walls. He got more than he bargained for. He drew a Changewind, and he was dead center in it, and he dropped all the way down to here. They say the whole plateau just vanished with everything on it, leaving only virgin-colored sheetrock.''

"Tesla?"

"Nikola Tesla, one of the types like Einstein, so much a genius we have units of measure in science named for him. He was obsessed with controlling the weather and, back before the turn of the century, and in full view of everybody, he did. But his device was banned, its principles still classified to this day, even to people like me, and experiments in that are even banned today in the Geneva Convention. The connection of weather and magnetic forces and fields should not be lost on you.''

"Well, I think I'm sort of following it," she told him, fascinated but not real sure. "It's still magic to me, though.''

"Magic has rules, Charley. That's why you need the charms and amulets sometimes or the magic words to focus the spell or anything else. Before the miracle can take place, the priest must incant and say *'Hocus Pocus!'* That's all a magic spell is, either in the legends and racial memories and religious rites that are all that's left in our world, and the spells here that do almost anything—if you can figure them out. Roy had a leg up. He recognized the spells here as being a variant form of his own mathematics. Unlike the ones here, he had his computer and much of his notes and a thorough grounding in conventional science and physics in particular. It's probable that the Akhbreed were mathematical geniuses with a high order civilization while ours was still in caves or maybe worse off. Over the years here, they lost much of their ancient knowledge, becoming fat and static, unmoving, comfortable with their spells and their empires. Most science vanished, leaving only the sorcery, as happened many times, apparently, with many civilizations. The main thing here was—the magic still worked, if you had sufficient mathematical aptitude to use it. The better your aptitude, the higher you rose in the magical priesthood. That's the difference between Dorion, here, and me. I can solve equations thousands of lines long in my head. He couldn't add two and two without pen and paper.''

Dorion bristled. "Come on! I'm not *that* bad!''

"Uh-huh. Well, it's higher math, I admit, but you can't

keep a ten variable equation in your head, so your spells have to be looked up and done step by step out of a cookbook. Your highest achievement was a unique formula that gave everybody electric shocks.''

"Okay, you two! Enough!" Charley responded. "Those electric shocks came in handy on this trip, sir, which is more than you did. I mean, if you knew all this and could sneak out, and you can fly and all that, then why did we have to suffer like we did all this time, and go through the hell we went through?''

Boolean sighed. "It's hard to explain. It was only a few months ago that, quite by accident, I discovered I was being conned. That the substantial and hostile Second Rank presences I felt all around the border were being faked. Roy came up with some kind of projection device. I can't begin to imagine what or how, but he did. It only betrayed itself as a convincing false signal when he had to do that close-in demonstration of how he could guide and project a Changewind over in Qatarung. It caused him to lose contact for a while with his illusion, caused all sorts of flickering in and out of it. Until then, I was convinced that I would have to face several of my colleagues and maybe Roy himself if I stepped out of there, and they sent that message loud and clear. Even when I *did* find out, it didn't do me much good. Between my duties here to an increasingly nervous king and country, as it were, and my attempts to find out just who was working for Klittichorn and what they were planning, I didn't have much time to spare. I was also trying to track down just where his projector was. In the back of my mind, I figured that if you all got in any real trouble I could break off and either get you out or send some of my adepts to do it. Then, when Sam just sort of vanished off the map, as it were, we went frantic. I'm afraid your side just got lower priority.''

"Thanks a lot,'' she said dryly.

"Well, without Sam this isn't going to mean anything. With her, then you have a certain importance as well.''

"Me!''

"Wait a while. We'll get to it. I think, in fact, that if we can beat them to Sam this might well all work out for the best. Enough for now. Suffice it to say that you aren't *crucial* to the scheme, but you are none the less important.''

He would say no more on it, and she finally didn't press, but it started her mind wondering like crazy and coming up with the most outrageous, and unappetizing, possibilities.

Eating with a Second Rank sorcerer was an experience as well. He just picked a clear, remote, uninhabited spot and set them down, and, almost with a wave of his arms and a few mumbled phrases of sheer nonsense, materialized a full table complete with hot dishes, silverware, and the right wines, all uninterrupted by company, weather, or even ants and flies. It was pretty bizarre, but they were the best meals any of them had enjoyed since Covanti hub. Nothing to wash or clear away, either—another few waves and incantations and it was gone.

Boolean could say what he wanted about physics and math and chaos theories; this was sheer fairytale magic.

It was at the first meal stop, too, that she discovered that the green fuzz had not only a life of its own, but a voice that was so deep and raspy it sounded like a small child speaking by continuously belching. Dorion described the creature, whose name was Cromil, as a small pea-green monkey with jackass ears and a nose that resembled an eggplant. A longtime companion of and familiar to Boolean and his remote "eyes," in much the same way as Shadowcat, he was not nearly the quiet type that the cat had been, although he disliked speaking around strangers more than he had to.

"You just *love* to show off, don't you, you big ham," Cromil croaked as Boolean did the meal with extra flourishes.

Boolean chuckled. "That's why I keep Cromil around. He keeps me in my proper place because he doesn't care what happens to him."

"You need me more than I need you," the creature reminded him. "Without me, who would act as intermediary with the netherhells? Who'd make the best deals with all those imps and demons you love to use?"

Now, at the one rest and sleep stop Boolean had decided upon for all their sakes, Charley and Dorion were both at last able to get themselves clean of days of grime and garbage. The sorcerer had merely picked, not materialized, the waterfall and pools, but he'd made certain that the water was both warm and pure, and he even provided her with scented soap. It seemed to Dorion that she was *never* going to get out of the water, and that she was going to compulsively scrub her skin completely off. He was out and dried off long before she first considered coming out, and that meant he had to play life-guard for her.

It was Boday, as usual, who gave him an answer. "Boday felt the same way after those foul beasts had her on the rocks back in the Kudaan," she whispered in his ear. "We all did, but Charley, she did not experience what we went through. Now she has. She is trying to wash them out of her. All of them out of all of her. She will not succeed, any more than Boday has even after all this time, but, let her try. Sooner or later she will realize that, once you have been violated like that, you can never wash it all away."

It explained much, but left Dorion with the same confusion over the sexes he'd always had. Charley'd been a whore, damn it. One, two guys some days, for a year, and after that she'd screwed almost anything with a male voice and it hadn't been anything *but* fun, and most of the countless guys she'd had were strangers, too, about which she'd known little or nothing. Hell, she even did sexy come-ons to the townies and border guards. And yet, somehow, that gang-bang orgy with her at the center back at the camp had been different, had really changed her. It was one thing for a violent-type guy to stalk and pounce on a woman, any woman, and force himself on her. That he could understand. But, damn it, if you're going to glory in being a sex object and advertise the fact, how'd this one really differ except that they were rougher, cruder, and smellier. It wasn't even the bruises and soreness she still had—it was something inside, like Boday said. There was something new—fear, maybe, although she still had guts enough to cross that camp and go into the null and a personality decisive enough to shape her own destiny if she could. Maybe it wasn't fear. Maybe it was doubt. Self-doubt.

Maybe it was just that the one night back there at camp she had to face what she really had become—and what she'd been all along—and she didn't like it. He wondered.

He'd been fascinated at what Boolean had been telling her. The man had always been very chatty, but Dorion had trouble following this story and all its references, even though Char-ley apparently knew what he meant. All those references, even though they didn't come from the same worlds. Who or what was an Einstein or a Tesla, and what was so wonderful about a Nobel Prize, whatever that was, that it would cause such misery? And what was so unusual about mysterious appearances and disappearances and frog rains and the like? Hell, they happened all the time. . . .

For Charley, the sudden rescue from the continual bottom of the heap she'd been forced into for so long had come first as a shock and now as a joy. She no longer was even all that nervous about falling off the damned saddle, although, tied in as she was and short of aerial saddle fights, there was little chance of that. Being able to talk with someone, even one of great power with a surface personality that was pleasing, masking something she knew she could never really comprehend, and being treated as an equal, at least for social purposes, by that man was something she hadn't really thought she'd ever experience again. It little mattered that he came from a world which had known far more wars and experienced even more tyranny than hers—whose last major war, except a few banana republic ones, was the one against the Germans and Japanese. Or that had apparently successfully somehow torn its way from England in revolution back in the Seventeen Hundreds sometime and as a result had had to fight a bloody civil war over slavery in the middle Eighteen Hundreds instead of being forced to obey the British abolition back in the Thirties, and had something called a Congress instead of a parliament.

But by their common times there were more similarities than differences. She knew Einstein and MIT and Cal Tech, and there were a lot more similarities than differences between them now from her point of view. He was no more out of touch with rock and roll, or TV stars, or fashion than anybody else who'd been stuck here and out of touch for thirty years.

But that did bring up the question of just how *he* had come to be here.

When Lompong had vanished along with all his project and a lot of technicians and army people and the like, there had been consternation. The only man who might decipher Lompong's work and figure it out was Lang.

Lang himself was fascinated with the result when he was told of it by high security people and couldn't resist. However, while there were gigabytes of material in Lompong's computer areas, how it all tied together was a mystery. Worse, thanks to his experience with Lang, some key material, perhaps *the* key material, was encoded in a way even Lompong's bosses didn't know about. Not until they tried to break it and wound up activating an insidious set of computer "viruses" that began to systematically destroy not only all the data but the entire data base series of the Livermore computer system, right down to the payroll information and budget trackers. There were backups, of course, but they had now destroyed two and had only one left. Lang looked but could not touch, even though he pointed out that data that was so highly protected was useless anyway unless the scheme was cracked. No deal. One had to remain—and that was the way it was.

Still, while nobody really knew how Lompong's mind worked, Lang had the closest idea, and he was able to do a lot of work, laboriously, interpolating from papers, conversations from associates not swallowed up in the "incident," and the disparate data bases you *could* use without the data being eaten. It was fascinating; so much so that he was on long leave from MIT and working full time on it. After three years, he thought he'd gotten at least the general idea behind what his old pupil was trying to do, and he was taking a break, driving to Las Vegas for a conference there—Boolean, it appeared, had no trouble with flying saddles but never liked airplanes—and it happened.

"It was late but I was feeling good, and driving always cleared my mind and got out my frustrations," he reminisced. "It happened very suddenly and at about seventy-five miles an hour. One moment I was on the Interstate, the next thing I knew I was surrounded by pitch dark and I had the damndest feeling I was falling, only slowly. I slowed to a stop, which did nothing, opened the window, and got the dry air of the maelstrom, although I didn't know it then. I opened the door, looked down, and closed it again and just stayed there, scared to death. I don't know what I thought—that maybe I'd crashed and was going to hell in an automobile or something. It went on and on and on, and then I landed, not hard but with a bump that bounced the shocks all to creation and me with it, and suddenly I'm sitting on solid ground surrounded by the damndest fog you ever saw right up to the door handles. Fog—in Nevada! Well, I knew I wasn't in Nevada and the only way to find out where was to drive there.''

"You came down in a null? But I thought Changewinds didn't cross nulls.''

"They don't, but the weak spots gravitate there before they dissipate, sometimes hours, or even days, later, so you always land *down* in a null, just as you did. It has a lot to do with magnetic fields but I think you'd need a lot more classroom before I could explain it to you. At any rate, I drove a while, and finally I saw the lights of a border crossing and drove right to it, and became the first, and to my knowledge, only individual ever to drive up to the Masalurian or any other entry station. I think the two guys on duty there were more terrified than I was. Naturally, I didn't know Akhbreed and they didn't know English, but they decided that the car had to be the product of a powerful sorcerer, so they treated me nice, gave me some wine and chocolates out of their own lunches, and sent word to the Chief Sorcerer in a hurry. The adepts at least knew there'd been a Changewind in the colonies the night before and figured some outplaner had been caught and they were right. Karl was an old Prussian from some world that I was never quite sure about, and my German wasn't great but it was passable, and that's how I started on the road to becoming the great and powerful Wizard of Oz.''

"Hold it," Dorion put in. "Even *I* know enough to know that the odds of you just happening on a Changewind that far up the outplane is about like the odds of all of us being carried off by giant moths.''

"Slimmer. I didn't just 'happen' into it, though. Apparently Roy had an even easier time of it here than I did at the start and he figured out the system in record time. Most important, he knew more about the Changewinds than they did here—here they were scared silly of them, since it was the one random event over which the spells had no control or effect. I know that some of his party and most of his equipment was smashed when he got here—and the rest was useless because of a lack of power—but he'd saved his portable computer, and he knew the mathematics of magic better than anybody, having independently reinvented it in what seemed to have been a streamlined and vastly improved version. He went after me, Dorion. Who knows how many nets he cast before he got me? How many disasters and disappearances and freak weather he caused before he finally figured out how to nail me exactly? He wanted me here, with him the master now, and me the cowering subject. It didn't turn out that way, though, first because it's tough to guide the maelstrom in the outplane and have any control over where the weak point drifts, shifts, and gyrates here. You can even shift weak points and come out in the wrong spot. I did that deliberately with Sam and you, Charley; Klittichorn did it by accident with me. And Karl was much too strong for him to take on right then, particularly since Roy hadn't made any friends here, either. Again, too strong too fast.''

''He learned, though,'' Dorion noted.

''Oh, yes. He plays the social and political game better than I ever could now. In fact, he has a much higher tolerance for what passes for intellect here than I do, and no real aversion to the system he sees. He doesn't care, so long as he's on top. Twice he'd been thwarted by mastering the technical and ignoring the social and cultural requirements; he's not about to get stung a third time. Underneath, though, he hates them—he hates all of them who don't acclaim him as a virtual god, as two-bit hacks like Rutanibir do. The Akhbreed system must revolt him; every time he saw it in action he must have flashed back to his own childhood under the terror regime. It finally occurred to him that he survived then by playing the tyrant's games until opportunity presented itself. Now he's played the Akhbreed and sorcerer's Guild like a well-tuned orchestra. There's only one person he really fears in all creation, and that's the man who cheated him twice. To him, I'm the only man who could possibly cheat him a third time—and he's right. But the deck's so stacked I'm not certain, even if everything now goes right, that I can do it. I only know I've got to try.''

''Not much chance of an all-out attack on everybody now, is there?'' Dorion asked hopefully. ''I mean, consider the losses here. A lot of the colonials aren't going to be too thrilled about signing up with him after word of this gets around.''

''You mistake him, then,'' Boolean responded. ''He doesn't

care about this rebellion, and he's no liberator. He's had to play that game as well to keep them loyal, and get the men and materiel he needed, and to keep the loyalty of the Storm Princess. But that child, when born, will screw him up royally. If he doesn't get Sam, he won't wait, army or no army, position or no position. He'll simply convince his people that all is ready whether it is or not, and if he wants something passionately he can do it. Take out the hubs and the majority of Second Rank sorcerers and let the rebellion come later, that's all. The Akhbreed can never hold the colonies if they don't hold the hubs anyway. He really doesn't care."

"Then—what is his real motive?" Charley wanted to know.

"I've caught up with him, I think, and corrected most or all of my wrong assumptions about his work. I got into his maelstrom and got you out and I managed to trigger the burst early on your world so you'd be sucked down in the center instead of destroyed. I think I know more about how this whole thing works than anybody alive except Roy himself, and that's the trouble. Klittichorn is an ancient Khmer deity from the pre-Buddhist days, one of many but a powerful one. He took the name, I'm convinced, not as a mark of humor, since he has none himself, nor out of nostalgia, either. Countless sorcerers have died or been horribly mutilated and destroyed going for the First Rank. The best have been sucked down through the netherhells to the Seat of Probability itself, where they have been crushed in a universe that could possibly fit in a sand bucket. I think Roy has cracked it. I think he may be the only mind capable of cracking it. I think the destruction of the hubs and the release of massive Changewind power, enough power, possibly, to destroy or transform beyond any recognition not only Akahlar but possibly the outplanes as well, as part of a plan. A careful, premeditated plan. There was always a touch of the Oriental mystic in him. He seemed upset that his own theories seemed to preclude any need for any gods at all.

"I think he wants to rewrite the bottom line. I think he wants to fill in the gap and redo the cosmos to his own designs. I think he's convinced he's found the way to the First Rank and the replacement of pure chaos with a true regulating governor. Having been convinced that there are no gods, he now intends to supply at least one. And if you want to know what kind that would be, well, all I know about Klittichorn the god is what he told us in conversations long ago about his ancient culture, and, as I remember it, Klittichorn was a god of absolutes not easily appeased, and human sacrifice was clearly part of his requirements.''

"Jesus!" Charley swore.

"Uh-huh, but if you need more motivation, consider this. It appears that the detachment of Khmer Rouge soldiers, who tortured and murdered his parents in front of him and kept him for over a year in a slave labor battalion, were composed mostly, or entirely, of young women, many if not most mere teenagers. He always exhibited a great deal of hostility towards women, and we weren't sure what was going on inside him. Unless he's mellowed, which I doubt, it must eat his guts out to have to play up to the Storm Princess. The conventional explanation around Princeton was that his experiences had made him a confirmed homosexual, but there were those who saw such hostility in him that they mused that he had the potential to explode in a different direction. Possibly as a rapist or serial killer of young women or something even more creative. It's a curious pathology, a mixture of hatred and fear. You can understand, I think, what it must mean to him that a young woman is his greatest threat, and yet that fear level is such that it might well explain why you two kept slipping from his grasp. I don't think he's exploded yet. I think he's tried to make himself an automaton, to even believe he's above sex and emotions of any sort. But—imagine if he attains First Rank, Charley. Not a god, but Roy Lompong with the powers of a god. What will keep him from exploding *then?*''

· 10 ·

Reunions

IT WAS RAINING out. It was usually raining out, at least half the time, between the jungle and the sea, and it didn't really bother her that much. She really didn't feel much like doing anything these days except lying around; keeping house for the boys was more than enough work for her, and if she really needed help she could shoot a simple flare and have one of the other wives run to her.

The place was as clean and straight as she could make it. She prided herself on doing it all each day, if only to prove to herself and to others that she was still capable of things. You had to keep at it; with the mud and constant dampness, any missed spots would be seized as high ground by mold and fungi and general jungle rot. At least now she understood why the people who were native to jungle areas hadn't ever bothered with much in the way of clothes or the like and had lived in simple huts of grass and bamboo. The forces of the living jungle, fed by the constant heat and humidity, attacked almost anything vulnerable.

And things *were* pretty loose here. The boys had one set of stock clothes apiece which they kept in a sealed trunk and put on just for important visitors, and they'd worn them that first day, but now things had gotten loose again and, frankly, the village was basically a nudist colony, which suited her just fine.

Bugs weren't a real problem so long as you kept the netting on the doors and windows and remembered to rub a potion on the stilts once a month so nothing wanted to crawl up it. The floors were of a rock-hard native wood that insects didn't bother, although it warped a bit and wasn't ideal in its primary use. The walls were of a bamboolike plant, the roof was some kind of woven grasses over a rust-proof metallic webbing, and it was waterproof. Inside ventilation was by a clever series of permanently netted openings that let some light and all the air through but caught most of the rain and all of anything else. It was enough that only a central oil lamp was needed to pretty well illuminate the place.

It had only a single interior, but it was fairly spacious, the only thing blocking free access was a thick pole rising from the ground below, though the floor, and up to the roof center. There were two sets of bunk beds over to one side—handmade affairs of the same wood as the floor, with criss-crossed and tightly bound vines providing the support for thin and well-worn mattresses. She didn't know what the mattresses were made of, but they looked like some kind of soft vinyl, the only plastic stuff she'd seen here and so it probably wasn't, and she had no idea what they were filled with but they held the human body, even her, fairly comfortably. They had ordered her a bed weeks ago, but she didn't care when it arrived. All four were seldom home at the same time and she had whichever lower she wanted.

Other than that, there was a large round table, also of the same irregular wood and looking hand-carved, with four matching chairs and one obviously cobbled from another set somewhere; a large chest with all sorts of clay pots, gourds, and the like, and another with a set of well-worn and dented pots, pans, plates, and utensils. A makeshift cupboard and shelves held some fruit, containers of dried meat, and some jar-sealed delicacies. Without a refrigerator or freezer there wasn't much else you could keep around. Food was caught or picked from the Company common stores which were constantly restocked, the men of the camp taking turns doing the required hunting, fishing, and the like. The women were supposed to plant and tend and pick the gardens and citrus grove, and tend to the *miriks*, a chickenlike bird that thrived here and gave regular fine-tasting eggs. Then they would pick up and deliver what they needed at the end of the day for the next day's food.

Cooking was done on a wood stove on the porch, where the smoke could easily disperse. It was of stone and reminded her of nothing as much as the most elaborate permanent backyard barbecue she'd ever seen. Still, with a little instruction from the other women, she'd had no trouble in mastering it pretty well, and getting to know the seasonings and oils and herbs and spices by eye, as well as how to cook without getting spattered or asphyxiated. She'd gotten real good real fast because she'd been a cook for Boday all that time, and because she was very eager to learn and please.

Over to one side was a partially finished project with the basic tools for the carpenter's job set in a case next to it. She'd always been a fair carpenter and the crib was taking real shape, but she was finding herself too easily frustrated and upset by little things, and she just hadn't been able to keep at it. She knew she'd let the boys finish it, although it bothered her. She was proud that she still did all the same work as the others, that she could be "normal." Of course, she had thought that she would handle the later stages of pregnancy better than she had; what was a little more weight and tummy when she already carried so much? It wasn't like that, though. After a while you hardly thought about the fat, but this was like a bowling ball that didn't move exactly the same as you did. Dead weight that shifted suddenly and wrongly and threw you off balance and made you permanently a little uncomfortable, and you didn't get used to it.

She heaved herself out of the chair, got her cup, and lumbered over to the door where there were two amphoras, each containing a supply of pretty good wine—one white, one red. Covantians seemed to live on wine, and to be able to produce a drinkable product somehow in the damndest places. They mostly looked kind of American Indian, but she was certain that they must somewhere have had common ancestors with the French or Italians. She didn't like drinking so much alcohol, for the sake of the kid, but these were deliberately fairly weak, and they were here and running water was not.

Central wells provided the water, which was taken in large gourds on the head back to each hut. She'd gotten quite good at carrying fairly heavy burdens on her head, and so each day as needed she'd climb down the ladder after lowering the vine-rope-supported platform that served as a kind of dumb-waiter, get her own food from the stores, and get what water she needed as well. The fact that she managed this while being now so hugely pregnant was a matter of pride to her, and she wanted to do it as long as she was the least able. It was one of her jobs, her duties. At least now, with the boys out on the boat for up to four days at a stretch, it was mostly just getting stuff for her, although she missed them.

It was a very primitive life, with no amenities, full of constant work just to keep in the same place, and yet she was happy and content with it. She did not want to do anything else or be anyone else. She understood her place, what was expected of her and what was not, all her duties and responsibilities, and it was all she wanted, all she could be. She, like the others, was the perfect Covantian wife, and the spell allowed for nothing less than true belief. She wanted nothing else because she could not; she acted and thought as she did because she could think no other way.

That went as well for her sexual nature. Women no longer attracted her; she could not really remember how they once did, although she remembered it. Men, who had never really attracted her before, now seemed attractive, alluring, sexy; their moves, even their mannerisms, fascinated her, and she felt real lust at times with all those naked guys around.

Of course, her now being hugely pregnant had only allowed for so much, and they were more concerned than she was about hurting the kid, but they'd had some fun anyway and she'd managed some oral tricks. Still, she dreamed and fantasized about after the child was born, when they could truly unite with her.

Oddly, those fantasies particularly pleased her, as did the unusual, for her, eroticism brought on by things even vaguely phallic. For the first time, she had feelings like the other girls had; for the first time, she was over on Charley's side with the "normal" folks. For the first time, she felt like she fit in, and it gave her an enormous sense of inner peace and a feeling of belonging. She had approached it at Pasedo's with her memory gone, but her sexual nature had still stood in the way.

Until now, nobody had really understood her, including herself. Even Etanalon's magic mirror had drawn its basics from her, and since she was confused so it could only work with what it had. It wasn't that she was this Storm Princess, or that she wanted to run from responsibility. It was rather that she'd always been an outsider, a totally square peg, even back home, and even more so in this far more structured and restrictive society. Nobody who didn't always feel different and abnormal—and was—could ever understand that, and only now, when she was in all ways as "normal" as the other girls here, or the ones she was likely to meet, did she herself truly understand her own longing.

If anything, she was more "normal" than Charley had ever been. Charley would look down her nose at this kind of life. She never needed or wanted a husband or anything that smacked of convention, that was clear from the way she'd gone and kept going on this world. The funny thing was, Boday was more a model for Charley, love potion or no love potion. Boday had talents, not all of which were of the noblest sort it was true, and she'd carved her way by force of will, brains, and without any magical powers, into a position where she was totally in control of her life, and really needed no one even in this traditional, male-dominated society. Yeah, that's where things had taken a wrong turn at the start. Boday and Charley were kind of natural partners, or at least soulmates; she hadn't even fit in with Boday. Not sexually—Boday had been straight until she'd gulped that potion, as straight as Charley—but even in that they both had the same basic lack of regard for men as anything more than sex partners and certainly no desire for long-term commitments. Not that Boday hadn't married guys—it was practically a hobby with her—but she dumped them just as quick when lust cooled down.

Well, that was the two of them. She'd had another option chosen for her, but it was one that meshed with and quieted her own inner demons. She hadn't even had any of those Storm Princess dreams since, nor did she feel the rain or other storms now any more than ordinary people had. Whatever powers she had were gone with her old life, and she felt freed by that as well.

She sat uncomfortably in a chair at the table and picked up a worn and weathered deck of playing cards. Cards here weren't like the ones back home; for one thing, they had ones to fifteens in five suits and looked more like Tarot cards than regular ones, but by removing the extras she could make a fifty-two card four-suited deck and, by now, she was more than used to the suits and knew the funny squiggles for the proper numbers. She shuffled the cards and dealt them on the table in the familiar pattern of Klondike like her father used to play. She knew and had played a lot of solitaire games from back when she was living with Boday. They were good time-passers when she didn't feel like doing much else, although lately she'd been taking them much too seriously. Somehow she wasn't in full control of her emotions any more, and it didn't seem to be the spell. The other girls said it was a natural part of the last stages of being pregnant, but it was the hardest of all to take.

Any little things that seemed to go wrong, even the most petty little shit, and she'd wind up crying and getting depressed for long periods. She'd bawled more at nothing the last few weeks than she had at any time since she herself was a baby. Sometimes she'd get suddenly feeling real insecure, even paranoid, and she'd huddle there and shake with fear and finally, if she couldn't stand it any more, she'd manage to get down and go over to Putie's as fast as possible just for company and a hug.

Other times, just as suddenly, she would have an enormous need to just be totally alone and get real introspective, like now.

It worked the other way, too. Sometimes with other people she just couldn't stop talking and talking even if she had nothing else really to say, and the littlest things would strike her as enormously funny, and she'd laugh abnormally long and hard to get the giggles and be unable to stop. And all the extremes might come one after the other, like somebody throwing a switch.

It bothered her, but she didn't really want to intrude on the others, particularly since Quisu was just getting over having her own kid, a boy with the lungs of a lumberjack, and had her own hands full, and Putie'd had hers, a daughter, just three days ago and was in pretty poor shape, while Meda was due any day now. All had their men, or most of them, around as well and that made her long for her own husbands, all of whom were out working double duty to fill in for the guys attending their own wives back here.

The fact was, nobody really knew when she was due. She'd not looked at a calendar, let alone a watch, in so long she had no sense of how much time had gone by except that it seemed like years and was definitely less than nine months.

For that reason they'd rigged up a bell on the porch so if she suddenly felt the baby coming, she could summon help in a hurry. They'd all offered to take her in while the boys were away, but with all those other men around she felt more comfortable here. It wasn't modesty, just feeling too much like a stranger intruding on somebody else. She'd seen and even helped with the babies, though, and she wanted her own real bad.

Still, she worried. She worried about her old friends and what might have become of them, and she worried about her own eventual safety, since she knew that while *she* might have changed, the child inside had not, as evidenced by the thunder and lightning all around the place when she kicked. Mostly, though, she worried about the impending birth. Not that she wouldn't be more than happy to have it over with, but she'd sat there by Quisu and then Putie, and it didn't look like much romance or fun at all. In fact, it looked awful enough that if she had some way of backing out of it, she certainly would have lost her nerve. Seeing the level of pain and discomfort it brought, and seeing, too, Quisu's almost twenty-two-hour labor, she knew now just why it was called "labor," and she didn't like that one bit.

She heard someone coming up the ladder and turned, curious. It didn't cause any alarm, since she knew all the people there were for a hundred or more miles in any direction, but she was curious as to who would be dropping by. She was quite unprepared for the figure that struggled in, using the doorway to steady himself. He looked like hell, his clothes were in shreds, and the shirt was heavily stained with blood.

"Crim! My God! Is that *you?* What are you doing here? And what happened to you?"

She went over to him and tried to help him to one of the beds, but he shook her off and collapsed in a chair instead. She immediately forgot her own thirst and offered the cup of wine to him, which he drank greedily and then tried to catch his breath.

"Been—protecting you," he managed. "Did a good job for a while, but it was finally too much."

She frowned. "Protecting me—from who?" She suddenly had a fearful thought. "I'm not going back, Crim. You can't make me!"

"I knew the situation, that's why I could only protect, not bring you out," he told her. "I wish I could—that would have prevented this, but that doesn't matter now. Nothing matters right now but the moment. How many people are there in the camp right now, besides you and me?"

She thought a moment. "Sixteen, counting the other girls. Why?" She began fussing with his shirt to see and perhaps help dress the wound, but he again would have none of it.

"Forget me now. If we don't act and soon, it won't make any difference if the wound's bad or not. Can you call the others? Get others here in a hurry?"

"Yeah, I got a bell, but—"

"Then do it! Now! All our lives depend on it! Theirs, too!"

She knew Crim well enough to take him at his word, and she went out and immediately rang the bell loud and long for all it was worth. When she finally decided that even the dead couldn't have missed, she went back inside. "Now—what's this all about?"

"Sam—if *I* could find you, *they* could find you. Klittichorn's already started the war. He attacked and destroyed Masalur. Boolean got away but it's ugly. Now a mercenary bastard I should have killed years ago named Zamofir is riding here hard. They've got repeating guns that can shoot hundreds of rounds a minute and they intend to get you and everybody else and just level this place, just to make sure."

"Zamofir! That son of a bitch from the train who was in with them raiders? Oh, I know him, Crim. How many?"

By that time the first of the camp people had appeared, with several more following. Two of Putie's husbands, Ladar and Somaz, and one of Quisu's, Dabuk, anyway, as well as Putie herself. They initially froze in hostility at the sight of Crim, but his condition told them he wasn't somebody to be feared. Sam told them briefly who the stranger was, and that he was trustworthy, and they listened with growing concern.

Ladar, a big, muscular man, and by agreement of the women the best-looking male body they'd ever seen, nodded. "How many are there?"

"There were twenty when they started, but there are only fourteen now," the Navigator responded with a touch of pride in his voice. "But they're mad as hell and they got nothing but blood in their eyes at this stage. I overheard them saying they were going to kill every living thing here and burn the place. I pulled two of the fancy rifles off the dead ones and got two boxes of ammunition as well. Hauled them on foot the last three leegs. They're simple to operate and you don't have to aim—they'll nail most anything within maybe a thirty- or forty-degree angle of where they're aimed. You have anything else to fight with?''

Ladar turned to Dabuk. ''Get back to the still. That stuff's pure grain alcohol. You remember the firebombs Jerbal used back in that raid? Make some. Figure what to do with the rest. Somaz, you and Putie go tell the others and have everybody meet here. This here and the mill across the way are the first two buildings they got to pass. You—Navigator. How much time you figure we got?''

''An hour, maybe a little less. Hard to tell today.''

He nodded. ''Might be just enough. All right, everybody— *move!*''

They put Putie in charge, getting the other women well back in the jungle they all knew, along with the two babies. They were just to go as far back as they could, far enough back so that the crying of the babies wouldn't attract anybody. Sam was ordered back, too, but she refused. ''No, this is my fight, my fault,'' she told them. ''If it wasn't for me, they wouldn't be comin' here. The others'll make out, but I want my crack at the bastards. Besides, if they get us and I'm killed, maybe at least they won't risk stayin' around to find the others, but if I'm not here, they'll stay until they find us.'' That last was the clincher.

Crim showed Ladar how to work the submachine gun and the big man took it and one box of ammo and set up in the loft above the mill about a hundred yards away across a clearing. Crim himself kept the other one, propping himself up behind the porch stove and cutting a hole in the netting big enough to fire through. Other men took their positions with baskets filled with fire bombs—small gourds filled with nearly pure grain alcohol and plugged with strips of cloth. The rest loaded rifles and pistols, all single-shot legal kinds, and waited in a line behind bales of hay. All seemed almost relieved that they didn't have long to wait.

They rode into the camp slowly, bold as brass, eyeing

everything like they were speculators out to see if the place was worth buying. Sam had a feeling of unreality about the scene, as if she had seen it many times before in countless western movies, where Constable Earp faced down the Clanton mob or a hundred old Duke Morrison films on late night TV. The only difference was, most gunfights were at dawn, not sunset. Damn! This was more Charley's style than hers. She couldn't help counting them, and suddenly came up short.

"Crim!" she whispered urgently. *"I only count ten!"*

Crim nodded. "One or two to watch the road just in case, and two more probably coming in on foot to cover them. We'll just have to take the hidden ones as they come. We got the high ground."

A man—one of Famay's boys, Sam saw—got up from behind a hay bale, rifle at the ready. "That's far enough, strangers!" he called out. "What do you want here?"

Zamofir, looking ridiculous and haggard at one and the same time, with his big waxed moustache and riding clothes, came a bit forward, but not too much. "Covanti's under attack," the little man shouted back. "A general uprising by the natives in a ton of colonies. We've been sent here to evacuate all of you to the hub until the crisis has passed."

"That so? We heard of the troubles but there ain't no natives around here, either. This ain't their type of place. And if we was gonna be evacuated, they'd send the army."

"The army's too busy handling the flow of refugees and setting up defenses. There's whole *armies* of rebels converging on the hub border, and massacres of Akhbreed throughout the colonies. They couldn't spare a troop of soldiers for this little outpost, so they sent us, instead."

Zamofir, she thought, was as glib and convincing as ever, and just as much a skunk and a liar.

"That's pretty good, you bastard!" Crim yelled down at him. "Zamofir, if I didn't know you so well, I'd almost swallow that myself!"

Zamofir suddenly went white and somehow slid, horse and all, back into the midst of the gang. "Crim! I—uh! Old friend, I know we haven't seen eye to eye on a lot of this, but . . . *scatter, boys! They're ready for us!*"

At that moment Crim and Ladar opened up a sudden, withering crossfire, and men and horses went down in a bloody mess in the clearing. Some who had bolted at Zamofir's first syllable made for the mill or the house, on the instinct that neither man would fire towards the other's position. It was also clear that they'd gotten more horses than men; machinegun fire was being returned from the midst of the clearing, behind the figures of horses, some still, some thrashing in agony. Bullets whistled through the house and mill and down the main road, and Sam beat a hasty retreat to the rear of the house, where the angle kept direct shots from hitting. Furniture, pans, you name it, started moving, flying, and shattering all at the same time.

She was ashamed of herself for cowering like this, and she was worried for Crim. It didn't sound like he was firing any more.

The firing at her didn't last long, though; she heard sounds like breaking glass outside and then the sounds of men screaming, and, cautiously, she made her way forward again to see. The men in the trees had started throwing firebombs down on the massed men in the clearing, creating a hellish fire, and individual shots picked off men, some on fire, who ran from the cover into the open

Suddenly there were sounds on the porch vibrating through the floor, and into the interior lurched a huge, filthy, bearded raider brandishing a pistol. He stood there, staring at her, and gave a laugh and then brought the pistol up, still chuckling. Suddenly someone appeared behind him, and, before he realized that anyone was there, he suddenly stiffened and bent backwards a little, the most incredulous expression on his face, then keeled over and collapsed on the floor, a big Navigator's knife sticking full into his back.

"The sun set just in time," Kira said with satisfaction. "Now, help me get out of Crim's shirt and jacket before I tangle and fall myself!"

Sam was almost too shocked to do anything, but Kira galvanized her into action. There was more shooting outside now, and a lot of yelling.

Kira got the rest of Crim's clothing off and then crouched down and looked at the situation outside. Although the sun had set, it was still very light, but there was little to see. The survivors of the raiders and whoever was still going defending the camp were all under cover now, and it was hard to tell who, what, or where, or even friend from foe.

Kira looked over at Sam and gave her a reassuring smile. "I feel like a native now. Crim couldn't haul much more than he did, so I guess I'm bare-assed and everything else for the duration."

Sam partly recovered her composure. "Crim—I didn't hear. . . ."

"Like I said, nick of time," the pretty woman responded. "That bastard got under the porch, climbed up, and pulled Crim and half the netting down. I guess he thought Crim was dead, and if sunset had been another five minutes, or those guys had waited until dawn, he would be. Now he's sort of suspended, at least 'til dawn." She sighed. "Wish I had something decent to fight with. Any weapons here except this one-shot pistol?"

"Crim had the repeater. The only thing we got is an old set of sabers, Jubi—one of my husbands—kept from his old army days."

"Get them. God, that horse barbecue out there smells awful!"

Sam fumbled and then opened the trunk. Although it was growing pitch dark in the house without the lantern, she knew her way as if it were the back of her hand.

Kira took both sabers, hefted them, then picked one. "This'll do. You take the pistol and shoot anybody who comes through the door."

"What're you gonna do?"

"A little hunt in the dark. This is my element, remember? And I'm fresh as a daisy." She started to duck out, but Sam called after her.

"Kira—what about Crim? Come morning, I mean. And you?"

"If help doesn't come before morning, then Crim will die," she responded calmly, as if referring to someone else. "And if Crim dies, I probably will, too. That makes the next few hours real precious, doesn't it?" And, with that, she slipped out.

Sam felt suddenly terribly guilty and panicky at one and the same time. This wasn't the way it was supposed to go, damn it! Would they never leave her alone? Now Crim and Kira

were gonna die for her, too, and maybe most or all of the
people she loved here! And all she could do was sit there in
the dark on the floor with a pistol.

Or could she? Suddenly she smelled smoke, not from
outside—that had pretty well died out now—but like it was
coming from. . . . *The house was on fire!* The bastards had
set fire to it, and maybe to other places in town. The four left
behind, and anybody who got away, now working to create
light and force the defenders from their own ground out into
the open.

And it was a good plan, since there was no question of her
staying where she was. She got up and carefully peered out at
the porch, or what was left of it. Was the one who set fire to
her place hiding under it? Damn it, what could she do? The
glow from underneath told her that the place would quickly
be engulfed in flames, but she'd also be silhouetted against
that glow when she got down. Jumping was out of the
question—not in her condition. Taking a deep breath, and
holding the pistol tightly, she let herself out over the edge of
the porch, turned as best she could, and dropped, landing on
her feet for a moment but then falling over. She forgot all her
physical limitations, all danger, picked herself up and made
for the darkest area she saw nearby, behind some bullet-
scarred trees.

She froze for a minute, then peered cautiously around it
and back at the house, where flames were now shooting
upwards. But—wasn't that somebody on the edge of the
porch? Who the hell . . . ?

The dark figure jumped effortlessly to the ground and then
began to look around. At that moment, two shots from somewhere crashed into the tree, one just above her head, shower-
ing splinters and wood fragments, and she gave an involuntary
cry. The figure heard it, turned, and advanced towards her,
holding something in his hand.

Sam looked frantically around but couldn't see where to
run. There was shooting in back of her and this character in
front. Damn it, she couldn't outrun them—she couldn't *waddle*
more than ten feet at a stretch.

"Come, come, Susama!" cried a familiar and unwelcome
voice. "The threads of our destinies have been criss-crossing
for a long time now, and then barely missing entanglement. It

is time now, my sweet,'' Zamofir almost sang to her. "Come out and I will make it swift and painless and then get out of this trap. Resist or make any trouble for me and I will carve the child out first so you can watch, and then I will remain until I have hunted down and killed all the other women as well. Your choice. Whatever, it is time.''

She took another deep breath, then turned, and stepped out into the fire's glow, facing him. Oddly, she felt calm, even relaxed, at this moment, and the moment seemed to hang stuck in time.

He was there, showing some blood so at least he'd been nicked a few times, and he was holding the other saber! My god! Did the man actually just *twirl* his moustache? Then he said, "You see, my dear, we are both survivors. We survive and triumph against even the most impossible odds. The trouble is, destiny allows only one of us survival at this juncture." He raised the saber in a sort of salute, then took another step forward.

Kira stepped out of the trees nearby, holding the other saber, blood very definitely on it. "Hers is not the only destiny entwined with yours, you pig,'' she said to him. "First you take me, and then you can have her.''

Zamofir froze, turned, and sighed. "I would think you more confident with a rapier," he said calmly, lowering the sword. "This, my dear, is more a man's weapon." And he leaped towards Kira, who blocked, and they were joined in a duel.

Sam knew she couldn't run any more, that all the fight had been drained out of her. She could do nothing now but stand and watch one hell of a duel, between an old-time movie villain and a naked beauty, with swords that looked left over from a pirate epic.

Clang! Clang! Thrust! Parry! Block! Clang!

With stray bullets still whistling occasionally through the trees, and by the eerie glow of the fire, the two of them fought their duel, and they were pretty damned good at it, both of them. Sam expected Kira to have the moves, the grace, the quickness, but not the arm and wrist strength for such heavy weapons. Clearly Kira did a lot of steady working out with weights—that explained some of the stuff in the wagon. Muscles flexed now, she was still gorgeous, but she had the arms of a female body builder.

Zamofir had some experience and more familiarity with the weapon, but Kira was younger, quicker, and had the moves of a ballet dancer. Sensing that Zamofir was tiring, she pressed in, again, again, again. . . . Now a twirl, a twist, and the little man's saber flew from his grasp and landed a few feet away on the ground. He crouched down, warily, and gave a furtive glance to it, as if he were going to try for it, then suddenly he laughed nervously, whirled, and began to run.

Kira ran after him, but not a runner's gait, holding the saber almost like a javelin, and, when only a few feet in back of him, she let it fly. The sword was thrown with such force that it pierced Zamofir's back and came right out his front, so that from his back you could see only the ornate hilt. He cried out, staggered, then managed to turn back to Kira and almost shrug.

"Just as well," he managed, coughing. "Better . . . a more honorable . . . death . . . than I deserved . . . than to face . . . the wrath . . . of Klittichorn. Never . . . underestimate . . . the power of . . . a woman, eh?"

He smiled at that, then collapsed forward, the sword actually popping up a bit from his back as he hit face down and lay still. Kira went over, put a foot on his back, and pulled the sword out, then came over to Sam. "*That* was almost worth dying for!" she proclaimed. "You okay?"

Sam was stupefied. "That was the most amazing thing I ever saw! Like you was Robin Hood or somebody!"

"I told you once I was a female jock, before I got paralyzed. Since coming back to life, more or less, I've done most everything to make up for lost time. He was right, by the way. I fenced a lot in college, but these damned things are heavy and awkward as hell. I think I sprained my wrist at least. If he'd been in his prime, I wouldn't have had a prayer, but I bet that was the first time he'd fought with swords in years. You don't use it, you lose it. Thank heavens."

"*Now* what do we do?" Sam asked her.

Kira sighed and shrugged. "I dunno. I figure your boys wouldn't shoot a naked lady in this place and I knew who the gang was, but as to who's winning and what's what, it's impossible to say. Unless we see something worth going after, I think we find a dark, secluded spot, sit down, and have a good cry.''

"But we can't know much of anything until it's light, and when it's light. . . ."

"Yeah, I know. That's why I'll do most of the crying."

The shooting had stopped completely within another hour, but most of the camp was either burning or had already burned, and there wasn't much to see. Nobody dared come out in the open yet, though; in the darkness and with pockets of flame, it would be impossible to tell who was who and make a decent count to see if all the raiders were dead—or if all the camp people were dead.

Slowly, though, one at a time, the surviving men of the camp made contact with one another. It took most of the night to count all the casualties. On the camp side, six dead, including Ladar, damn it, cut down and shot in the back from his loft position by one of the guys who'd snuck in just for that, and three wounded, none critically—although it looked as if Somaz might well lose both legs, and Kruwen, another of Quisu's husbands, appeared paralyzed from the waist down thanks to a wound in the spinal area. The girls and the babies were okay, certainly, but, ironically, it looked as if the only family left intact was Sam's, whose husbands were still out in the boat and blissfully ignorant of all this. That made her feel doubly guilty, almost unbearably so. It wasn't right that she'd been the cause of this, however unwillingly, and that she alone should survive with her family intact.

By now she was cried out and felt drained and sick, yet her mind was going 'round and 'round. There was no end to it. If Crim and Zamofir had found her, then others would, and that horned bastard would never stop, never, until he killed her and maybe saved the baby to raise, to try again with a Storm Princess raised from the cradle to do his bidding. Now, too, they wouldn't just send mercenary gunmen, they'd send sorcerers and demons.

The wedding spell inherent in the ring was a simple spell, meant for simple folk and for common situations. It was designed to eliminate all complications, not cause them, but cause them it now did. Her duties as a Covantian wife were to love, honor, and obey her husbands, to keep house, relieve the burden of their chores, do whatever was in their best interest, at whatever sacrifice. Her duty to her child was to bear and raise and protect it, and allow it to grow up healthy and strong.

But if she remained here, remained loyal and faithful, she would bring down more terror on this place, and certainly death or worse upon her own husbands. If she tried to pick up and go on, they would find her, and her child would either die or be taken to an evil monster to raise.

But she couldn't run. Not any more. Not physically, not emotionally. She'd be found out anyway. The only solution was to face and defeat the threat, and to do that she would have to be her old self, the surrogate Storm Princess. Had she still had those powers she could have brought lightning down to fry all those bastards, and rain to quench the fires. Had she been the Storm Princess, those men wouldn't be crippled, or dead, and Crim and Kira wouldn't be facing certain death at dawn having given everything to protect her.

But then the ultimate act of love, of sacrifice for her husbands and child-to-be, was to give all this up. The ring and its spell was preventing her from doing what its own logic compelled her to do. She felt its grip on her weaken, felt waves of dizziness and confusion, and sensed somehow that it was locked in a logic loop from which it could not escape. The conflicting demands it was making on her were sending waves of nausea and making her feverish, her emotions running the entire range, her mind beset with complete confusion as to what she could do and should do, until she couldn't stand it any more. It pushed her over the edge, and the only thing she could do to stop it, she did without even thinking about it. She pulled the ring violently from her finger, tearing the skin, and threw it away, and then she collapsed and passed out.

Sam awoke with vivid memories of all that had been until she'd looped out or gone nuts or whatever had happened. She reached over to her ring finger and felt it. There was a bandage on it, but no ring. She had sensed it more than remembered it, but that in itself was strange. She didn't really feel much different. Oh, she knew now what she had to do, if at last she was allowed to do it, but she still felt real affection for those four men and for the others as well, and still thought of the camp as home. Short of Boday's place, it was the closest to a real home she'd had since being dragged to Akahlar.

But there was a difference, and it was again something she sensed, felt, rather than directly experienced.

The power was back. It was raining now, outside wherever she was, and she could sense, feel the storm, join with it if she wished.

She suddenly opened her eyes full and looked around with a start. It was the cottage! *Her* house! And she was in her own bed, and nothing was burned and nothing was out of place! God—had it all been a terrible nightmare? But—no, what about her finger? The return of the powers, of self-control? Had she somehow had the ring torn from her or taken from her and hallucinated the rest as a result?

It *had* to be, because it was day, and there was Crim, coming in the door, and he looked okay! Even his buckskins were clean!

He grinned when he saw her staring at him like she was seeing a ghost.

"Not dead yet," he assured her. "But it was a near thing."

"But—but—Did I dream it? Didn't it happen?"

"It happened," he assured her. "All of it. This is a clean set, by the way—in spite of what you've often accused me of, I *do* have more than one set of clothes. They just had to be retrieved."

"Never mind the clothes! You had a couple of holes in you big enough to run through, you had maybe half your blood, you fell off the porch, and who knows what else. You were a dead man at dawn!"

"That happened as well. It all happened, Sam. I can show you where the dead bodies are stacked, including Zamofir's. I was proud of Kira, even though I had always hoped I could do the slimy bastard in myself." The smile faded. "Also six very brave men are laid out over on the floor of the mill, awaiting a proper funeral. Their wives insisted on doing it all themselves, along with the six who survived. Strong sorcery can rebuild a town that burned and repair the worst of wounds, but it can't raise the dead no matter what the legends say.''

She sat up straight. "Sorcery! Boolean!"

"Yes. He got here two hours before dawn—thank the fates. Kira damn near had a heart attack when he showed up. Not alone, either.''

She suddenly felt a shock. "God! I must look awful! My hair . . . .''

"You look fine, or at least normal. Relax.''

"I—Boday?''

He nodded. "And Charley, too, and a very odd fellow named Dorion, and Boolean's familiar whose name is Cromil and who looks like a green monkey and likes to insult people.''

"I—I'm not so sure I'm ready for Boday yet.''

"Relax. She's on guard duty overlooking the road right now and she can't come back here until I relieve her. But you'll have to face her sooner or later. How do you feel about it?''

She sighed. "I—I really don't know. I haven't been able to get my head screwed back on right yet. I just need a little time, that's all.'' She paused a moment. "Can I first see the other women here? I—I sort of feel responsible. Maybe I can help.''

Crim nodded. "But be quick. Boolean wants us out of here as fast as is practical. Even now Klittichorn dispatches Sudogs to see what has been happening here, and he must know that as of now the child still lives. Boolean is powerful—even I hadn't realized how powerful until I saw what he did here—but that power has limits. He's not the only one with power, and they can and will gang up on him if they think they have him cornered.''

She nodded. "I can take care of the Sudogs," she assured him, "but you're right. I've brought enough misery down on this place. All right—let's go.''

The place was so fully restored that it made it all the more jarring to see the corpses laid out in the mill. At least Boolean's healing powers had extended to the wounded; there would be no amputations or paralysis. It did not, however, end the sadness of the men who died bravely defending what was theirs.

Sam had come there mainly to comfort the others, but as she looked at Ladar and the others she'd come to know so well, bloody and still, she suddenly found herself filled not with sadness nor even guilt but with anger. All that time, until she'd finally faced up to that Changewind back in Covanti, she'd been running away. Running away from herself, running away from duties, responsibilities, burdens. She hadn't asked for them, of course, but they were hers none the less.

These guys hadn't run. They'd stood and bravely defended all that was important to them, even to paying the ultimate price. It wasn't fair that she had all this dumped on her, but it wasn't fair that she'd brought death on them, either. They hadn't questioned fairness; they'd done what they had to do to save her and their wives and their camp and all that meant anything to them.

She walked back out to where Crim was waiting and looked up at him. "All right, let's see this big-shot wizard," she said determinedly.

Seeing Charley again was something of a shock, too. Not just the brown skin-deep dye job, but Charley was so thin she looked almost emaciated, and she seemed, well, a whole lot *older*, somehow. Well, Sam reflected, maybe *she* was a whole lot older now where it counted, too.

She kind of liked Dorion on first impression. True, he wasn't much on physique, with pot belly and thinning hair, but there was a certain kindness and gentleness in him that came through right from the start, and the way he doted on Charley was more than the slave ring thing. Anybody could see he was in love with her; anybody, that is, but Charley.

Boolean was a different sort of shock. A man of medium height and build, with a gray-black neatly trimmed beard and deep-set, heavily lined blue eyes, he looked so, well, *ordinary*. Even Charley, who couldn't see the man as he was, had come up with the right impression at the start. The guy looked like a high school science teacher, and sounded much that way, too.

At his suggestion, they went back to her place and sat down, just the two of them, to discuss what happened next. She offered, as host, to make him some tea or coffee, but he just chuckled, snapped his fingers, and they both had just what they wanted right in front of them.

"The man who could do miracles," he chuckled. "Child's play, really. Once you determined the rules and the math and approached magic here as you approach any other scientific discipline, it just all sort of comes naturally. I've never tired of it, and it's as much fun, and just as fascinating as it was the first time. The only thing is, the more you can do, the more godlike your powers become, the more frustrated you become by those things you can't do. Those dead men out there. I could animate their corpses, but I couldn't bring *them* back or restore *their* bodies. They're gone. It's what keeps driving us to push the limits, and what destroys most of us in the end."

She nodded. "But what's next for us, on the practical level?" she asked him. "I mean, let's be realistic here. I can't be positive here, but I think I'm in my eighth month. I can't seem to keep my emotions in check, I haven't got the stamina, and I can't run or fight worth a damn, and as near as I can figure out, the only way to end this madness is to literally walk into the lion's den and face them down. *She'll* be in peak condition and totally in control, and she has Klittichorn for protection. I won't be able to get near enough to lay a glove on her and you know it. On top of that, she can sense the kid. I can't even hide out in a group. I'm willing to do whatever is necessary, but I can't see how I can do it, all things considered. Not until after the baby's born."

"I understand the problem," he replied seriously. "Our related problem is that we can't wait for the birth. He's going to jump the gun at almost any time from right now to no more than a week or two at best. His timetable was already upset by the problems involved in the attack on me. His generals are amateurs and they're now seeing the results of their mistakes. You can train armies of specific worlds rather well, but when you have to simulate conditions, and then mix various races with their own tribal chiefs and loyalties you get a mess. I think the effect on him would be to accentuate the positive and ignore the negatives. He did destroy a hub civilization and break the hold of a sorcerer. He's desperate now. If the child is born, the Storm Princess's powers may be weakened to the point where she couldn't handle multiple

Changewinds, or perhaps not put them and keep them where they're supposed to be. He can't do it one at a time. His power is limited, the same as mine. The next time he's got to do it, if not simultaneously, at least continuously. Speed and accuracy are at a premium for him right now. Everything he's built all these years, and all his dreams, face ruin unless he acts now.''

"But how can I do anything?"

He sighed. "You've heard from Charley and Dorion what the battle and its aftermath was like, what a mess this all is, what horror it is bringing. I don't know whether we can stop the process now. As soon as he feels we're after him he'll jump the gun and do it, and we can't wait because he could jump the gun anyway, thanks to your own biological clock. There is a way out of this, though. Wait a moment."

He got up and went outside and looked down at the clearing. "Charley, will you come up here?" he called. "Dorion, help her out and come up, too. I may need some assistance here."

Charley got up and in, with Dorion's help, and was taken to a chair. She was puzzled, but willing to listen.

Boolean took a deep breath. "Charley, you know the problem. We have to hit them before they hit everybody and make us irrelevant. I'm sure Klittichorn would have done it all as soon as he got the data from Masalur, if he didn't also have to play some politics with the Storm Princess and others. We have to hit him and get him the first time. There will be no second chances. And we have to do it soon."

"You know where he is?" Charley asked him.

Boolean nodded. "I know. I didn't know, exactly, until he hit Masalur, but I was able to identify and follow his threads back. That's what I was doing, and is the gain we got from Masalur's suffering. It's not close, which is why, even using the flying spells, we must leave immediately. Even with Sam and I in the best of shape, it's a question whether we can do it alone, or with just the forces that we have, even if we make it in time. As it stands, we have less chance. Sam hasn't the mobility or the control she should have, and the child is a dead giveaway. Sam needs a way out."

She nodded. "So?" At the moment she had no idea where he was going with this or what it had to do with her.

"I can't snap my fingers and make her into a peak Amazonian warrior. Well, actually, I could, but not without destroying the child. I'm just now beginning to realize why there *is* such a thing as a Storm Princess, why she comes up in other worlds as well, and why Klittichorn just didn't preempt this threat and have his own knocked up. Too much deduction with too much hunch, but I think I'm on the right track. The Storm Princesses are the only true 'naturals' in magic, and the only ones with influence over and immunity from the Changewinds. I think, somehow, they're safety valves—natural regulators—essential to keeping some kind of order. How and why it evolved this way is something we may never know, but, like gravity, it's still there. There's some evidence to show that the death of any of the Storm Princesses anywhere, even on the outplane, is followed by a long period of natural disasters, cataclysms, wars, you name it— until a new one is born. By killing so many in the outplane, Klittichorn has provided the evidence and pattern that this is true—at the cost of who knows how many lives or even civilizations. What will happen when he looses so many Changewinds at once on a weakened outplane is something I can't imagine, nor can he. The difference is, I care and he doesn't.''

"I'm with you so far,'' she told him. "I just can't see what it has to do with me.''

"Both of you think back, to that first time, in the Tubikosan caves, when we first had a talk. When I transmitted, through the icon, a blood-mixing and sealing spell that turned you, Charley, into a physical twin of Sam's.''

They both nodded. "I remember,'' said Sam. "It seems a hundred years ago.''

"It wasn't a mere appearance spell. I had to fool not just someone who knew what the Storm Princess looked like, I had to fool magicians, Sudogs, ones with the ability to see through mere appearances. Anyone short of the highest levels of the Second Rank, who could recognize the spell for what it was. It did more than make you physical twins on the outside; it made you true twins, genetically identical. You still are. The difference in appearance between the two of you may seem great now, but it's a difference in weight—and how long you've been like that and adjusted to it—and experience and, of course, in Charley's case, Boday's alchemy made a stunning difference. But, you see, I had to guard against spells and alchemy, so I had to make those with the power be confused, and they see people differently than the average person does.''

"Wait a minute," Sam interrupted him. "If she's actually me down to that level, why isn't she a Storm Princess, too?''

"Good question. There are two answers to that, both relevant. The first is that no one can create a Storm Princess by sorcery. It can not be done, or Klittichorn would have dispensed with his right off and things would be a lot more complicated. Second, there is more than the physical involved here, there is an entire pattern. Notice how the common peasant marriage spell removed your powers yet it didn't change you physically one bit, Sam. It is physical, mental, and psychic, and all must have certain elements exactly right or the balance is destroyed and the rest is ignored. Charley is physically you, no matter how dramatic the difference seems sitting here, but she is nothing like you either mentally or psychically in the areas that seem to count. One of them, quite clearly and unexpectedly, is sexual in nature, something I have been puzzling about since that was shown. There's got to be a reason for that. In many ways, it seems to be part of the key to this overall puzzle, a key that I am afraid Klittichorn has worked out ahead of me, as usual. But that's beside the point for now. The bottom line remains that Sam's current physiology can't be touched for fear of harming her child, yet it places her at great risk and extreme disadvantages in any showdown. We can't just transfer the needed elements to Charley, who's better suited for it, since one can not give away magical gifts of that sort.''

"Yeah, well, Sam wouldn't be much use blind, either," Charley noted.

"She wouldn't be blind. Her psychic self has the power. That's why she's been exposed to much magical energy herself and yet never suffered from the problem.''

Charley suddenly pushed back a bit from the table. "Oh, no! I think I see now where you're going with this and I don't like the route one bit.''

Sam looked at Charley, frowning, then at Boolean. "Well, I don't," she said. "Somebody want to let me in on this?''

"From a magical viewpoint," Boolean patiently explained, "the two of you appear identical. The differences, psychic and mental, are, therefore, easy to factor out completely when you two can be compared side by side like this. Were you not physically the same, all the differences could never be so clearly identified. Since they can in this case, I could transfer those differences."

"Differences? What the hell do you mean?"

"He means," Charley said softly, "that he can take your mind and soul and whatever and put it in my body, and mine in yours. And I get to carry the kid and keep their eyes off you two sneaking up on them while you get in my body. Isn't that about right?"

"I couldn't have said it better myself," the sorcerer replied. "It's an ideal solution shaped by the threads of destiny. And it's best for both of you. Sam gets the mobility and loses a telltale marker; you get out from being a blind, dependent woman without status whose body is good for only one thing. Sam's body also has other attributes. Thanks to the demon of the Jewel of Omak, wherever he now is, she doesn't get sick. No hostile organism can live inside her. Fleas, ticks, mosquitoes and other parasites die when they bite her. In spite of her weight, her blood pressure is perfect, her heart strong, her veins and arteries cleaner than a newborn's. Wounds heal quickly, damaged tissue regenerates."

"So *that's* why I was able to run like that, build those muscles, lift those weights!" Sam exclaimed.

"Well, it didn't hurt," the sorcerer replied. "So where is the problem, Charley? Are you afraid of the process itself?"

"No, no. Not after what you've pulled off so far. I believe you. But—to be fat without even having had the pleasure of eating my way up to it, and pregnant at the point where it's all work and the fun's long past—I'm not so sure I can handle that. Yeah, I'm frustrated here, and it seems like I always have a cold or I'm scratching little bites, but—jeez, Sam. What do you weigh now?"

"Last time I checked it was about two hundred and sixty pounds," she responded. "At least I think I got that from figurin' the halg and stuff."

"Two . . . And when you add the kid and the water weight. . . ."

Sam was astonished. "Jesus, Charley—I can't *believe* you! Ever since you got the way you are you been paranoid about weight. You always were, but it got to be a mania. I got to tell ya, Charley, you don't look real glamorous to me right now. You look fucking anorexic! I ain't no more thrilled about having that body of yours than you are havin' mine. I never liked bein' fat but I kind'a got used to it. The only real hangups I kept were about my health, and now I find out that's no problem at all! I'd be givin' up shit, too, you know." She grabbed her breasts. "I'm at least a forty-four D and I love 'em. Most of all, I'd be givin' up havin' the kid, and I want this kid bad."

"Yeah, but it's *your* kid, not mine. And it's the only one between us!"

"Not necessarily," Boolean cut in. "There's nothing physically wrong with Sam's system. It's Storm Princesses who are prevented from having but the one child—related in some way to that regulatory function I mentioned. You wouldn't be a Storm Princess. There's no reason to believe you would not remain fertile."

"You mean," Sam asked him, "if that spell here had stuck and I wasn't a Storm Princess, I could'a had more kids?"

Boolean shrugged. "Who knows? If you were taken out and stuck here, though, I doubt if it would have been a long or happy life once Klittichorn won. Here—or in Albuquerque, for that matter."

"Yeah, but who would screw somebody that fat without magic?" Charley asked acidly.

Behind her, Dorion said, too low for her to hear, "I would." To him, the resemblance was more marked than could be seen by each of them, and the idea of Charley in Sam's body was, somehow, something of a turn-on.

"So, this is the great Charley Sharkin," Sam retorted. "Bright, ambitious, liberated, and all that. The new woman, right? So what's she do? Finds out when she's turned into a whore and a bimbo that she *loves* being a whore and a bimbo, sellin' herself and actin' cute and dumb and all that. Shit, Charley, I thought I was given a raw deal here, but you're actually *happy* with the deal you got. You just want it improved so you can go on bein' Little Miss Fuckalot until you're big enough to become a madam and sucker in more poor kids. Another Boday, maybe. And to think I always looked up to you—"

"Hold on! Hold on! It's not that *simple*," Charley protested, then took a moment to compose herself. "Sam—*it's all I have*."

Sam sighed and looked at Boolean. "Well, if we're really twins now, and you got the power to rebuild the town and heal the wounded overnight, couldn't you just take off the spells that kept me fat and make her thin and pretty?"

"I could," the sorcerer admitted, "but not right off. I don't dare mess with any of those without risking messing up the biochemistry and possibly harming or even killing the kid. I'm not *that* good. Afterwards, if any of us survive this, and the child's born, well—then anything is possible."

That put a different face on it for Charley. "You really mean that? If I keep like that for another month or two, and bear her kid, then the weight and all can be taken away? I mean, if you fail after all this, it won't make any difference anyway, I guess, so otherwise I pay the price of a couple of months like that and then wind up better than I am now." She shrugged. "Well, I guess we'd better do it, then, huh?"

"Jeez," Sam sighed. "This is gonna confuse the hell out of Boday. . . ."

· 11 ·

Allies, Answers, and Questions

"WHEN DO YOU want to do this?" Sam asked Boolean, a bit nervous in spite of it all.

"Ordinarily I'd have to set up a lab," he replied. "Prepare primer potions to ease the transfer, do a lot of provisional spells, all that. But because you two are true twins, created in the lab for this purpose, so to speak, I think I can do it on the fly, right here and now. It'll save time and ease the stress. Just lie down there, side by side, heads towards me," he instructed. "Dorion, you assist as needed. Sam, I know it's uncomfortable, but bear with it."

"*Everything's* uncomfortable at this stage," she responded, but managed to lie down with some help from Dorion. The magician then guided Charley to the right spot and positioned her as well, then stepped back. He felt oddly mixed emotions at this, but while Boolean had removed the ring from Charley's nose he'd made no move to remove Dorion's. Dorion was stuck if Charley went along, and probably even if she didn't—Boolean's power was far greater than the simple spell that bound the former magician.

He also couldn't avoid a little straight professional curiosity in spite of the personal involvement. The fact was, this wasn't one of the spells they ever taught or talked about in magician school.

Boolean went over to them and stretched out his arms, hands palm down, over each of their faces, and concentrated.

"Now, each of you just close your eyes and go to sleep," he told them softly. "In a nice, deep, pleasant sleep, with no thoughts, no worries, no cares. Just a nice, deep sleep."

They were both out, with soft smiles on their faces, and,

oddly, like this and so relaxed, they really *did* look a lot alike.

Boolean turned towards Dorion and said, "I *hope* it's this easy with twinned people and I don't require the prep. Otherwise we could have some very hairy results." And then he winked, and turned back to the two sleeping women. He knelt down behind their heads and placed one hand on the face of each of them. Neither moved or seemed to notice, their breathing heavy and regular.

Dorion felt suddenly uneasy about this, thanks to Boolean's comment. Up to now he'd had so much confidence in the man's power he hadn't doubted, but Boolean was right. Doing this by spell and sheer force of will, with no intermediate medium for the soul except himself, was damned dangerous. He would have to draw both souls, both consciousnesses, even memories, from the bodies into his own as the medium and then switch them with no losses—and pretty damned fast, too—without mixing them or letting them touch in any way, either each other or his own.

The sorcerer took a deep breath, let it out, took a second, let out a bit, closed his eyes tightly, and began.

His body began to tremble slightly, and gobs of sweat broke out on his forehead; his teeth were tightly clenched together and his face contorted into a terrible grimace.

To normal human eyes nothing else was happening, but to Dorion's magically attuned eyes, the great juggling act was clear.

Both women's bodies took on a sudden pale reddish glow. It was all over, except for the different colored mass in Sam's abdomen which had a few slender psychic tendrils to her.

The two large masses coalesced, growing smaller and smaller and yet more intense, and the tendrils from the fetus grew long and wispy, like a few strands of spider's web trying not to let go in the wind.

Now came the tricky part for Boolean, as the two centers of bright energy, now burning with an intense red-white fire, egg-shaped and compact, were drawn into the sorcerer's two hands, then up the arms and into Boolean's own body. He was going to pass them very close—too close for any eye to follow—and Dorion watched as they drew closer and closer, the thin webs from the fetus seeming too tiny and tenuous now to possibly hold.

Now, carefully, the orb from Charley slid just atop the one from Sam, so that Charley's gently brushed by and made ever so gentle contact with the thin tendrils from the fetus and continued on to the other arm.

There! The wispy links had transferred! They were now contracting, getting a bit stronger and thicker as Charley's orb flowed now past the shoulder and down the arms towards Sam's body, while Sam's orb, now free of the contact, went towards Charley.

He'd done it! *The hell with Klittichorn!* Dorion thought in intense admiration and wonder. *That's the greatest feat of unaided sorcery anyone has ever seen!*

Now the orbs passed through the heads, out of Boolean's body, and began to lose their distinctive shapes and some of their intensity, flowing into first the head and then through the rest of the two bodies, fading, fading, until they were finally mere auras such as everyone had.

Boolean suddenly expelled his breath, which he'd been holding for at least the couple of minutes that seemed to have passed, and gasped for air, then removed his hands and fell back.

Dorion was to him in an instant. "Master Boolean! Are you all right?"

Boolean's eyes opened. "For a brief moment, right there in the transfer, my soul, which was still diffuse, intermixed with Sam's," he managed, still a bit out of breath. "I am afraid, Dorion, that I am now cursed to sexually prefer only women." And then he grinned and sat up.

"I have just witnessed perhaps the greatest feat of mind control in all history," Dorion growled. "Why is it, then, that I still want to wring your neck at this point?"

Boolean's grin remained, and he managed to stand up, then make his way back to the pair who still reclined there sleeping. He examined his handiwork and nodded to himself. "It *was* tough, a lot tougher than I figured on," he admitted. "The transfer's complete and successful, but I don't think I want to do that again without the full paraphernalia and a lot of time and prep. I had some mild chest pains at the transfer point and I almost lost my concentration wondering if I was going to have a heart attack or a stroke. One more like that and it'd kill me.''

Dorion stared at him and saw how suddenly old and tired he looked and realized that this wasn't a put-on. ''Are you certain that you are still up to Klittichorn? Or that *she* is?''

''I can't ever know that until we try it, Dorion. There will be enough time between now and when we get there for me to do some self-repair and reconditioning, though. As to Sam— yes, I think she is, now.''

''How long are you going to keep them in the trance?''

''The longer the better so it settles in,'' the sorcerer responded. ''Anything from Crim or Boday yet?''

''I'll check.'' Dorion stepped outside and looked around, but it was still quiet. He went back in and reported, ''Nothing yet. Want me to go check?''

Boolean nodded. ''Do that.'' He turned back to the two sleeping forms, looked down at them, and gave a soft chuckle. ''I really feel sorry for those four husbands,'' he muttered to himself. ''Not that she'd enjoy herself like she did, moving back from oral to anal. I'd sure like to leave Charley here if I could. Be good for her, too, to find not just one but many men still wanting her no matter what her weight or condition.'' He sighed. ''Well, can't solve everybody's problems, I guess.''

He didn't dare leave her anywhere near here or anywhere that anyone from the rebel camp was likely to spot her. The four guys would just have to suffer, but he made a mental note to make it up to them, if he could, at some point in the future. Decisions, decisions—that's all great power ever really brought you. Decisions without irreversible consequences or accountability.

It was fun to be a sorcerer.

Charley awoke slowly from a very erotic dream and turned slowly to one side. Suddenly she felt a shifting down in her abdomen and it unnerved her and she woke up. Somebody else—Sam—was waking up next to her. She looked over and was startled first to realize that she could see again, in the normal, colorful way, and that excited her. What she was seeing, though, bothered her a lot.

She had never really seen herself properly and in full color with the chocolate brown skin and blue-black hair, and it didn't look right. In fact, Sam was right—God! She'd been skin and bones! Funny it hadn't felt like that. . . .

With a shock she suddenly realized that she was seeing her own body in full living color and three dimensions, yet as a third party. Somehow, deep down, she hadn't really believed it was possible, and certainly not like this. Hell, it was still *light* out!

She shifted uncomfortably and ran her hands over her own body as it now was. She remembered how fat Sam had been, but it seemed even more gross, if anything, now.

She tried to get to her feet and found that it took something of a balancing act to do so. Dorion came over, put out his arms, and she took them and let herself be pulled unsteadily to her feet. Christ! It felt like she had a goddamned bowling ball in her stomach, and something in it shifted slowly when she did, but not in the right ways or at the right speed. She let go of Dorion and tried walking a few steps and it, too, felt awkward and weird.

The weight and feel of the breasts also surprised her. They felt like they weighed a ton of dead weight each, shifting when she walked but complicating the balancing act required to maintain equilibrium with the bowling ball in her belly, and the extra padding wasn't any real help, either. Her thighs rubbed together tightly every time she took a step, and produced motion in her ass as well. God, she was *gross!*

"God! This feels *weird,*" she heard Sam say. "Jeez! I feel so light it's like I was eleven years old again! It just don't feel like I'm all here no more. I guess I got more used to that body than I thought I had. Wow! This is *strange!* I'm actually inside your body, just like it was mine! Uh—how you feelin', Charley?"

"Like a beached whale. I think these tits are more like fifties than forty-fours. Jeez—when did you weigh yourself last?"

"Back in Tishbaal. It was the last scale I saw. I could'a done it on the mill scales here, but with bein' pregnant and all it didn't seem worth it. Boy, that's strange, seein' yourself like this, from a different pair of eyes or whatever it is I'm seein' with at the moment. It's different than a mirror. It's real and not backwards."

"You went like this and didn't have screaming fits?"

"Aw, you get used to it pretty fast. Not the kid—you always know that's there. But like Boolean said, you don't get sick, and you don't get clogged. Bigger lungs carryin' more oxygen, so you can't exactly do things fast but you can do 'em pretty good."

"I gain three times my weight at least and I don't even have the fun of eating my way up to it. It's not fair!"

"Yeah, well, at least you can eat whatever you want and all you want now," Sam noted. "Huh! These eyes are kind'a odd. You see like this when you was in this body?"

"Unless it was something of magic or another plane all I saw was gray, unless I used Shadowcat," Charley told her. "Why? What do you see?"

"Everything, but not quite. The colors are funny. Things look sorta' fuzzy and all, and all the colors are pastels or something, and there's a glow to most everything. Real strong from you and your buddy, there." She stared hard at Charley. "Hey! If I concentrate real hard I can see your insides! Wow! X-ray vision!" She hesitated and looked at Dorion. "Would it hurt the kid if I checked her out?"

"No," Dorion told her. "You're not really using your eyes to see in the old pattern or old ways. You're not really seeing just with them at all. In fact, if you concentrate hard enough, you can see what's in back of you, too. It has a lot to say for it, but it's also limited in vital areas. Those of us with The Sight can't read ordinary books—takes a special kind of ink and paper to see right—and there's a lot of color shift, and a lot of blurring with much motion. You can see things others can't, but there are tradeoffs. You'll learn them. The glows are the auras or spiritual components of people and things. You get pretty good at recognizing specific things by their auras alone."

Charley looked at Dorion. "Then why couldn't *I* see like that?"

"You have to have the power as well. Just three percent of the Akhbreed have it, and they're born with it. You either have it or you don't, and, even then, you never find out unless you're subjected to the intense radiation from dealing with the netherhells. Only ones with really strong natural power see it from the start."

Sam looked now at Charley's distended abdomen and concentrated and, to her immense surprise, she *could* see the fetus in the womb. "Gee—looks just like the films in sex ed, only in three-D and living color," she commented. "This is neat! Kind'a gross in parts, though. And it *glows* real bright." She felt a sudden shiver run through her. "What the hell?"

Boolean reentered the hut and saw what she was doing. "You felt it, huh? That's what the enemy feels as well every time some random part of the power is given off by the child, even though unborn. She can feel you, too, looking at her, and is reacting. I'd stop it for now." He turned to Charley. "And how are you making out?"

"Awful," Charley moaned. "Like a ton of bagged water is inside me all shifting around, dead shifting weight below, slow and awkward. I can't even see my own feet."

Boolean passed a hand in front of her eyes and suddenly Charley's face went blank, staring forward.

"The more you move, the more you will learn about and compensate for the body's limitations and these will be automatically and subconsciously incorporated into your normal movements until, within your limitations, you feel totally confident and can walk, sit, stand, or lie without even thinking about it. When you reach that point you will think of it as your body, your child, and accept it as normal and not think much about it, accepting it and its limitations."

"Jeez! Where were you when I needed you?" Sam muttered.

He turned to her. "Just a simple spell, like hypnosis, only it won't wear off so rapidly, and by the time it does it'll seem natural to her. It's no panacea, but anyone who can adjust so well to blindness should have little trouble with this. More gradually, the biochemistry of pregnancy will begin to influence her thinking as well. Of course, I could cast a really fine spell so she'd be perfectly happy and all that and do all sorts of other things, but casting individual spells on human beings is kind of like making pacts with the devil. You never can be sure you've covered all the loopholes and the ones you don't are often doozies." He turned back to Charley, did another wave of his hand, and she came back to full consciousness and frowned.

"Huh! Had a little dizziness there for a moment. It's okay now. Let me move around and do a few things and get the real feel of this. I'm not going to be much help, but if I'm going to survive the next couple of months, I want to be as self-sufficient as possible.''

While Boolean and Sam huddled over what was going to be done next, Charley was active, trying out all sorts of things, the ever-concerned Dorion at her side should she need assistance. She even went out and managed to climb the ladder down and back up again, although not without some difficulty. At the end of an hour or so she reported, ''You know, this isn't as bad as I thought at first. I guess my hormones are flowing or something, but I'm starting to get the hang of this. It's not like pregnancy is an abnormal condition or something—women's bodies are designed for it. It's just that I suddenly had to take it on in full bloom rather than grow into it gradual like.''

''Don't push yourself,'' Sam told her. ''We don't want to lose the kid.''

Charley shrugged. ''If we were really that delicate, then we'd never have gotten out of caveman days. I'll manage. I'm actually less dependent now than when I couldn't see, by a long shot, and I just picked up and moved that heavy chair over there without thinking about it. You got real muscles under all this fat. I couldn't have moved it before.''

Sam nodded. ''I kept working out as best I could using weights. There's nobody else around here half the time to move the heavy stuff and do the lifting. I got pretty good around this place carryin' heavy stuff around on my head, but first I had to lift it up there. I'm havin' the opposite problem now discoverin' how weak I suddenly am for anything. When I was with Crim I practiced with swords; now I don't think I could lift one.''

''Compare notes later,'' Boolean told them. ''Now we have to plot our move. It's already late afternoon and we can't dawdle here any longer or we'll begin to attract some visitors with real power.''

She nodded. ''Nothing personal, Sam, but I think I want to be gone before your four husbands get back. I don't think I could explain this to them—or maybe it wouldn't make much difference to 'em. But where are we going? And how? You think it's safe for me in one of those—saddles?''

''You'll be fine in the saddle, and I'll be watching out for you," the sorcerer assured her. "In fact, Sam's the one we'll have to watch for a bit. As to where, we are going to go briefly to a small town in Covanti hub where I need to contact some people and update them and see if there's anybody left out there with both brains and guts. After that I'm going to put you in some safe hands well out of the field of battle, and Sam and I are going north for a while."

"Hey! Wait a minute!" Charley objected, suddenly hesitant. "First of all, I haven't any clothes! If we're going someplace where strangers are, I don't want to be like *this!* And, second, what about Boday? She's technically married to Sam but she'll think *I'm* Sam! This is bad enough without having to deal with *that!*"

"Yes, and what about the other people here, and my own husbands?" Sam added worriedly. "They're good people. The boys may be a little rough but they're not really bad."

Boolean thought for a moment. "Well, Charley, we'll get you some clothes when we need them. You didn't seem to mind being undressed before."

"Yeah, well, I didn't have this body before."

He ignored the comment. "As for Boday—well, Cromil has informed her of what we did, although I'm not sure she'll believe it until she sees it for herself. I can probably ease belief by simply separating out that simplistic marriage spell that caused so much trouble late in the game and transferring it over to Sam. Here—I'll do that now." It took maybe ten seconds and a bit of odd gesturing, and Sam actually watched as he reached out and grabbed the slender red thread of a spell she'd never seen before as if it were a real thread and attached it to her. "There. Uh—Sam I hope you're ready for Boday now."

"Yeah," she sighed. "If she'll accept me this way, sure, why not? I hate to admit it, but I actually missed her."

"As for the locals here," he continued, "well, that's going to have to leave a void, that's all. There are, after all, suddenly far fewer men than women. They might miss you, but I don't think they'd understand how complicated the problem was. It's best you just, well, vanish. I wish I could do more, but time's wasting away."

"But, won't Klittichorn eventually send other forces here?

I really do care about them, you see. All of them. I don't think they should suffer any more.''

"Don't worry about them. They'll be okay—unless Klittichorn wins. Then I wouldn't give a plugged nickel for anybody. You see, there's not much chance they'll send anything but supernatural forces the next time, and those will be looking for impulses from the child. They won't find them, and they will move on. Right now, they can't afford mindless vengeance with you again on the loose and in full power—the Storm Princess will know that, probably already does. They haven't the time.''

Sam wanted to believe it—hell, she *had* to believe it. She took one last look around the place, sighed, and walked out onto the porch, opened the netting, and climbed down the ladder. Odd how easy it was to do that all of a sudden. She was tending to overcompensate and almost turned her ankle at the bottom. *Hav'ta get Boolean to do one of those adjustments on me,* she thought. She had never been this thin or this weak. She felt *tiny,* and she wasn't sure she liked the feeling.

She turned and saw Boday standing there a bit uncertainly. The artist sure looked different without the neck to toe tattoos, but, in a way, she almost looked, well, *normal.* No, better than normal. She was still tall and thin, but she was tight as a drum and look at those *muscles!*

"Hello, Boday," she said, feeling a bit awkward.

"Charley? You are seeing? Or is it . . . has he . . . ?" She grinned. *"Susama!"* And then there was a rush to her and Sam was picked up and hugged and darn near killed by Boday, who'd picked up real muscles herself and damn near crushed the now tiny Sam.

"All right, all right! We've got to go!" Boolean called to them. "Dorion, you help Charley down and go over to the saddles where we parked them. Boday, you and Sam will ride together—you'll both fit very nicely in one of the saddles now, I think—and can renew old times then. I've already mentally summoned Cromil and he'll bring Crim in. Probably Kira instead by the time we're ready to go. That may simplify matters. . . . Hmmm. . . .''

"He always does that—thinks aloud on the practical level," Dorion told them. "He can formulate a spell in his head that

it would take a good magician a day just to read, but unless
he does that he can't remember to put on his own boots.''

The saddles looked both more and less intimidating to
Charley when she could see them. Just ordinary saddles,
although when Boolean nodded towards one it rose into the
air. It was clear right off that no matter what her and Dorion's
preferences were, there was no way even Cromil, who was a
foot high and weighed maybe twelve pounds, could fit on one
with her as she was. Boolean lowered one to the ground, she
got on and got as comfortable as possible, and then it rose
maybe three feet in the air. She had some initial trouble with
balance but managed to stay on and finally decided that she
could handle it.

Charley turned and was surprised to see a very pretty
young woman, dressed in a tight black stretch pants outfit and
pistol belt, walk in as Cromil scampered up, jumped, and
perched on Boolean's shoulder. Boday, too, seemed startled
by the strange woman's sudden appearance.

"Oh, I forgot about Kira," Boolean said apologetically.
"This is the master swordswoman who did in three of the
raiders and dueled Zamofir to the death last night."

Charley frowned. "Where'd *she* come from? And what
about the guy with the sexy deep voice?"

It was Kira's turn to look confused, and Boolean had to
explain, "I had to make a switch in the interest of all concerned. *That's* Sam and *that's* her friend Charley. Probably
the only two people in the cosmos who even share the same
fingerprints. And that's Boday, about whom you've probably
heard much over the past months."

Kira gave a wan smile. "And people have problems with
me sometimes. Well, glad to meet you. And—Charley—Oh!
this is going to be very difficult for me! I'm so used to one
being the other. . . ."

"*You* are!" Charley muttered.

"Well, you'll meet Crim in the morning in the flesh. Right
now you might say he's with us in spirit. Don't bother to
figure it out. I am certain that if someone wants to explain,
they will."

Now that's *the kind of body I would kill for,* Charley
thought, looking at Kira. She made Sam—or Sam in Charley's
body—look positively plain. That woman would be glamor-

ous in a pigsty. Seeing the way even Dorion was looking at
this Kira suddenly made her self-conscious and jealous. Worse
when Boolean said, "Dorion, you'll double up with Kira for
now so I have one less saddle to juggle. Use hers over
there—we're donating the horse, Kira. Hope you don't mind."

"No, these people need all they can get. Well! I can't think
of any time I had a ride with a naked man. You want front or
back?"

Charley fumed inside but couldn't really say or do anything. Any order she gave Dorion would be nullified by
Boolean anyway, so what was the use? But he better damn
well not get so much as a hard-on or he was gonna regret it
later!

All set, they rose high into the air, giving Charley some
really bad moments, then set off in a line. After the first
hours, Charley had the hang of it, but she sure wished Dorion
and that woman were in front rather than in back of her!

She was actually somewhat surprised at her feelings seeing
Dorion with the woman. She tried to dismiss it as simple
jealousy based on what she looked like now as opposed to
what she had looked like, or thought she had looked like.
Good lord—was she really *that* thin? Somehow she always
felt just a little fat, a little not right, no matter what. Maybe
Sam was right—maybe she *had* gone overboard. Well, Sam
could fatten up that body now. At least she didn't have to
worry about it in *this* body, with that spell that would make
any diet useless. Maybe, at least, she could enjoy the next
two months pigging out, if she was anyplace she could pig
out. Ice cream . . . chocolate. She hadn't had those since,
well, since she'd been back home on her own world. If they
lost, well, hell, why diet? And if they won, Boolean would
eventually make her look great again with no strain. It was a
no-lose period.

But Dorion. . . . Well, he *was* kind'a cute, really. Overweight, yeah, but still with the tightest, cutest little ass. . . .
He had a crush on her, sure, but in all that time he'd never
taken advantage of her. In his own way, he was kind of sweet
and a little shy. If that slave spell of his came off, with her
looking like this, though, what would be his feelings then?
Maybe that was it. The insecurity of being this way. That's
what it had been, she knew, all along. Being blind and

dependent but beautiful and sexy had given her some measure
of power and security. They could be appalled at her liking
the old way to this, but in her old society, as well as in
Akhbreed culture, looks outweighed anything else most every
time. Nobody ever seemed to look beyond, look inside. That
was even this hangup the Akhbreed had with the Changewind
victims. Those Masalurians, at least according to Boolean,
still had the same minds, personalities, souls, whatever. They
just looked really bizarre now, but no more bizarre than the
native colonials had looked, nor than the Akhbreed looked to
the colonials.

But something in the back of her mind wondered if maybe
she wasn't just as guilty of that. She'd never once put the
make on Dorion, who was no worse-looking and better-
looking than some or most of her old "clients" back on
Tubikosa, but she'd fallen overboard for the handsome, sexy,
romantic Halagar, Mister Macho, and look at what he'd been
inside. Could that train of thought be right? Could she be just
as guilty of what she condemned others for behaving? It was
a troubling thought.

They passed over the border once more, this time far easier
than going the opposite way. Even the magic sight was gone;
the null just glowed in the same way it had when she'd first
seen it, but enough so she could see the rebel emplacements.
There seemed a *lot* more of them.

The Covantian side seemed, paradoxically, smaller than
she'd remembered it, although admittedly her memories were
colored by her limited sight and condition at the time. It had
just seemed that there had been wall to wall guys down there
when they'd crossed the first time, and now it was the kind of
makeshift, thin line like the rebels had back then. But the hub
ahead was so dark that for a moment she thought she was
going blind again.

For Sam, the whole place was alive with a glorious glow,
and when they crossed into the hub itself the countryside was
not dark, but lit with a dim but beautiful spectral glow.
Everything, it seemed, had some kind of aura, and each was
unique, both by class and by shape within that class. It was
beautiful—but where were the lights? There were vineyards
and farms and whole towns down there. Even though it was

growing late, there should be lights. Was it a limitation of this new vision, or was something very strange down there?

"I think they're getting smarter than Klittichorn gave them credit for," Boolean's voice came to them. "At least, it seems so. Maybe, just maybe, somebody's gotten paranoid about Changewinds in the hub. There's only a few people and some animals down there. Probably civil guards making sure nobody gets any bright ideas about looting. Either Grotag got the shakes after all, or the kings and nobles did."

"But—you mean it's been evacuated?" Charley asked him. "If so, where would they go? And how?"

"Well, it's just a hunch, but the rebels didn't have enough to mass on every border and left only token forces on one before hitting Masalur. If the one opposite is uncovered, as it might well be, then we'll find they've moved the mass of people to the outer ring and into a safe and secure colony, a bit dispersed and with the bulk of the army to protect them. It's smart. If anybody hits Covanti they're going to cream the best vineyards in the cosmos. If it isn't hit, they'll eventually move back in only a little worse for wear. But to hit 'em in the colonies with precision like they used on my hub, they'd need a Second Rank man of their own on sight to aid in spotting, and they don't have enough to go around at all, let alone spare. If everybody's doing this, he's going to have a real empty victory. Of course, everybody won't, but it looks like the smart ones may get through this. Well, we have to pass very near the center of the city. If Grotag's still holding down the fort we'll know who's scared and who's stupid, and it's the loyal Second Rankers he's really after anyway."

The center city showed lights, but the population was far less dense than it should have been. Clearly a fairly large number of people had decided not to move, or to take the chance, or that the risk was in somebody's head, but, still, there couldn't have been more than ten or fifteen percent of the people left. The exception was the big castle in the center, which, to Sam, Dorion, and Boolean, blazed with a light so bright it was almost impossible to look at.

"So Grotag's still at home and holding fast," Boolean noted. "Well, thank the Lord for civilian government and some common sense. It goes to show how useless power is without brains. A few top adepts could hold that shield convincingly and Grotag could protect himself and his people at their side. What a jerk!''

Once beyond the city, there seemed to be far more activity and a lot more life, and it increased as they closed in close to the border. Clearly the evacuation was still in progress and this was the side possibly left undefended by the rebels. They weren't going quite there, though, but angled off to the north, skirting the border, and came upon a town that looked very normal and undisturbed and still with some life in it. The border towns *would* be the last to go in any event, of course, and might not, since they wouldn't be at Ground Zero or near it. The country areas of Masalur hadn't been touched by the Changewind except for one narrow swath towards the exit point. These people were just as safe at home.

Down now, not quite to the town, but to a small house on top of a hill overlooking that town, settling down right in the front yard, as it were. Sam and Kira recognized it at once, but it was strange to the others.

Boolean got off, and Dorion slid off his and came over and helped Charley up off hers. She made almost a tearing sound when she did rise, as if she'd been glued to or stuck to the thing.

There was a light on in the front window, and before anyone could approach the front door, it opened, and a pleasant, sweet-looking gray-haired little old lady toddled out and looked at them, then smiled sweetly.

"I've been expecting you," said Etanalon.

Etanalon looked around quizzically at the group. She nodded to Kira and said, "Her I know, but you—" pointing to Charley, "you look like the one who was here but you are not. And you," she went on, pointing to Sam, "you I know as well. Oh, dear. Has the mirror erred? Have you starved yourself for months to get to that state?"

Sam laughed. "No, it's Boolean's tricks. We're kind'a twins, and Boolean switched our bodies around."

Etanalon sighed and nodded. "Ah, yes, that explains it. You, skinny one, should eat something. Anything. I have some find food and snacks in the kitchen." She looked again at Charley. "But you, my dear . . . I sense great conflict and unhappiness in you. Perhaps we might do something for you." She turned to Dorion. "And you, young man, should get some pants on!"

"No time now for all that should be done," Boolean told her. "I want to be out of Covanti entirely before a good search is launched. Anybody else?"

"Yobi will meet us en route," she told him. "It is cutting it close, but what can Klittichorn have up there? We know the rogues and mental midgets he employs in the field, so what sort of competition can he have on hand?"

"Probably adepts he elevated himself without going through the niceties," the sorceror replied. "That makes them unknowns and thus more dangerous. The best guess I have is that he uses three of them on some kind of mock-up of Akahlar to triangulate and hold the position, then he opens the weak point and the Storm Princess captures and guides the storm. But that still leaves their four Second Rank against our three. Not good odds when one is Klittichorn and the other three are Klittichorn hand-picked and trained."

"Bosh. What kind of experience can they have? Those three have most certainly been concentrated in their training on the single goal of making this work. You have a mental hang-up on Klittichorn, though, which could prove our undoing. Are you certain you wouldn't like to face the mirror?"

Boolean gave a dry chuckle. "I'll handle him, don't worry."

Sam looked at Etanalon wide-eyed. "You are going to help us? I thought you were above this sort of thing."

"No one should be above crushing evil, dear," the sorceress responded. "I have been sitting here treating the individual ills of Akahlar so long, I seem to have temporarily lost my perspective. Just as I could no longer work for the system I found oppressive, so can I not sit idly by while whole masses of people are destroyed or driven mad. Some madnesses are such that they do not know they are mad and so will never seek treatment. Klittichorn is the sort of insanity that visits its madness on the innocent. The man is suffering but he is taking it out on everyone else. I can not sit idly by and let that happen. It was the two of you who made me doubt, but only when Masalur was so brutally assaulted did I realize that Boolean was right."

"I'm going to need to use your lab to get in touch with my people and make certain everything is set up," Boolean told her. "Sam, you come, too. We want to discuss a few things. The rest of you just hang loose; raid the pantry if you want, but I'd suggest sleep."

Etanalon, Boolean, and Sam went into the back and down into the depths of the hill where the sorceress's laboratory was, leaving the rest.

"Yobi, too," Dorion breathed. "I can hardly believe it! She hardly ever moves from her lair for *anything*."

"I think Boolean's right," Kira told them. "I think we should pick some comfortable spots in here and get what rest we can. We don't know just when we'll have to move long, hard, and fast. I don't sleep—nights—so I can keep a sort of watch. I know this place and I'm used to it."

They gave Charley the couch, but she found it too uncomfortable to sleep, and felt a little too keyed up. The others, from Boday to Dorion, had no such problems, and Kira was back snacking in the kitchen. She hauled herself up after a while, feeling a need for fresh air, quietly opened the door, and walked outside.

It was a beautiful night and, with the town below, an almost picture postcard scene. The air was warm, with just enough of a gentle breeze to make it pleasant; the kind of atmosphere and setting that made the troubles seem as distant as home, and allowed you to pretend, if only for a few moments, that nothing was wrong.

A strange, small shape moved nearby, startling her and causing an involuntary cry.

"Sorry," said the strange voice of Cromil. "Didn't mean to make you jump, although sometimes it's fun scaring folks."

She relaxed. "That's all right. I'm surprised you're not down with *them*, though, and that you're talking to me."

The little green familiar spat. "Nothing but boring crap down there. No interest at all to Cromil. Just talking about ways to get themselves killed is all. Got to hand it to him, though. If anybody can pull it all off, Boolean can. Suckered you good, didn't he?"

She frowned and looked at the tiny shape in the darkness. "What do you mean by that?"

"You never figured out how his mind works, have you? So pleasant, so chatty, you'll hand over your jewels and beg him to steal the rest. Gets so complicated sometimes he crosses

himself up—almost did with the two of you. Had all this in
mind from the start, he did. Surprised he actually got this far,
though. The others all wound up bad.''

''Others?''

''Sure. Your friend wasn't the only Storm Princess dupe he
managed to snatch from Klittichorn's grasp. Not many, but a
few. Took bets on 'em, we did, only neither of us would bet
that your friend would be the one to make it this far.''

''Bets? What—what happened to the others? Where are
they?''

The little green monkey shrugged in very human fashion.
''Some dead. That's the easiest state to accomplish in this
place. Others trapped, caught by Klittichorn's men, or spells,
or whatever. Started you all off pretty equal and pretty low,
he did. Wound you all up and let you run. Put the pressure
under you when he had to, otherwise just let you run. Set you
far away from him and sit there and tell you to find him. Kick
you in the ass if you sat down or gave up. A kind of race in
the end. First one to reach Boolean wins.''

Her jaw dropped a bit. ''But—why? You mean he could
have pulled us to him at any time? That he *caused* all that we
went through?''

''Not specifics. Bailed you out when he could, but mostly
you were on your own. See, the winner gets to go up against
the Storm Princess, right? Practiced, accomplished, one tough
broad, driven by hate. Think of yourself when you got dumped
here. Would your friend have been any match for the Storm
Princess and sorcerers then? Would she even have understood
the dangers or her own self? She'd have been a patsy. Chopped
to pieces out of ignorance, hang-ups, you name it. Took
education, see? Had to learn about Akahlar, about wizards
and spells and all that stuff. All of you were naive, dumb,
impractical airheads—typical teenagers. No good to go against
them. You had to learn the rules, learn what evil really was,
and to separate it from stupidity, which often looks the same.
You had to fight some battles, get victimized, even abused.
Not planned—we just knew it would happen. Could you
cope? Could you survive? Help out when we could and you
couldn't, sure, when we could, but that's all. You're the only
two that made it.''

She sighed. When she saw how close she and Sam had

both come to buying the farm, it was even more sobering. Right up to the last minute. . . . She wasn't sure if she was elated or depressed as hell by the news. "I see," she answered. "Both of us had to be degraded, raped, tortured through spells, chased by gunmen, undergo fire and flood—all as a *test?*"

"Not a test—an endurance contest. It wasn't totally random, either. The more you progressed, the more the destiny threads pointed to your friend. Boolean took something of a chance when he ordered the Demon of the Jewel of Omak to make certain she got pregnant. He had to know it would start a chain reaction that would lead to this point. However, there were indications Klittichorn was attempting to find the proper mate for the Storm Princess—strictly for the one purpose, of course, but satisfying the rebel's own sense of propriety and quieting disturbing rumors about her having a stable of female slave lovers, which was true but politically inconvenient—and your friend, thanks to her weight and her unconventional mate and lifestyle, seemed safest at the time."

"The demon . . . *made* her get pregnant?" Charley was appalled.

"Well, it's not as bad as it sounds. It simply implanted in her mind a natural curiosity about the normal way of doing things and the fact that she could use the hypnotic powers to do it, so, at the point when she dropped an egg, as it were, at the exact prime moment, she did it with one of the wagon train crew. You remember that."

In a way, it was a relief, even though it galled her to think how Sam had been so manipulated. At least the child wasn't a child of one of those gang-raping monsters. It was rape, of course—by Boolean, sort of—but so long as Sam didn't *know* it and thought it was her idea, Sam wouldn't think it so. That didn't really help Charley's own feelings, that Boolean had treated Sam as a thing, a piece of meat, the same way Halagar had treated Charley, but facts were facts, and now *she* had the kid inside *her*. So had she been sort of raped by this third hand? It was too complicated an issue for a night like this.

"But almost immediately after we were all caught in the flood, most of the train was killed, there was the capture, the tortures and rapes, and then we were split up in the Kudaan. Some help Boolean was there in our survival.''

"He didn't plan it that way, but who would have expected Sam to use her powers so soon? Or that the mercenaries under the Blue Witch would hit that particular train in their search for Mandan gold cloaks to sell to the rebels? The mess happened, and it took Boolean and Yobi to straighten it out, that's all. When the two of you surfaced at Yobi's without Sam, Crim was contacted to track her down. Until then he'd been tracking you, thinking you were all still together.''

"Yeah, but we were only found and rescued because Dorion happened to see us and saw my resemblance to the Storm Princess. Lucked out is what you mean.''

"Crim would have tracked you, most likely, in the end. Luck is simply an amateur's term for the threads of destiny that are woven at conception. It's why some people have 'miraculous' escapes and others die in freakish happenings. The threads can be aborted by conflict with others, but Boolean read Sam's and it was a long thread. He and Yobi intervened, got Sam out of Pasedo's, got her mind mostly back, and she'd learned a lot about herself during that period—and so had you.''

"So why didn't Boolean just order Crim to take us to Yobi so we'd be together again and then bring us to him, or him to us, right then?''

"Because you weren't ready. You were by now hardened survivors, but you were not ready. Sam was still at war with herself; she was still spending almost all of her time trying to escape her destiny and her obligations rather than facing them willingly. The same went for you, really, so together you would just reinforce each other. You both had grown hard, pragmatic, questioning, but neither of you looked at anyone else, not even each other. You were still turned inward, without a sense of obligation or any willingness to sacrifice for the common cause. It took Halagar to make you see what you'd really become, to see what others perceived you to be, what you thought you wanted or could accept. For Sam, it was easier. She always felt an obligation to others, to her friends, but her lack of ego, of self-esteem, of self-acceptance, and self-worth was driving her mad. In desperation, we had a magician refer her here, to Etanalon. It made her accept herself and resign herself to her duty, but no more. We decided we had to go with what we had, but the unexpected diversion that allowed her to feel normal, turned out to be a blessing even though it panicked us and almost cost us the game.''

"Normal? Four husbands in a jungle house in the sticks?''

"Normal to *her*. It gave her something besides a lifetime with Boday to fight for. It showed friends, people she was closed to, dying—and for her, basically. It put *her* in the position of seeing others do what was expected of *her*. It broke the last barrier. She's ready now. In many ways she has far more experience and toughness than her foe. And you were right there, also ready, to play your own part.''

Her eyebrows went up. "Me? What part? I was a decoy, maybe, but if it wasn't for my own thinking I'd have drank a potion back in Tubikosa and become permanently a mindless courtesan. I practically did, anyway.''

"Well, it was your body, not your mind, that was important in the plan. You were, after all, an add-in, a bonus, there to give Sam the body she needed when the time came, and take on hers and keep the child from harm. We needed only the receptacle, and with only the receptable the transfer would have been easily done. That you remained mentally alive as well actually complicated matters. Had we not been able to keep an eye on you, so to speak, we might well have had to make other arrangements.''

"An eye . . . Dorion, you mean?''

"Of course not. Shadowcat. Like me, your familiar existed both in this plane and in his native one. There distance and even duration are meaningless. He and I discussed everything. We agreed that you should not betray your true self to Halagar lest he beat or possibly kill you. You were far safer when you appeared to have no mind and presented therefore no threat. He truly liked you, which is rare for a familiar. Perhaps too much. He was not supposed to kill Halagar. Boolean would have retrieved you upon his return from seeing what was done to poor Masalur. It caused much consternation that you had vanished, and we overstayed there seeing if we could pick you up on the impulse to come to him. Because of that, Zamofir got there first and all the bloodletting was made necessary. Again, it worked out, as those with true destiny tend to do, but that was the way it was. Because we were late Sam learned duty and sacrifice. Because you finally reached a point where you would rather die, naked, blind, and alone, in a foreign wood than return to being a slave and object in the camp, you learned much, too.''

"You make it sound so cold, so calculating, so callous,'' she said, shaking her head. "Like we were pieces of meat with no rights and no say. Just dolls to make over and play with and never mind the suffering and pain and degradation. Our lives, our *minds,* really meant *nothing* to your master except possible means to his end. And he got just what he wanted, which grates on me. I sit here, fat and ugly and miserable, surrogate mother to somebody else's baby, and Sam's going smiling into maybe worst than death. Somehow, that really pisses me off.''

"That's how wars are fought these days. Maybe they have always been fought that way, with the little folks being ordered to charge into the enemy lines. If they don't they get shot as traitors. If they do, they get shot by the enemy, all so their body can be used as a shield and stepstone by the next guy to get another couple of yards. Yours is an interesting race, that climbed from the muck by little murders, and as you grew in power and experience they became bigger murders. Now you have reached the point on many worlds where you can murder your whole species in a matter of a few minutes and that makes you the zenith of human civilization. Here a madman—and there are always madmen in a society built on murders to scale—intends to install himself as master and then as god. My race has sat back and watched, occasionally intervening over the years to get a better view, in utter fascination at this, and some of us spend eternity arguing the points you people raise. You object to being a tool, an object, pushed, shoved, and manipulated by powerful forces beyond your comprehension in the cause of stopping something horrible. Yet if those powers did not do so, would we not be guilty of allowing the greater crime to happen to the greater number? It is a fascinating point. Even your gods reflect this. You are pawns of omnipotent beings. You pray for mercy, for forgiveness, for victory in battle, and the death of your enemies. You sacrifice to them, either really or symbolically, with blood and ritual cannibalism. You are *born* pawns. It is in your nature. It is only when you notice that you are that you object."

She looked over at the tiny figure in the darkness. "Just what *are* you, Cromil?"

"An alternative reality. One from a universe so different that you could not even comprehend it, where the very laws of nature are so different as to be madness to you, as yours is to us. In the long distant past, we learned to use the weak points created by the out-rushing Changewind, and, being curious, we tagged along. We need form here, so we take form here; otherwise it is all incomprehensible madness to us. We deal with the powerful, the high priests or sorcerers or whatever. We give some service, they give some things we want. It's worked out pretty well over the years."

"And what *do* creatures like you want from us?" she asked it. "To satisfy curiosity? To explore? More knowledge? Blood? What?"

Cromil's answer stunned her and stung her and she reeled from the impact of its words.

"Amusement," it said.

For a while she said nothing more to the creature because there was nothing more to say. Who was whose god, and who was whose plaything? Who pushed who, and for what motives? Was anybody, even Boolean, even Klittichorn, really free, really a master of fate, really in control?

"You going to tell anybody any of this?" Cromil asked curiously.

"Maybe. Maybe not. It's not exactly what Sam needs to know right now, and your own feelings I suspect are pretty well known to the sorcerers."

"Oh, yes."

"Tell me—does Klittichorn have a familiar?"

"Oh, they *all* do. It's kind of necessary to the higher functions of magic. We're very loyal to whichever side we happen to be on, you see, but we tend to stay out of the showdowns. We prefer to watch."

"I'll bet." She yawned in spite of herself. "Well, you've depressed the hell out of me, anyway. I guess, for everybody's good, I ought to try to sleep."

"Your role in this, except for mother, is about to end," the familiar told her. "The big show is about to begin now. We are actively wagering on the outcome."

She picked up a rock and threw it at him, but it missed.

To Charley's surprise, they flew next to Masalur, but only Boolean and Cromil went to the hub; the rest, under Etanalon's powers, went east, where she and Dorion had thought of going, and into a colony world that seemed peaceful and virgin. They flew out over a broad, sparkling blue, tropical ocean, landing eventually on a good-sized island, perhaps thirty miles across and twenty miles wide, the largest of a string of isolated volcanic islands. The place looked like those pictures in the magazines of tropical paradise; of coconut palms and virgin sandy beaches, with banana and mango and other tropical fruits—or reasonable cousins thereof—growing wild all over. It was a gorgeous place, the only inhabitants of which appeared to be birds and insects.

There was one structure on the island; a small but comfortable-looking beach house overlooking a picture postcard tropical lagoon. Inside they were surprised to find two bedrooms with big, comfortable, modern beds with spring mattresses, plus a living room and dinette area and something of a den overlooking the lagoon itself, all comfortably furnished if not with the best, then with homey touches appropriate to the setting and decor. Rattan chairs, that sort of thing. The bathroom was an outhouse—somebody had even carved a half-moon in the door—showers were available at a pretty tropical waterfall about a hundred yards into the jungle, in back of the house. There were oil lamps, storage places, and an outdoor covered grill. No electricity or immediate running water, but it looked like somebody's idea of a perfect tropical hideaway.

Boolean arrived about six hours behind them; by then they'd already found the ponds that trapped the fish at low tide, and were feeling quite pleasant. The sorcerer, however, was not alone.

The two creatures were both almost cartoons of extremely erotic girls, but they were not—at least not the way Charley and Sam and the Akhbreed thought of girls. For one thing, they were absolutely identical twins. For another, they had incredibly smooth pea-green skin that seemed almost to lack pores, and glistened a bit in the light, with lips of darkest green and

emerald eyes in a sea of pale olive. What appeared to be thick
if short dark green hair had the consistency and solidity of
brambles, not hiding at all ears like delicate, tiny seashells;
and their feet each had three wide, webbed, almost birdlike
toes. They had four thin arms that seemed a bit more rigid
than human arms and ended in three long identical fingers
that closed on things almost clawlike, but were soft and as
dexterous as human fingers, and the lower set appeared to be
on ball joints, able to reach forward or back equally, and four
small but firm breasts, the top pair looking normal but hanging just slightly on the lower pair. And, odder still, they had
thin, prehensile tails that did not come out of the spine but out
of the point between the vagina and the rectum, about a foot
long and ending in a structure that looked like a . . . well, penis.

They were the objects of a lot of attention, and it was good
they were not self-conscious about things. Everyone had the
same thought: *so these were what the Changewind made of
the Masalurians. . . .*

"Folks, these are Modar and Sobroa," Boolean told them.
"Don't ask me which is which now, but you'll tell when talking
to them. Modar used to be six-two and all male, and Sobroa
was about this size and the best-looking female adept I ever
came across. They were among the small staff who volunteered
to maintain the shield and defenses and remain at their posts."

"If our form shocks *you*," said one, in a strange, two-
toned kind of voice, "think of what it was for us to suddenly
find ourselves this. I hope you will get used to us, because we
have not yet gotten used to us and we learn more every day. I
fear it will be years before we learn everything."

"What matters," Boolean told them, "is that Sobroa was a
trained healer and a midwife. She has no powers now, but she
has delivered a *lot* of babies and she knows basic first aid and
medicine. Modar was my librarian and something of a romantic and dreamer on the side. He found and mostly designed
this place, and there's nothing about it he doesn't know."

"Do you like it?" asked the other one, in a voice that was
identical to the first yet somehow different in tone and accent.

"It's *beautiful*," Sam responded. "Was this a kind of
retreat?"

Boolean nodded. "When we had to get away—me or any
of the staff—we came here. There's no shipping to speak of

on this world, and the population is concentrated in the less tropical climate zones for reasons that would be obvious if you saw them. These islands are a thousand miles from anyone and are likely to stay that way, at least for a number of years. Food, water, all the basics almost fall into your lap. But since it's a Masalurian colony, I highly doubt if anybody would look for you here. Anyone here now is welcome to remain here. Charley, you, and Dorion, of course. Just remember that you are the guests of Sobroa and Modar, they're not your servants. We will be leaving in the morning, and we won't be back until it's done."

It was tempting, really tempting, but first Boday, then Crim, talked to Boolean.

"Boday has not found her Susama to once more give her up. She will go, and if she can be of help to the last she will do so! And if, by miracle of miracles, she survives, she will immortalize the greatest battle in the history of the cosmos!"

"Just not knowing would drive us nuts," Crim told him. "Maybe we can do nothing, and maybe we're crazy, but I want to be there at the end, and I feel inside that Kira does as well. We already almost died for this."

"You both are welcome and may be useful," Boolean told them. "But, remember, if it's you or the enemy, you'll be left to the fates. And if it turns out that you can do nothing, then stay out of the way. Now get some sleep."

The goodbyes were tearful, with Charley doing a lot of hugging and kissing and crying and breaking up Sam and Boday as well, but then it was time. They who would remain watched the others climb on their enchanted saddles, rise up into the burgeoning sunrise, take one last loop around, and then become tiny specks and vanish in the warm light of day.

Dorion looked at Charley. "You wish you were going with them, don't you?" he asked her.

She just smiled and didn't answer.

"Well," he sighed, "so do I. May the gods who brought us all to this point be with them still."

High in the air over the sparkling blue ocean, Sam felt her breakfast remaining lumped in her throat, but she looked ahead, not back. She hadn't slept much, but she felt very wide awake, very keyed up.

My god, it's really happening, she told herself. *Here we go!*

· 12 ·

The Citadel at the Edge of Chaos

WHEN KLITTICHORN HAD dubbed himself the Horned Demon of the Snows he wasn't just doing it to make himself sound colorful.

All her time in Akahlar, Sam had spent in the subtropical or tropical belt, until she'd almost forgotten there was any such thing as winter or that cold meant like the inside of a freezer, not merely a bit of a chill after an intense rain.

Their journey northward had turned steadily if slowly colder by degrees as they passed each border or hub. Boolean was able to put in a perspective she could somewhat understand by asking her to think of Tubikosa as perhaps northern Australia or New Guinea; Masalur would be somewhere around northeast Africa, maybe Egypt, although with a lot better rainfall. Klittichorn, however, had his domain in the equivalent of northern Sweden or perhaps even Iceland or Greenland, up near or on the Arctic Circle.

It was hard for Sam to think of Akahlar as a planet like Earth—in fact, the planet Earth itself. It was too different, too exotic, without the land or sea or other areas to make any comparisons. The intense pull and hold of the Seat of Probability, like a giant sun on a different and lower dimensional plane, held Akahlar where it was, and had also slowly, over the millennia, pulled the other Earths "nearest" to it down so that they intersected for short periods, one atop the other. The hubs and nulls were the only places where, because the worlds were round, the intersection did not take place, and, as such, they were the only parts of the real world of Akahlar that had been able to develop.

Other than the increasing cold, the other thing Sam noticed

as they travelled northward was that the intersection points, the parts of the colonies that overlapped Akahlar's reality, grew shorter and more irregular, often much longer on one side of a hub than another. Beyond the Arctic and Antarctic Circles, there was virtually no overlap, just ice and snow and occasional nulls to nowhere in patches here and there. It was for this reason, as well as its hostile environment and remoteness, that Klittichorn had chosen it. Almost no one lived there; just about no one wanted to go there.

But in the region he had picked there were high volcanic ranges providing unexpected warmth among the glacial ice, and the means to tap geothermal heat and power. In a small valley surrounded by glacier-clad volcanic mountain peaks, he had built not just his home and laboratory but a small city, populated by those who were the outcasts of Akhbreed society. Here the political malcontents, the magicians with grudges real or imagined, the disgraced soldiers and criminal classes, could gather with absolute immunity and safety and with a level of comfort and protection that a similar area like the Kudaan Wastes could not provide. Here resided the cream of the outcasts; not merely Akhbreed but colonials as well, picked up by Klittichorn or his agents from their own worlds and brought here to help their master plans.

Klittichorn's great, dull-red castle, with its menorahlike eight towers, dominated the scene. It was not merely his own home and base, but the workplace for many of the people. Below it, on the valley floor, stretched the comfortable and hyper-insulated houses of the people—heated by geothermal steam which also provided their hot water and even their cooking medium—stretching out on either side of the central greenhouses wherein were raised the best food crops adequate for all their needs. Beyond, the massive herds of reindeer and other arctic animals provided the sources of meat as well as the work animals for the society. Just viewing it from the air, as frigid as it was, the region impressed the hell out of all of them. None, not even Boolean, had seen it before.

There were six of them now; all were clad in layer after layer of heavy furs, gloves, you name it, to withstand the bitter cold, but while it was enough to keep them alive and out of harm's way from the elements, it didn't make any of them feel warm or comfortable.

Yobi had joined them in the air over Hanahbak, a thousand miles to the southeast, her great lower bulk covered with a tremendous fur cloak. She looked as if she were just floating there, a being who was her own craft, and if she used a saddle or other conveyance they had not seen it.

"Is that it? Is that where we have to go?" Sam asked, now used to being able to talk through muffled layers and masks and still have the same power of speech as if they were all sitting together comfortably around a fire inside a snug lodge.

"No, I just wanted to take a look at what he'd built," Boolean replied. "I think we're all impressed, although it doesn't really surprise me. He never did anything halfway."

"The scale of it surprises and shocks me," Yobi put in. "I had this picture of a frigid castle redoubt in the middle of wastes, not a somewhat grand city. Didn't you say the fellow was from a *tropical* place?"

"He was, but humans are very adaptable," the sorcerer responded. "He could never have accomplished all this in the south, not with all the people and politics and the Guild snooping about. Besides, look at the steam slowly rising from the ground all around. There's plenty of heat available here for almost anything you need. I bet inside those places, even the castle, it's as warm as Masalur. And if you look at the way the heat shimmers go, the odds are you can get from almost anyplace to anyplace using heated underground tunnels there. Unless you're into skiing or herding reindeer, you might never have to go outside or feel the cold."

"Then where is the man himself?" Crim asked.

"Not far, but better hidden and independent," Boolean told him. "In fact, I think we'll find a reasonable place to make camp here, and then send you and Boday to check it out for us."

"Why not everybody?" Sam asked him.

"I think he knows we're near, or coming," the sorcerer responded, "but I don't want to give him any free shots at us. He has monitoring spells all over here to detect people like us, but he feels he has nothing to fear from ordinary, nonmagical people. Not that there won't be some guards, so care will have to be taken, but to present the three of us to him within sight of his headquarters would be to draw targets on ourselves and give him a few free shots. No, let's keep him guessing as to our strength and location and true nature.''

"You don't think he'll panic just by the awareness that we are close?" Yobi asked, concerned.

"Not so long as the Storm Princess knows and feels the presence of the child half a hemisphere away, no. He seeks godlike powers, but there is no way he can have godlike omnipotence. I think our little trick with the switch will fool him because it's too subtle and too unprecedented. I know the way his mind works as well as anyone, at least on the surface level."

They set up a camp back out of the weather in an old lava tube. The outside was freezing and nasty, but heat radiated from the walls within the tube, creating a frozen waterfall where it broke to the outside and some level of comfort within.

Crim surveyed the tube. "Comfortable, but I feel very vulnerable in here," he commented. "If anybody discovers we're here, they could just magically turn the lava back on, or even give us a wall of water, and we'd be through."

"That kind of magic is always telegraphed," Yobi assured him. "We have enough to prevent that sort of thing, so relax. More important is the two of you and whether you can really handle those flying saddles without one or another of us propping you up. You'll have to go in low and be very unobtrusive."

"Will he not see the spell that makes the saddles fly?" Boday asked her worriedly.

"Probably not. It's too minor a spell and there are probably thousands around a place like that. It would be drowned out by the weight of all those already laid on, much as a whisper is drowned by the roar of a crowd. Take care, though. If any of the sentinels that are almost certain to be guarding the place spot you, then all bets are off."

Crim looked a bit nervous. "You sure we can do this and be back before sunset? I don't want Kira to come out under these conditions."

"I fear we will be deprived of poor Kira's company, but for perhaps an hour or so, if that," Boolean told him. "It is late spring here and we're close to the Arctic Circle if not slightly past it. If we are, we won't meet her at all, for this time of year the sun does not set there. Were we in the Antarctic, we wouldn't see you. Cheer up, my friends. We may be in the jaws of death, but at least for now we are absolutely safe from vampires.''

Crim and Boday did a bit of practice flying around the peaks and valleys near the cave and both decided that they were pretty confident.

"It'll take you about a half hour to get there," Boolean told them, "and spend only as much time as you absolutely need to get the feel of the place, its tangible defenses, looks, and the like. If you are not back here within three hours we will have to assume that you were seen, possibly captured, and we will go immediately. Understand? Boday, I'll expect you to be able to sketch it when we get back, with Crim's memory as a check. Temporarily, you'll have to be a realist. Accuracy counts. The odds are, when we go in, we'll only get the one shot. Either we go all the way, or that's it.''

She shrugged. "Boday is great at all art. She will do what you wish and better that you dream!''

Sam hugged her. "Take care, now. If we're all gonna die in this, don't you be the first.''

Boday laughed. "The Gods of Chaos have woven our destinies too tightly! Boday has suffered too much to die now before she achieves immortality through the works she has yet to create! Come, big man! Let us see this fortress of evil!''

Sam watched them go, feeling nervous for both of them and also for what would come after. She felt guilty realizing that, of all the people here, there was a hierarchy of expend-ability, and she was the only one absolutely sacred.

Now they could only sit in the volcanic warmth, munch on a few cookies and some strong drink brought along for this, and wait. There was something strangely ridiculous about huddling fur-clad in a cave with these three master sorcerers, who could restore a town overnight, heal the most gravely wounded, make saddles fly, and do all sorts of miracles, all of whom were also huddling here in furs and looking as miserable as she felt.

"It's the fat, dear," Etanalon said to her.

"Huh?"

"You feel colder than you ever have. I can see you shiver-ing like you had a fever even in this relative comfort and warmth. You probably know that most people who are native to cold areas have yellow skins. The yellow is a layer of fat, even on the thin ones, that provides extra insulation, but fat is a premium to them. You have fleshed out a bit on the journey here, but you still eat like a bird because your friend starved that body and shrunk that stomach to the size of a walnut. One wonders about young girls' sense of proportion when they will starve themselves rather than dare be pleasantly and comfortably plump. In hard times, the fat women survived to have babies, the thin ones died out. In many societies a bit of plumpness is considered sexy, but, these days, everyone seems to want to be a skeleton. I believe that if I were a goddess, I'd make a new standard for beauty.''

Yobi gave one of her cackles. ''Imagine you or *any* of us as gods and goddesses! I suppose I do somewhat resemble some of those monstrous idols some societies worship, but I'm afraid I'd die laughing at prayers to statues of *me*.''

''Admit it. You're here because you think our friend out there has found the key,'' Boolean noted, pointed a finger at her. ''For ten thousand years at least sorcerers have tried for that state, and failed, mostly miserably. The lucky ones died. Godhood. The ability to summon and *direct* the forms of order out of what Chaos sends. Not random, like the Changewinds, but deliberate. Yet, like the winds, generalized, or as specific as the simplest and most direct spell. The power to right wrongs, change minds, mold and shape civilizations, create.''

''And destroy,'' Cromil commented, peeking out from a fold of Boolean's coat. ''You're talking about a man—or woman—having the *power* of a god. There's more to being a god than that. You're afraid Klittichorn's going to get the power. Big deal. Would you really be any better at it—any of you—or just different? Power doesn't confer wisdom, nor make you omnipotent. It just makes an ordinary person with an extraordinary love of power able to exercise it, with all his or her hang-ups and problems.''

''The voice of wisdom from the netherhells,'' Boolean commented dryly.

''Figures. We been talking with people like you for thousands of years and nobody really heard anything from us they didn't want to hear,'' the familiar retorted.

"I suppose that demons and imps and the like could do better at it, having all that wisdom and a superior civilization," Yobi said sarcastically.

"Of course not. Why do you think they call it the netherhells, anyway, and why's everybody around here always cursing somebody to go to Hell? You know what Hell is? It's *boring*, that's what it is. Deadly dull. That's why we have to come up here to have any fun."

Sam shivered and looked around the cave. "Yeah, ain't we got fun."

"Like, who says this guy would ever be the first one to reach First Rank, anyway?" the familiar went on, ignoring the commentary. "All those universes, all those worlds, and they all got all those gods. Old men in the sky, creatures with wings, creatures that demand sacrifices and have like eight arms, fish gods, horse gods, you name it. Jealous gods, philandering gods, gods who curse men for not being cruel enough in war in their names—who are looked upon as ending war and bringing heaven to earth anyway? We've had our *fill* of gods up here. That's why demons are never on God's side. All the gods are jerks, that's why. So what's one more jerk in the cosmos?"

Boolean looked down at him, frowning. "I wish I knew when you were being cynical and making trouble and when you were telling the truth."

"I think it would be too damn complicated to be a god," Sam commented. "Even if you *were* pure of motive and the power didn't corrupt you, which it almost surely would. I mean, every time I think about somethin' I really would want to change—hate, envy, greed, jealousy, hunger, war—I can't figure out how to do it, unless we make everybody everywhere like, well, the Changewind did to Masalur. They're all absolutely identical, not even sex to cause trouble, in a place you described to me as a swamp that seemed pretty much the same. If it's warm all the time and everybody looks the same there's no need for clothes, or fashion. If they make their own food inside, somehow, and maybe only need to drink water or something, then there's no hunger. Probably no government, neither, since when everybody was the same who would follow somebody when you couldn't even tell who was who?"

"I have a feeling that Masalurian society is going to be

more complicated than you think," Boolean noted, "although, I must admit, it'll complicate itself because their minds didn't change and they already think differently than ones born and raised like that. Still, the one thing that's not identical is their brains. Their I.Q.s and their aptitudes will be different. In all the colonies and in all the parallel worlds of the outplanes not corrupted by the Akhbreed, we find more cultural similarities than physical ones. Geography, resources, needs of all kind shape competition which heads to the rest, and having only one sex doesn't solve that problem if it still takes two to make a baby. The human need for companionship, closeness, seems overpowering even without the baby thing. Otherwise homosexuals would never feel jealousy. No, I'm afraid you're right. The only way to cure the ills of the human condition, even with godlike powers, is to make people inhuman, either machinelike or perhaps incorporeal beings like the demons and imps, who are so bored they come up here for their entertainment and often meddle just to cause trouble and see what results. Still. . . ."

"Still, you'd like to have the power and find out," Cromil finished smugly. "Only if you can't have it, you sure don't want the good old Horned One to have it, because his vision of insanity is different than *your* vision of insanity."

"Enough, imp! You can be sent back home for a very long time!" Yobi snapped.

Boolean looked over at Sam. "Wouldn't you really take a crack at it, if you could, though? Be honest."

"Only if I had to," she sighed. "Honestly—power like that without the genius to figure out all the angles to using it . . . well, you'd just be some kind of corrupted power monger, or you'd be real careful how or if you used it, 'cause you might not figure all the angles. I think I'm more scared of what it would do to me, or what I might do to lots of others, to want it. I got more sense than that."

Boolean shifted uncomfortably in his furs. "I know I'd always be warm," he muttered. "Still, the puzzle drives me nuts. I've always been able to do anything Roy has, to understand or come up with anything he has, *after* he's worked it out and told me it's possible. The elements are all there, like pieces in a puzzle, but they all don't fit. Okay, we need a Storm Princess because she's immune to the Changewind, and we need a sorcerer because the Storm Princess's abilities are natural and couldn't cope with the massive variables involved in actually shaping reality. And we need power—lots of power. Lots of Changewinds, not just to knock out or nullify the other Second Rankers but to feed—what? Storm Princesses are some kind of power regulators just by their very existence, temporizers of the Changewinds, safety factors on each world. But why in hell are they all lesbians? What can the sex preference have to do with it all? It's insane. Yet you take that sexual preference thing, the least of it all, and the magic goes away. Why?''

Not even the one with all the attributes had the answer. Still, Sam had to wonder. Her? Little Sam Buell? Somehow protecting her world from the major effects of the Changewinds depended on her just being alive, living there someplace? Made no sense at all. And whatever it was, it came natural, like breathing. It wasn't something you thought about or even necessarily knew you had.

She had a sudden thought. *Wait a minute—this Storm Princess, the one just over there, wasn't an unconscious regulator. She* had *been, but not now. She drew that Changewind right into downtown Masalur hub! She made it march round and round until it covered maybe two thirds of the hub. That's what this was all about, wasn't it? Somebody who could* control *the Changewind, deliberate like, not like breathing.*

Like she had done. She'd already done it with regular storms. She'd banished the Sudogs, called lightning down to fry a gunman, summoned a great storm in the Kudaan, and then, in Covanti, she'd stood her ground and actually *deflected* a Changewind! She could control the storm like any other, and was immune from its effects other than getting wind-blown and wet. But she couldn't speak to the Maelstrom, which was still just a great storm and not something with thought and deliberateness. Its effects were random, like any storm's; the order that formed from it, bizarre as it might look, held together, made sense, thanks to those laws Boolean talked about. The ones concerning how the universes formed out of one big bang and how snowflakes are so pretty and intricate. A god could somehow talk to those forces, shape those laws, so they formed or did what he or she wanted. It would be like giving a mind, a brain, to a Changewind maelstrom.

All these sorcerers spent half their time doing miracles, making magic, and none of them *believed* in magic. It was all natural laws and math and all that. The whole idea that one girl in each world was born with these powers and did this regulation bit, identical girls, they explained simply by noting that regulatory mechanisms always developed in nature, and that the results of the laws of chaos didn't necessarily make sense, they just accomplished what they had to.

"Boolean?" she prompted, and he looked over and raised his eyebrows. "Who are the Storm Princesses in the world that aren't human. Akhbreed types, or whatever you want to call people like you and me? How can there be somebody like *me* in worlds where people breathe water or have horns and tails and all that? Who are *their* regulators?"

"Huh? They don't have them. Or, if there was a common ancestor or thread to the Storm Princess mold, they've been able to mutate or change somehow. That's always been a mystery, of course. Maybe you don't really have to be physically identical. Maybe you only have to be physically identical within the same racial stock. None of the Akhbreed are native to here, after all. They dropped down in the more violent maelstroms of the prehistoric past from up around our area. The others, too, must have regulators of some kind, I suppose—unless there are other factors so that they don't need them and we do. Who knows? One can only study the system that chaos sticks us with, we can't read any master plan into it. I know of a few attempts in the ancient literature to find what regulates the others, but they never came to anything. Still, it's another part of the puzzle, isn't it?"

It was—but not as lightly dismissed as he made it seem. Of course, who was she to think on this, when big brains like him couldn't figure it? Still and all, she doubted that those other universes *had* Storm Princesses, at least not on Earth. Maybe someplace else in each big universe humans like them appeared and with them a Storm Princess. Maybe so. Or maybe all those other Earths had something that only the humans lacked.

The little demon said there were lots of gods. Did he mean it? And, if so, which kind was he talking about? The kind of

God she was dragged to church for, or the kind the ancients worshiped that looked like a big Buddha with horns, or what? Or did he see any difference between the worlds of humanity and those who were something else? What if Cromil was telling the truth? What if there really were gods? If those universes had gods, then they wouldn't need Storm Princesses for protection and regulation and all that, right? They'd go from the whims of chance to the control and will of their god.

Fifty million monkeys pounding on typewriters would, given an unlimited amount of time, write the works of Shakespeare.

Her science teacher back in tenth grade had used that as an example on why the Earth was how it was. The universe was so big, it just happened, that's all. Boolean's chaos shit in a nutshell, only her old science teacher hadn't dreamed how big a place it really was.

So fifty million monkeys, given enough time, would write Shakespeare. So the universes, given enough time, would— *develop gods?*

This was getting too heavy for her and she didn't like where it was going, but she couldn't really stop. She didn't have much education, much understanding of things, but maybe all these folks had too much. Suppose, just suppose, in each universe, the system said there'd be a god, or many gods—who knew?—to regulate, to control the Changewinds, to stabilize things like they were never stable in Akahlar. But suppose, just suppose, that whatever made gods didn't always work. It worked most of the time but not all the time, particularly when you got way out, where the rest of the humans were. Suppose all the things needed to make a god just never got together, or never got together *right* there? So they just kept floatin' around, never comin' together. . . .

My god! All the holy wars and all the church singin' and all the Hallelujahs and monks and missionaries. . . . All for different gods created out of need or out of some visions from other universes or maybe out of folks' minds 'cause they knew they ought'a have at least one. All for *nothing?* And her mom joining that real fundamentalist sect and even gettin' divorced from Daddy 'cause he thought they was phonies and all that. All for *nothing?* And her science teacher was right that there was no god, just natural laws, but he was wrong, too. *Most people had gods, but we don't!*

It was such an emotionally unnerving concept that she said nothing about it, didn't even want to bring it up to the others. Maybe it wasn't true—exactly. But, somehow, deep down, she thought it had to be at least part of the answer. And old Klittichorn had figured it, and he'd spent all that time getting together all the things needed to make a god of the Akhbreed, and that was what he was planning to do. . . .

Damn! What sacrilege! What a horrible, horrible thing to even *think*. But she couldn't stop thinking it, even though it made her feel sick and empty inside. Did all Akhbreed lack one, or just some? Oh, jeez. . . .

She just *couldn't* be right. Even if she somehow pushed her own emotions and beliefs aside for the sake of argument, she knew she had to be wrong. *I mean, these people here like Boolean—Professor Lang—are all big brains who been studyin' this their whole lives. I never even got to graduate from high school with my C average and I didn't have the brains for college, anyways. This is crazy thinkin', me pretendin' I got more brains than I got, that's all.*

She wouldn't say nothing to the others; no use in getting laughed at.

Crim and Boday were back in a little over two hours, looking frozen to death. The sorcerers risked a bit of magic to warm them and soothe frostbitten areas, and they were soon able to talk about what they had seen—and what they had not.

Boday took the charcoal pencil and paper from her saddle pack and began to sketch. "You see—on a plateau, like so, with downward slopes and then high mountains around. It does not look like much, except for this bulge here in the center, but we think most of it is underground."

"There are fortifications along the downward slope into a V-shaped notch valley before the high mountains begin," Crim elaborated. "Hard to tell just what they were, but they looked dug in and sheltered. There's no question it's the place, though. There's no snow on top of it. Not a bit. You can see the warmth coming from it, and there's almost a little snowstorm where it meets the real cold air, but the stuff that falls never freezes."

"We think the main entry is here, below the plateau, in the sides," Boday continued, as the sketch took on a remarkably detailed look that seemed almost three-dimensional. "It appears that there is a bridge that can be extended, *so,* making a connection to a fairly wide trail *here,* which is snow-covered but passable if you knew it."

"Except for a few rough edges here and there, it looks kind'a like a flying saucer," Sam commented. "Jeez! How the hell do we get *in* there?"

"We know Klittichorn has very few Second Rank people with him," Yobi remarked, obliquely addressing Sam's question. "The odds are, unless he has one or two spares, they would all be needed to focus the mechanism when they begin their dirty work. I am quite confident that the three of us can take the operators, Klittichorn included, or that we can take whatever spare people—who would be lesser, more inexperienced types—who would be left to guard and run defenses. The trouble is, we can not take both. Their combined power would require at least another three or four as strong as us."

Etanalon nodded. "I agree. From here, even now, I can sense the power level against us. Klittichorn is strong, but so are each of us. The others are mere shadows, but together they are formidable, particularly under their master's direction. If we are to have a chance, they must first be divided."

Boolean nodded, then looked first at Etanalon, then at Yobi. "You know what that means? We have nothing we can draw them out with—they know their strength and time is running out on them. They could go at any moment, but certainly no more than a week to ten days. After that, the child might well be born. They're not going to split themselves up now for any cause at all, or they would have sent some of them after Sam instead of Zamofir. In fact, if we wait for them, they'll have gathered in any of the others they might still have out there and be stronger. We must hit *now!*"

Yobi nodded back to him. "Yes, I think we understand what that means. The only way to have them divided is to have them divide themselves. That means Klittichorn and probably three of his best directing the war, which, once started, they dare not break off, lest they have the whole of the Second Rank up here and on our side regardless of what they do to the hubs. And, I agree as well, we know not how many others might be coming here in preparation for the big attack but surely there are some. We can not wait."

"It's agreed then," Etanalon chimed in, "that the best and only practical method is to provoke them into starting the war now, pulling their strongest to its commission and allowing us to enter dealing only with the second rate."

"Yes, but how do we provoke them?" Boolean asked. "We go in frontally and they'll know it's only we three—they can read the power as much as we. They won't panic—they've been at this too long. They'll just gather together and meet us head on."

Sam's jaw dropped as she couldn't believe what she was hearing. "You mean—after all this, you're gonna let it *happen?* You're gonna actually *make* them do it? Start the war? Kill or transform millions and millions of innocent people? Give him his crack at godhood?"

"We see no alternative, dear," Etanalon responded gently. "Hopefully we can prevent it from covering the whole of Akahlar, depending on how strong his outer defenses prove to be. But without Klittichorn as the will and the glue, it will fall apart in the end, and those of us with great power can aid in picking up the pieces and reregulating the system as we've always done, much as I hate to get back into *that* end of the business. It's either this or we must quit and sit here and wait for him to first win his war and then claim his First Rank status."

"That's what it's always been about, hasn't it?" Sam said accusingly. "You—none of you—really care, deep down, about the lives that will be destroyed, the civilizations and cultures shattered, the people who will be enslaved and all that. It's Klittichorn you've been after all along. Nothing else matters. He's the first one you all are convinced really can make himself a god and you're scared of him. If not you, then nobody. That's it, isn't it?"

Boolean sighed and looked her straight in the eye. "No, Sam, that's not it. Or, rather, that *wasn't* it. I swear it. And it didn't have to be it, either. It didn't have to come down to just us on the edge of a frozen world in the middle of nowhere having to make this decision. There are literally close to a thousand Second Rank sorcerers in Akahlar. A *thousand!* If we had just one percent of them here—just ten—this wouldn't even be a contest. We could shatter that place and fry him and that would be the end of it. One percent! But he's caressed them and cajoled them and fooled them and wined and dined them and fed their prejudices and when all else failed put real, genuine fear into them. He's played to greed, like Grotag getting an empty promise, he believed that his own hub and staff would be spared and that he'd increase his powers and holdings under the new order. He's played to an ancient, corrupt system that so takes its powers for granted that it believes itself invulnerable, and played it like a symphony orchestra. And that leaves three of us—one social pariah, one exile, and one retired researcher—and the three of you to do it.''

"But, surely *some* of them . . . !"

"In what I think is our common history, give or take a few years, one fellow went from a laughingstock in a beer hall to ruler of a large and powerful country that prided itself on its intellectuals, its culture, and its sophistication. He turned it into a gangster state that had a relatively weak army and weaker navy and he scared bigger, more powerful countries, or buffaloed them, or lied and agreed to everything they wanted and then did the opposite, in a massive con job that resulted in the most horrible world war we have known. Klittichorn's turned the same neat trick here. And, like his predecessor in my own world, when he eventually must go to war and his power and strength and aims are no longer possible to hide, then he must go for broke. He has to hit them hard and fast before they can organize, figure out who's hitting them and how, and bring down massive concerted force to stop him. To do that at this stage they will all have to admit they were stooges, fools, and dupes, and pretty openly and obviously. That's pretty hard to do when you're used to being a demigod, and, once he starts, that's the only time allowance he has. Sure, we wanted to stop it, but we didn't have the weapon until now and we don't have the allies even now. This is the best we can do. We can't stop him, we can only hope to salvage what wreckage he makes and minimize it.''

"But—"

"No buts! The choice has changed from preventing him from wiping out anybody—to preventing him from wiping our *everybody*. Once you're in there, you wrest control from that Storm Princess! You send those things out where they can't do more damage here, and where they will be tempered in the outplanes. You get her and take control and save everybody and everything you can. Now, that's all we can do. The alternative is to do nothing. Is that what you want?''

She sighed and sank back down on the floor of the cave. She wished she had an answer, an instant plan that would solve it all, but there was none. He made too damned good a case. "No, that's not what I want, damn it. I'm just sick and tired of every decision, even life and death, bein' made for me with any choice I got limited to ten seconds or less." She sighed again. "All right—so how are you gonna get him to jump the gun?''

"One thing at a time. Let's first make sure we're rested and well coordinated and know just what we're trying to do.''

Crim looked at him. "What about us? Do Boday and I just hang loose and freeze to death, me making sure she lives long enough to do battle sketches?''

"Uh-uh. You wanted in, you're coming. You take those machine guns you got so fond of with you. Now, you stand in front of a Second Rank sorcerer, even a good adept, and empty the clip at them, and they'll laugh and freeze the bullets or turn them to raindrops or something. But if they're taking on me, or Yobi, or Etanalon, they won't even *think* about you. They'll be on magic sight and won't even *notice* you. If that happens and you see us engaging, then you don't hesitate. You blow 'em to Hell.''

Crim nodded. "That sounds like my fantasies come true. I always wanted to nail some sorcerers. And if we get in to wherever they're doing their thing? We won't be much use in *there*, I suspect, and they're bound to have a few folks with guns of their own.''

"Military stuff, probably. You're better than they are— typically, the average general hasn't shot anything except maybe clay pigeons in years. Keep 'em off us, and if you see the Storm Princess, open up. She doesn't have that kind of magical protection.''

"Yeah, but neither do I," Sam noted nervously.

Boolean chuckled. "Uh-huh. Well, you've eavesdropped or your alter ego in there enough. If you were dressed pretty much like her, you might even pass for her. Sure, they might catch on if they put two and two together, but they'll hesitate.

They may take no chances at all and divert fire from you—I would in their shoes. If you can act the part, even for a little, you may just throw them for a loop."

"I—I don't know. My dialect's more of a peasant sort than hers, and right now she's fatter, although I suppose with some clothing choices we could fake that. But her hair, that sort of thing."

"Perhaps," suggested Etanalon, "we could minimize that whole confusion. If we knew exactly what she looked like now—right now—it would be a simple matter to adjust your looks to hers. The acting we will leave to you, but I suspect little of it will be required. The *presence*, as it were, is enough."

"Yeah, but how're we gonna know what she looks like? I mean, the last time I tried that mindlink bit she heard me, screamed, shut me out, and sent a Changewind after me."

Etanalon smiled sweetly. "Ah, but, my dear, you weren't hypnotized by an expert sorceress, who could subtly guide that link."

"But she'll know I'm close by. They were able to send a Changewind after me in Covanti. . . ."

"That's because she was able to turn to Klittichorn right then and there and have *him* trace the link," Etanalon told her. "We will go patiently this time, until she is in the right environment. And we will eventually send her a vision, but with confirmation that you are not close but far away, since the child is far away. Tell me, have you ever attended a live birth?"

"Two. Putie and Quisu. I had nightmares about my own for a week after that. One part of me didn't want to go through that at all, the other wanted it over and done with. Why?"

"Perfect. You fantasized based on what you saw. Well, that's all we're going to have you do again, my dear. And we're going to let that young woman in the redoubt there in on that fantasy. Oh, yes, we are. . . ."

The Storm Princess awoke suddenly with a series of very odd sensations, most of them unpleasant. First was the convincing feeling that she had suffered some kind of major menstrual flow and that her bed was now wet with a thin, yet mucousy substance she could still feel draining from within her. Almost immediately, she felt the muscles deep within her contract in spasmodic fashion.

Alida and Botea, her two female slave consorts who generally shared her bed, stirred into wakefulness as she abruptly sat up.

"Alida! Botea! Awaken and switch on the lights!" she commanded, even as she was pulling the covers from the bed and examining the satin sheets for any signs of wetness. She found none, which troubled her even more than if she'd found it, nor did anything seem amiss in and around her vagina. The lights, when they went on, confirmed it.

There was nothing there. Nothing.

A dream? A vision? Or another of those shared things? She felt intermittent short bursts of weakening powers within her, not serious but more frequent than she'd ever known, and that, tied to the nightmare, gave her alarm.

She got up, pushing one of her consorts out of the way, and went immediately to the wall intercom and pushed the red button. Even Klittichorn slept—everyone assured her of it—but he somehow was never asleep when she had to see or talk to him.

"Yes, Princess?" his voice came back, clear and awake.

Quickly she described the vision and the sensations to him, and he was not pleased, but also not easily panicked. "Sense the child, the source of the interference. If your duplicate is close by, then such a thing could be transmitted to force us into hasty action."

"No," she assured him. "It is far away, still distant, remote. The interference I felt there was real, but it was still far away and easily handled."

"Hmmmm. . . . Very well. Get dressed and meet me in the War Room as soon as possible. And, if you feel any more of those muscle spasms down there, let me know and tell me how far apart they might be."

"Lord Klittichorn—if this is no trick, then what might it be?" She was genuinely worried about herself now.

"Silly fool! First the water breaks, and the amniotic fluid drains out. Contractions start either a bit before or almost immediately after that, leading to the birth. Either my guess as to impregnation was wrong or the child is coming early, which is not unprecedented. This is the first time that psychic link has worked to our advantage in warning us. We must seize the initiative now. You may feel no more contractions, but if the link still is sending them, the time between is critical. Once the babe is born and the umbilical cord severed and she takes in her first air and cries out to the world her existence, your power and control is diminished by at least half, and that's far too much. Get dressed and hurry down to the War Room. I will summon the others. Take any of the elixirs I provided depending on your wakefulness and physical strength, but eat nothing.''

"I shall do as you ask," she responded, then turned and looked at the two waiting slave girls. "The brown and red saffron ensemble," she told them. "Now!"

She went over to the dresser, sat on the seat, and began to comb her hair and make herself presentable to the world. The slaves came back with the outfit she wanted, which was comfortable yet imposing, the trim on the dress just touching the knee, but with matching leggings and short, comfortable boots. The pair helped her on with it, then one fixed her earrings while the other brushed her long, flowing hair.

She was not fully satisfied, but it would have to do. She got up, examined herself in the dressing mirrors, decided that she could go out like this, slipped the gold ring with the huge ruby on her ring finger, kissed the girls, and walked out, up a short flight of stairs, then down a main hall. She had not touched the elixirs; if she needed any chemical help to do this, then she was not up to it in any case.

She was almost to the main doors of the War Room when she felt another slight twinge down there. She hadn't timed it, but guessed it could be no more than fifteen or twenty minutes from the initial one.

The big red double doors opened before her automatically and she strode into the center of the fortress, the War Room, with its tiered layers leading down to the central circular floor and the great suspended globe of Akahlar in the center. Klittichorn and two of the others, as well as a few slave attendants and the Adjutant, were all there.

She felt curiously awake and excited, as if this was the moment she had waited for and prayed for all her life. *Soon, ghost of my mother, soon,* she thought with some satisfaction.

Now, this very day, the empire of the Akhbreed who killed you and destroyed our beloved people will be no more.

Etanalon snapped her fingers and Sam came out of it with a start. "Huh? What?" She clearly remembered the vision but not being put under.

"Mission accomplished, I believe," Boolean announced, "although I thought you were taking a big chance going that close in to Klittichorn, Etanalon."

"Well, I wanted to see what the place looked like. It's quite impressive, you know. I'll attend to the makeover of Sam, here. The rest of you be fully prepared to move just as soon as we sense full radiated power from that contraption of his. Once they are committed, we want to move as swiftly as possible. The sooner we get in and get to them, the more hubs and lives we'll save." She turned back to Sam. "Ready?"

"I guess. Won't he sense your use of sorcery, though?"

"I think old Klittichorn's got more on his mind than us right now, dear, and so long as he still thinks you're far away and the power use is slight, what matter now? Stand by. This will tingle for just a wee bit, and then you'll have to depend on me for major warmth until we are inside. It is cozy, but it is not an outdoor outfit."

She felt the tingle, but felt no different—only slightly chillier. She looked down, though, and saw that she now wore the outfit, right down to the cute boots, that the Storm Princess had put on in the vision. She felt her ears and found earrings there, and her hair was longer, softer, and fuller than it had been. She, too, felt a bit fuller, and she noticed that her ring finger now had a duplicate of that mega-ring the Storm Princess had put on. She understood now that Etanalon had somehow shared that vision and manipulated it, and had made her over into as close a double of the real Storm Princess as possible.

Crim and Boday checked their weapons and ammunition belts, and Boday clapped her whip to its strap brace on the side of her belt. To top it all, both had quivers full of crossbow bolts on their backs and very fine-looking crossbows in hand.

"Not the machine guns at the start?" Sam asked Crim.

"Uh-uh. We talked it over. If there are any routine guards

out there, we want to take them out silently. Leave the machine guns until the alarms go off.''

Boolean looked approvingly at Sam. "A perfect double. Incredible. My genetic spell was right on the money, proving at least that I am a genius. One thing, though—it's unlikely you'll get close enough to get the chance, but by no means should you touch the Storm Princess. Anything else is okay, and, remember, she's as mortal as you are. That goes both ways.''

. "Huh? Why no touching?''

"Just a feeling. There's an old legend, back home as well as here and elsewhere, about what the Germans in my native world deemed *doppelgangers*. It was said that everyone in the world had, somewhere, an exact duplicate, and if the two ever met and made contact, they would both cease to exist. It's unlikely that there really are many doubles, but people *have* fallen through outplanes to ones below—it's happened many times, enough to be recorded. There's a possibility that there is some kind of difference at the atomic or molecular level that would in fact cause two duplicates from different worlds to cancel one another out. I'm not positive, but why take chances? If we can get that close to her we can nail her a hundred ways. Why sacrifice yourself?''

She nodded. "Well, I'm in favor of that sentiment. Now, how long do we have to wait?''

"Who knows? Not long, I hope. We've started his clock counting down and he wants to attack before the explosion. We all shared the vision of that room, which pretty well confirmed our deductions of what it must look like. I noted the pentagrams, too, Cromil. Some of your buddies are playing in this on his side.''

"Aw—he's always had the *prohjjn*—the Stormriders—with him, and their Sudog pets. Probably just gonna use them to confirm his kills, that's all. They can't do much damage now.''

Yobi's great, hooded head shook slightly. "I would like to know the importance of the small red dots in the hubs on that globe of his,'' she commented. "They weren't regular enough to be aim points.''

Nobody else had noticed them, including Sam. "Nothing we can do or know about it until we're there,'' Boolean pointed out. "Still, didn't underestimate the bastard. *Whoops!* On your marks, ladies and gentleman! Looks like they switched on the juice!"

"Give it a couple of minutes to make certain it's not a test, or not some ploy to draw out potential attackers," Yobi responded nervously.

"Hey! Don't I get a gun or a sword or something?" Sam asked, more nervous than they were, and maybe a lot more now that she saw these high-power sorcerers were scared, too.

Crim gave a half-smile. "You never could shoot worth a damn. We had you on the rifle coming along, but a rifle wouldn't be much use there and would blow the disguise. And your arm strength now isn't what it used to be. Your looks and the probable ignorance of most of the staff in there as to what's going on inside the War Room is your best defense. If you need a weapon, Boday or I will get you one somehow."

"Yeah, thanks. I think."

"I think it's on for real," Yobi pronounced at last. "That is one hellish amount of power being pumped out of there and in to there as well. Thinking time is done, people. Let us go, and may the gods of Akahlar and the misdirected prayers of its foolish people ride with us!"

This time Sam rode in front of Etanalon, who provided some kind of shield that kept out the wind chill and preserved at least some warmth. Still, it was cold and she was cold and she wasn't sure whether she'd like to freeze to death or go into the jaws of that fortress.

They fanned out; Crim on the left, then Yobi, Boolean in the center and slightly forward, then she and Etanalon on the right, and finally Boday on their right. A sort of V-shaped flying wedge, going over the glaciers and snowy peaks. One more rise, and then it was before them, looking very much as Boday had drawn it only bigger than Sam had imagined it. She had also thought that Boday had exaggerated the smooth, almost plastic-looking appearance, but it really did look unreal, like some humongous giant kid's lost toy.

She, too, felt curiously unreal at this point. From a troubled teenager back in the land of television, cars, rock and roll, and shopping malls, to a fugitive running from storms that chased her and bad dreams that plagued her, to the descent through the maelstrom to Tubikosa, the initial safe haven and then, betrayal by Zenchur, the strange spell of Boolean's, the kidnapping of Charley and her sale to Boday, the love potion that turned Boday into her lover, the strange life they'd led in which she'd grown fat and bored, the demon of the Jewel of Omak, the wagon train, Hude, the great storm and flood, the torture-rape, rescue by Charley and the demon, the fleeing from the mercenaries, Pasedo's and a strange new peasant's life as Misa, then Crim and Kira, Yobi, the great overland journey and her mental breakdown on it, Etanalon and her magic mirrors, then the unexpected life with four husbands and an extended family in a primitive place, the attack by Zamofir, the rescue, the body switching ploy, and all the rest—it all seemed, somehow, like something in a dream, a panorama, that had a few good parts but was mostly nightmare.

All forcing her here, forcing her to this place in this time, going against the cause of her suffering and the suffering of millions. Yet, somehow, even as they closed on the place, she felt curiously distanced, more observer than key participant and guest of honor.

Guest of honor at a funeral, anyway.

Suddenly, just in front of them, there was a great rumble and roar and they halted almost immediately. She knew what was coming, felt it coming, and was the only one among them who did not fear it; in fact, she had to shout to the others to close in and not to break ranks.

The great central maelstrom of the Changewind burst through ahead of them, a tremendous, tubular gray-white funnel reaching from the outer perimeter of the "saucer" upwards until it gathered and reached the clouds. The air rumbled and it grew suddenly quite dark, and lightning and thunder began to fill the frozen skies.

Instantly, Sam seemed to know what to do. What was a terrible nightmare to the others was to her a source of power, of strength.

"Etanalon! Let me take the lead and everybody come as close as you can to us!" she shouted above the rising winds and sudden blizzardlike snows stirred up by the great white thing before them. "Boolean! It's okay in the middle, remember? You told me that! They're still there! They're keeping this one right where it is, feeding on it, using its power!''

"Yeah, fine," he responded nervously, "but while I could *project* myself inside, there's no way for us to physically enter now! He's beaten us!"

"The hell with that!" she shot back. "Look at the waves from the Changewind radiating outward, warping the very mountains! But they do not touch us because I won't let them! Now, if you all got the guts, let's go in there, and kick their ass!"

"What—how?" Yobi asked, sounding even more panicky than the rest.

"Right through that motherfucker! You asked me to trust you and you forced me all this way—now you put your trust in me and in *my* hands or it was all for nothing! Come on!"

For Boolean, once he'd made the decision to press on, it suddenly became a matter of extreme academic interest to him. *Of course! Of course! That's how he does it! Draws a single great wind up through the netherhells and holds it just below Akahlar with a magnetic repulsor. Keeps it there, building, letting off "steam," as it were, by opening small, mostly random Changewinds all over the place. This place— not Greenland, not Iceland! Northwest Territories, by god! It's the damned magnetic north pole!*

The Changewind wasn't attracted to this place, it was *repelled* by it, diverting it southward. The inplane angle must be . . . yes, yes. *I see it now! I see how he's doing it! Son of a bitch! What a great mind did I help destroy.* . . .

They approached the maelstrom, tiny specks against the vast and turbulent atmosphere around them, and, as they did, all but Sam and Etanalon closed their eyes, although they would have never admitted to it one another, gritted what teeth they had, and waited for the end.

There was sudden dead silence and calm. "We're through," Etanalon breathed, with obvious amazement. "We're inside the Maelstrom itself! *Physically* inside."

They set down on top of the saucerlike mesa, feeling like ants on a concrete slab, slid off, and looked around. To those with the magic sight, the raised domed shape in the center seemed alive, radiating fingers of blue-white magical energy, fingers that went up and then contacted the edges of the Maelstrom and mated with it.

Boolean dropped to his knees, took out a small pocketknife and scraped a bit at the "saucer."

"Mandan gold," he told them. "The whitish color were oxides and residues. This place just isn't coated with a thin layer of Mandan, it's *all* Mandan—at least the outer shell. Protect the rebel troops my ass! He's been taking what those rebels and gangs bought or stole and melting it down and reforming it!"

"Yeah, it and the Maelstrom protects them from everybody but me," Sam noted. "Uh—I hate to mention this, but while we're safe here, how in hell do we get *in* this thing? The Maelstrom sort'a form fits around it and there's all sorts of flyin' debris down there. I can keep the storm off our backs easy enough, but I sure can't deflect *that* shit. And there don't seem to be no entry up here."

Yobi was still unnerved at being within the one thing she could not control and the only thing she really feared, but she had regained some self-control and this coupled with a desire to get the hell off of here.

"The Changewind protects against sorcery," she said a bit unsteadily, "and Mandan gold against the Changewind, but Mandan gold is no protection from sorcery." She picked a spot, pointed a long, gnarled finger at it, and a beam of pure white magical energy sprang from it and struck the surface of the "saucer." It began to neatly, almost surgically, burn a neat path right through the top.

"Get ready, everybody!" Boolean warned. "All this energy might disguise us, but the odds are about even that somebody's gonna be down there to find out about the hole in the roof!"

· 13 ·

War of the Maelstrom

THEY FLOATED DOWN through the hole, which was wide enough for both Crim and Boday to drop first, Crim with the machine gun ready, Boday with the crossbow, to cover both angles. They appeared to have dropped into a fairly large office, but nobody was home.

Boolean dropped next, then Sam, Etanalon, and, finally, Yobi, whose bulk nearly filled out all the available space. Still, she turned, looked up, and made a series of passes over the roof. The section she had cut out quivered a moment, hanging as it was by only a metallic thread, then went back up into the sealing and reversed the cut. The roof was once again solid and intact.

"Electricity, intercoms—nice place," Boolean noted. "All the comforts of home. But this was never a sorcerer's office. One of the political or military leaders, most likely."

Yobi closed her eyes in concentration, then opened them again. "The door leads to a smaller outer office which also accesses other offices," she told them. "All the offices here are vacant, but the hallway outside passes more, and some of those are occupied. I sense no major power as yet within the immediate region. Do any of you?"

"No," Boolean responded. "Crim, Boday—your job. Go!"

Boday's eyes were glazed. "Boday feels like the star of an action epic that will live forever," she said with awe, and, with Crim, they made their way, wall by wall and door by door, out and into the hall and then down. In the first office there were two senior officers in full uniform and a half a dozen lower-ranking military of about as many races, all pouring over maps and dispatches and seeming very busy.

"The hell with the crossbow," Crim muttered, back against the wall next to the doorway. He threw the safety off the machine gun, checked the clip, then turned so he was framed in the doorway and let loose a volley. Bodies, chairs, and papers flew everywhere. They both rushed in and while Crim finished two that lay moaning with short bursts, Boday found a fencing sword and ran another through.

The noise attracted others, who were met with a hail of gunfire as they rushed to see what the problem was. When no more people came running, Boolean stepped into the hall, raised his arms, and blue-white lightning snaked from his hands and the bodies shimmered and vanished. Vanished, too, were his furs and buckskins; now he wore the shimmering emerald green robe of his office, and, somehow, he looked both younger and radiant in a powerful sort of way. For the first time, he looked to Sam like the kind of sorcerer she'd expected to meet, and she grew a little more confident. He grinned, turned to her, bowed, and gestured for her to emerge.

"Seems to me if you can do that and look like that, you don't need Crim or Boday or me," she muttered.

"I don't like to waste it. I may need every bit of it and won't have any time to recharge. Onward."

She held her breath and began walking as regally as she could. Boday and Crim emerged and fell in behind her, and none looked to see what the sorcerers were doing. They reached a down stairway, and she didn't hesitate, but paraded down it. When she reached the landing she saw two men, one kind of frog-faced and the other with a turtlelike red- and yellow-spotted head, at the bottom with automatic weapons ready. They almost opened up, but their eyes widened when they saw who was coming down.

"Why do you train weapons on me?" she thundered in her most imperious, spoiled-brat tone. "Have you gone mad?"

They stood and snapped to attention. "Pardon, Highness, but we thought, that is, we heard. . . ."

She strode past them and, behind her, Crim took the one on the left and broke his back and Boday punched in the throat of the one on the right. Even as they both collapsed, Crim muttered, "Too easy so far. Much too easy."

"Perhaps they are as stupidly confident in their own winds

defense as the sorcerers of the hubs are with their shields,'' Boday responded hopefully.

Sam checked the floor and saw that it seemed to lead just to more offices or people's rooms or whatever. No sign of the wide hallway with the double doors. She decided to go down another flight, and they followed. The place *couldn't* be *this* empty, could it?''

''If he's paranoid enough it could be,'' Boolean said from behind them, reading their thoughts.

Sam reached the next floor and pressed on the big wooden door leading from the stairwell to the floor itself. It opened easily and she thought she recognized it as leading, maybe from the opposite side, to the grand entrance. She strode on, the door closed behind her, and only then did she turn and realize that nobody had followed.

At almost the same moment, from the opposite stairwell, two figures emerged, dressed in black robes. A man and a woman, both young-looking, both clearly adepts of power. She stood there a moment, feeling totally exposed, and wondering what to do, hoping they wouldn't spot her—but they did.

''Highness,'' said the woman, sounding startled. ''We thought you were already in the War Room. We were going in to observe.''

''They are still focusing the beam,'' she responded, hoping what she was saying made any sense. ''I took advantage of it to retrieve something I had forgotten.''

That seemed to puzzle the adept. ''But—your quarters are over *here*. I—'' The other, male adept poked her with his elbow and she suddenly realized the way she was sounding. Who were *they*, who called the Storm Princess ''Highness,'' to question her?

''Come, Highness. We are all going the same place,'' said the male diplomatically, and she had to walk out into the hall while they started walking behind her.

Jesus! Now what? she wondered, trying to figure something out.

At that moment there was a crackling sound behind them, like a massive electrical short, that caused them all to freeze in place. The two adepts and Sam all turned, startled, and saw a resplendent Boolean standing there, flanked by Etanalon in robes of shimmering silver and looking to Sam like the Good Witch of the North.

There was an immediate and near blinding exchange of crackling energy between the adepts and the invading sorcerers, and, slowly, the black robes seemed to catch fire and burn with the intensity of a torch. In less than thirty seconds, both were nothing more than heaps of black ash on the great carpet.

"Oh, dear! Now they're going to have to get that cleaned," Etanalon remarked with seeming sincerity.

"Sorry to leave you like that," Boolean said to Sam. "We had some unexpected and unpleasant company back there and there was a nasty little spell on the door to take care of." There were the sounds of shooting and an explosion behind them in the stairwell, the sound echoing eerily in the stillness of the hall. "It seems, though, that even the defensive spells here can't tell you apart from the real thing."

"No, but we can," said a crackling male voice from just behind her back. Sam turned and saw two robed figures step out from alcoves or side stairs or someplace on either side of the big double doors that had seemed too close before and now seemed an eternity away.

One of the sorcerers wore a yellow robe embroidered with elaborate Oriental-like designs in shimmering red; the other violet, with trim in silver. Both hoods were down, revealing one very old cadaverous man's face, the speaker, and the other, the one in violet—well, it looked more like an animated death's head.

"Nice to see you, John. You're looking quite well," said the yellow-robed sorcerer. "And you, Valentina Ilushya, have never looked more beautiful."

"Sorry I can't say the same for you, Franz. And if that's still Tsao, I double the regret," Boolean responded. "You look dead on your feet, Tsao."

Sam suddenly realized that she was in the midst of the crossfire and carefully edged over to one side. Tsao pointed a skeletal finger in her direction and a bolt shot from it, but Etanalon flicked her own finger and it deflected, allowing Sam to get clear.

Boolean sighed. "Well, this explains some of my political troubles, anyway. I always figured you for treason, Franz, but not to be subordinate to anyone else, least of all Roy. And Tsao, you were never the political type. Not since I beat you out of Masalur. Is that it? It's just revenge against me?''

"For a hundred years I served that old man," Tsao hissed in a voice that sounded more reptilian than human. "A century! And in a mere eight years you became his favorite, you usurped my rightful position. Twenty years I spent in exile because of you!''

"That's because you were an incompetent toady, Tsao. And because it just so happened I had my own portable computer in my trunk when I got here. Took me three years to get the current matched, but after that you didn't have a prayer. Reinventing the three-pronged outlet was the bitch. You don't have a prayer now, either, Tsao. Or do you think Etanalon is more your speed? I never fought you, Franz, but treason always motivates me.''

"We do not have to beat you!'' Tsao hissed menacingly. "We need only kill your bitch, or perhaps turn her into a toad or something. You may kill us, but you will then not have the power to stop what is going on in there!''

"Oh, I don't know,'' Boolean responded. "Let's you and him fight and see.''

Instantly the entire hall was ablaze in beams of magic energy, not mere lightning as with the adepts, but brilliant, blinding yellow and white light like searchlights, emanating from all four sorcerers. And in the center, where the beams clashed, equidistant from the now darkened, still forms of the sorcerers, figures took shape. Weird, demonic figures, misshapen, horrible, like the gods of some ancient tribes suddenly come to life, and they battled one another with psychic swords and hand-to-hand, or hand to claw or tentacle or whatever contacted what.

For the fighting shapes were constantly changing: wolflike, jaws glistening, spectral heads and snouts closed on dragon necks, and many forms were too nightmarish and too bizarre to figure out.

Rather quickly it seemed that two were getting the upper hand, smashing and then hacking at the other two almost at will, more and more, over and over, until it almost was like kicking a guy after he was down. The figures of the losers began to shrink, first to dog size, then cat, then mouse, until heavy psychic feet stomped on them and crushed them into pulp. Sam could only watch, terrified, unable to move out of the alcove, and wondering who was what.

As quickly as it had begun, it was over, and for a moment all Sam could see was the same four figures standing there, looking exactly the same, but unmoving. To Sam's astonishment, Boday suddenly walked between Boolean and Etanalon and right up to the enemy pair standing there. She looked at one quizzically, then the other, shrugged, and pushed the yellow-robed one over. He fell and shattered, like porcelain, on the floor. The other she also pushed, and he fell and shattered as well, only into a foul-smelling black dust.

Boolean sighed and turned to Etanalon. "Well, that wasn't bad, was it?"

"I was out of practice," she responded. "It took more out of me than I would have liked. Where in the world is Yobi?"

"She comes," Boday assured them. "She had to take on another one in the fine robes of the masters along with two adepts. Crim, by the way, found some *wonderful* little bombs on the soldiers we took out down there. You pull this thing and throw and a few seconds later they blow up and shoot little tiny pieces of metal all over the place. We thought they might form a nice introduction to the room down there."

"Grenades, huh? Worth a try," Boolean said, thinking. "Sam, you okay?"

"All but my heart. I think that's in my mouth," she said shakily. "Are we gonna hav'ta go through more of that in there?"

"No, it'll probably be a lot harder. Ah—here's Crim. Boday said you found grenades—throw bombs."

He nodded. "Four of them, anyway. Say, Yobi was having a tough time with those guys back there. If I hadn't been able to take one of 'em out while they were all concentrating on her she'd have had it. Why didn't you. . . ." He suddenly saw the remains of the two sorcerers. "Oh. Never mind."

Yobi came thundering through the door, partly shattering it, looking winded. Of the trio of sorcerers, she was the only one who looked as bad as ever, but, of course, she could never be accused of looking ordinary.

"You know who that slimy little twerp was?" she thun-

dered. "Bolaquar! Vice Chairman of the Guild itself! No
wonder nobody'd listen to us!"

"Well, that was Franz—Golimafar," Boolean responded,
pointing. "And that thing over there was once Hocheen—you
remember him. You sense any more big shots on our back?"

"No, but lots of adepts are about. You were right about
the soldiers—mostly headquarters types. Couldn't shoot straight
even at a target *my* size. Not too many folks here, unless the
rest are all in there. I guess somebody rushed 'em into action
before they were ready."

"Yeah, well, speaking of rushed. . . . You feel up to the
rest? Yobi? Etanalon?"

They both nodded. "Let's get it over with while I'm still
sharp," said the silver-robed sorceress. She looked at the
great doors. "That's a mean set of spells on there, though.
Could take some real effort breaking through and set off all
sorts of alarms to whoever's in there."

Boolean turned to Sam. "Well, I guess that's your job,
then, Sam. This time, *don't* close the damned door behind
you. Leave it open for us to come in."

"You think they're not layin' for us after all *that?*" she
asked him. "Damn, you two would'a woke the dead with that
fight. In fact, lookin' at the one guy, you probably did."

"No, that's insulated in there," Etanalon told her. "If they
knew, reinforcements would have come out—if there's anyone in there to reinforce. We can't get any sense of who's in
there or what's happening, and if we can't, they can't."

"Crim, Boday—you roll in to the right and left as soon as
Sam's through," Boolean told them. "Crim, give Boday two
of those grenades. Yeah. Fresh clips. Okay, Sam, you open
that door, get behind it, and stay behind it until you hear four
explosions or we tell you to come out. That should protect
you from them, and maybe the surprise and shock will nail a
few or take a couple of sorcerers' eyes from that globe in
there back here, screwing up the system. The two of you roll
in as soon as the things explode and you blast anything
blastable. I doubt if you'll be able to nail anybody actually in
the area around the globe. They're bound to be shielded. You
just keep the slaves and military boys and whatever off our
backs, and when your ammunition runs out, head for cover
and stay there—understand?"

They both nodded. Sam looked at the pair and shook her head. Crim was really grim and serious about this, but Boday was having the time of her life.

The alchemical artist looked over at Boolean and asked, "That shield any barrier to us or just to magic types?"

"Everybody inside, as far as shooting or the like goes. Anybody who steps outside is dead, though."

"Even the Storm Princess?" she asked.

"Hmmm. . . . No, you're right. If the Storm Princess emerges from that well down there, she's all yours. Sam—stay back and unobtrusive if you can. The odds are once we've joined they won't be able to tell you and the real Storm Princess apart on the magic level, so you'll be relatively safe. If we can break that shield, or the Storm Princess comes out, you get in. Send those Changewinds elsewhere. Understand?"

Sam nodded, not quite certain what she could do or how but willing to play it by ear. This was the big one, and her major job right now was to open that damned door. She went over to it, took a deep breath, and pushed.

It didn't open.

"Try pulling, dear," Etanalon suggested. "That also leaves you out here, where it's safer."

Sam felt foolish, pulled the door open full, and then stood behind it in the hall. Boday and Crim rushed in, threw the grenades, and came right back out again. Sam almost slammed the door and inside she could hear four muffled reports. Then she opened it wide again and they went back in, shooting anything they saw.

Boolean led, then Etanalon, and finally Yobi, they strode past the bodies of the dead sorcerers and into the great hall. Sam, feeling suddenly alone and more vulnerable out in the hall than in the eye of the storm, came in after.

The surprise conventional grenades and subsequent machinegun spraying had been far more effective than they'd dreamed it could be. Not prepared for trouble, watching the show blow and fascinated by it, adepts, some probably quite powerful, as well as a number of rebel officers in fully festooned uniforms, lay dead or dying all around. No amount of armor will protect someone who didn't put it on, as the bloody remains of black-robed men and women attested.

The place looked like a miniature of the Roman Coliseum

with a roof on, but the main floor was untouched by any of the carnage, any of the action above or outside. There they stood in their pentagrams, staring at that huge globe representing Akahlar, the hubs brightly glowing against the gray, semi-transparent skin of the rest, and something was happening.

Almost a third of the globe's hubs, from Arctic to Antarctic, were blackened, their lights out, as if crossed off on somebody's battle map, in a great and ugly crescent that was widening even as the globe was slowly turning.

Sam watched from the top row of seats, spellbound, sickened by what the sight entailed. And then she looked down and saw *them*. There they were—the man in the crimson robes with the horns on his head and *her*, standing there, eyes calmly fixed on that spinning globe.

She looked back at Klittichorn, feared Horned Demon of the Snows, most powerful and evil of sorcerers, and all she could marvel at was that, even in her visions and nightmares, he'd looked as huge and imposing, and now—hell, he wasn't much if any bigger than *she* was. A little, tiny man, which even the horns didn't help get much bigger.

She could see, too, for the first time, the magical shield that protected them even at this stage; clear, almost totally transparent, but present sort of in a shimmery effect produced by the lights and the fact that it wasn't still but in motion.

"He's got a spin on it somehow," Yobi noted. "Makes it hard to burn a hole through."

"It's got to be going on its own momentum," Etanalon noted. "If we can speed it up a bit rather than slow it down, we might be able to present the same face if we can match its revolutions per minute. What do you say, Boolean?"

"Well, if we can't brake it somehow, maybe we can get it going so fast it'll burn a hole in the floor. Let's give it a go."

"Wait a minute!" Sam almost shouted. "Look at them! They don't even know this all happened, or that we're here! Just gimme one of the machine guns and I'll go down there and blow their fucking brains out."

"They know, dear," Etanalon assured her. "They just don't consider us relevant right now. We are about to make ourselves relevant. Hold on."

The shield seemed to pick up speed until the reflections were just tiny lines of light apparently suspended in the nothingness above the floor. Beams of red-hot energy shot from all three, converging on a single spot, and it began to create a black streak that widened more and more.

The three sorcerers on the other side broke off their concentration, came out as a group, ducked under the black streak, and lined up against the trio in the seats. This time there was no introductory chatter, no insults, no nothing. The battle was immediately joined, and it nearly filled a quarter of the hall. Crim just barely got out of the way of the field of fire, and Sam walked around the top to the opposite side, away from them, and tried to think.

Boday crept up to her. "So, Susama, how do you think it is going?"

"Who the hell knows?" she muttered. "At least they've had to temporarily break off from the looks of it. *Holy shit, Boday! That means—*"

At that moment the walls supporting the entire War Room seemed to collapse in a roar, knocking her briefly forward and tumbling Boday most of the way down to the pit. She rolled, turned, and saw that those walls, perhaps the whole building, no longer existed.

The Maelstrom was contracting onto them!

She rolled, concentrated, and began to push it back. *Oh, no you don't, bitch! I beat you once, I'll beat you again!*

On the opposite side where the sorcerer's battle was taking place, the strategy of the defenders was clear. They had their backs to the stage, as it were; Yobi, Etanalon, and Boolean all had their backs to the wall. Contract the Maelstrom down into them while pressing them or holding them in place and you engulfed them in a power they couldn't resist, couldn't change, and couldn't keep from being subject to.

Sam could help them, immunize them, but that would put them on the outside once more with her, undefended, on the inside. And where in hell was Klittichorn?

Damn it all, this wasn't right! *Feel the storm, become the storm, control the damned storm!*

Now she was there, inside the storm, as the heart of it, but not alone. She felt and sensed the other's presence, the only other in this, *her* domain, who dared to be there, where even Klittichorn dared not intrude.

"*You can not win this time!*" the Storm Princess taunted

her. *"The last time it was I who was remote from the storm attacking you at your center! Now it is you who are remote and the storm is here, around me, where I can squeeze your friends!"*

With a shock, Sam realized that, while they certainly had seen her, they *still* thought that she was back in Masalur or someplace like that because of the child's impulses. They—even the Storm Princess—thought she, on scene, was Charley!

She flicked her vision around to where the sorcerers were joined. Still three to three; Klittichorn seemed off to one side, fiddling with something but not joining the fight, depending on the Maelstrom to finish them off. What was he fiddling with? Some kind of portable computer! He was running his shit through to see how to keep the thing up until he could get back to ruining the world!

Once started, he can't stop until he's done it through, the words came to her. He didn't *dare* shut it down, so now—my god, the winds were still coming, only running wild!

Still, first things first. She turned her attention back to where her opposite number had never deviated attention from—the wizard's war.

Yobi in particular was only inches from the slowly tightening wall. For a moment Sam wondered why she didn't just contract quickly, but then she realized that there was only so much you could do and keep control without overrunning your own people. First things first; the Storm Princess was right.

Sam reached out to the storm wall and pulled a segment out. It seemed to her like taffy, and she made it a mentally formed fist aimed straight across from one side of the closing circle to the other, right through the defending sorcerers.

The Storm Princess saw it and tried to block, but so unexpected was the action that she deflected the Changewind segment only slightly, so that it sliced right through the middle where the sorcerers' psychic selves were battling! There were screams and some or most were affected in some way, but it was impossible to tell who or how many.

"Damn it!" she screamed to the Storm Princess. *"Stop it! This is madness! Madness! They didn't kill your mother or your people, you stupid little bitch! Klittichorn ordered it to get your dumbass support for this! He suckered you like he*

suckered everybody else! Can't you see he's getting you to
slaughter your own people in order to become a god?''

The plea didn't work, but it took the Storm Princess's mind
off the attack, and somebody over there was still clearly
fighting somebody now that the Changewind element had
passed and dissipated, and now even the Storm Princess
would be hard-pressed to tell who was who—they were fighting at an angle to the winds, on the same level!

''Quiet, whore! slut! Usurper! Do you think I am stupid? I
am a Princess, daughter of a god and the Storm Queen, my
mother. You are but a reflection, a distorted, ugly shadow of
my own godhood! I alone am anointed by the gods and by my
mother, who is now a Goddess above us all, to rule an
Akahlar I remake because it pleases me! What is even
Klittichorn to me now? I need only close the Maelstrom
completely, and then there will be only one, no other!''

Jesus! What a stupid, demented asshole! Sam thought,
incredulous. And yet, and yet—something in what she said.
If Klittichorn was the big brain, the guy who figured all the
angles, he must also have figured that she'd nail him at the
end of this as well. How could he stop her? Unless. . . .

The hell with this. Where was this mad princess? There—
still on the floor, maybe ten feet from Klittichorn. And—
somebody else? Who? The battle over there seemed to be
over. Who the hell was that?

Klittichorn turned away from the portable computer, got
up, and looked straight at Boolean. The green sorcerer looked
terribly old and near exhaustion, his formerly dark hair and
beard now white, but, the fact was, while Klittichorn had fought
no battles, he didn't exactly look in peak condition himself.

"Hello, Roy," Boolean said softly. "You came very close
to pulling it off."

"Well, Doctor Lang, I would not have had this turn out
any other way, assuming that we had to meet at all," the little
man in crimson responded. "It is fitting that you should be
here for the end."

Boolean looked up at the spinning globe. "Impressive
gadget, Roy, but I make only a quarter of the hubs gone.
Your three sorcerers are gone, and even I can't tell which
Storm Princess is which at the moment."

Klittichorn chuckled. "You are weak, Doctor Lang. Too

much has gone out of you. All you have done by this is murder about a hundred million people instead of letting them be transformed into something different. And that will be sufficient for me. I did not want to murder them, but you forced me to do so. Then I will dispose of the pitiful wreck that is all that remains of you, then I will achieve First Rank, and bring logic and order to this chaos as my destiny commands.''

''What do you mean, murder?''

''You see those red dots up there? Each one represents a bomb, each scientifically worked out as to its placement, geography, and kilotonnage to completely eradicate all life within each of the hubs. The timers began the moment we activated the full system. Naturally, any that we were able to cover in the more merciful Changewind manner were transformed along with the lands and people and are no more. The rest—they will begin going off any time now. The signal has been given, was given, the moment I had to shut down the progression. You can not believe how long I have planned this, covering every eventuality, even this. Nor do I care which little bitch is which. Either one will do.''

Boolean blanched. ''Roy—have you gone mad? *I* dishonored *you*. I admit that. Perhaps in a few minutes I will pay the price for it. I don't think I deserve it, but at least I can understand how it would be justice to you. But—you're talking about *genocide,* Roy! My God, would you dishonor your own parents? Have you looked at yourself, Roy? I no longer see the face of the victim, I see the face of the Khmer Rouge there, murdering, slaughtering millions of their own. How can you become like *them,* Roy? How can you give those who murdered your family and enslaved you for so long the final victory?''

''I reject your pitiful moralizing!'' Klittichorn snapped back. ''The man you knew is no more! *I* have replaced him! *I,* in human form, have become the incarnation of Siva, the Destroyer of Universes! What is done here is nothing compared to what I do merely for sport! The girl, can you not recognize her by her mastery of such energy as Durga, the Goddess of Death? And your girl her other aspect, Kali? Soon we shall combine, we two, in the Dance that Heralds the End of the World, and lose our Earthly aspects, having done our duty, and resume our rightful place at the left hand of Isvara Brahman, there to witness the timeless recreation of a better world! You see everything only with the blind eyes and arrogant ignorance of the westerner! You who so polluted and defiled poor Cambodia that I had to send the dark children to wipe them out, to purge them of the west and its evil! Come! Let us do our little dance, corrupter of souls, so that I may get on and do mine!''

My god! He is totally mad! was the only thought Boolean could make before the onslaught of sheer, brutal power struck him, and the battle was joined. It was, right off, a battle he knew he must lose, for he faced fanaticism and madness along with brilliance and power, while he defended weakly and from a position of guilt. *No! Purge the guilt! Don't think of Roy Lompong! Think of those bombs, those millions of people . . . !*

The Storm Princess tightened the ring some more, although she could sense no life forms within the Maelstrom not inside the stage circle. Klittichorn was locked in battle; the others seemed weak, irrelevant, and not near enough to her. Her battle was not with the likes of them, but with the Usurper battling quite strongly from afar. No—suddenly there was one, quite close, just opposite her. For a moment she took her mind off the Maelstrom and looked with her eyes.

It was like looking into a mirror, and she was startled at the sight in spite of herself. Sam was not at all startled; she saw just what she expected to see, and she didn't like it one bit.

"So, little decoy, they send you at last as if to frighten me," the Storm Princess muttered between clenched teeth. "In a way I almost feel sorry for you, as insignificant as you are."

Sam smiled grimly at her and began walking slowly towards her. Their eyes met, and there was something in Sam's eyes that suddenly caused doubt, even fear, inside the thoughts of the Storm Princess. She took a step back as Sam continued to advance, oblivious of the Maelstrom around them.

"Mother protect me!" the Storm Princess muttered. *"You're not the decoy! You're. . . ."*

Back around the side of the great spinning globe, Sam pressed on and the Storm Princess retreated. They made a quarter of the circuit, and then the Princess found her back to the wizard's battle and stopped, with no way out except through the storm, and that would be no out. The storm and its most terrifying effects were as nothing to either of them. But what lay beyond now? Not the building, certainly, and possibly not the mountains, either. Cold, no matter what, for that would require changing the whole planet's position and tilt to alter, but what? A chasm hundreds of feet deep? A glacier? Some alien horror?

Sam knew now what she had to do. "We must touch, sister. You know what that does? It cancels us both out. We cease to exist, to the betterment of this and many other worlds, maybe. I ain't afraid no more, 'cause it'll mean something. Nothin' I ever done or hoped to do ever really meant somethin' before." She stepped forward, and the Storm Princess looked panicky for a way out.

Suddenly something snakelike seemed to come out of nowhere and wrap itself around the Storm Princess's throat. It wasn't hard enough to strangle her, having partly caught the collar, but it surprised and held her, and she was pulled with some force to a strangely familiar dark shape just beyond.

So sudden was the whole action that it startled Sam and stopped her dead in her tracks, only a few feet from the Princess. She stared, confused, and then saw who it was.

"Boday! What the hell . . . ?"

Boday had slipped the whip off the confused woman's neck but held her now in a sort of wrestling grip, forcing the Storm Princess's mouth open and her head back, and then stuffing a small vial into her mouth. The Princess swallowed it involuntarily, then cried out and sank, unconscious, to the cement floor of the stage area. Boday bent down, picked her up, and grinned at Sam.

"Don't you worry about her," Boday said with a smile. "She'll never do anybody any harm again. Let me past and you go help out Boolean. I think he's losing bad. Just remember when it's done to leave me a way out of here!"

She stepped back and let Boday go by to the far side of the globe, confused as hell but not questioning it.

She was at Klittichorn's back, but she could easily tell that he knew she was there and also that he was winning. In fact, the magical sight was a sea of crimson, with only a small glow of green left that was even now contracting more and more.

"Soon he'll be smaller than me," she heard Cromil's amused voice near her. She turned, furious, and a wisp of Changewind lashed out from the Maelstrom like Boday's whip and caught the little creature dead on. He screamed and then vanished into the storm, whether dead or simply banished back to his own strange universe she couldn't know.

Still, her fury had caused that, and without even thinking about it. She turned again and brought just the nearest side of the Maelstrom wall inwards, touching but not harming her, and engulfing the brightly shining orange mass.

Klittichorn, an inch from victory, seemed to sense it and suddenly whirled. "No! Not yet!" he screamed, and it was on him. She held it there, just where it was, then rolled it back to see if she had caught anything but the sorcerer in the mess. Where Klittichorn had stood was now a mass of solid ice. Pink ice. If it was random, it certainly appropriate. Just beyond was the little left of the stage area, and on it lay a green robe, collapsed like an old rag doll.

She rushed over to him, heedless of the cold, almost slipping on the ice, and bent down. He looked horrible, more like that walking skeleton he'd faced down outside than anything like the man he'd been. Still, as she could see by the very tiny glow still within him, he was not dead yet, but he was dying and he knew it. Still, somehow, he saw her or senses her, and he tried to speak.

"A-bombs," he gasped, sounding like a voice from beyond the grave. "He put A-bombs in all the hubs he didn't change!"

She looked up at the globe, still incredibly spinning around on its theoretical axis. "Is there any way I can get rid of them? There's still a lot of Changewind energy here."

"Not focused," he managed. "Need the others. No way out. Yobi . . . gone. Etanalon . . . gone. I go now myself. Millions will die. . . . Horrible nuclear waste. . . . He thought . . . he was . . . already . . . a god."

"Oh, my god!" she breathed, and then something snapped inside her. "No, damn it! Don't you die on me now, you bastard! Join me! Join me in the Wind!"

She let it wash over them as she clung tightly to him, but this time she didn't ward off its force. "Join with it," she told him softly. "Join me and join with it. Mate with me and the Wind!" And she kissed his skull of a face and picked his brittle body up and clung tightly to it.

She held his pitiful shell in passionate embrace, a passion she did not feel but knew somehow was not really necessary, and let the wind take them both, melding them together within the Maelstrom. She felt the clothing dissolve, their very bodies seem to melt and meld into new forms, and she felt him understand and accept her and she accept him, and together they merged with each other and with the wind.

Her mind and his mind exploded and joined, creating something new, something unique, something great, but something only her half could shape. It was all so clear to Her now! Everything!

And the irony was that Klittichorn's pitiful, mad dream of godhood would not have been his to claim, but that of the Storm Princess, who alone was the Shaper of What Was. It was the feminine who gave birth, even to gods.

In Sam's own, simplistic way, she had guessed the key. Chaos created gods and goddesses like snowflakes, each different, each unique, each the protector as well as the ultimate ruler of their worlds. But even that was a random process, the fifty million monkeys creating into infinity produced not the works of Shakespeare but a system by which the man and the works might be created. But not every snowflake was perfect, and not every copy of Shakespeare was, either. In some worlds, perhaps for physical reasons—perhaps for no particular reason but chance—the process had stopped short of the final creation. Stability had been achieved, regulation established, short of local godhood.

There the elements had not merged, the opposites that created. The being with the power to call the Winds had to mate with the being who could command them, and the two had to merge with the wind and become something newer and greater than any of the three. How early had it been, in the other planes? In the trees or in the oceans, perhaps? Simpler gods for simpler times and more rational development.

But not just any god would do. It had to be a fusion of opposites, the cerebral and emotional, the male and the female, the old and the young, and countless other variables and elements had to merge. This did not necessarily make a perfect local god, nor even a great or wise one, but the patterns created by the order formed from the creation out of Chaos did not mandate that.

Akahlar had been created out of that first great explosion, but not as it was now, nor even the way the others had been formed at the time. It had been a vast, empty place upon which the other realities, the other universes close at hand, had fallen, compressed by the pull of the Seat of Probability after the great explosion's force had passed. Its compressed and compacted state had ground out the nulls and created the overlaps with countless worlds around the few untouched areas, the hubs, and it had been populated from the outplanes long after things had settled and developed for billions of years.

The ironic thing was that those who became its masters had come from worlds where the gods were created by the minds of men, not the patterns of Chaos. Violent, fierce people unregulated and untempered by anything above them. In them, the elements to form the gods did not truly exist, although the need for them did and took form in ancestral yearnings for such beings. In their worlds, and perhaps only in their worlds, the prototypes for the gods continued to be fashioned and born as the patterns dictated, but never to understand, never to unite, never to form the whole that was required. And there was a reason for this.

They were from the far outplanes, the last of Creation, where the Changewinds weakened into shadows of themselves and their power was greatly diminished. Humankind multiplied and occupied their Earths, further separating and making unlikely that the elements, any of the elements, would ever meet, unite, or comprehend what the patterns urged. For it was always the female element who sought out and chose her lovers, and the pattern had gone slightly awry; for the woman always took their lovers from their complements, not their opposites, rarely uniting with a male at all and even rarer with the Changewind.

Yet there was a kind of stability imposed, as even apart the separate elements maintained an automatic, unconscious regulation, keeping the worst of the Winds at bay, and only when they died or were removed before the patterns forced another element to be born, somewhere, in their world, did the Winds have true free reign, producing the improbable elements that might give the world an Alexander, a Caesar, a Napoleon, or a Hitler, or, conversely, a Buddha, a Jesus, or a Gandhi.

Only here, in Akahlar, where the magic was real and accepted and taken for granted, had the line of the female become institutionalized, mother choosing mate for all the wrong reasons and bearing another and yet another version of herself, and using the powers of the Winds while ignorant of her own place or the meaning of things, believing themselves goddesses while actually being but an element of the divine.

She looked down upon the ruins of Klittichorn's fortress and saw that there were in fact survivors down there, survivors whom She recognized and identified. She reached out a spectral hand to them and created for them an avenue and an ice bridge to safety beyond. She was about to do more but She felt a sharp and painful disturbance within Her, one She did not fully comprehend, being above pain now, or so she had thought. The survivors would get out; she would have to come back to them later.

At the speed of light she was at its source, a great, horrible explosion sending horrible thunder and searing fire outwards over a vast radius, obliterating, even atomizing, much of what its blast touched. She dampened it, pulled it upward, kept it from doing further harm, but now there was a second, and She knew what She was facing.

Too late on the first, She froze the second as it was forming its mushroom shape, suspending it there, then went methodically from hub to hub, pulling the power of the Winds to render the other bombs useless junk. Only then did She return to the first, and discover that there were in fact limits to Her powers. Even this universe was vast, and She was but the Goddess of Akahlar. She could not roll back time, but She could undo much of its effects.

Frightened people, frightened armies, frozen in the vision of that second bomb, were now unfrozen; the great, irregular mushroom shape stopped billowing upwards and instead seemed to them to solidify. On a shaky, bent foundation stem the structure could not stand; it toppled over and fragmented as it hit the ground over hundreds of square miles, burying the hub and its defenders and attackers knee-deep in chunks of true mushroom.

For the first hub there was less hope; it was already a
blackened plane, with the bare charred remnants of what had
once been a great kingdom and great seat of empire. There
she could do some things; within limits even raise the dead,
as little was truly impossible now, but she could not spin it
back, could not take that explosion back, and far too much of
it had gone. Better now to simply contain the damage and
limit its effects to what had already occurred, spinning the
dust and radiation outward into the netherhells between the
outplanes where they would hardly be noticed. Let this burned,
dead hub become then a place of pilgrimage, a grim reminder
to the millions who survived through the bravery of a few as
to what great power can really do, and what price might be
paid for turning one's back on evil.

For they could have stopped this; the high and mighty
Akhbreed sorcerers in their towers and in their lairs, but they
had chosen to believe what they wanted to believe and to
compromise with evil, succumb to evil, or turn their eyes,
ears, and brains away from it, and ignore it until it was too
late. They had shown how weak and fallible their power was,
how they misunderstood the fullness of their charge to protect
their people. They had let their sense of power replace their
common sense, and so had failed both their people and
themselves, and now they sat smug and fat in their castles,
congratulating themselves that all was now well and that
someone had done for them at great sacrifice what just a few
of them could have done with no sacrifice required at all.

She reached down to them, as they sat in their towers as
before, ignorant of just what horrors they and their people had
been spared, and touched them with the breeze they could not
control, the one power to which they were subject. The office
of Chief Sorcerer was herein abolished; now they were revealed by their loss of power as just the pitiful old men and
women, frail and scared and very ordinary, as they always
were, but now stripped of their cloaks of invincibility and
forced to appear with their minute souls bared to their people.

The shield came down. There would never again be shields
to keep subject populations separate and in check, coordinated by the masters of the hubs. She knew that this would
cause much death and suffering, that the wars would now
rage for a while, and that the Akhbreed and the most militant

of the colonials would be a long time finding a peace, but they would be forced eventually to an accommodation, for they needed each other, and the vast majority of colonial races understood that as well. If the Akhbreed would let them, some of those races would fight at its side in the defense of a broader, freer organization, less kingdom than interdependent commonwealth. The Akhbreed who refused alliance would die, or be overthrown by those who saw survival and the future as overwhelming prejudice.

She cried for those who would die and those who would never learn, and most of all for the innocents caught between, but this was the sort of hard decision that her other half could make and the only long-term solution. She would be able to help, to guide them, to perhaps minimize the appalling losses, but the War of the Maelstrom might take a generation to sort out the world of Akahlar.

When She had time to learn all Her powers and Her limits, to study what could be done and how best to do it, some provision might be made for the innocents. Nor was She still naive enough to believe that the system She envisioned for Akahlar would evolve on its own. Something would have to be done to give them a guide, a nudge in the right direction. Prophets and teachers might be quite useful to develop here, and perhaps a book to guide them and give them the plan.

For a moment, She wondered if this was the way it always worked out, that others suddenly thrust into Her position had not done much the same.

But there had to be one place of safety, one point of shining sanity upon Akahlar, if only as an example. A holy city within a centralized hub, perhaps, to train those not only of the Akhbreed but also of the natives to carry the message and the plan, safe from wars and revolutions and barbarism, so that no matter how ugly things got there was one source for putting it right.

Masalur! Astride the equator, near the center of the greatest kingdoms. Masalur, who had known both the horrors of war and subjugation and the wrench of the winds; who had an almost unique core population that remained intact, a bridge between the opposites, between the changelings and the whole, between the rebels and the Akhbreed, between the male and the female, and whose old government had allowed, however

reluctantly, the experiments with native self-government and
self-sufficiency and whose colonial populations as a result
had, in the main, eschewed the fight and caused Klittichorn to
have to import dissident armies to help.

Its magically charged hub, with its swampy core and its
large and strange population, surrounded by a ring of Akhbreed,
would be a holy place. In this hub, the weapons would not
work, the spells would not hold, and judgments might be
rendered directly by Her until such time as a new form of
government could evolve, a multiracial government, to teach
and give example to the world.

This kind of responsibility had been the sort that Her
feminine half had been fearful of and had not wanted; that her
male half had wanted above all else but with no clear direction as to what he wanted that power for. Now he would
provide the drive, the joy of power, and she, through whom it
must be filtered and accommodation reached, would tempo-
rize and shape and guide it. Together, the three in one, the
male, the female, and the Wind, might well make something
worthwhile, something great. And if She could not banish the
horrors of the world and the darkest parts of the human soul,
then at least She might provide justice.

*Lonely figures, like tiny dots against a sea of white, crawl-
ing, clawing their way forward, yet freezing, without a place
to go. . . .*

*Other creatures, strange and hideous yet impervious to the
cold, clawing around the edges of what remained of Klittichorn's
redoubt.*

Two in particular drew Her interest; the others could claw
and mew and stalk each other through eternity on that ice for
all she cared, and dream only of what might have been.

She reached psychic fingers down to them, to the two
strange figures back on the ice and to the tiny dots fighting
their losing battle against the elements, knowing, at least,
what to do with them. But she held them suspended, for a
brief moment, in the netherworld between the ticks of the
clock. She had something else to do first, one last obligation,
one last, personal bit of housekeeping, before She withdrew
to oversee her grand design, knowing that in the times to
come She could no longer afford such personal attachments,
that the greater good would come first.

*   *   *

There was a sound, like the gentle tinkling of bells in the breeze, that woke Charley up. She sat up in the bed, frowning, for it was quite dark and the snores around told her that she alone had heard what it was and come awake.

For a moment she thought it was just the child, now perhaps only days from being born—and that would be a relief! She hadn't slept too well these past couple of weeks as it was because of that.

Something formed in front of her bed, out of the darkness; a shimmering mass, and two strange figures, semi-transparent, superimposed over a seething mass of clouds formed there. The vision made no intellectual sense; the smaller figure superimposed on the larger seemed paradoxically to be the greater. A small, yet increasingly familiar feminine form, atop a larger, more imposing, father figure.

"We had to come back, for just this once," the female figure said.

She frowned, unsure whether she was dreaming this or what. The others apparently heard nothing and slept on. "Sam?" she said, hesitantly, "Is that *you?*"

"It is and it isn't," the figure replied. "Once I was Sam, and he was Boolean, but it is becoming harder and harder with each passing moment to tell one from the other. Our time is short, and full integration of my three parts proceeds at a pace even I can barely comprehend, so this is the last time this will be possible."

"Sam—what happened to you? Up there . . . ?"

"I can't explain. The results will be apparent to you all in the days and years to come. Let it suffice that Klittichorn is dead, and while there may well be others like him in the ages to come, none will ever again pose the kind of threat he did. The others will be returned here shortly; they can give you as much as any person can about what happened. This last visit is for me alone, for the sake of what has gone before."

There was a sudden blurring of the images, and the figure struggled to come back and retain full focus and form.

"The time is shorter than I thought," the Sam figure told her. "We must go."

"Go? Go where? Sam—where are you? What happened to

you? Will I see you again?'' *And where'd you get that vocabulary?*

''I can't explain and it makes no difference anyway. You were always bright; you will be able to figure out a little of it. The rest you will simply not believe. It doesn't matter. Only false gods are dependent upon belief. That's none of your concern. I came here just to see you this last time, and to tell you a few things about your own self.''

''What? What's this all about, Sam?''

''The child is no longer a Storm Princess, just a beautiful little baby girl who will need love. The position of Storm Princess has been abolished. It is redundant. Love her, Charley. Think of her as your own.''

''Uh—yeah, okay, Sam. But. . . .''

''You have a lot of potential, Charley, that you either threw away or had thrown away. You have a second chance now. Tell me, would you rather go home, now? Have the baby in a real hospital, live in the world you grew up in?''

Charley had thought about that for a long time but had never expected to be asked the question when it meant something. ''No, Sam, I don't think so. I don't think I could just pick up, not as somebody else, which I am now, after all this here.''

''Then remain in Masalur, Charley. Here there will be no more war, no more slavery. Trust me on this. The rest of Akahlar will be in foment for many years, perhaps a generation or more, but not here. And here, as the creation of Boolean the Great, surrogate of Sam, you'll have additional position, power, and prestige. Nor will you be alone. What wealth you need you will find; what you do with your life and how you spend it is your own affair, as they should be. But you'll make your own choices from here on in; they will not be imposed. Farewell, Charley. Remember us fondly. And if our daughter ever asks about Sam Buell—lie.''

''Sam—you should know. . . . Cromil told me. All that hell we went through, all that shit they put us through—most of it was deliberate. Sam! They *used* us!''

''We know, Charley. We have a far better understanding of it and source of information than Cromil. Charley—just, well, don't waste yourself as a bimbo any more. Make some right choices for a change. Live your life and enjoy it. For our sake—and for our daughter. Don't stay blind to everything, now you can see. Farewell, Charley. We didn't ask for this, didn't want it, but we couldn't avoid it. Live a life like Sam still dreams of living, and know, curiously, that she envies you.''

The vision flickered again, this time worse, the white smoky background seeming to reach out and swallow them up.

"Sam! Wait!" But the vision had vanished, gone into the darkness.

"Damn you, Sam!" she grumbled. "I'm still *fat!*"

· 14 ·

Aftermaths and Beginnings

THEY WERE SCATTERED along the beach like bits of flotsam and jetsam washed in from a storm, although the sky was sunny with just a few fleecy clouds and had been for many days.

It was Dorion who found them, while out walking along the shores of the lagoon and trying to decide on the meaning of things. Charley had had a vision, or so she said; Sam had come, sort of with Boolean, almost as ghosts, to announce both a victory and a farewell, yet the promise of Charley's weight loss had not been fulfilled. A dream? Perhaps, but why had Charley, who had never been able to master the language, awakened now speaking flawless Akhbreed? And acquired a voice that was still her voice, but a bit higher, softer, definitely in the feminine registers, and kind of sexy? A dream? A new spell? Or, in fact, had things truly changed, and, if so, how?

And what about him? Sometime yesterday, he was suddenly aware that the spell binding him as her slave had simply vanished; the ring was not inert, just a piece of jewelry, and in a very silly place for jewelry. She hadn't known, and he hadn't told her, although their relationship remained ambivalent. She was so hung up on her looks she couldn't seem to think of anything else; so long as that was so, the fact that she *thought* the ring bound him was sufficient to keep him there and on hand, not allowing her reason to dismiss him.

Suddenly he stopped dead on the beach and stared. By the gods—the beach was littered with *bodies!* He broke free of his shock and ran to the closest one and stared down at it.

This one was familiar, although a bit different-looking; Etanalon had never looked so radiant, and the silver robe did wonders for her. He bent down, fearing she was dead, but she stirred, frowned, then opened her eyes and saw him, and then she smiled.

"Help me up, Dorion, if you please," she asked him kindly, and he did so. She looked around. "The others?"

"I see more over there. You were just the first."

She nodded. "Let us check them." She yawned, stretched, and stamped her feet to get herself going. "Not bad for an old ice monster," she muttered to herself, and followed him.

Next, bundled in furs and sweating like a stuck pig in them under the tropical sun, was Crim, looking like he needed a bath, shave, and a very long rest. Etanalon checked him out while Dorion went to the next figure down. Crim opened his eyes and did an imitation of Etanalon waking up. "Huh? What? Where . . . ?"

"Hey! There's a real pretty naked lady over there!" Dorion shouted, and Etanalon left Crim to manage and rushed over to the next patient. Dorion turned over the nude form and gasped; the sight also startled Etanalon, even though she might have expected it.

"It's *Kira!*" Dorion breathed, then looked back at Crim, just making it as far as sitting up. "But—I thought—" His head went back and forth between the pair. "How . . . ?"

"Their curse is ended, undone to the core," Etanalon told him. "Yet she as well as he are whole, and in the prime of their half-spent best years." She chuckled. "If you think *you* are shocked, imagine what it's going to be like when they see each other!"

They heard a familiar voice cursing and rushed to the next figure, who was even now getting up on her own. Boday groaned, stretched, then looked around, saw where she was and saw the others, and grinned, then immediately began shedding her own fur clothing and boots. "Hey! You two! Victory is sweetness and Boday has become legend!" she shouted exuberantly. She looked around. "Have you seen someone who looks a lot like my darling Susama?"

Etanalon came over to her. "Uh, Boday, I'm afraid you won't be seeing Susama any more. You see—"

"Ah! Boday knows that! She understands! The fates never intended that her Susama should be limited to being the wife and love-slave of Boday! No, I said somebody who *looks like* her.''

"No, I—wait a minute!"

The fancy clothing was unmistakable now, and before either Dorion or Etanalon could reach the unconscious form, Boday was there, turning her over, brushing the woman's hair back and the sand from her face. She twitched, then sighed, then opened her eyes and looked at Boday.

"I love you," sighed the girl who looked like Sam, eyeing Boday as if the alchemical artist were a true goddess.

Boday smiled. "Boday knows you do, her little Princess! Ah, never again will Boday have to worry about who will cook her meals, mend her clothes, clean the place, or assist and provide whatever Boday needs. That's all you want to do now, isn't it, my Princess? Now and forevermore!"

"Yes, my darling," the girl who looked like Sam responded.

Both Etanalon and Dorion stood there, staring. Finally it was Dorion who said, "That's not—*is* it?"

Boday looked up at them and grinned broadly. "Once, yes, she was called the Storm Princess and filled with hate and madness, but no more. Never more. Now she is filled only with love and devotion for Boday!"

"But—how?" Etanalon wanted to know.

Boday shrugged. "A little taste of the whip, a bit of a choke hold, and an entire phial of Boday's own special ultra-powerful, quick-acting love potion, which she fixed up in your own lab over the evening we spent there. It was not intended for this, but there they were, face to face, my Susama and the Princess, and then the fates placed Boday, at just the right angle, with all the means at hand! So Boday saved Susama and the Princess, which allowed Susama to save Boolean, which allowed them both to save the world and make of Klittichorn some kind of ice sculpture or whatever. Boday has claimed her own rewards; no thanks are necessary, even if, in the end, *it is Boday who saved the world!*"

The alchemical artist paused, looked back at the princess, then at them, and shrugged. "After all, what else is she good for? Her powers are gone, and she's not well equipped to go to work for a living. This way at least she is useful, and happy."

Dorion was about to say something, thought better of it,

then averted his eyes and caught sight of something, or someone else, still further along. "Who can *that* be?"

There was an enormous cloak of familiar brown cloth, but the figure filling it was almost lost within the vastness of its folds. The cloak was familiar to them—clearly it was Yobi's—but the woman inside was not. Although middle-aged she was still something of a beauty, stately and statuesque, not at all grandmotherly or matronly like Etanalon.

"Who is *that?*" Dorion asked. "And where's Yobi?'

"That *is* Yobi, dear," Etanalon replied. "That is the Yobi who attained the Second Rank, before she paid the price of her researches and her battles and went places and did things that so terribly changed her. It is Yobi before she paid her terrible price, now given a second chance at it. I believe she will need a smaller, grander cloak of rank now."

Dorion shook his head in wonder, then got up, leaving Yobi's recovery to Etanalon, turned, and looked back up the beach. "I had wondered what would happen when they saw each other in the light of day," he said, smiling. "Look."

Etanalon turned and saw, back up the beach, the figure of a tall, handsome man in a long embrace with a young, naked woman, each holding the other as if they were afraid to let go.

"That's sweet," the sorceress commented. "I was so afraid that after all this time they'd be sick of each other."

"I'll go tell Charley and the others," Dorion shouted, starting to turn for the house halfway around the lagoon. "Boy, we're gonna have one *hell* of a party!"

Yobi groaned, opened her eyes, saw Etanalon, and went through the whole routine. The old sorceress allowed herself to be helped up, and only then did she look at herself and realize the change that had been wrought. "Oh, my!" she muttered. "Oh *my!*"

"Yes, dear, but I'd think very seriously about playing those demon games any more," Etanalon cautioned. "I seriously doubt if anybody will give you a third crack at it."

"We still—we have our powers back?"

"About like before, it seems to me. Neither magic nor the rest were abolished, only limited in their range and scope, which is reasonable. Akahlar depends too much upon people like us to wipe us out now, and I get the distinct impression that there are far fewer of us in the Second Rank than there were yesterday. Don't you?''

''Indeed. But not everything works. The boy, Dorion—he still had the ring in his nose but it was just a ring. No power. No enslavement.''

''That's not permitted in Masalur, I think. We'll have to divine the rules once again, but that's a fascinating chore. You know, I doubted right up to the end whether or not we weren't stupid suicidal idiots for going against all that, but it seems to have worked out nicely that we did. Except for that brief horrid transformation on the ice, we—you and I—came out of this pretty well. In fact, I'd say that we are probably right now the *de facto* heads of the Guild, whatever's left of it.''

''Just as well,'' Yobi noted. ''Otherwise we'd be stuck forever in this island paradise.''

They joined Boday and her new escort, which amused Yobi no end, and continued on up the beach towards the house. They passed Crim and Kira, who didn't seem to be aware that anyone else was there, and decided not to disturb them.

Etanalon looked over at Boday and her fawning lovesick princess and said, ''You know, something's been bothering me since I heard your version of events, Boday. Why did you go down in my lab and spend so much time mixing your love concoction at that point? Not for this end, surely. You can't see the future. Might it have been in the back of your head to secure the love of Susama once and for all?''

''Oh, no! Boday understood the special position of her Susama. Why do you think she never slipped Susama the potion during all that time in Tubikosa? Boday did not come on this journey, give up everything, for *her*. It was to renew herself, to fill her emptied soul, and that it has done. No, she spent months in the company of that pair up at the house, and hours in talking sense to that silly girl there who had no sense of what was truly important. It was the idea that, if the opportunity presented itself, a few drops, perhaps, in a farewell toast, to cement a deserving relationship, as it were. It was concentrate, by the way. My princess here probably swallowed enough of it to make love-slaves out of the whole of center city Tubikosa, but that's all right. She had a lot of hate to smother.''

Etanalon looked at the house. "And did you manage it?"

"No, there was no opportunity, which is why it was still in the belt." She reached down and pulled a small phial out of her leather belt, held it up and looked at it. "There are still a few drops in there. Probably more than enough. Perhaps it will be done yet."

"No, hold off," Yobi interrupted. "Ever since she got here people have been making most of her decisions for her, so that the few she could make couldn't help but be a bit wrong. It will be sad if she keeps to that pattern, but it is her choice to make. At least she's earned *that* right."

Charley shared the shock, surprises, and joy at having them back, and did not let them alone until each of their stories was drawn out and compared. Boday was already sketching, and dreaming one day of an entire panorama in oils, perhaps a diorama depicting the epic fight against the forces of evil that had saved Akahlar.

During one of Charley's frequent trips to the outhouse—it seemed like she had to pee every ten minutes these days—Etanalon followed her in conversation, and during the course of it let slip that Dorion's slave spell was nullified, gone. Apparently, although he had to know, he had neither told her nor acted any differently.

She shook her head in wonder. "Why? Why would he do that? Pretend to still be my slave?"

"He loves you, dear. You know that. He gave up what little he had for you. Surely that must be obvious."

"Yeah, I guess so, but . . . , well, he could do a lot better than me if he was just a little more assertive. He *is* kind of cute, you know. I mean, I'm *fat*, and any moment now I'm gonna be a *mother* to a kid by a father long dead now. Either one would be bad enough, but both together is a hell of a burden to stick a guy with. I mean, he's not really in love with me; he's in love with some little slip of a courtesan who could charm the balls off a pawnbroker's sign. That girl's gone. The closest to her is the one Boday's got, and she's kind'a out of circulation. You yourself examined me and told me the spells were still there, so I'm not gonna change. Who the hell would want a five-foot-two-inch 50-42-50 butterball, never mind one with a kid?''

What she said was true, as far as it went, but it wasn't because of the Omak demon's curse. Someone had undone all that and rewoven an elegant new spell, one so fine and so carefully tuned that it was beyond even the best of Second Rank sorcerers. Without harming the child in any way, or affecting her, Charley had been carefully redesigned, reengineered from the inside. Nothing showed, but her bone structure, muscle tone, everything, had been finely tuned so that her current weight and stature was her normal condition. When not pregnant she would be exceptionally strong, unnaturally healthy, free of all the diseases and maladies that plagued all but the best magicians, able to climb, lift, run, and lots of other things—without feeling any more winded than someone in peak condition. But she was also exceptionally fertile, able to bear many children, if she chose to do so, without stressing the body the way it did many women. She was under no spells or charms; a skillful weaver of the winds had changed her as surely as the inhabitants of Masalur hub had been changed, yet she was still Akhbreed. Someone, who thought Charley had learned every lesson except the most important one, had wanted her to look that way.

And that was why, in spite of the fact that a skilled sorcerer like Etanalon could in fact have granted Charley's wish, she neither did so nor suggested the possibility. There was something potentially great in Charley that everyone seemed to sense when she was being herself; Charley alone could not see it because she was too busy looking in the mirror to look within herself. Sam had been helped by mirrors; to Charley they were her curse. Why begin questioning the judgment of the First Rank now?

"Is it really so terrible being fat?" Etanalon asked her. "Why do you want to be thin? Not for health, surely. That is a good reason for some but not for you. Do you feel so terrible this way?"

"Yes. No. Well. . . . It's the way other people see you, react to you. Other women, guys. I mean, what kind of man would be interested in me looking like this? And I think other women might be worse yet. I know how I used to feel when I looked at some fat girl. Sure, I love not constantly dieting and not worrying if I want some bonbons, but it's just not me.''

"And you really believe that Dorion is in love with an idealized vision of your outside, that he is not in love more with your inside? With what he sees inside you?''

"Now, maybe, he thinks so, 'cause he's been so cloistered and shy and all, but I saw the way he looked at that Kira.''

"Happily married men have been looking like that at bodies like Kira's since there were women and men to look at each other,'' the sorceress responded. "And women like you look at bodies like Crim's in that manner as well. Or bodies like that Halagar's, never considering what's inside. But they rarely want to settle down with one like that. They just look, like one appreciates fine works of art or the beauties of nature.''

"You really think I should give it a try with him, then?''

"It's your decision, and you've known him longer and more intimately than I. If you are that unsure, get Boday to mix you up a love potion, but I don't think you'd want to do that to anyone else, and I don't think you'd be happy that way. But, if I were you, I might give it a shot. You could do worse, with a nearly instant newborn around, you are very quickly going to find his measure and his commitment.

"I—I'll have to think about it, that's all.''

"That's all one can ask another to do in these matters, dear,'' Etanalon replied with a smile.

"I can't believe it! They're all over the place!'' Dorion was both excited and stunned beyond belief at the discovery. "I mean, I never saw 'em before, but you just kick a rock and there's a diamond the size of a child's rubber ball, or a ruby fit for an idol's navel, or an emerald the size of a small melon! The island's *crawling* with big gem-quality stones!''

Charley nodded and smiled. "Well, at least now I know what she was talking about when she said we would have all the wealth we needed.'' Gold and silver were common in Akahlar—any competent alchemist could make them from common lead—but gem-quality stones, flawless, with perfect luster, almost ready for the cutter, were very rare indeed.

This had followed on the heels of Yobi and Etanalon's visit to Masalur hub to check things out, their sorcery protection against anything they might be likely to find. What they had found, though, was far different than what they had left. The slavery spells on the Akhbreed survivors, who numbered more than three hundred thousand people, were all broken and ineffective. They had then risen up collectively against the remaining skeletal force of Hedum and the other nurbreed conquerors, joined unexpectedly by forces from the transformed millions of the inner hub who had once been their brethren, and overcome them, only to be joined by forces from no less than eleven colonial worlds, accompanied by Akhbreed who lived there—the very worlds where Boolean's experiment in self-government had been permitted and encouraged. More races were coming out now and, after testing the political and social winds, were blowing the way of the colonies, and tremendous pressure was being extended even now on the nine unconnected Masalurian rebel worlds.

They had not waited for peace. A compact had been drawn up by the pragmatists and those horrified by what had occurred. Masalur was being reconstituted as a republic, a form of government known in some remote areas of the colonial worlds but never among the Akhbreed, with each race of Masalur who signed brought on as an equal partner with equal voice and representation in a kind of parliamentary assembly still mostly on paper. The entrepreneurs, the Navigator's Guild people in the region, and others were already starting to redevelop commercial ventures, often in partnership now with locally owned, and in a few cases hastily formed, native corporations. A combined army, for defense of the republic rather than for subjugating it internally, was being assembled under former officers, and was having to be talked out of carrying their "revolution" to other kingdoms while their own was still being born.

Revolution by example was being preached instead. Without shields and Chief Sorcerers, and with the Akhbreed's vulnerability exposed by the wars and revolutions, such an arrangement could be offered as the only viable alternative to civil war and the breakdown of services and authority. The rebels, in the main, didn't want to revert to primitive ways and tribalism; they wanted what the Akhbreed had, and the smartest among them understood that the Akhbreed alone knew how to harness the power of water for electricity and engineer sewage systems, running water, and the rest. Much blood would be spilled, and centuries of hatred and oppression could not be overcome in a night by high-sounding principles and promises, but it was a start.

It wasn't perfect, and not everybody went along right now, nor was everybody satisfied, but it seemed a damn sight better to those on the island who heard about it than anything else in all Akahlar. Those without sorcery had a meeting to discuss just what they wanted to do in this new world.

Boday pointed to Charley. "Boday still remembers the brillant undergarment you and Susama created which more than financed our journey. Surely there are other such ideas that can be found, developed, licensed. Whole new vistas are opening up! Imagine, if you will, if we could just convince the four-breasted Masalurians that these 'bras' were good! And think not only of the Akhbreed and Masalurians but of all the races that products can now be developed for!"

The project interested everyone. Crim, for example, was a member of the Navigator's Guild, and could arrange for coordinated transport. Kira could wine and dine and charm the pants off the most hard-hearted businessmen and politicians. Dorion had no powers, not that he'd lost that much to begin with, but he had his Guild membership and lots of contacts there.

"But you're going at it all wrong," Charley told them. "Sure, we might actually manage it, but then we'd become Akahlar's greatest corporation, with an economic hold on it. Our company would become a pseudo-empire, stronger and possibly with less heart in the end than the old ones and more powerful. No, what we want to do is to start with some ideas that show the way, and provide a center, perhaps in Masalur hub itself, in the remaining outer circle, where everyone with creativity could come, both to share ideas, learn, and to test and market their own new products and ideas. Making money gets boring after a while. Becoming the intellectual and artistic center of the whole world, though—*that's* exciting!"

Kira, Dorion, Boday, even the two Masalurians, were fascinated by the concept but still not clear about the details of her vision.

"Isn't that what the great University hub is for?" Boday asked her.

"No, no! I'm no talking about education and I'm not talking about theory, both of which that probably does fine. I'm talking about a forum and an outlet for the ones who graduated from there, and those who never got the chance to go but still have great ideas."

'Can you picture it for us?" Kira asked her. "Show us, somehow, what you mean?"

Charley smiled. "I'm not the artist you are, Boday, but gimme that pad and I'll show you what I have in mind. And it's only the start of it. Surely, sometime, hopefully soon, *somebody* in Akahlar will invent air conditioning. . . ."

The Mother of Invention was pregnant again, but she didn't mind even if some other people thought she was overdoing it. Misa, now eleven and in the process of turning from adorable to sexy and dangerous, had been partly responsible for it, teaching and giving to her mother as much or more than her mother was giving her, and being an unexpected joy. That had been compounded by the arrival of Jonkuk, now nine and the spitting image of his father at that age although with a highly extroverted personality, but, damn it, who would have suspected that Dorion would be so phenomenal in bed?

Not that he really believed it yet; after all, if your wife's had a little prior experience with, maybe, two or three hundred other guys, you would tend to think you were being flattered, but there was something to be said for the fact that she had been absolutely faithful now for eleven years, and why she had Joni, age six now, and Petor, age three, afterwards, and they probably wouldn't stop with the one on the way, either. They both loved kids, particularly theirs, and, hell, they could afford them.

Not that it had slowed Charley down. The concept of day-care and an equal spot for women in the policy-making body that controlled the entity known throughout Akahlar simply as The Mall had been laid down from the start. After all, three of its seven-member board were females, and two more were sort of all of the above.

Stepping into the Grand Promenade, with its large grass and tree-lined park going down the middle between the two long rows of multilevel shops, galleries, and boutiques, she stopped to look into the windows of some of the fashion galleries. They were catching on quickly to the potential business here; the traditional chadoorlike garb of even the most conservative kingdoms was giving way to modernity with the collapse of the Chief Sorcerer's authority and the failure of the old religions to keep pace with the revolutionary new conditions present on Akahlar.

It had started with just this section, but even now it seemed to go on and on in all directions, less a collection of shops and stores than a small city in its own right, with its own electric power and its own population just to staff the place and keep it clean and perfect. Fashion and cosmetics tailored to a thousand races, but even if you foreswore clothes altogether where you were from, there was something here for you. Inventors here had created a kind of escalator system previously unheard of; others were trying different methods of cooling and compression, even electricity from solar energy. There were toys galore, and shops selling everything from sports stuff to commercial fishing gear. They liked to brag that there was nothing you could not buy at The Mall, and two-thirds of it could be bought nowhere else, although the best and cleverest products were now being copied and imitated.

There were playgrounds for the kids as well, and separate day-care for the employees and those guests who had them. All the staff was multiracial, and it was surprising how easy it was for even the most hidebound old Akhbreeds to accept that when they were here shopping for a new creation or a stunning coat or the latest in jewelry creations. And going up now were the resort hotels that would make this a true destination community, and they were listening right now to proposals for creating a water park and to another fellow who appeared to have independently reinvented the amusement park.

She walked by two young Akhbreed women, skinny and slinky in obviously newly bought tropical fashions including sandals and the latest inventive rage, sunglasses, and they gave her a look that could only mean, *Hey, you fat, barefoot slob of a baby factory, how dare you be in a place like this?* It no longer particularly bothered her. In fact, her one fond wish was that someday one of them would actually make a comment like that and she could reply, *"Hey, skin and bones! While you're still trying to score in bars, I got a great marriage, great kids, and, on top of that, I own this fucking place!"* Nobody ever had, but there was always hope.

The fact was, she *was* comfortable with herself. True, she'd still like to be 36-24-36 and not worry about it, but not if she had to trade what she had to get it. Not if she had to trade *any* of it.

Kira shouted her name and waved, then came and joined her. She was still what Charley would want to look like, what *any* woman with any taste would want to look like, although she was starting to show just a little wear and tear. Kids, even with housekeepers and day-care, will still do that to you, although Kira hadn't been quite as gung-ho as Charley on that score, having been a bit gun-shy having her first baby just a few days past nine months after seeing her first sunshine in years.

Kira, in fact, was just back after a couple of months on the road with Crim and the kids setting up some new delivery contracts, and she was just seeing some of the new projects after being away.

"Am I going crazy, or is that building-sized mural of Boday's on the North Wall being redone again?" she asked, shaking her head.

Charley chuckled. "Yeah, our big attraction. *War of the Maelstrom.* I don't think she'll ever actually finish it, but it keeps getting more grandiose and, I suspect, less realistic as she goes along."

"Well, I remember the initial one had her as just a tiny figure down in the corner, and now it seems like Boday is the star of the entire painting. Before we're through we'll have an entire building side that's nothing but Boday in a reclining position, whip in hand."

Charley laughed. "Well, the rest of the Board will have something to say about that. Still, her gallery's going great guns, even if I can't figure out a damned thing in it—I mistook a fire box for one of their creations the other day. And I'm somewhat afraid that her body painting studio is going to catch on and become the next real fad."

"Well, not for me it isn't. How's Dorion and the kids?"

"Except in one department, I think Dory was born the wrong sex. He absolutely adores the kids, loves cooking and keeping house, and seems perfectly content to let me run the business end while he stays home. Of course, he keeps writing those epic first-person accounts of him and the great sorcerers that nobody will publish, but it keeps him occupied. It's the only blessing to my failure to ever learn to read Akhbreed, although he's pestered me to teach him how to read and write English. And, of course, he's created a whole range of ingenious children's toys and games for our kids that have wound up being successfully marketed. I think that's his true secret—he's never wanted to grow up, and now he doesn't have to.''

"Not Crim. He's getting sick of being on the road half the year, coming home and having his own children ask for his identification. That's why we all went along on this last one—and I think it will be the *last* one. Lately he's been talking about building a new chain of world-specific malls in the provincial capitals and other hubs. We have to go that route soon, I think, or the Masalurians will run out of places to live.''

Charley leaned back in the chair and sighed, looking around at it all. "You know, sometimes I really can't believe that such a nightmare as I was cast into turned out like this! God! You know, this place, this life—me, my family, all of it—is more than I ever dreamed of achieving when I was a kid. I keep living in fear that one day I'm gonna wake up or be awakened and find this was all a dream or some hypnotic trickery. So far, though, it and you have all still been here. And it just keeps getting better.''

"Well, at least nobody's come up with television yet. I have hopes that it won't happen in our lifetime but you never know.''

"Oh, I dunno. The idea of a Hedum variety show fascinates me. Still, I look around and I wonder what Sam is doing now. If she's finally happy, or if she still exists as we understand it, and if at least she knows what we've done here. I think she'd love this place.''

"You know there's actually a large cult movement growing around her, complete with prophets and visions and holy books?''

"No! In the other lands?''

"Uh-huh. And creeping this way, I'm afraid. Masalur's holy ground to them.''

"Jeez! Well, I hope they don't expect me to be their high

priestess and interpreter, or decide that all this is profaning holy ground or something. You know, that vision I had, all those years ago—it was kind'a like she was gonna become a goddess, more or less against her will. There was some sadness in her, like she always just slightly missed the boat her whole life. Be kind'a weird if she was, huh? If that cult really was worshiping a live one? A god created from a teenage girl who never wanted anything but a normal life in absolute obscurity and a half-baked old physics professor? Hell, you always think of being a goddess as having no troubles at all, no pain, no worries, and anything you want. I'd like to do it, just for a little bit. Point my astral finger and say, *'From this point on, the more chocolate you eat the more weight you will lose.'* ''

Kira laughed, and then remarked, "You know, it *is* something to think about. Between the two of you, *you* might have had fun as a goddess, while the one who might well have gotten it, would carry it as a burden." She sighed, "I don't know, though. Maybe, if you must have a god, that's the kind of attitude you want your Supreme Being to have."

Charley shrugged. "Yeah, well, maybe I *am* living the life she so much wanted, but I love it and if Sam's up there in the great beyond looking down at me with jealous eyes she can just eat her heart out."

The sky, which only a moment before had been a clear blue one, suddenly went dark, and storm clouds suddenly rumbled overhead, and there was the feeling of the barometer dropping and the distant sounds of thunder.

"Only kidding, Sam!" Charley said loudly to the sky. "Only kidding!"